Manic Pixie Dream Earl

JENNY HOLIDAY

KENSINGTON
PUBLISHING CORP.

kensingtonbooks.com

KENSINGTON BOOKS are published by

Kensington Publishing Corp.
900 Third Avenue
New York, NY 10022

ISBN: 978-1-4967-4510-1 (ebook)
ISBN: 978-1-4967-4509-5
First Kensington Trade Paperback Printing: June 2025

10 9 8 7 6 5 4 3 2 1

Printed in the United States of America

The authorized representative in the EU for product safety and compliance
is eucomply OU, Parnu mnt 139b-14, Apt 123
Tallinn, Berlin 11317, hello@eucompliancepartner.com

To all the manic pixies out there.
I always thought you got a bad rap.
Here's to starring in your own stories.

A palace made out of crystal seems mighty fragile to me, if you ask me.

—Ted Lasso

A Manic Pixie Dream Girl (MPDG) is a stock character type in fiction, usually depicted as a young woman with eccentric personality quirks who serves as the romantic interest for a male protagonist. The term was coined by film critic Nathan Rabin after observing Kirsten Dunst's character in *Elizabethtown* (2005). . . . The term has since entered the general vernacular.

—"Manic Pixie Dream Girl," *Wikipedia*

Chapter 1

The Ghost of Hamlet's Father

When his friends arrived to fetch him for Earls Trip 1822, Edward Astley, Viscount Featherfinch and heir to the Earl of Stonely, was not at the ready.

"*Featherfinch*," Archie said censoriously after being announced by the housekeeper. And when Mrs. Moyer wrinkled her nose ever so slightly, curtsied, and departed, Archie—Archibald Fielding-Burton, Earl of Harcourt and Effie's best mate—said his name again, albeit much less formally: "*Effie*." He threw up his hands, but if there was resignation in the gesture, there was also affection.

Effie smiled, letting the pleasure of his friends' arrival seep through him like watercolor across canvas. "We are for Brighton today. I have not forgotten."

He had forgotten.

"I'm nearly finished my packing."

He hadn't even started.

"At least he is attired this year," said Simon Courteney, Earl of Marsden and Effie's other best mate.

"There is that," Archie said.

"I *told* you, I had a most unfortunate encounter with a malevolent patch of hogweed last year just before our departure." Honestly, one's friends find one composing a sonnet naked in one's own bedchamber *one time*, and one never lived it down.

"What are you doing out here in the stable?" Simon asked. "And what . . ." He turned in a slow circle, taking in the chaotic contents of what had until recently been home to Effie's father's horses. "In God's name." He stopped turning and pointed. "Is that?"

"Indeed," Archie said. "Is that a torture device?"

"That," Effie said, "is a printing press." He regarded the contraption that had become the bane of his existence.

And now he was going to have to leave it behind for a fortnight. "A broken printing press, alas." He patted it as if all the beast needed was a little tenderness when he knew full well the bloody thing had it out for him.

"It might even be haunted." Effie cocked his head, considering what sort of creature would haunt a printing press, especially a very old one such as this. "I think I shall give this press a name." He patted it again. "I hereby christen you Hamlet, Prince of Denmark."

"Why Hamlet?" Simon asked.

What Effie said was "It's a pun. Prince of Denmark, but also 'prints'—P-R-I-N-T-S of Denmark."

What Effie thought was *Because Hamlet was haunted by the ghost of his father.*

The boys smirked, and Archie asked, "More to the point, what are you doing with a printing press?"

"Nothing at the moment. Did you not hear the part where I said it's broken? This . . . clampy thing here"—he patted said clampy thing—"is meant to close down on this plate, but it isn't cooperating. Which I suppose explains why it was such a bargain."

"What are you *planning* to do with a printing press, then?" Simon asked. "Once it's fixed?"

"I can't tell you."

"Clearly, he's meant to be printing something," Archie said. "The question is, what?"

"I can't tell you." But Effie had an idea. He ought to have thought of this earlier. "I can, however, ask you a question."

"I am all anticipation," Archie said.

"May I store Hamlet in your stable?"

"I keep horses in my stable. Astonishing, I know."

"May I store Hamlet in your house, then?" Archie was the master of his own house. He could do whatever he wanted, including storing a broken printing press in a seldom-used parlor.

But, oh, there was a flaw in Effie's logic. Archie was the master of his own house, yes, but Archie's sister-in-law, Olive Morgan, was often in Archie's house, and if she caught wind of the addition of a printing press to the furnishings, she would know exactly what was going on. And although Olive Morgan was as dear to Effie as a sister—dearer, for although Effie was fond of Sarah, they weren't close—Olive could *not* find out about this.

He turned to Simon. "May I store Hamlet at *your* house?"

"I suppose so," Simon said mildly.

"Hold up," Archie said. "I haven't said no. I was merely mentally rearranging the furniture in the library. We shall store this contraption there."

"My house is better," Simon said. "It's just Mother and me. When you're in Town, Archie, your house is full. And your mother might be upset by the addition of such a machine. It *does* resemble a torture device."

"No," Archie said, "*your* mother will be scandalized by the addition of a torture device to her domestic tableau. *My* mother will not even notice. She rarely leaves the music room these days."

"Oh, Archie," Effie said.

Archie's mother suffered from an affliction of the mind, and it had worsened in recent years. She didn't recognize her own son anymore, yet Archie remained devoted to her. It was difficult for him to leave her for a fortnight for their trips. Effie had been so caught up in his own machinations that he hadn't called on the dowager countess since the family had arrived in Town. Which might have been some time ago. As had been established, calendars were not Effie's forte.

"He asked me first," Archie said, bickering with Simon over the press, and Effie smiled. More watercolor traversing canvas, veins of color crossing previously blank space. That was the boys for you. They had no idea what Effie needed a printing press for, yet they were vying over who would hide it for him.

"We will discuss the matter in Brighton," Effie said. "The press can remain here for now. It needs to be gone before Mother and Father are back, and that isn't for. . . . What day is it?"

"It is the eighteenth of September," Simon said. And with a flourish—or as much a flourish as the overserious Simon was capable of—added, "The first day of Earls Trip 1822."

"And so it is." Effie clapped his hands together. "My favorite fortnight of the year."

Mostly.

Historically.

He did rather dislike having to be away from home for so long these days. What if he missed a letter?

But, he reminded himself, she wouldn't write to him. He'd told her about the trip this year. She knew he was going to be gone and for how long. In fact, he'd promised her a detailed accounting of both the Royal Pavilion and the seaside.

"Why don't we discuss the fate of the printing press over tea before we depart?" Simon asked.

"We don't need tea." Archie pulled out his timepiece and frowned at it. "We've port in the coach. Let us make haste."

"Hold up." Effie put his hands on his hips. "You've made a wager again this year, haven't you? About how long it was going to take to extract me?"

"Of course not," Simon said, even as Archie said, "Can you blame us?"

"If only I knew which of you would end up storing Hamlet, I'd throw the wager in your favor."

Cheered by the good-natured bickering that broke out, Effie led the boys across the garden and through the house, rebuffing Mrs. Moyer's offer to send a maid up to pack for him. "I will need a trunk, though, thank you."

They almost made it upstairs when the butler announced visitors.

"Mr. John Lansing and Miss Eleanora Lansing."

"Dash it," Effie muttered. He had been to a ball yesternight, and he'd forgotten to instruct the staff that he was not at home to visitors today. Callers always came out in droves after a night out. He was, if he did say so himself, the life of the party.

"My lord." Miss Lansing blushed as she curtsied, and Effie might have been mistaken but he rather thought Mr. Lansing went a little pink, too, as he bowed.

The Lansing siblings were the last people he wanted to see just now—or ever—but he could hardly shuffle them off now that they were face-to-face.

"We best have that tea after all," Simon said, after introductions were made, and no one but Effie noticed the face Archie pulled.

"Did you enjoy the ball, Lord Featherfinch?" Miss Lansing inquired.

Had he? He didn't quite know. Effie used to love balls. Music, gaiety, dressing up, dancing. He'd had a fine enough time last night, he supposed, though he had been stuck playing cards with Mr. Lansing for what had felt like an eternity.

"It was a lovely party," he finally said, and thus began thirty interminable minutes of chatting about the various personages who'd been assembled. He had trouble caring. He couldn't even get himself exercised over an analysis of the outrageous gown worn by a visiting Italian baroness.

"It was so kind of you to dance with me twice, my lord," Miss Lansing said.

The word wasn't *kind* so much as it was *forgetful*. Miss Lansing had hinted that she'd like him to sign her dance card early in the evening, so he had, and a little later, her brother had done the same, and Effie had complied, not remembering the earlier encounter. So he'd ended up dancing both a quadrille and, unfortunately, a waltz with the young lady.

"Yes, wasn't it?" Mr. Lansing was doing something with his

eye in Effie's general direction that Effie supposed was meant to be winking but looked more like an early sign of an impending seizure.

"I do so admire your coiffure, if I may be so bold," Mr. Lansing went on to say. "When my sister asked me to escort her to visit you today, I resolved to tell you as much."

"Thank you," Effie murmured.

He stifled a sigh. This happened. Women flirted with him. Sometimes men did, too. Usually, he flirted back. It was an enjoyable enough way to pass the time, and what was life for if not enjoyment? He was aware that as the heir to an earl, he was no doubt attracting people for reasons other than his sparkling wit and legendary head of hair, but what of it? The days had to be filled somehow.

The Lansing siblings began hinting rather heavy-handedly that they would like him to make an appearance at Vauxhall that evening.

"We could take a walk," Mr. Lansing said, his eye once again signalling either romantic interest or impending doom.

Effie was accustomed to such overtures from both ladies and gentlemen, but he'd never been the recipient of such from a pair of siblings. He wondered idly what Mr. Lansing's endgame was. To marry his sister to Effie, thus gaining proximity? If so, he wondered whether Miss Lansing was in on the plot.

How exhausting.

But, again, how interesting that he regarded it so. A year or two ago, he would have found this brand of low-stakes drama diverting. He was never stirred to desire by these kinds of overtures, but he would have played along with one or both siblings, just to amuse himself. Now, he just wanted to escape.

Handily, he had just the excuse. "You will forgive me, but I must take my leave. Lords Harcourt and Marsden are here because we're about to depart on a holiday."

An interrogation followed: Where? For how long? Would he bring Miss Lansing a memento? Would he bring *Mr.* Lansing a memento?

"I should never have gone out last night," Effie said when he and the boys were finally liberated and climbing the stairs toward his bedchamber. "I forget that as amusing as a ball can be, the aftermath is decidedly less so."

"Poor Effie," Archie said. "So handsome and eligible and charming, you can't go anywhere."

"I've been thinking," Effie said. "If women become old maids at a certain age and are considered on the shelf, why isn't there an analogous state for men? I am nearly thirty. Will I reach a point at which the marriage-minded schemers will leave me be?"

"I don't think so," Archie said. "Regardless, I imagine at some point your parents will force your hand."

"Curiously, neither has said a word about it. One would think that since I am such a disappointment to Father, he would be anxious for me to marry so that he may influence the next in line for his precious earldom." Father's silence on the matter, especially as the years ticked by, was very strange, but Effie considered it a blessing, so he didn't question it.

"Here we are." Effie held the door to his bedchamber and gestured the others in ahead of him.

"I thought you said you'd nearly finished packing," Archie said, looking stern, or as stern as Archie was capable of looking, which wasn't very.

"Why don't we have some more tea sent up? Or some port—we can get started early," Simon said. "We shall repose while you pack."

"Repose!" Archie protested. "He needs to pack, and we need to go!"

"Go!" called Leander from his cage by the window, drawing the attention of all three men. "Go!"

"I thought he didn't talk," Archie said.

"Yes, well, he's found his voice," Effie said with exasperated affection.

His new macaw was quite a bit more talkative than his predecessor, Sally, but at the same time he managed to say a great deal less of import.

"But he only says random words, single-syllable ones, at that. He will hear a short word he fancies, and that's all he'll say for days. He's done 'No' and 'Tell,' and now he's added—"

"Go!" shrieked the bird.

"You see? One word at a time. You can't have a proper conversation with him like you could with Sally."

"I wouldn't say I ever had a proper conversation with Sally," Simon said, leaning over and peering into Leander's cage. "The most that ever happened is she said 'Hello'—grudgingly—in response to a greeting."

"That was only because Sally didn't like you," Effie said.

"Hmm." Simon, apparently unbothered by the knowledge that Effie's dear departed pet had thought poorly of him, pulled out his timepiece. "What about that port?"

"What has happened to this room?" Archie, seemingly having forgotten that he was in a hurry, was looking around as if he'd never seen the place.

"How do you mean?" Effie asked.

"It looks as if a rainbow fell from the sky and took up residence."

Effie's bedchamber *was* rather in disarray. The dressing table at which he had made his toilette last night was littered with ribbons and tinctures. He had been trying on different waistcoats, and he'd left the rejects strewn about.

Simon, from over near the mantel, pointed to the flowers bedecking Effie's ormolu clock. "What are these? They're as big as a man's fist."

"Dried peonies. Aren't they magnificent?"

"Where are the black roses that used to be here?"

"I felt a change was in order."

"And where is the painting that used to hang here?" Archie had made his way to Effie's dressing area at the far end of the room. "It was an odd image—a monkey sitting on a dead woman's chest."

"She wasn't dead; she was dreaming. And it wasn't a monkey;

it was a demon. That was a reproduction of a Fuseli entitled *The Nightmare*. And to answer your question, I took it down."

How to explain why, though, which was what Archie was actually asking. When Effie had first seen the image, years ago in a book his mother brought home from Italy, he'd recognized it. Not because he'd seen the painting before, but in the way one recognizes that which is familiar. That was the magical, horrible-wonderful potential of art, to show us what we already know. To be a mirror.

But then one day last spring, he'd thought: *Art can show us the familiar, yes, but can it also wear a groove in our souls, turning the familiar into the* expected? *If one has nightmares, need one remind oneself visually of that fact every time one enters one's bedchamber? Might doing so even* prime *one to have nightmares?*

The nights had been getting so much worse. He had been desperate to try anything to get the nightmares—if one could even call them that—to stop.

But like the printing press, the nightmares were difficult to explain. He might be able to do it in Brighton, after a drink or four, but now, here, he didn't know how to tell the boys about any of it.

Happily, he didn't have to. Archie moved down his line of questions. "What have you replaced it with? And isn't this a rather unusual color for sky?" He tapped the painting's gilt frame. "Who painted it?"

"I did."

The boys made admiring murmurs, and Simon made his way over to join Archie. "What do you call that color?"

"I don't know, exactly. It is very like a liqueur my mother is fond of called Chartreuse. She imports it from France. I believe it is made by monks."

Effie was a trifle surprised no one questioned the concept of a green sky. When he'd painted his first, it had been an accident. He'd been sipping the liqueur in question, and somehow, its color had made it onto his canvas. Then he'd just kept doing it. He wasn't sure why, only that it almost seemed as though the sky came out of his paintbrush that color, without any apparent forethought on his part.

"Who is that woman?" Archie asked.

Effie hesitated. "I imagined her."

It was not, strictly speaking, a lie. He did not know what Julianna looked like. He knew the components of her visage, based on her own reporting: brown, almost black hair that curled more than she preferred when it was down; green eyes; "tall for a woman." But one could invite a dozen ladies fitting that description to tea and end up with a drawing room full of a dozen different-looking ladies.

So, no, the woman against the chartreuse sky was not Julianna. It was an idea of Julianna.

"This is extraordinary," Archie said.

"Indeed," Simon said. "It feels as if she's looking at you. Into your very soul, even."

That's because she is.

Effie did not care, though, for the notion of Julianna, or this Julianna avatar, looking into Simon's soul. Looking into anyone's soul but Effie's.

Still, he was chuffed by the praise. "It is my best work, I think. Which of course is not saying a great deal. We all know that my skills with a paintbrush are generally on par with those of a girl in the schoolroom. A very young one. I ought to stick to poetry."

"But you persist," Archie said. "It is admirable."

Simon nodded at the painting. "And, apparently, efficacious."

A knock heralded a footman with a trunk.

"Go!" Leander screeched, and Effie began tossing apparel into the trunk.

Before too long—Archie still lost the wager, though, thanks to the Lansing siblings—they were ready.

A pair of footmen took the trunk, and Effie picked up Leander's cage.

"Surely you are not bringing that creature with you," Simon said.

"I have to. He's only recently learned to vocalize. If I leave him alone for a fortnight, he's likely to backslide." When no one said anything, he added, "He needs someone to talk to him."

"Cannot a maid talk to him?" Simon asked.

"Do I trust a maid to talk to him?" Effie asked. "To feed him, yes, but to tend to his education?"

"He has a point," said Archie, suppressing laughter. "I imagine your maids have better things to do with their time than talk to birds."

"And look how big he is!" Effie said. "He needs regular exercise outside of his cage. Can I trust *that* to a maid?"

"Oh, for heaven's sake," Simon said.

The three of them bickered good-naturedly about avian intelligence or lack thereof as they descended to the foyer.

Whereupon they ran into Father and Mr. Nancarrow.

Effie's first impulse was to think, *My goodness, are we* ever *going to get out of here?*

His second impulse was to panic.

The second impulse won out. The sight of the earl filled Effie's ears with the roaring of an imaginary sea.

He did not want to be the sort of man who panicked when encountering his own father, but here they were.

To be fair, he did all right when he had time to prepare, when he knew he would be meeting his sire. So perhaps he was merely the sort of man who panicked when *unexpectedly* encountering his own father.

And also the sort of man who held his pet macaw behind his back when unexpectedly encountering his own father.

When the cacophonous waves receded, the boys were in the process of making greetings to his father. The panic subsided, soaking into the sand with the waves, because of course his father would behave in the company of Effie's friends, highborn as they were.

"Harcourt, Marsden," Father was saying, "may I introduce Mr. Nancarrow, who has recently come aboard as steward at Highworth."

Mr. Nancarrow dipped his head at the earls as Simon said to Effie's father, "My lord, I am happy to meet you here. I was hoping to gain your support for an act we shall be introducing in Parliament next session . . ."

The rest of Simon's speech was drowned out by the crashing of another wave. A larger one that brought with it not just panic but also terror. Terror not unlike the sort that had shoved Effie, gasping, from slumber to wakefulness more often than not these recent months.

Or perhaps not that sort. Nightmares subsided when one awakened sufficiently to grasp that the tendrils slithering through one's mind were merely of the phantasmagorical variety.

The panic was back because Effie remembered that the printing press was in the stable. Father's driver was no doubt encountering it now. The last Effie had heard, Mother and Father were in Campagna until early October. He had thought he had more time.

He forced himself to think, to return to the conversation at hand. What would Julianna do, in his shoes? Simon was droning on about prison reform, and Archie and Father were paying polite attention. Effie turned to the new steward and said, lowly, carefully, "Mr. Nancarrow, might I have a word?" Kenver Nancarrow had struck Effie, on the few occasions they'd been in company, as a reasonable, even affable, sort of man. He was also Effie's only hope.

"Yes, of course, my lord."

Effie caught Archie's eye as he ushered Mr. Nancarrow into a small parlor off the foyer and hitched his head ever so slightly in Father's direction, willing Archie to receive his silent message.

Archie didn't nod, at least not with his head, but he turned to Effie's father and said, jovially, "I've been thinking of a trip to Naples. My wife and I honeymooned in northern Italy last year and we'd like to go back. There is so much to see. We never got farther south than Florence. What time of year do you think is best? Is July too warm?"

"Mr. Nancarrow," Effie said, shutting the door softly behind him and setting Leander on a side table. "I must prevail upon you to assist me in a somewhat sensitive matter."

"Of course, my lord. I will help however I can."

Would he, though? Effie didn't have the true measure of the man. He well knew that affability sometimes papered over other, less pleasant qualities.

It mattered not. Effie had no choice. He did not want Father to find out there was a printing press in the stable. Either Mr. Nancarrow would help Effie in this matter, or he would not. If he elected not to help, Father would discover the press. Yet if Effie did *not* prevail upon Mr. Nancarrow, the same outcome was guaranteed: Father would find out about the press.

Therefore, the only course he had was to ask this near stranger for help.

Cheered by this uncharacteristic application of logic, he decided the best way forward was forthrightness. "I wasn't expecting my father back so soon. I have been storing a printing press in the stable. He . . . won't be happy about it, and I think it better he not discover it." He paused, considering whether to summon forth an exculpatory lie. *I am fixing up the press to donate to the Church. I am printing self-improvement tracts for wayward heirs.*

He could think of nothing that wouldn't sound ridiculous. And had he not just decided on forthrightness? "I was planning to move it elsewhere after I returned from the holiday on which I am about to depart, but now . . ." He turned his palms upward in a wordless appeal.

"Think no further on it, my lord. I shall go round back and confer with the grooms. I am certain we can find somewhere else to stable the horses for now. Where had you been planning to move the press?"

"To the home of the Earl of Harcourt, Number Four Hanover Square. Of course, he is also holiday-bound with me, but if you explain that the press is from me, the countess will receive it."

Clementine would, he was all but certain. He could only hope her sister was not in residence. But if he had to choose between Olive's discovering he'd bought a printing press and Father's discovering the same, he would choose Olive a thousand times over.

"Consider it done, my lord."

Effie allowed himself to relax a touch. "Thank you, Mr. Nancarrow. Be warned that the press is quite heavy. You'll need several men. And it's broken, so there are . . . bits and bobs loose. Take care." *Beware the ghost of Hamlet's father.*

"If I may say, my lord, that is a fine bird you've got there. Is it a hyacinth macaw?"

"Oh, yes!" Effie had momentarily forgotten that he was carting Leander through this crisis. "You must know exotic birds, given that you identified him on sight."

"*Anodorhynchus hyacinthinus,*" Mr. Nancarrow said. "Native to South America, I believe?"

"Ah . . . yes." In truth, Effie did not know. He'd procured Leander from the same merchant who'd sold him Sally, and he hadn't been made aware of any providential details.

"Studying birds is a particular hobby of mine," Mr. Nancarrow said. "Though I've never seen a bird as fine as that outside the pages of a book. Does he talk?"

"Go!" Leander said, as if on cue.

"He says a few words," Effie said as Mr. Nancarrow laughed in delight.

What a curious creature—Mr. Nancarrow, not Leander.

Whatever relief Effie had experienced in Mr. Nancarrow's easy company disappeared as they reentered the foyer. Effie felt as though his ribs were calcifying, making his movements awkward and unnatural. He edged along the wall as best he could so as to not draw Father's attention to Leander. With a small nod at Effie, Mr. Nancarrow slipped out the door.

When Archie, who was still quizzing Father about southern Italy in the summer, caught sight of Effie, he said, "What good luck to have encountered your father. He's made several improvements to my hypothetical itinerary."

"How fortuitous," Effie murmured, smiling blandly as his father looked up, brow knit. Effie knew that look. Father was trying to remember if Effie had been standing there all along. It used to wound him, when he was a boy, to know he was that forgettable in his father's eyes. For as a boy, he generally *had* been standing there the whole time. As he'd grown, though, he had come to understand that invisibility came with benefits that could be exploited—for example, the opportunity to arrange for the covert relocation of a printing press.

"If we want to make Brighton by nightfall, perhaps we ought to make haste," Effie said, affecting a nonchalance he did not feel. "Perhaps you can call on our return, Harcourt, and continue your discussion. Will you still be in residence, Father?"

"Brighton?" Father said, frowning. He looked rather . . . yellow. Put out, though Effie could not imagine why.

"Yes," he said, "our annual trip."

"Annual trip?"

Effie didn't say, *Yes, Earls Trip 1822.* The fanciful appellation for their holiday would not go over well with Father, who, in addition to lacking any sense of humor whatsoever, would almost certainly have pointed out that Effie was not an earl but a mere viscount. He was the heir to an earl. A very unpromising heir. To put it mildly. Which, to be fair, Father would do, given that they were in company.

Effie didn't say anything, just smiled blankly.

Archie said, "Yes, sir, the three of us have developed a bit of an annual tradition—a fortnight of holiday in September."

Never mind that this was the ninth annual Earls Trip and Father had just now noticed.

Father's eyes traveled down to Effie's feet and back up to his face. "What on earth are you wearing, boy?"

Boy. Effie winced. He was eight-and-twenty. He was not a boy. He felt the word as the prick it was meant to be, the *y* at its end a sharp pin sliding into his guts. But to complain, to react at all, would only prove him deserving of the moniker. It was a paradox he often found himself in with Father.

Chartreuse skies, he reminded himself. *Chartreuse skies.*

The answer to Father's question was that he was wearing a dismayingly unremarkable pair of buff pantaloons, a perfectly acceptable black coat, and a wildly ridiculous waistcoat of pink and violet striped sarsenet. But Father had eyes, so the boy said nothing.

"I've brought Mr. Nancarrow to Town," Father said after several beats of silence, perhaps after not getting the reaction he'd wanted, though Effie would allow for the possibility that he was overestimating how much thought his father expended for him.

"Yes," Effie said, because *he* had eyes. He did rather wonder what business the steward of the family's Cornish estate had in London, but as long as some of that business involved the relocation of a printing press, Effie didn't see that it was any concern of his. Father had made it quite clear matters to do with the estate, with the title, generally weren't.

"Thought I'd acquaint him with the goings-on here in Town," Father said.

"I thought you were in Italy," Effie said.

"Just long enough to see your mother and Sarah settled."

"I see. Well, we must be going," Effie said quickly, but he immediately regretted the almost desperate tone that had crept into his voice. He didn't like this feeling that he was slinking away. He didn't know what to do about it, though, other than to follow his instinct to pull Leander's cage out from behind his back. It was incredible that Father hadn't noticed Leander to begin with.

"Go!" Leander screeched, attaining a heretofore unheard-of pitch, and Effie didn't know whether to laugh or cry. At least he was no longer hiding.

"I hope I may count on your support for a gaols act next session," Simon said to Father, as if there *wasn't* an overlarge blue macaw screaming at them.

"I'll consider it," Father said tightly.

He would not consider it. Effie could tell from his tone.

One compensation for when Effie inherited the earldom was that he would vote however Simon told him to.

They made their goodbyes, Father wondering aloud where Mr. Nancarrow had gotten to. Effie led the way down the front steps, all but threw his valise at the waiting footman, and flung himself and his bird into Archie's coach.

The boys joined him, and they all sat in silence for a moment until Simon said, "That was very . . ."

"Painful?" Effie supplied. "Uncomfortable? Anxious-making? Odd?"

"I haven't seen your father for a long time" was Simon's only answer.

"Nor have I," Effie said. He turned to Archie. "Change of plans. The printing press is—one hopes—making its way to your house. Ought we to detour there and warn the countess?"

"Will she be told it's from you?"

"Yes."

"Then we needn't bother. Clementine will take it in stride."

Effie, too, had thought Archie's wife would be unfussed by the arrival of a broken printing press to her fine London townhome. It was part of what made her such an excellent person. "Is your wife's sister staying with her at the moment?"

"No. Olive and Sir Albert are at Hill House," Archie said, naming his wife's family's country house.

Good. With any luck, Effie's secret was safe. Though it wasn't luck, was it? It was Mr. Nancarrow. Which was rather remarkable given that Effie's secret was several hundred pounds of iron and wood. Effie allowed himself a degree of relaxation. It would take a while before he could unbend fully. But respite was coming. That was the beauty of an Earls Trip.

"Let us *go*," he said. "Let us go *now*."

"Go!" Leander agreed.

A footman stuck his head inside before they could do that, and Effie's heart sank. Another delay. What could this mean but that Mr. Nancarrow's mission had failed?

"We are *going*," Effie said in a low voice to the boys. "Whatever happens, we are *going* on the trip."

"Why would we do otherwise?" one of them asked. Effie wasn't sure who, because he was occupied bracing himself. He straightened his spine and raised his eyebrows at the footman, trying to affect a pose of aristocratic impatience.

"A letter has just arrived for Miss Turner, my lord."

Effie fell over himself lunging for the letter, belatedly regretting the fervor with which he received it.

"Thank you." He tucked the letter into his pocket, the effort of not immediately tearing it open almost too much to bear. Usually, he fell on one of Julianna's letters like a hungry vulture at its first meal in days.

He turned to Archie. "Let us go."

Archie gazed back at him for several silent beats.

"Please," Effie added, allowing a note of the desperation he felt to creep into his tone.

Archie nodded, rapped on the ceiling, and they rumbled blessedly off.

"Who is Miss Turner?" Simon asked.

Archie, for his part, said nothing, just regarded Effie with a quizzical expression.

When Effie didn't answer, Simon pressed further.

"Turner was your mother's maiden name, was it not? Are you corresponding with a relation of hers?"

Effie knew the question was disingenuous. The footman had said a letter had come *for* Miss Turner, not *from* Miss Turner. Simon was as quick as they came. He hadn't missed that.

After a moment of silence while Effie floundered silently, Archie, who had continued to gaze at Effie with a curious expression, said, "Perhaps we ought to stop at my house, after all," He turned to Simon. "What do you think?"

"I think you were right the first time," Simon said. "The countess will be surprised by the arrival of a printing press, but she will find a place for it. She's quite unflappable."

"Yes, you're right," Archie said.

Simon had brought a newspaper into the coach, and it was resting on the seat next to Archie. Archie picked it up and handed it to Simon and got out the beads he worried with his fingers as a way of keeping his mind calm.

Effie had the sense that Archie, with the question and the newspaper, had been purposefully distracting Simon from the matter of the identity of Miss Turner. Effie was grateful.

Grateful and a little guilty. He didn't like to hide things from the boys. They didn't do that.

He was ready to confess. But he needed that drink or four, the quiescence that only an Earls Trip could provide. They would settle in at their destination, and once he'd got the rhythm of the place, of the holiday, he would tell them about it.

About *her.*

The letter in his pocket felt warm, which he understood was impossible. But it was crying out to him. It *wanted* to be read.

He ordered himself to hold off. Did he want to read the letter hastily and surreptitiously in a close carriage, or did he want to savor it? Let his fingers trace the embossed header on the cream-colored stationary?

Miss Julianna Evans, Editor
Le Monde Joli

Before diving in, he would allow his gaze to slide languorously over her sharp, small hand. Her *u*rs were always formed so similarly to her *w*s, making *turn* into *twn.* Her uppercase *G* was nearly indistinguishable from her uppercase *S* when she was exercised over her topic and therefore writing quickly.

Next, he would jump ahead and take in her signature, which for quite some time now had been simply *JE*. He still remembered his elated shock the first time she had signed off that way. The familiarity implied by the use of mere initials never failed to give him a thrill.

So, yes, he would wait and read the letter in Brighton.

He eyed the boys. Both were still engaged in their solitary pursuits. Leander, whose cage was on the floor near Effie's feet, had fallen asleep, lulled by the rocking of the coach.

To distract himself from Julianna's letter, Effie decided to work on his "Advice for Married Ladies" column for the December issue of *Le Monde Joli*. It was due the middle of next month and would have to be posted shortly after he returned home.

The coach was too jostley for him to write, but he took out the letters he intended to answer. He would reread them. Ponder the predicaments presented therein, and in so doing, return to himself.

Dear Mrs. Landers,
   I am the mother of two daughters and four sons ranging in age from ten years to two months.

Dear lady, he thought. *Stop right there. I already know what your difficulty is, but I fear there is no settlement.* He returned to the letter.

My husband is a barrister and works long hours. I am grateful for the living he provides our family, but by the end of the day, I am at my wit's end. Everywhere I turn there is a child in want of something. Small hands always grasping, grasping, grasping. Yesternight, I asked my husband to hold the baby so I might step into the garden and breathe the first fresh air of the day, even as day became night. He refused, telling me that child-rearing is women's work. It's not that I disagree, but what woman will be around to do said rearing when I have lost my wits?

My dear Mrs. Landers, I am in despair, and that is understating the matter entirely.

Yours sincerely,

Bound for Bedlam

He smiled at the moniker she'd chosen. When "Advice for Married Ladies" debuted a year ago, the initial batch of letters they received had been signed with their writers' real names. Julianna had decided to use descriptive pseudonyms, and they'd had fun naming their correspondents. Gradually, correspondents had begun naming themselves.

He flipped to the next letter.

Dear Mrs. Landers,

My son spilled castor oil on two of my husband's three shirts. The oil will not come out. Have you any advice?

Cordially,

Mrs. Frank Lewiston

That one would be easy enough, though he would have to name her. "Oily," perhaps. On he went.

Dear Mrs. Landers,

Is there ever a circumstance in which a wife might be justified in spending Christmas with her own family? My mother is taken quite ill, and I fear this Christmas may be her last. I should like to spend it with her. The dilemma is that my husband is equally bent on spending the holiday with his family, as we always do. I have offered, variously, to take the children with me, or to leave them with him—his reasons for needing me to be at his family's home have changed from not being able to look after the children on his own to not wanting to be away from the children on Christmas—but he isn't having it.

My mother is my greatest champion and confidant. I do not know what to do. Please help.

Cordially,

Home for Christmas

Poor lady. Yet how lucky she was to have a parent she considered a champion and confidant.

Dear Mrs. Landers,

I must confess from the outset that I am not a married lady. I was to be. If everything had happened as it should have, I would have been married last week.

My betrothed did not appear at the chapel at the appointed time. We—my sister, my parents, the vicar, and I—waited and waited. Eventually, my father dispatched a messenger to the home of my erstwhile betrothed—his family is from the next village. The man came back and reported on a conversation he'd had with my fiancé's parents. They said he had left on a tour of the Continent, and what's more, they knew nothing of a wedding—or of me.

I fear I am losing my grasp on sanity. This was the same man who'd met my family numerous times, who made quite an impassioned speech when he asked for my hand—after securing my father's permission. And now he is gone without a trace.

I have read your column with great interest since its debut. I always find myself agreeing with your advice, and I have no one whom I may ask this question. My mother is horrified and intent on pretending the betrothal, not to mention the wedding-that-wasn't, never happened. My father paces the drawing room muttering about bounders. My sister seems to be worried that being left at the altar is infectious and will somehow damage her prospects—she is eleven. No one seems to care about me and the ghost of my betrothed.

Is my heart broken forever?

Sincerely,

Miss Heartsick

"What are you reading?"

Effie was startled out of his epistolary reverie by Simon's question. He shoved the letters into his satchel. "Nothing."

Simon narrowed his eyes. Fair enough: his skepticism was entirely justified.

"I am reading a letter," Effie amended.

"From whom?"

"I have . . . a few correspondents."

"Such as?"

"Olive Morgan." It was true. Since they'd struck up a friendship on last year's Earls Trip, Effie and Olive had written each other long, heartfelt letters, and in fact, he had her latest with him as he intended to answer it from Brighton. Olive was the only person alive who knew about Effie's feelings for Julianna. That was because Olive was also a "Miss Heartsick." She and Effie had commiserated on the matter of having given one's heart to someone impossible.

"That looked like more than one letter," Simon said. "Are they all from Miss Morgan? And who is Miss Turner? You never answered that."

Goodness, Simon was inquisitorial today. "Does anyone know if the king is in Brighton?" Effie asked by way of distraction.

"I sincerely hope not," Archie, whom Effie had thought wasn't paying attention to the conversation, said. "The possibility of such is the potential fatal flaw in our plan this year."

His Majesty had long been devoted to the seaside town of Brighton, and, in fact, his ever-growing palace—which was the raison d'être of this year's trip—was Brighton's crowning jewel.

But the same royal favor that had made Brighton a destination also made it . . . a destination.

"I'm sure we've never been anywhere so fashionable on an Earls Trip," Effie said. "By all accounts, the king's dinners last for hours. It sounds as if quite a society has been established. Did you know there are balls at both the Castle Inn and the Old Ship? Apparently the proprietors have agreed to alternate nights."

Simon made a strangled noise.

"Indeed," Archie said wryly.

"Well, what if the king *is* in residence?" Effie said. "It isn't as if we must make ourselves known." Of course, Mother would have an apoplexy if she learned Effie had been in Brighton the same time as the king and had not gotten himself an invitation to court. "We can skulk around and see the sights incognito, evading all inducements to join society. I suspect the balls are more summertime amusements, anyway."

Once again, Effie could hardly believe he was hearing himself plot to *avoid* a ball. Fond as he was of fashion, art, and dancing, he was generally not one to miss a party.

Was he?

Perhaps the problem was that Effie did not know who he was anymore.

"We could devise disguises," he added, trying to interest himself as much as the others. "That would be diverting, would it not?" Goodness knew, he could use a diversion. Existential crises did grow tiresome.

"I share an aversion to crossing paths with any of the Upper Ten Thousand, much less the king," Simon said. "If it hadn't been for my fervent desire to see the Pavilion, I'd've picked somewhere far less populated."

The friends took turns planning their holidays, and this year's had been Simon's.

"Well, I for one am heartily in favor of the indulgence of fervent desires," Effie said. Simon in particular had so few of them. Or perhaps it was only that he *expressed* so few of them.

Simon pulled a folded bit of newsprint out of the book he was reading. "The spherical dome is built on a cast-iron framework weighing sixty tons. Isn't it remarkable? How can something so heavy appear to soar toward the sky?"

Leave it to Simon to have fervent desires related to engineering.

As Effie made noises of appreciation, his attention snagged on Simon's book. "What are you reading?"

Simon snatched up the book, but it was too late.

"A *novel*? And one of Miss Austen's at that!"

"It was lent to me by Miss Brown," Simon said defensively.

"My Miss Brown?" Archie asked.

"She's hardly *your* Miss Brown, but yes."

Miss Brown was Archie's mother's companion, a young lady with a scholarly bent. Effie wondered when Simon had been in a position to receive a book from Miss Brown but concluded that Simon, not caught up in self-inflicted melodrama as Effie was, had no doubt been diligent about calling on Archie's mother when the family was in Town.

Chastened, he slumped against the squabs and looked out the window. Archie and Simon conversed a bit about the book in question, for Miss Brown had also recommended it to Archie's wife. Eventually, as silence fell inside the coach, the rumbling of wheels and snorting of horses the only sounds, Effie patted his pocket where Julianna's letter was smoldering and allowed himself to indulge in the sentiment he usually reserved for late at night, under cover of darkness.

Longing.

He closed his eyes and imagined a chartreuse sky. A woman with eyes a few shades darker.

"Ahem."

He wasn't sure how much time had passed when Archie's throat-clearing pulled him back to the corporeal reality of the journey. The landscape had changed. They were surrounded by farmland, the cobblestones of Town having given way to a rutted dirt road.

"Oh," Effie said, "is it time for the rules?"

"It is," Archie said, "but I wonder if we ought to scrap them, or amend them."

"Why would we do that?"

"Well, I'm not sure there's any point in trying to prohibit you from writing poems and Simon from talking about Parliament."

"You're just saying that because you've brought a gun." Effie wagged a finger at Archie. "That was ill-done of you. You can't be waving a gun around Brighton."

"I haven't brought my fowling piece," Archie protested.

"He hasn't brought his fowling piece," Simon said to Effie. "But you will note he hasn't said he hasn't brought a gun generally."

"I did note that," Effie said as Archie made vaguely indignant noises.

"Do you recall that we're staying in Hove?" Simon asked.

Effie did not recall. "What's Hove?"

"A fishing village a few miles west of town. We're staying in a house owned by a friend. It's empty this year." Simon smirked. "But unlike last year with you at the helm, I have established that it is provisioned and staffed."

"Yes, yes." Effie waved a hand dismissively. "We had a fine time last year in the end." He narrowed his eyes at Archie. "Some of us more so than others."

"My point," Simon said, talking over Archie's grumbling, "is that the house is rather isolated. It's on the edge of town and has access to a secluded beach."

"Oh, so Archie *has* brought his guns."

"I have not!" Archie protested, throwing up his hands. "I haven't hunted since last Earls Trip."

Effie chuckled. That was the influence of Archie's new wife. The Countess of Harcourt, née Clementine Morgan, loved animals so much she refused to eat them. "When was the last time you had a pork chop, or a leg of lamb?"

"It has been a very long time," Archie said, "and I am looking forward to consuming both this fortnight." He paused. "I think."

"As for the rules," Simon said, "we ought to have the ceremonial recitation of them even if we're being rather more relaxed about infractions these days."

"Yes," Effie agreed. "It's tradition."

And wasn't having traditions with people you adored one of the sweetest parts of life?

"All right." Archie passed out tumblers and sloshed a few fingers of port into each.

Effie marveled at how he never spilled a drop when he did this, despite the lumbering of the coach. That was Archie: graceful, agile, athletic.

Archie cleared his throat theatrically. "Gentlemen. Welcome to Earls Trip 1822. Allow me to remind you of the rules. Number one: every time Marsden says the word 'Parliament,' he must down a dram of whisky. Number two: Featherfinch is strictly prohibited from writing poems, unless they are naughty ones. And should you be harboring any concerns that I fancy myself above the law, we come round to number three: Harcourt is not permitted to shoot anything." He rolled his eyes. "Which there is no danger of, because he hasn't brought a gun."

Effie and Simon jeered good-naturedly.

"And finally," Archie continued with a flourish, "the most important rule of Earls Trip . . ."

They spoke in unison. "What happens on Earls Trip stays on Earls Trip."

Leander awakened and added, "Go!"

Chapter 2

Editorial Independence

Mr. Glanvil was running late.

Mr. Glanvil was always running late, though, so Julianna wasn't sure why she was so aroused over this particular occurrence of tardiness. But as she sat outside his office attempting to edit a recipe for teeth cleaning and whitening, she grew increasingly agitated.

He was the one who insisted on these weekly meetings. Meetings that, even when they commenced at the appointed hour, were a waste of her time. When he made her wait to see him, the affront compounded but not usually to this degree.

She sighed and set down her papers.

It was because Effie was bound for Brighton.

It made her happy to think of her dear friend turning her face to the sun, letting the sea water and air do its good work.

She and Effie had corresponded, in recent months, about the concept of holidays. Effie took quite a lot of them. Which was unsurprising, for Julianna suspected that Euphemia Turner was the daughter of a gentleman. Perhaps even a member of the aristocracy.

Julianna, by contrast, did not take holidays. She could not afford to, in more ways than one. While her modest savings might have permitted a short jaunt to a place like Brighton, she pinched every penny. Ambition required sacrifice.

That's what she told herself, anyway.

More to the point, she couldn't afford the time away from the magazine.

The magazine above all.

Julianna had a few adages she lived by, a collection of directives that shaped her thinking and therefore her behavior. *The magazine above all* was paramount among them, a kind of secular First Commandment.

She *had* considered taking a holiday. In the summer, when the July and August issues were combined and the editorial and production schedules therefore less harried than usual, she might have, for example, hopped on a London-to-Brighton coach and enjoyed a brief respite. She had long wanted to try sea-bathing. Something about the sea called to her—theoretically, for she had never seen it.

But she didn't have anyone with whom to travel. If she wanted to make such a journey, it would have to be alone.

Could she even get away with it? She was unmarried. She didn't have a maid.

Pish. She ordered herself to abandon such fancy. She wasn't going anywhere. She didn't *want* to go anywhere. *The magazine above all.*

She just . . . got distracted sometimes by the crashing of imaginary waves on an imaginary shore.

The door to Mr. Glanvil's office opened, and the man himself appeared.

"Julianna! My apologies for keeping you waiting. Allow me to introduce you to Mr. Ryan. He's a whaler out of Massachusetts, and we've struck a deal to ship whale oil here."

Mr. Glanvil had inherited his late father's shipping business.

Unfortunately, he had also inherited Julianna's late father's magazine.

"Mr. Ryan, my sister, Miss Julianna Evans, edits a little magazine I own."

A little magazine.

Julianna's head burst into flame as she dipped into a curtsy. "Mr. Glanvil and I are not related by blood," she said calmly as her head burned. "My mother married his late father seven years ago."

"Mr. Ryan runs whaling ships out of a place in America called New Bedford," Mr. Glanvil said, appearing not to have heard her disavowal of him. "Whaling ships! Can you imagine?"

That *was* interesting. The head flames began to die down.

She turned to Mr. Ryan with newfound interest. "I wonder if you or one of your associates could be persuaded to write an account of a whaling mission for the magazine? We often publish travel accounts, tales of adventure."

"Come now, ladies have no desire to hear about a whale hunt." Mr. Glanvil turned to Mr. Ryan. "'Tis a ladies' magazine we are speaking of, you see. I imagine a whale hunt is rather bloody."

"It is indeed."

"All the better," Julianna said. Blood sold magazines.

Mr. Ryan's eyebrows rose as Mr. Glanvil chuckled. It was false laughter, meant to signal that Julianna was in jest. Mr. Glanvil did this quite a lot. Apparently, having a "sister" who said absurdly amusing things was preferable to having a bloodthirsty one who commissioned reports on whale hunts.

After seeing Mr. Ryan off, Mr. Glanvil ushered Julianna into his office, which was dominated by an overlarge desk. This tableau always brought to mind a boy sitting at his father's desk, playing at being a man—which wasn't that far off the mark given that Glanvil Shipping had been started by Henry Glanvil Sr., who had sat behind this very desk.

Julianna missed Glanvil Senior. Which was remarkable. She had spent *years* resenting the man her mother married after the unexpected death of Julianna's father, founder of *Le Monde Joli*. After Father's death, the magazine had gone to Mother, and things had carried on quite well for two years, Julianna stepping up to edit. She had learned more than enough from her father to continue without him, though she had missed him dearly. She still did. His perpetually ink-stained fingers, his brow knitting as he peered through thick spectacles at copy he found puzzling, his expansive sense of what was possible—for both the magazine and for his daughter. They had always planned that she would succeed him. When it happened, she'd been bereft but prepared.

But when her mother had remarried, her property, including the magazine, had gone to her new husband—Glanvil Senior. Whom Julianna had disliked from the start.

But not as much as she disliked his son.

Senior had allowed Julianna to carry on editing mostly unimpeded, though he had embraced the proprietor role. He had always been looking for "efficiencies" and never let her reinvest the magazine's profits into improving it. She recalled more than one battle over the annual fashion spreads she wanted to have colored. How was one supposed to report accurately on the latest dresses being shown in Paris if one had to do it in black and white?

She hadn't known how good she'd had it.

"I can scarcely believe it's time for another editorial meeting," Glanvil Junior said. "How the days fly by." He went around his man-desk and made a show of getting out a nameplate he kept in a drawer and setting it out.

Henry Glanvil, proprietor, Le Monde Joli

He always did this at the start of their meetings, chortling as if he intended the gesture to be amusing, even self-deprecating.

It boiled Julianna's blood. It wasn't enough for him to play shipping magnate? As much as his "little magazine" phrase had irritated her just now, it wasn't inaccurate in a fiscal sense. The magazine's annual budget was nothing against that of the shipping company.

Why, then, did he care so greatly? Glanvil Senior had only required Julianna to meet him once a month, to acquaint him in broad terms with her plans for the upcoming issue, and to inform her that her proposed budget was too high.

Glanvil Junior insisted on weekly meetings. He wanted to be

updated. He wanted to opine on the editorial outline. He wanted to hear himself talk.

Of course, he also spent a fair amount of time informing her that her proposed budget was too high.

"Is everything in hand for the production of October?" he asked.

"Yes. I'm off to the printer after this to check the proofs." She would be late, in fact, on account of having had to wait so long for Mr. Glanvil.

"And November? How is the report from the Lake District?"

"It came in, and it is well written." She handed him the story. Well written was about all she could say on the matter.

Julianna liked to publish travel reports, but she preferred they be from exotic destinations, places her readers were almost certainly never going to get to see. Mr. Glanvil, by contrast, favored accounts of "respectable holiday locales."

Not that there was anything wrong with the Lake District story. It had been written by a lady married to a minor aristocrat who had an estate near Penrith. She was content—nay, eager—to see her name in print, and that name would sell magazines. Julianna had titled the story: "A Peeress's Guide to the Lake District: Baroness Cartworth Opines on the Sights and Delights That Await You."

"Oh!" Mr. Glanvil exclaimed. "Look at that, a listing of recommended inns."

"Yes, I thought that since everyone is familiar with the Lake District in a broad sense, we might as well make some specific recommendations."

"That was a good idea."

"Yes." She waited for it . . .

"I had a hunch that would work. Better to extract the most practical information and set it apart visually."

"Yes," Julianna said, aiming for mildness of tone despite the fact that the head embers were stirring, fanned back to life by Mr. Glanvil's hot air.

He did this: took credit for her ideas. She told herself it didn't matter. The result was the same—the story would run, and no one would know or care about the intellectual power struggle behind it.

"And this issue's moral essay?" Mr. Glanvil asked.

Le Monde Joli had not published a monthly moral essay before Glanvil Junior's tenure as proprietor. It had occasionally printed pieces that grappled with specific ethical considerations—the notion of a sugar boycott, for example—but that was as far as it had gone. Julianna was of the opinion that between church and life under the thumbs of fathers and husbands, most ladies did not require additional moral instruction.

"'Notes on Gluttony,' I think I shall call it," she said. Julianna's little rebellion against the monthly moral essay was to give it a dull, too-literal title that, with any luck, inspired readers to skip it. It was an odd, unpleasant feeling, wanting people *not* to read part of her magazine. "It has been commissioned but isn't in yet."

"Who is the author?"

"Mrs. Ann Smith, the wife of a rector in Penrith." The rector of her Lake District correspondent's parish, in fact. Julianna often found writers this way, by asking existing writers for ideas and introductions. Everyone thought editors sat at desks with ink-stained hands and stared at words all day, but much of her job was about managing people, making connections.

"Why can't the rector write it?"

"I beg your pardon?"

"Why the rector's wife and not the rector himself? Musings on one of the cardinal sins would seem to mean more coming from him. He is closer to God, is he not?"

"I take the point, but I believe Mrs. Smith will be in a position to provide commentary from a uniquely womanly point of view."

"Well, she may write it, but put her husband's name on it."

And that right there why Julianna was content—nay, happy—being a spinster.

"As I have explained," she said, as mildly as she could, "I prefer to have as many lady correspondents as possible. Female bylines resonate more with my readers."

"You mean *my* readers."

This was a problem. A real one. Had Mr. Glanvil merely been a self-regarding blunderbuss, a man who fancied he'd earned the status and wealth he had inherited, that would have been one thing. But when he put that "proprietor" nameplate out, he *meant* it. The jovial manner in which he did so was an affectation. He owned the magazine. That was a regrettable truth. But beyond that, he seemed to think that meant he owned its readers. That he owned *Julianna*.

Julianna had gone into Glanvil Junior's tenure as proprietor thinking she could manage him, and for the most part, she had. But he had a streak of cruelty in him. She had learned that he had to win a certain amount in order for that cruelty to remain dormant. Hence the monthly moral essay, among other concessions.

"I shall do as you suggest." She had to swallow a lump in her throat to get the sentence out. The embers in her head had been doused with water, leaving only a sodden pile of ash.

That was the worst part of all this. She detested the fact that he could make her feel this way: melancholy, and a little bit scared. She preferred the immolating effects of the ire he usually inspired. She tried, in her dealings with Mr. Glanvil, to stay angry. But sometimes, as today, she left his office feeling . . . small.

But she would not cry. Julianna did not cry.

As she emerged into the sunshine and bustle of the Strand, she clutched her reticule to her chest to ward off pickpockets and ordered herself to be cheered. Nothing lifted her spirits like a trip to the printing house. Even after all these years, seeing the pages of her magazine—*her* magazine—printed and drying never failed to give her a thrill. A magazine was a little miracle. That Mr. Gutenberg's innovation, the words and art of so many talented people, and her own editorial acumen if she did say so herself, could come together and produce a tome that was at once uplifting and informative, and do it every month, was a wonder. Nothing had ever or would ever make her prouder.

Nothing was more important to her. If she had to make sacrifices, "Notes on Gluttony" among them, to keep the magazine alive, that was what she would do.

She turned her face toward the uncharacteristically warm September sun. Effie had once said that feeling the sun on one's skin was like being agreeably prickled by the tiny fingernails of benevolent fairies, and Julianna thought of that every time she had occasion to be outside in the sunshine, which wasn't often. She worked long hours in the office, and at home she tried to make herself unobtrusive. The former helped with the latter. Julianna lived with her younger sister. Amy and her husband, Arthur, had four children and very busy lives. They were kind to Julianna, but she was exquisitely aware that she was a charity case—which was ironic because she worked days as long in duration and as many in number as did Arthur.

The point was, Julianna didn't spend a great deal of time out of doors. She rarely felt the agreeable prickling of tiny fingernails on her cheeks.

By the time she reached Grub Street, her disposition had improved. She was done with Mr. Glanvil for a week, and she was about to have her first look at October.

The bell on the door heralded her arrival, an arrangement that had always struck her as futile, for if the presses were going, they drowned out the bell—and the presses were always going.

She made her way to the back of the shop. As much as she'd enjoyed the sun on her skin, she liked this better. The dim light, the smell of ink, the thudding of ink balls being mashed over plates: there was nothing better.

She looked around for her pages. They ought to be hanging by now. All she saw was what appeared to be the middle pages of a newspaper. She squinted at them. It was the *Weekly Star*, a middling publication.

"Ah, Miss Evans."

"Mr. Cabot." She dipped an abbreviated curtsy as the proprietor approached. "How is October?"

He wiped his hands on his apron. "Well, that's the thing . . ."

"What's the thing?"

"There's been a delay."

She pressed her lips together and got hold of herself before asking, with what she hoped was merely a tone of mild interest, "May I ask why?"

He reached up and ruffled one of the drying pages. "The *Star*'s expanded by four pages."

"Goodness, how fortunate for them." What she would do with four more pages. She told herself not to be envious. Perhaps she could write December's moral essay on the topic. Under a male pseudonym, of course. "Professional Envy When One Isn't Supposed to Have a Profession to Begin With."

"As a result," Mr. Cabot said, "I wasn't able to print your pages today as planned."

Julianna schooled her expression so as not to display the irritation she felt at this development. She hated when this happened. Her "little magazine" was deemed less important than the papers, even the mediocre weeklies. "All right. When can you do it?"

"Not until the middle of next week, I'm afraid."

"No!" she cried and immediately regretted the outburst. She constantly strove to disabuse people—and by "people" she meant "men"—of the notion of the hysterical female. She understood that her job was small, relatively speaking. She grasped the economic incentive of a printer to keep his presses optimally occupied. She understood that the combination of both those facts sometimes meant shifts in the schedule, the displacement of her jobs. But the middle of next week was too far. It would mean delaying the publication of October—she had some slack built into the production schedule, but not that much.

Her printing job was small, but her magazine was not "little."

Having composed herself, she said, "The middle of next week is too late."

"I can refund your deposit if you'd like to go elsewhere."

She *would* like to go elsewhere. The problem was, where? Mr. Cabot was her third printer in as many years. At every shop, she encountered the same difficulties. Unforeseen delays, shuffled schedules. At least Mr. Cabot was polite.

She sighed, mentally rearranging her calendar. "Middle of next week, you say? What day? Wednesday?"

"Better say Thursday," he said. "You may inspect the proofs in the morning and give me your corrections, and I'll have your job done by the end of the day Friday."

"Very well," she said tightly. "I shall return next Thursday morning. Shall we say nine o'clock?"

Mr. Cabot agreed, but Julianna did not take her leave immediately. She gazed at him, waiting for him to apologize. *I am sorry I failed to fulfill my end of our contract, Miss Evans. My apologies for disrupting the publication schedule of your little magazine.* She wouldn't even bristle—much—over the "little" qualifier if it came in the context of an apology.

The qualifier did not come, because the apology did not come. Why had she ever thought it would? When had a man with a printing press ever apologized to a woman with a little magazine?

Julianna's spirits were very low by the time she reached her sister's house in Barton Street.

"Is that you, Julie?" Amy popped her head into the foyer as Julianna let herself in. "What are you doing here this time of day?"

Julianna recounted the news about the printer. "I find myself at loose ends as a result." She had nothing to do the rest of this week. Or next, until nine o'clock on Thursday morning. It was currently Wednesday, which meant she had seven days to fill.

Julianna had never been particularly talented at idleness. She didn't have hobbies. She didn't do needlework or play the pianoforte. Those were the pastimes of gentlemen's daughters, and she was not one. Neither was Amy, despite appearances to the contrary. Amy had married above her station.

"Is there anything I can help you with?" Julianna asked. Amy was wearing her spectacles, something she did only when Arthur was out of the house. She was probably going over the household books. Arthur was the youngest of seven, and though his family was genteel, they were not landed, and he had been making his own way since he was a young man. He made a good living as a barrister, but with four children, three of them girls Amy was determined to debut in society, economizing was necessary. Economizing that Arthur wouldn't have to see.

Mr. Glanvil paid Julianna a pittance of a salary. He pretended his masculine mind was uniquely suited to managing the magazine's books, but Julianna knew what it cost to produce *Le Monde Joli*. She knew how much revenue it generated.

She knew how much blunt Mr. Glanvil was pocketing as a result of her labors.

She tried to give the aforementioned pittance of a salary to her sister every month, but Amy wouldn't hear of it. It wasn't out of solidarity with Julianna, necessarily, despite the fact that Amy shared Julianna's dislike of Mr. Glanvil—though she called him Henry, which Julianna had never been able to bring herself to do.

No, Amy's refusal came from a place of pride. Amy, ever aware that she had married up, often seemed to Julianna to be playing a part. A bit like Mother had with Glanvil Senior—both the marrying-up bit and the playing-a-part bit.

Though of course "marrying up" could mean different things. Father had been an infinitely better man than Glanvil Senior, so in that sense Mother had married *down* the second time around. Julianna's father had been kind and hardworking, and they had been happy and hadn't wanted for anything.

Unless what you wanted were gowns and a second housemaid and dancing lessons for your daughters.

"Are you going over the books?" Julianna asked Amy. "I could help. You know I've a head for numbers."

Amy pocketed her glasses. "I was merely going over menus with Cook."

"Perhaps I could take the older children out for an ice since I find myself unexpectedly unencumbered this afternoon? My treat."

"That's kind of you, Julie, but you keep your money. You've earned it." The sisters weren't overly close, but to her credit, Amy never said anything condescending about *Le Monde Joli* or about Julianna's work. Amy had grown up with the magazine, too. Not in the intimate way Julianna had, but she had been there. She still read it every month, often complimenting Julianna on some aspect or other of it.

While Julianna was, theoretically, happy to keep her money—she had impossible ambitions to save for, after all—she knew Amy could do with the extra income. It was the role Amy was playing that necessitated her refusal. Her sister was the sort of person who bent the world to her will. She thought things into being. It was admirable, in a way. Amy didn't want to see herself as the kind of person who needed money from her sister, therefore she wasn't the kind of person who needed money from her sister.

"Besides," Amy said, "I'm taking the girls to the park this afternoon. You ought to take the opportunity to rest, Sister. You've been working such long hours of late, even for you. Perhaps your mishap with the printer is a blessing in disguise."

Julianna could have hinted that she'd like to come along to the park. Amy would have responded by inviting her. Amy probably would have bought them all ices afterward, just to prove a point.

So Julianna would not invite herself along. She would stay home. For the next seven days. Eating her sister's family's food and reading their newspapers and creating work for their servants. Taking up their space.

Julianna divested herself of her gloves and began the trudge to the small parlor at the back of the drawing room that had once been Amy's sewing room.

"Oh, Julie," Amy called as Julianna was about to disappear into her cave. "A package came for you." She nodded at the small table near the French doors that separated the drawing room from Julianna's room.

"Thank you," Julianna managed, though inside her chest a flock of birds had taken flight. There was only one person who would send her a package here at the house.

Clutching the package to her chest, she pulled the doors closed behind her and collapsed onto the bed that took up most of the floor space in the room. There was nowhere else to sit, but a mere chair would not have contained Julianna's expansiveness anyway. Her anticipatory joy required room for her limbs to fan out. She felt like a cross between a starfish and a girl.

She smiled. That sounded like something Effie would say.

She sat up and used a letter opener on the packet, forcing herself to be careful and precise because she was a careful and precise person.

Inside, she found a folded . . . newspaper?

She turned it over and gasped.

No, it was a copy of *Archer's Lady's Book*.

Julianna had heard about the new American magazine, which was, as far as she knew, the first of its kind that country had produced, the Americans being rather behind in such matters.

But Americans were so bold. So enterprising. She could not wait to see what kind of ladies' magazine an American would publish.

The cover featured a series of illustrations of ladies in various contexts—in gardens and drawing rooms and such. Under the title was a small circle that contained the words *Edited by Mrs. Emmeline Archer*. Envious and depreciative sentiments swirled together in Julianna's mind. Imagine having one's name printed on the cover of one's magazine! Julianna's name was inside hers, but underneath and in smaller type than that of Mr. Glanvil's.

But, she considered, *why* have the editor's name on the cover? What need did it serve? Did readers care that their magazine was edited by Mrs. Emmeline Archer? Perhaps they did, if Mrs. Emmeline Archer was a personage of some repute.

Before Julianna opened the magazine, she read the letter that had come with it. It was written in dark-green ink in Effie's familiar, loopy, expansive hand. She smiled.

My dearest Jules,

A friend of a friend made a trip to America this past summer and I requested the enclosed, knowing you have been wanting to see an issue. It arrived yesterday, and though I'd said my previous letter would be my last until I returned from my holiday, I simply <u>had</u> to send you this before I left. I must admit, though, that I didn't send it on <u>yesterday</u> because <u>I</u> spent the day reading every word inside it. I am all anticipation to learn what you think of it. I am certain your opinions will be more informed and refined than my own, but my initial impression is that it isn't nearly as good as your magazine. I say that most earnestly. You have a way of coaxing out the best in your writers without inserting yourself overmuch in either the process or the prose, whereas look at Mrs. Archer with her name front and center! What purpose does that serve?

Julianna smiled. She and Effie were always so aligned in their thinking.

Though for all I know, she is well known among American ladies. Perhaps her name alone sells magazines. Perhaps it is akin to a magazine being edited by Mrs. Fitzwilliams.

Julianna's smile deepened at the way Effie's thought process was a mirror image of her own, but with a fanciful flourish at the end that was uniquely Effie.

Can you imagine a magazine edited by Mrs. Fitzwilliams? First, it should contain a menu for a dinner party featuring seventeen removes. Then, a column entitled "Counterintuitive Advice for Marital Harmony, or How to Make a Man Wild with Desire by Ignoring Him."

Oh, and do you know, I have heard rumors of secret tunnels between the Royal Pavilion in Brighton and Mrs. Fitzwilliams's residence! Apparently there were times the then regent was seen breakfasting with her on her balcony when the last anyone had seen of him was the previous night in his own palace. So perhaps Mrs. Fitz's magazine can also contain some architectural drawings. What do you think? "Architectural Drawings to Aid in Clandestine Affairs"?

Julianna's smile turned to outright laughter.

Speaking of Brighton, I am resolved to write a poem per day on my holiday. When I return, I shall mail you the whole stack.

I jest. I shall choose the best of the bunch and toil away at it endlessly over the next several months and talk about it so incessantly and oppressively that you lose patience and command me send it to you—which I shall then do, of course, as I always have and always will do whatever it is you command, my dear friend.

Farewell for a fortnight. Brighton will be less bright without your letters.

Yours,

Effie

Julianna, letting the hand that had been holding the letter fall on the bed, resumed her starfishing. Oh, how she was going to miss Effie.

But she was being ridiculous. It was a fortnight! How many letters would they normally exchange in a fortnight?

She'd meant the question rhetorically, but she could check. She sat up and extracted from beneath the bed the box in which she kept Effie's letters. She added this latest to the front—she filed her letters in reverse chronological order.

The answer, over the last fortnight, was four letters from Effie.

Their correspondence had not always been so frequent. She pulled the first letter, from the back of the box, dated five autumns ago. She hadn't started keeping Effie's letters until after they'd forged a friendship beyond their relationship as editor and writer. She remembered the day this particular letter arrived. She'd realized, with a shock as bracing as an unexpected clap of thunder, that Effie had, somehow, become her closest friend. And a woman keeps letters from her bosom friends in a way an editor doesn't from her writers.

She returned the five-year-old letter to the box and pulled out the next one. It was dated three months later. She pulled out some more. The gaps between letters grew smaller as the months and years wore on. Presently, Effie was writing her twice a week. She was replying only half that frequently, but that was only because of the expense.

She put the box away. Julianna would miss Effie, but she could endure a letterless fortnight.

'Twas a pity much of that fortnight was going to contain very little work to do. Certainly, there were numerous small tasks she could complete, perpetually neglected matters she always shoved aside in favor of more urgent demands. She could tidy the office, for example. Start planning with Charles, one of her engravers, for the next few months' worth of engravings.

She slumped back on the bed, less a gleeful starfish this time and more a mindless one. Starfishes, she imagined, were probably quite stupid.

But perhaps not so mindless, not so stupid, for an idea arrived. Arrived with such force she felt almost as if someone had slapped her.

It was a wild notion. Very unlike her. Impulsive and profligate and irresponsible.

She was back up in a flash, scrabbling under the bed, deeper this time, fanning her arms out until her hands made contact with worn leather.

She extracted the pouch and counted her money, the coins she typically pinched so tightly.

Did she dare?

Dear Amy,

I've decided to seize on my period of forced idleness and pay Mother a visit. I haven't been to Reading since Easter, and even though it has been two years since the late Mr. Glanvil's passing, Mother is still so melancholy, drifting around the halls of that drafty house with only the servants for company. She never could stand to be on her own.

I expect I'll be back Wednesday of next week at the latest, though perhaps sooner—you know how Mother and I tend to rub along well enough for a few days but then find ourselves in a conversational morass that sometimes necessitates a premature departure in order to preserve the geniality of future relations.

My point is that I've gone to Reading, and I don't know when I will be back, except to say that it shan't be later than Wednesday next.

Your sister,
Julianna

One of the benefits of being mindless, Julianna considered, as she hastily packed and hailed a hack, was that one needn't stop to question one's spontaneous choices, or to fret about having lied to one's sister. One simply moved through space, more body than mind, a starfish drifting in the waves.

And when one arrived at the Blossoms Inn, one merely had to count out one's money for a return ticket on the London-Brighton coach and find a bench on which to wait for the departure of said coach.

It wasn't until they were underway that Julianna's logical mind reawakened. As it fired to life, the reality of her uncharacteristic decision began assailing her. Her breathing became shallow.

What had she *done*?

The answer was that she had spent a quarter of her savings on a ticket to Brighton!

Julianna was saving to buy a printing press. Or, she corrected ruthlessly, she *had* been. Even without contributing to her sister's household, Julianna's salary was so low that it would take years for her to save enough. And who knew how much lodging in Brighton would cost?

If she'd wanted to be profligate, she could have spent a considerably smaller sum on postage. She could have written Effie as often as she wanted, letting her thoughts spill onto a second page without regard for the increased cost.

Well, it was too late now. She attempted to put her extravagance out of her mind and to resign herself to a seaside respite in Brighton.

How would she find Effie?

And assuming she did, then what? Was she going to be ill-mannered enough to gate-crash her friend's holiday? Intrude upon her family? Or her circle of friends?

Julianna did not know with whom Effie was traveling. For as intimately as Julianna knew Effie, their friendship existed in a bubble. She knew the contents of Effie's heart, but she did *not* know the contents of Effie's day-to-day life. Effie talked about her sister, Sarah, but not a great deal, and she referenced her parents only in the vaguest terms. When Julianna probed, her inquiries went unanswered. Effie's next letter would contain a poem, or a pressed leaf, or a vastly amusing anecdote, and the question would be forgotten by both of them.

Julianna had, uncharacteristically, not been so circumspect with the details of her family situation. She had confided in Effie about her frustrations with Mr. Glanvil—with both Misters Glanvil. Effie knew that Julianna felt like an interloper in her sister's household. And when Effie had inquired about whether Julianna had ever considered marriage as a solution to that particular problem, Julianna had written a very long letter explaining why she hadn't and wouldn't.

In short, Julianna had sliced open her chest and allowed Effie to see her heart. To see the tender, beating core of her.

While Julianna couldn't quite bring herself to regret how forthright she'd been—surprisingly, the slicing open of her chest had brought a kind of relief rather than the pain she might have expected to follow from such a surgery—she did sometimes wonder if the degree of her openness had had an inverse effect on the degree of Effie's.

Euphemia Turner was hiding something, and Julianna was almost certain she knew what it was: her friend was of noble birth, and she didn't want Julianna to be made unsettled by the knowledge of such. There was much evidence supporting this conclusion.

Effie's vagueness with respect to her parents.

The fact that she sometimes wrote to Julianna from Cornwall and sometimes from London—and she never cross-wrote her letters, and they always came in envelopes that doubled the price of posting them.

How apparent it was that she'd had an excellent education. The daughters of working men did not, generally speaking, have Effie's knowledge of and knack for poetry.

And, most damning of all, the bank reported that Effie had never cashed any of the drafts Julianna had sent her in payment for her work.

Julianna felt as if she and Effie were sister birds living in adjacent but separate cages. They knew each other's song intimately, but there were bars between them.

Julianna wanted to know what her friend was hiding, because she wanted to know her friend, to know her with no veils or equivocations—or bars—between them, but she had, historically, feared that to inquire too directly, to allow her curiosities to shade into demands, would cost her the friendship. She had considered pressing the matter anyway, attaching a disclaimer: *If you are the daughter of a peer, I shan't be angry or alienated or envious. You'll still be you, and I'll still be me, and nothing will have to change.*

Except she knew that wasn't true. Effie surely did, too. Society wasn't like that. *Life* wasn't like that. Daughters of peers were not bosom friends with women like Julianna.

Which no doubt explained why neither of them had suggested they meet in person, even now that Effie had been resident in London for so long. Julianna had considered it, had even had quill poised over paper to propose exactly that, ready to risk her most important friendship.

Something always stopped her, though, something beyond the possibility of Effie's not being entirely who she pretended to be. Julianna couldn't quite put it into words, but it had something to do with a feeling of foreboding that overcame her when she thought of actually meeting her friend in the flesh. As if it might change everything.

She was being nonsensical. She shook her head. It was time to stop this madness and meet Effie. So, yes, Julianna was going to gate-crash her friend's holiday. Not for long. She did not intend to be rude. Just long enough to open the doors to the adjacent cages and say hello properly. If there were consequences, she would bear them. She could no longer live in this limbo.

That settled, she began to consider what her strategy ought to be. Where would she look for Effie? And what about the more immediate problem that Julianna did not know what Effie looked like?

Well, she corrected herself, she knew what Effie looked like, to a point. She had described herself: long dark hair. Different color eyes—one blue and one brown, which would certainly aid in endeavors of identification should Julianna get close enough to her friend to look into her eyes. A tendency toward the fanciful when it came to her wardrobe. A fondness for old-fashioned court shoes. The latter was more evidence of Effie's being highborn, for who but an aristocrat would wear such gaudy and impractical shoes if she had to actually *do* anything in them?

Sometimes Julianna asked herself how it was possible that her closest confidant, her dearest friend, was a person she had never met. But it didn't *feel* that way.

To be fair, it wasn't as if Effie had a great deal of competition. Julianna was, due to the nature of her employment, friendly with a great many people. She wrote scores of letters each month to assign stories and deliver editorial instructions. She was friendly with the banker who issued the drafts with which she paid her writers. She was friendly with the woman who worked at the receiving house where she posted her letters.

Friendly was not the same as *friends*.

Julianna did not have friends. Not the way Amy did. Amy took tea with her neighbors and visited the shops with Arthur's brothers' wives. More than once, Julianna, having heard peals of laughter from the drawing room, had entered it only to cause the roomful of ladies to go dead silent.

What if she couldn't find Effie? What if she got so close but had to return home as far away from Effie as ever? What a waste of her money. Her time. Her sentiment.

By the time the coach stopped at the halfway point, Julianna had made herself quite melancholy.

They alit for a short respite, and she walked around the yard of the coaching inn and gave herself a stern talking-to. What was done was done. Her money could not be unspent. Time could not be unwound. Therefore, she must put her mind to having an enjoyable holiday, regardless of whether she managed to locate Effie.

Sea-bathing. She would concentrate on sea-bathing. She had been curious about it since she'd read about the practice gaining popularity in Brighton. It had been an idle sort of interest, though, because why allow oneself to want something one can't have? That was another maxim Julianna lived by: *You can't miss what you don't let yourself want.*

Therefore, she hadn't wanted to sea-bathe.

But now she could try it. And she would *see* the sea, too. Walk along it and stare at its vastness.

She dug in her reticule and produced the wedding band she often wore when she was out and about alone. Julianna would never be a wife, but being a "widow" afforded a lady a certain amount of freedom, and she had found that the existence of a dear departed husband, even a fictional one, often aided in her work. She suspected the same would prove true on holiday. For instance, a spinster, even a spinster of eight-and-thirty with a great deal of experience of the world, might not be allowed to sea-bathe without her mother, or a maid.

Back in the coach, she closed her eyes and attempted to visualize a flame. Julianna had read about the technique in a book written by a professor at East India College who'd been an acquaintance of Father. It was meant to be practiced every morning, and with time and diligence, reportedly led to "enlightenment." Julianna had yet to achieve that exalted state, but the exercise reliably focused her mind when she was distracted.

Today, as per usual, enlightenment was not achieved, but alas, neither was focus. The attempt yielded only slumber. It wasn't until the ostler shouted, "Brighton! End of the line!" that Julianna awakened. Well, if one could have neither enlightenment nor focus, a nap was a not-unwelcome substitute.

She smelled the sea the moment she alit. The air was heavy and tangy and salty and *wonderful*. The sun was shining, and the sky was a brilliant blue.

"Which way to the sea?" she asked a boy leading the horses off, and she went in the direction he pointed, reasoning that if she walked long enough, she would eventually reach it.

She took in fine town houses and green parks on the downward-sloping streets. When she finally glimpsed the sea peeking between buildings, she realized she'd *been* seeing it for some time. She thought she'd been looking at the sky.

She passed an inn called the Old Ship as she traversed the final stretch toward the water, making a note to return and inquire about a room. It looked like a fine hotel. Perhaps Effie and her traveling companions would be lodging there.

A few more steps, and she arrived at her destination at the end of the earth, buildings and other assorted man-made detritus behind her. She stepped onto a pebbled beach and marveled.

There were two shades of blue ahead, two wide stripes, one of sea and one of sky, meeting up in the middle in what looked like a poorly sewn seam between two patches on a quilt.

Even in London where she could hardly see it, Julianna understood that the sky was vast. She had not been prepared for the sea, too, to be so boundless. There was more water than she could fathom, steely and beautiful and blue. That water touched America and the Far East. It was home to shipwrecks and fanciful animals. It was the cure for any number of maladies if one believed Dr. Awsiter's claims about the sea right here in Brighton. She had thought such claims a grift, but now she wondered. It seemed possible that this much water could do anything. Perhaps it could even remake a person.

There were people all about, strolling and talking and laughing, but she was alone in the ways that mattered. No one need witness her body being turned inside out, her ribs cracking and vulnerable in the salt breeze. She was a pillowslip being turned in on itself by a wash maid, beaten with a stick and hung to dry in the curative sun.

She was in a new world. *She* was new. She had not misspent her funds after all.

Chapter 3

From the Mouths of Birds

"Shall we drive through Brighton before we turn for Hove?" Archie asked as they made a quick stop a few miles out of town to stretch their legs.

"Oh, yes, let's," Effie said. "We can take the measure of the place. Although perhaps we *ought* to have brought disguises. What if the king *is* there? What if someone recognizes us?"

"No one is going to recognize us," Archie said.

"Of course you are right," Effie said archly. He tapped the side of Archie's coach as he climbed back inside. "This grand vehicle emblazoned with the livery of the Earl of Harcourt won't give us away in the slightest."

"We merely need get to the house," Simon said with an air of tried patience, as if he were a harried mother and Archie and Effie quarreling children. "Hove has the advantage of being home to a mere three hundred souls, and the house itself is on the outskirts. We shall be quite anonymous once tucked up there. Then we may come and go between Brighton and Hove on horseback."

"It is almost akin to being a character in a novel of intrigue," Effie said. If one had inexplicably ceased to enjoy balls and parties, intrigue might be the next best thing.

"The last thing I want to do on my holiday is feel like I'm a character in a novel of intrigue," Archie said.

"To each his own." Effie sniffed jestingly.

After some discussion, the gentlemen agreed to make a brief stop at the foot of Brighton, where it met the sea, to take in the prospect.

"With the caveat," Simon said, "that we take a circuitous route down to the sea so as to avoid glimpsing the Pavilion."

"Is the Pavilion not the point of this trip?" Archie asked.

"It is, which means I want to take it in properly, all at once and not in passing en route somewhere else. I prefer to be overwhelmed all at once by its symmetry and majesty rather than assailed by bits and bobs of it as we drive by."

"How poetic of you," Effie teased. "But I understand perfectly."

"How lovely," Archie said a few minutes later as they climbed out of the carriage in front of a hotel called the Old Ship, which to Effie's dismay did not look like a ship whatsoever. It seemed a lost opportunity. "Shall we walk down to the beach?"

"What a beautiful day," Simon said. "One forgets, in London, how very much sky there is in the sky."

"How very much sky there is in the sky?" Effie echoed. "I take it back, Simon: You are not poetic whatsoever."

It was so lovely to be bantering with his friends. Effie could feel something inside himself, some taut inner part of him, opening.

"I never claimed to be a poet," Simon retorted. "There's only so much room for poetry in this group, and you have already contributed more than is indicated."

Effie snorted and hurried to catch up with Archie, noting the delightful crunching beneath his feet as he stepped onto the pebbled beach. The birds were so loud here; their caws unfurling over the sound of the wind were simultaneously jarring and satisfying. Perhaps he should not have left Leander in the coach. Then again, it would be rather cruel, would it not, to show a caged bird what life might have been like had he been born a common gull rather than an exotic, expensive macaw?

"We ought to try sea-bathing while we're here," Archie said.

"Have you never been in the sea?" Simon asked.

"Not since I was a child. We used to travel to Lydd-on-Sea with . . ."

Their conversation faded as Effie stared at the horizon. He wasn't looking at the sea anymore, though. There was a woman alone at the edge of the water with her back to them. She stood a hundred yards out, and she was wearing a pale-gray coat and a straw bonnet adorned with a ribbon of the same faded gray. She was right in the middle of his prospect, almost as if she were centered in a painting. He could put a frame around the whole thing and hang it on the wall and it would make for a very compelling image.

He watched as she took off her bonnet. Her hair was very dark and pinned up. There was something about her posture, the way she carried herself, that seemed . . . familiar. He shook his head, certain he did not know a lady who would wear such a lackluster dress, much less on the beach in Brighton.

If he had thought for a moment that he knew her, it had only been wishful thinking.

He tilted his head up as she had done hers. Besides, the sky was the wrong color.

"I have something to tell you both!" Effie shouted as soon as they were back in the carriage. "I must do it immediately upon our arrival in Hove!"

"Tell!" Leander screeched.

"Not now," Effie said to the bird. "Honestly, did you hear what I *just* said? I can't tell anything now; it must wait until we're in Hove." He said to the boys, "Forget speaking in complete sentences. I would be happy if the creature would only *listen*."

Neither Simon nor Archie spoke. He had shocked them with his earlier outburst. And/or his one-sided conversation with a bird.

Effie had resolved to tell the boys about Julianna on this trip, but he'd intended to wait a few days, to let the rhythms of the holiday settle first. But after their brief seaside stop, that curious feeling of opening had continued to the point where he felt a terrible urgency to confess, as if the secret were alive inside him and had begun clawing its way out. Perhaps that's what that feeling of hardness, of calcification, he had experienced at home in the foyer with Father had been: the bars of a cage. Bars that were now dissolving thanks to the salt air and the gentle barbs of his friends.

How had he kept this from them for so long? And more to the point, *why*? These two were his closest friends, his "found family," to use a perfectly lovely phrase Simon had coined.

Effie was going near out of his head thanks to this business with Julianna. His longing for her, of course—always, his longing for her—but also the tragic impossibility of the situation. His lies—to the boys, and to her. How miserable he was.

How happy he was.

How completely befuddled he was.

The boys would help.

After recovering from their startlement at his outburst, Archie's countenance became open, inviting; Simon appeared serious, bordering on skeptical, but that was his way.

"By all means," Archie said. "If you have something to tell, we are keen to hear it."

"You must give me a drink upon our arrival. Several drinks. Then I shall tell you everything."

Archie did as instructed, as well as he could, anyway. The Hove house, unlike Quintrell Castle of last year's holiday, was well staffed. A housekeeper, a footman, a groom, a cook, a kitchen maid, and a housemaid awaited them, and it took some time to fend them off. They wanted to know what the lords wished to eat for their evening meal. They wanted to know when the lords might next require horses. They wanted to know if the lords would like to inspect the bedchambers that had been made up for them and deem them suitable or no. They wanted to know if the lords would enjoy a tour of the garden, or perhaps a guide to show them the way to the beach. They wanted to know if Leander required any special care, or diet.

"Thank you kindly," Archie said after they'd endured a tour. "I am sure whatever arrangements you have made for dining and sleeping will be more than suitable. You will not find us demanding guests. And while we look forward to exploring, we are fatigued from our journey and for now would prefer to repose in a private room. Perhaps with some"—he looked at Effie—"Scotch?"

Effie made a choking noise. He would drink Scotch if nothing else was on offer, and indeed he had done just that on last year's Earls Trip, but in truth he hated the stuff. One might as well drink a bog.

"Ratafia?" Archie tried, and Effie nodded vigorously.

If the housekeeper found the request odd, she said nothing, and after a few minutes, she arrived with several bottles of the sweet wine. "Shall I take your bird, my lord?" she asked.

"Thank you, no," Effie said. "I could do with some old linens for my room, though. He will need to spend time outside his cage, but I shall confine him to my bedchamber, and protect its furnishings with anything you might see fit to lend me. Does anyone in the household paint? At home, I use inexpensive muslin for this purpose."

"I have to say," Archie said, "Mrs. Mitchell took that in stride. I don't know many a housekeeper who would be so sanguine about a houseguest announcing that their giant pet bird is going to shit all over the house."

"I think," Simon said, "that you underestimate the eccentricities of the average nobleman."

"Do I?" Archie asked. "Ought I to take up an idiosyncratic yet destructive pastime?"

"And," Simon said, ignoring the question, "I believe the purpose of the linens was so the bird will *not* shit all over the house."

"Point taken, but perhaps if one travels with a creature that is going to shit erratically, one ought to bring one's own linens."

As he listened to the boys banter, Effie poured himself a glass of ratafia and downed it before delivering glasses for the others and returning to the sideboard to refill his own.

Simon made a face as he took his first sip. "We ought to have asked for Scotch as well, so—"

"I am in love with a woman named Julianna Evans!" Effie shouted, unable to keep the secret-creature inside anymore—the bars of his chest-cage were dissolving, after all—and equally unable to keep his voice down, though he wasn't sure if it was glee or dismay that had him yelling. He said it again, at a more suitable pitch. "I am in love with a woman named Julianna Evans." Then, for reasons he couldn't explain, he lowered his voice yet again, making the last entry in his spoken trilogy a whisper. "I am in love with a woman named Julianna Evans."

The boys were silent, which was fair. It was a lot to take in, even for him. He had never said those words aloud before. Perhaps that is why he'd needed to repeat them twice over.

"I am in love with a woman named Julianna Evans!" Leander shrieked, and after a beat of collective shock, the three of them fell into laughter.

"Yes, I *said* that," Effie said. "Several times."

"There's your complete sentence, though," Simon said.

Effie laughed again. "I can only surmise that Leander was waiting for his first sentence to be one of great import."

"Are you going to tell us more?" Archie asked.

"Yes, such as: Who is Julianna Evans?" Simon asked.

"She is my editor at *Le Monde Joli*," Effie said, his words extinguishing the amusement provided by Leander's interruption. "I have never met her, but we write to each other quite a lot, and I am not sure how I am to survive a fortnight without word from her!"

He had shocked them. Well, he had shocked Simon, whose mouth was hanging open like a haddock. Upon further reflection, Archie didn't look shocked so much as quizzical. Assessing. As if he were piecing together a puzzle.

"Say something!" Effie cried. "Why aren't you saying anything?"

"We are surprised," Simon said after a beat of silence.

Had Effie made a mistake, confessing the contents of his heart? He hardly thought the boys would care that Julianna worked for a living. Had he misjudged them?

No. This was Archie and Simon.

"Ef," Archie said gently, "please, won't you come and sit?"

Oh. Yes. Effie had made his pronouncements from where he was standing by the sideboard. His skin prickled as he crossed the room. Was that . . . shame?

No. He refused to be ashamed of any of this: of whom he loved, of confiding in his friends. It was more of this mixed-up-ness, this sense that he was changing into someone new, someone he did not know. The only conclusion he could come to was that he was mightily befuddled.

His friends gazed at him for a moment after he'd settled, making him feel unpleasantly like a boy under his grandmother's quizzing glass.

Archie leaned toward Effie with his forearms on his thighs. "You will forgive me if I overstep, but if I am surprised, it is only because I always rather thought your . . . inclinations did not tend toward ladies."

Oh. *Oh.* Effie looked at Simon, who raised his eyebrows in a way that seemed to signal concurrence.

"You are not wrong. Yet you are not exactly right, either." Effie paused, trying to think how to explain. "We have all heard of gentlemen who prefer the company of their own kind." Would they understand what he meant? He didn't get the impression that Simon and Archie attracted the Mr. Lansings of the world the way Effie himself did. "Do we all know what I mean by 'prefer the company'?"

"We do," Archie said with an amused glimmer in his eye, and Simon nodded his agreement.

All right, then, onward. "To the extent that I have yearned for the company of anyone, I have never made a distinction between ladies and gentlemen."

"I see," Archie said.

"But at the same time, it is rare for me to . . . prefer company in that way. Increasingly rare, the older I get. I suffered the odd childhood infatuation, but it has been years."

In fact, when they were young, Effie had, for the briefest of moments, thought he fancied Archie. Archie had been so good at archery, and so dedicated to antagonizing Nigel Nettlefell, a boy whose principal hobby was being unkind to Effie.

But the sentiment had come and gone like a cloud over a picnic on a windy day; there was no point in dredging it up now. Archie was his brother in all but blood, and Effie cared little for blood. Where had blood ever got him?

"I always thought it was because I am an artist, a poet," he went on. "There is so much beauty in the world, and so much ugliness. There are big sentiments everywhere, just waiting to overwhelm one. The sunrise and the fall of an army. Revolutions and new planets being discovered. Did you know that there are great rings around the planet Saturn? There are who knows how many planets in the sky all around us, and some of them are *ringed*! Just the other day I tried to paint those rings."

"And?" Simon asked.

"I remain a better poet than painter. But I persevere." He paused to refocus his thoughts. Saturn was not the point. "What I am trying to say is that while I understand that for many people, love—and desire—are seemingly animating forces, to me they have historically seemed so . . . small. Inconsequential, even." He understood now, though, what all the fuss was about. "Was I that out of step?" He turned to Archie. "I must have been, for I watched you absolutely lose your mind over Clementine Morgan last year."

"I did not lose my mind."

"You did, and I am not sure you've found it yet."

Archie sent an appealing look at Simon, who merely lifted his glass and said, "May you never find it."

Effie said, "Miss Austen says, 'To love is to burn. To be on fire.' I had never felt that before. Mind you, she also says, 'We are all fools in love,' and I rather think I am already accomplished enough on that front without adding love to the pot."

"You are speaking in the past perfect tense," Simon said. "You said, 'I *had* never felt that before.' But you do now?"

"I do now," Effie affirmed.

"For this Miss Evans," Simon said, his tone gentler than was typical for him.

"Yes. But it was *not* like in novels. I wasn't in love with her from the start. It was only once I got to know her rather intimately that I was . . . struck. But struck I was." Effie put his head in his hands. He had so much love in his heart. If this was what love felt like, love was exhausting. "I have come to understand that for me, a bond of friendship is a precondition for love."

"What is the difficulty here?" Archie asked. "This would seem to be a happy revelation, no?"

"The 'difficulty' is not singular," Effie said through his hands. "My situation is beset with numerous difficulties. One, she does not feel the same." He lifted his head. "Two, I could never marry her. I could never be with her."

"Because of your father? Your title?" Archie asked.

"Yes. Miss Evans works for a living. She lives with her sister but aspires to become a woman of independent means. I would argue she already is, except her stepbrother is proprietor of her magazine and pays her a wage not at all commensurate with the value of her work."

"So how will she ever become a woman of independent means?" Archie asked.

"She wants to buy a printing press."

"Ah," Simon said. "Certain things have suddenly become clear."

"The notion was born because she sometimes has trouble getting her magazine printed to her specifications," Effie said. "For example, a year or so ago, she had a regular slot with a chap on Grub Street, but he started printing pamphlets for the abolitionists and told Miss Evans he could no longer accommodate her. While she sympathized with the pamphleteers' cause, she struggled to find a new arrangement." He paused to wonder how October, which should be off the press, was looking. "And even when she can find reliable printing services, her stepbrother—the proprietor who profits off her toils—often will not allow things like a color plate when one is clearly called for, and—"

He was getting carried away. He needn't mire the boys in the details. "If she owned a press, she could print the magazine exactly as she liked."

"It sounds as if she has a head for business," Simon said.

"Oh, she does. She is artistic *and* cunning." Effie put his head back in his hands. "Artistic and cunning and employed." He thought of another "difficulty." "And eight-and-thirty years old."

If the boys were scandalized by the ten-year age gap, they said nothing. But perhaps the silence that settled was indicative of their shock.

"You could walk away from your family," Simon said after a few moments. "Some do."

"Yes, but I'd still be earl when Father dies. I can't walk away from the title, even if I could bring myself to abandon the responsibilities associated with it—which I can't. As much as I loathe the idea of inheriting, and even if I don't care about Father, I *do* care about Sarah. I care about the estate. There are twenty-seven cottages at Highworth, and thirty-four servants. That's not even counting the staff at the London house. We have a great many people depending on us."

No one said anything, because there was nothing to say. Effie was well and truly stuck. He sighed. "It's academic anyway, as she proclaims she will never marry."

"Where have we heard that before?" Simon asked, raising his eyebrows at Archie, and Effie had to smile through his dismay. They had heard it on last year's Earls Trip, from Archie's now wife.

Archie grinned. "Yes, for what it's worth, that particular impediment may not be as intractable as you believe."

"Regardless, all these difficulties are not the point. They are indeed disqualifying, but there remains a larger reason I cannot be with Miss Evans. A more immediate and unscalable . . . obstacle." *Obstacle* seemed an anemic word given the circumstances, entirely insufficient to describe the fortress his lies had built.

"And that is?" Archie asked.

"She thinks I'm a woman."

Archie and Simon erupted, exclaiming and talking over each other. There. He had finally shocked them.

Archie got up and fetched a second bottle of wine from the sideboard. As he was opening it, Simon made a show of going for the third, which made them all laugh.

"You'd better start from the beginning," Archie said when they were all refilled.

"What about dinner?" Effie said. "Aren't you hungry?"

"You're more important than dinner," Simon said.

"Yes," said Archie. "Tell us the story now, and we can consider it as we dine. Perhaps there will be some solution you have yet to think of."

Effie's throat tightened. His friends were the best of men. He couldn't think why he had kept this from them for so long.

"When I submitted the poem she initially published," he said, recapping what they already knew, "I did it under a pseudonym."

"Yes," Archie said.

Effie had known that publishing a poem under his own name would cause more trouble than it was worth in his family. And publishing a poem under his own name in a ladies' magazine? All hell would have broken loose.

"I signed it E. Turner," he said.

"Ah!" Simon exclaimed. "Your Miss Evans is corresponding with 'Miss Turner.'"

"You will recall that *Le Monde Joli* published a handful of my poems over the next few years. Miss Evans and I corresponded about the poems, but gradually, our discourse became more personal.

"One day a letter arrived in which she signed only her Christian name: 'Julianna.' She said she hoped she wasn't being too familiar but asked me what mine was." He could still summon echoes of the thrill he'd experienced on reading that letter—the progression from "Miss Evans" to "Julianna" to "JE," had truly transported him. "I regret this now, but I equivocated. I told her, 'My friends call me Effie.' She must have decided 'Effie' was a diminutive for 'Euphemia,' for she thinks that is my Christian name. To my discredit, I have never corrected her."

"Why ever not?" Simon, always the sensible one, asked.

"I imagine," Archie said, "that the longer it went on, the harder it seemed to disentangle yourself from the lies you'd spun, lies that initially seemed minor."

"*Yes.*"

Archie understood.

"Miss Austen was right," Archie said. "Love does indeed make fools of us all."

"You will perhaps recall how I'd sent that first poem around to a great many publications. I received rejections across the board from everyone except Miss Evans. She wrote me with her acceptance, and she had a few minor but exceedingly thoughtful suggestions that improved the work enormously. I was thrilled."

"I remember," Archie said, and Simon murmured his agreement.

"I didn't realize until I saw the poem in print that *Le Monde Joli* was a ladies' magazine."

"With a name like that?" Simon exclaimed.

"What is wrong with the name?" Effie, a bit indignant, asked.

"Not a thing," Archie said soothingly. "It's merely that it sounds somewhat feminine."

"An appreciation of beauty being an ability limited to the fairer sex?" Effie shot back, his affront growing. But he stood down. They meant no ill, and their way of thinking was commonplace, if baffling. "Regardless, yes, I did not know it was a women's magazine until it was too late. I imagined that, like you, Miss Evans would assume her readership was exclusively female and therefore that I was, too. I should have corrected her when I sent in my second poem, but I was afraid she would reject it." He heaved a sigh. "Eventually, I became less concerned about the poems and more afraid that she would reject *me*."

"You talked at the end of our trip last year about needing to get back to Highworth because you were waiting for an important letter," Simon said. "Was it from Miss Evans?"

"It was indeed. I was waiting on an editorial assessment of a poem she had agreed to print. She had written to accept it but said that she wanted to let it simmer and would write again in a week with her thoughts. That is a particular phrase of hers. 'Let it simmer.' Isn't it clever? Think how much better a soup tastes on the second day, having had longer to simmer."

He caught an amused glance shared by the others. He wasn't sure what was so diverting. "I was certain the letter had arrived in my absence, and I wanted terribly to read it, and also not make her wait too long for my reply."

"Why hadn't you simply told her to write to you at your London address?" Simon asked.

"I'd spent the summer at Highworth, and she had been writing me there. I did consider writing and telling her to reach me in London from that point onward, but I worried about the possibility for confusion. What if she didn't get my new direction in time and she sent her thoughts on my poem to Highworth while I was in London?" He paused. "And honestly, I didn't want to be in London at that point."

"Why not?" Archie asked. "You used to be quite devoted to the entertainments of the city."

"I didn't want her to know who I was. Well, she *knows* who I am."

She knew him in all the ways that mattered, as well as the boys did. Perhaps better. "But I didn't want her to know I was noble-born. I had been representing myself as a country . . . person. To suddenly mention a second home in Town would have outed me as not a country . . . person."

"But you're in London almost exclusively now," Simon said. "So you must have outed yourself as not a country person, if not as a man."

"Yes." He was confusing them. "In the last year, our correspondence has become much more voluminous. Whereas it generally took a letter a week or two to come or go from Highworth, in Town I can drop a letter at a receiving house in the morning knowing she will have it in a matter of hours. I also realized that while I hadn't given any thought to the cost of all these letters, it was costing her twelve pence to send one to Highworth. In London, we can use the penny post and it's only three pence." For a single sheet, which was all she ever sent him. "And when I learned that she was saving for a printing press, I came to understand that writing to me was very dear for her. I could no longer justify time spent at Highworth."

"But you aren't tempted to see her?" Archie asked. "Now that you're both in London?"

"Did you not hear what I said? She thinks I'm a woman!"

"Yes, but could you not see her from afar?" Simon queried.

"Skulk around as if I'm the main character of a novel of intrigue you mean?" Effie said tartly.

"You sounded rather keen on doing just that a while ago."

"Yes, but that was merely as a holiday diversion. I *do* love dressing up. This is different."

In truth, he had considered the idea and discarded it. So many things could go wrong. To begin with, he did not trust himself to see her from afar and not swoon in the street where he stood.

But more elementally, what would it get him? He *knew* her. He couldn't have her, but he *knew* her. Seeing her would only make the yearning, the unrequited longing, worse.

Julianna had a few precepts she seemed to live by, or at least they functioned as aphorisms she frequently quoted. One of them was *You can't miss what you don't let yourself want.* He had tried, these recent months, to keep that one in mind.

"Why is it different?" Simon asked.

Effie didn't know how to explain it to them without making himself pathetic—though he wasn't sure why that mattered. He *was* pathetic. "It's a bit like your not wanting to see the Pavilion just now, Simon. You didn't want to see it casually, in passing. It wouldn't be right. It wouldn't be enough."

"Ah. I understand." Simon paused. "But the difference is, I will eventually see the Pavilion in all its glory. I will be satisfied."

"Yes," said Effie. "That is precisely the difference."

After their evening meal, Effie took Leander upstairs to put him to bed. He stood in front of the cage and said, "I am in love with a woman named Julianna Evans." He said it several times over, varying his tone. He wasn't sure what his aim was in trying to get the bird to say it back. Was he merely trying to reinforce the creature's expanded syntax, and if so, why now, on night one of an Earls Trip when his friends were waiting for him?

Did some perverse part of him want to hear out loud how hopeless his cause was?

He threw a sheet over the cage, and on his way back downstairs, he observed that, hopeless causes aside, he felt better than he had in days. Weeks. There was something about unburdening oneself to one's friends that made one feel lighter.

Of course, six glasses of ratafia did tend to have that effect, too.

He rejoined the boys in the drawing room, where they sat by a roaring fire, chatting and smoking. They nodded at him and offered him a cigar, which he declined, and carried on talking about a horse Archie was thinking of buying.

Effie appreciated how the boys absorbed him into the room, into the discussion at hand. That they didn't press him to discuss Julianna any further. He was glad he'd told them, but he needed a moment to adjust to having the knowledge out there, hovering in the world like a honeybee at a flower, rather than existing merely in his head.

When the talk of horseflesh dwindled, he asked, "If a ghost were to haunt a printing press, what sort of ghost do you think it would be?"

"The ghost of a printmaker, I should think," Simon said.

"That's a rather literal answer." Though had he expected otherwise from Simon?

"The neglected wife of the printmaker who never gets to see him because he works such long hours?" Archie suggested.

"That's more like it. But in that scenario, she would resent the press, would she not? It does not seem to follow that she would elect to haunt it for all eternity."

"Do ghosts have a say over what or whom—or whether—they haunt?" Archie asked.

"I take the point," Effie said. "Perhaps they don't."

"Why do you ask?" Simon said.

"Do either of you know the Earl of Stanhope?"

"Not particularly," Archie said.

Simon shook his head. "Nor do I. Not well, anyway. Why?"

"He has invented a new type of printing press. I gather that a system of compound levers means it requires less strength to operate than a traditional press. I should very much like to get my hands on one."

"So if, theoretically, a lady and her . . . friend had one of these presses," Simon said, "they could operate it themselves."

"Perhaps," Effie said, suddenly feeling glum. He had been thinking along those lines, but there was no "friend" in his imaginings. He merely thought that if Julianna had a small, sturdy handpress, she might not need to employ a puller. But he really didn't know. Because he didn't know how much less "less strength" was, and he didn't know anything about Julianna's vigor or lack thereof. Was she slender and delicate? Or sturdy and hale?

He had to amend an earlier thought. He'd been thinking—and

saying to the boys—that Julianna knew him. He'd meant that she knew him, and he knew her, *elementally*. Regardless of his deception, of the fact that she thought him a lady, their *souls* knew each other. And while that might be true, it was disconcerting to think he did *not* know enough about her physically to know if she could operate a hand press. He knew what she'd told him, that she was tall and had dark hair and green eyes, but those were but the most general of descriptors.

He ached to know her. The corporeal form of her.

Was this desire? If so, it was as exhausting as love.

"So you are trying to procure a press for your Miss Evans," Archie said, drawing Effie's attention back to the conversation at hand.

"Yes, but all I have been able to get is the piece of rubbish currently taking up space—a great deal of space—at your house. I can't seem to get it to work, and not because I lack the strength. It's broken—something is wrong with the screw mechanism as far as I can tell. That's why I named it Hamlet. I've decided it is haunted."

Simon said, "Perhaps you ought to name your press Dogberry, or Bottom, after one of Shakespeare's more inept characters, rather than the one who was haunted and went on to destroy everyone he loved before dying tragically himself."

"Hmm. I shall consider it."

Eventually, Simon went to bed. He always retired early. Usually, Effie and Archie conversed into the evening, but Archie surprised him by asking, "Have you got any copies of *Le Monde Joli* with you here?"

"I do. I have the most recent issue."

"May I read it? I've read your poems in the magazine, of course, but I'd like to give it a closer look."

"Of course." Effie was touched. Archie, by his own account, had trouble with reading. But part of the beauty of a magazine was that it presented information in different formats. September contained the latest installment in a serialized novel about a runaway heiress but also an engraving of a scene from *Tom and Jerry, or Life in London*, a wildly popular stage adaptation of the equally popular book, not to mention the medical advice column Julianna so hated, which this month contained a wretchedly compelling essay on the dangers of neglecting one's teeth. Teeth, and the many things that could go wrong with them both medically and aesthetically, had proven, to Julianna's mystified dismay, a perennially popular subject.

When Effie returned with the magazine, Archie went to sit with it in a wing chair near the fire. He looked up before diving in and said, "Simon won't say it, but he is beside himself to see the Pavilion. Can we go tomorrow?"

"Yes, of course, and we shall go properly, in Simon's way. Take it in all at once, or what have you. We shall look at it, and our hearts shall be shattered."

His own drama aside, Effie understood the aim of this trip. They had come to Brighton so Simon could see the Pavilion. Simon never asked for anything for himself, so accustomed was he to being the seldom-seen, and, not to put too fine a point on it—but Effie was putting a fine point on it because he was affronted on Simon's behalf—unloved third son of the late Earl of Marsden. Simon had never expected to inherit, but here they were.

This was Simon's trip, was the point, and Effie had so far made it all about himself. He would correct course. Tomorrow, they would go to the Pavilion and be overcome by the mathematical beauty of it.

With Archie occupied, Effie took the opportunity to pull out his lap desk.

Dear Bound for Bedlam,

My advice for you is threefold, and I shall dispense it in descending order of urgency.

First, you must not have any more children. Six is quite enough. Take yourself to see a midwife and express to her your desire to prevent subsequent children. If you do not know how to find a midwife, ask a housemaid or a kitchen maid. I am assuming the wife of a barrister has one or the other, if not both. If I am mistaken, please write me back and I shall provide more specific instruction privately.

Effie did not know how he would discover the correct instruction to pass along, but he would find a way. Olive would know someone who could help. She had aided him in other situations in which his qualifications fell short of what was required to properly advise his correspondents.

Second, and this will require a bit of subterfuge, you must remove yourself from the situation temporarily. And by "situation," I mean your family. All of them, with the possible exception of the youngest child if that child is reliant on you for nourishment. Your mother has taken dreadfully ill. Or your sister. Someone has taken dreadfully ill, is the point. You are needed at the bedside. You will not be gone long, but you must go.

And then, you simply leave. Perhaps, if this proves impossible to imagine saying to your particular husband in your particular situation, you leave a note. Either way, you leave. For a day, two if you can manage it. Your husband, your children: they will survive. The aim here is for your husband to understand, in a visceral way, the weight of the yoke you wear. This is not something you can tell him; you must show him.

Third, time is your friend, dear lady. When despair has you in its grasp, close your eyes and imagine yourself twenty years hence. Your children have left your home, which is quiet and peaceful. Except of course when they come to visit, some of them bringing their own children. (The cries of one's grandchildren, I think you shall find, are significantly less vexing than the cries of one's own children. And grandchildren have the benefit that after an interval of spoiling them, you can hand them back to their parents.) From the center of your present storm, picture this lovely future. Children home to visit, to dote upon their dear old mum. As for your husband, he is either retired, and reminding you what first drew you to him (unless what first drew you to him was his raven hair and slim build. I regret to inform you that both are lost forever) or he is . . . absent.

Could he say "dead" instead of "absent"? He would make a note in the margin and ask Julianna.

She would almost certainly say no, but she would be amused by the question. He often annotated his "Advice for Married Ladies" letters with asides meant for her.

Though in this case, he truly did mean "dead."

The point, dear reader, is that time marches on, which is both a blessing and a curse. Your charge is to focus on the blessings associated with such. This, too, shall pass.
Yours,
Mrs. Landers

When he was done, a kind of resigned calm settled over him. Archie was flipping the pages of *Le Monde Joli*, his forehead wrinkled in concentration. Simon was tucked into his bed, probably dreaming of Parliament.

This was where he belonged, with his letters and his friends.

For now, all was right with the world. Or at least as right as it could be.

Chapter 4

A Flock of Seagulls

Julianna's heart shattered when she saw the Pavilion.

She had not thought the Pavilion would be all that it had been trumped up to be.

She had been wrong.

She had never seen anything like it. The eye was drawn first to the large spherical dome at the center, flanked by two smaller versions of the same. They, along with the structure's many minarets, rose into the sky, spires liberated from churchly confines. The largest dome appeared to have windows in it, as if someone had thought to carve out portals to the sky.

She spent ages walking a slow circumference around the building, taking in the balconies and colonnade of the north face, the building's broad eaves. There was also a stable rising from the gardens that looked like a palace on its own. She ought to disapprove of such a lavish building being used to house horses, but she could not. It was too beautiful.

It wasn't just the buildings enchanting her. Though Julianna knew the Pavilion had been under construction for some time, had been remade more than once, it somehow looked as if it *belonged* in the tranquil gardens surrounding it, as if it had grown up from the ground along with the flowers—an absurd sentiment, she realized, given the building's Asian inspirations. No building in England looked like this.

Yet the whole was harmonious, nature and man-made structure looking as if they had always been there together.

She hadn't believed it possible to be so delighted by architecture. Spellbound, even.

Yesterday she would have thought Brighton's ability to transport her would be limited to the sea it perched on. And that would have been enough. She'd had an almost religious experience, standing at the edge of so much blue.

But here she was, again, transported.

She wasn't sure how much more her heart could take.

Tracking down Effie was beginning to feel beside the point.

She had set out to see the Pavilion this morning because she'd known the architectural marvel was the main draw for her friend, but as with the sea yesterday, she'd forgotten Euphemia as she gazed at such a vision. She'd forgotten *herself*, and it turned out that sometimes, forgetting oneself was *wonderful*. It achieved almost the same sensation as trying to visualize the flame. One became not an individualized person so much as a part of a larger whole.

"Julianna?"

And just like that, she was an individualized person again.

She glanced around to try to discover who had spoken her name. The gardens were full of people strolling, but no one here would know her.

Unless . . .

No, the voice had been distinctly masculine.

She shook her head. She must be imagining things. Perhaps she was having a religious experience. She had read about people being transported by the Holy Spirit. She didn't care for the notion.

Time to go back to the hotel. She was hungry. Lunch would exorcise the phantasmagoric voice in her head.

She hitched her reticule higher on her wrist and set off.

There was a gentleman ten or so yards off the path she was

walking. Well, there were three gentlemen ten or so yards off, but two of them were looking at the Pavilion. One of them, the one in the middle, was looking at her.

A flock of seagulls went screeching through her head, flapping against the back of her eyeballs with sinewy wings.

Effie?

No. Of course not. She shook the gulls loose, sending them back into the sky where they belonged. She had, for a moment, gone mad.

But then she heard the gentleman say, "Yes." Or perhaps she didn't *hear* him, perhaps she only *saw* him, saw his orchid lips form the word.

With what was he agreeing, though? She had not uttered his name aloud—she'd thought—so there was no reason for him to be saying, "Yes."

Yet she saw the word on his lips again: *yes.*

Julianna thought of herself as level-headed. Unflappable, even. Right then, though, nothing felt level. Not her head, not the ground beneath her feet. And there was much flapping, the head-gulls making another cacophonous fly-by. She closed her eyes for a long moment, took a breath, and tried to see the flame. Tried to stabilize herself, to quiet the birds.

When she opened her eyes, she was able to consider the gentle-man with a degree of detachment. The first relevant fact was that he was a *gentleman.* So whatever she thought had been happening before, she'd been confused. The fact of his gentleman-ness, of his sex, would allow her to study him impartially. Perhaps she knew him. Perhaps he had written for her, years ago, or for Father. She had quite the roster of correspondents, contemporaneous and historic.

The gentleman had long, lustrous dark hair. It was not pulled back into a queue but loose around his shoulders, making him look utterly striking, if a bit old-fashioned.

She dropped her gaze to his feet. He was wearing Hessians. They were made of fine brown leather but were otherwise unremarkable. His breechcs were a similarly unexceptional buff, the color of tea with too much milk in it.

But as her assessment moved upward, she noticed, peeking out from beneath his coat, a waistcoat of brilliant blue silk shot through with black thread, as if he were harboring a peacock against his chest.

I confess a weakness for fine fabrics. I used to favor black, but lately I have been finding myself drawn to vibrant colors. The other day in a shop window, I admired a bolt of brilliant blue silk shot through with black thread. It looked as if someone had taken peacock feathers and transmuted them into silk. My first thought was, Julianna would think this a silly fabric indeed. But I questioned myself. For wasn't it you who told me, when you ever so kindly rejected my last poem, that "silly" and "beautiful" need not be mutually exclusive?

They were suspended, Julianna and this peacock man, both of them frozen in place as surely as butterflies pinned in mounting cases. Well, this man, in his finery, was a butterfly. He was an Adonis blue, its azure wings edged in black. Julianna was a moth. A gray dagger, drably mottled with a tendency to blend into its surroundings.

She shook her head. It was impossible.

Wasn't it?

With great effort, she unpinned herself from her mounting case. She took a step toward him, then another. He took a step back, then another, as if he'd been instructed by some higher being—the spirit who had visited her previously, perhaps—to keep a consistent distance between them.

She advanced on him until she was close enough to see his eyes.

One was blue, the other brown.

And though his whispered, "Yes," earlier had sounded placid, his eyes didn't match that tranquil tone. They were wide with astonishment.

The shrieking gulls that had been streaming through her head circled back and came to a stop. Hovered. She could hear their breakneck bird hearts, tuning like instruments in a symphony, until they became one single note.

As she watched, waiting to see what the birds would do, what *she* would do, the man's countenance changed, astonishment giving way to dismay. His brow knit, and his eyes filled with tears.

She took another step. He tried to compensate, but he ran into one of his companions.

She took another step, gaining on him as his colleagues took note of his situation. They became confused as they registered his upset and began looking around for its cause.

They were speaking to him, but once again, she knew that only because she *saw* them doing so. Her head was filled with the gulls, their heartbeat note pressing against her eardrums.

She wondered if he heard them, too, if she could make herself audible over this avian plainsong.

Did she even need to speak, though? This man had, somehow, someway, seemed to *hear* her thoughts earlier.

"Effie?" she said, or thought—she wasn't sure which.

He gazed at her for a long time. She could feel the other gentlemen's attention, but she could not break eye contact with her Adonis blue, else he would fly away.

"Effie," she said again, or thought again. Either way, she had answered her own question. "*Effie.*"

Finally, he spoke aloud. "Yes." The tears that had been threatening spilled over as he added, "I'm sorry. I'm so sorry."

She had found Effie. Well, Effie had found her. She had come to Brighton hoping to find Effie, but Effie had found her first. Or perhaps they had found each other.

Everything made sense now. She smiled. How could she not? Here was Effie.

"It's all right, my dear," she said, and she covered the last yard between them, held open her arms, and he stepped into them. Effie. Her Effie.

* * *

Effie smelled like cloves. Julianna hadn't expected that. If anything, she would have expected citrus, or lavender—something light but not cloying—to accompany the personality of her long-time correspondent.

Cloves, though. Cloves were so much deeper, more complex. So much darker.

He held her tightly. She held him tightly. She never wanted to let go. She never wanted to leave this spot, with her feet on the earth and Effie in her arms and the sea in the distance.

Until her feet *did* leave the spot, as Effie, to her utter astonishment, lifted her off the ground and twirled her around.

She laughed, startling herself with the sound. When was the last time she had laughed? Laughed not sardonically or resignedly but genuinely, guilelessly. The world spun, rotating around them, and she wished it would never stop.

It did, though, and too quickly. Effie set her on her feet, grabbed her hands, peeled off her gloves, and turned her fingers over. They were stained with ink. "Aha!" he exclaimed in triumph. "Ink! I got that right, at least."

I got that right, at least.

She wondered if he was adjusting to the gap between the idea of her and the reality of her. Perhaps she didn't smell the way he'd thought she would.

"Ahem."

It was one of Effie's companions, the tall, graceful one, staring censorious daggers at them. The stare lasted only a beat before the man darted his eyes back and forth, seeming to want to draw their attention to their surroundings.

Their *public* surroundings, surroundings in which Effie had de-gloved Julianna with a degree of familiarity polite people would find scandalous.

Scandalous because Effie was a *man*.

"Yes. Right." Effie dropped her hand suddenly, as if it were a hot pan he'd mistakenly grabbed without protecting his hand. As if Effie, this fine gentlemanly version of Effie, had ever touched a pan. Still, something had shocked him, and unpleasantly so. His countenance changed, clouded. He looked as if he were going to be ill.

She put her gloves back on.

He took a step back.

"Miss Julianna Evans," Effie said, his voice taking on an air of formality that didn't sound like him—though she did realize what an odd notion that was given that she'd heard his voice for the first time mere seconds ago—"may I present . . ." He trailed off, looking pained, though she did not understand why. Were his friends criminals?

He stood taller, as if steeling himself to a task and began again. "May I present Archibald Fielding-Burton, the Earl of Harcourt, and Simon Courtenay, the Earl of Marsden."

Earls! Effie's friends were earls! She would almost rather have had criminals.

Julianna did not care for being shocked. It wasn't the way she wanted to present herself to the world. So she said, archly, even as she dipped a curtsy in response to the pretty bows made by Effie's companions, "Perhaps you ought to introduce yourself, too."

"I am Effie," he said seriously, even as his companions snickered over her retort.

"Not short for 'Euphemia,' though, I presume." The joy and wonder she'd initially felt on seeing Effie was receding in favor of pique.

After a pause that stretched out long enough to confer discomfort, he said, "Not short for Euphemia." He spoke quietly, almost sadly. "My Christian name is Edward. 'Effie' is short for my title, which is Featherfinch."

"You are an earl, too?" The pique was growing, though she wasn't sure why. She'd had her suspicions Effie might be the daughter of an aristocrat. And since it turned out Effie was not and had never been a daughter, why shouldn't he be titled?

"A viscount. It is a courtesy title. My father is the earl."

Effie continued to stare at her with such intensity, it seemed as if he were trying to convey a silent message. She had no idea what it might be. Perhaps they—Effie and Jules—only worked on paper. Perhaps Miss Julianna Evans and Edward Astley, Viscount Featherfinch, could not survive the confining realities of the corporeal world.

She wanted to ask him questions. A great number of them. Was he sometimes in Cornwall because his family had a house there? Was he the eldest son and therefore heir to his father's earldom?

Had he written those poems?

She tried and only half succeeded in swallowing a gasp at that last thought. She could cope with his being a man, a peer, even, but what if he had deceived her regarding matters of authorship?

She could easily imagine an aristocrat—one prone to misrepresenting himself, as it turned out—amusing himself by playacting at being a poet. She could hardly bear to think it. If Effie had not written "E. Turner's" poems, she would be devastated. If all the stirring words he had sent her, all the words she had printed, were not *his*, she didn't know how to come back from that.

"Perhaps," Lord Harcourt said, making Julianna realize she was once again comporting herself less than ideally given the public nature of their encounter—she and Effie had continued to gape at each other while she underwent her bout of mental turmoil— "we ought to find somewhere to . . ." He trailed off as if at a loss. She knew how he felt.

"Have tea," Lord Marsden said firmly.

"Yes," Julianna said, breaking with Effie's gaze, a rending that required some effort. Tea. A perfectly regular thing to do in the afternoon, and she *was* hungry. "I'm staying at the Old Ship. It's not far."

"I suggest," Lord Marsden said, "that we find an establishment a trifle less . . . prominent."

"We are endeavoring to not make our presence in town known," Lord Harcourt said conspiratorially. "In case the king is here. I don't suppose you know if he is? I understand you're somewhat of a newspaperwoman."

Effie and his friends—his earl friends—were trying to avoid the king. It boggled the mind. "No. I believe His Majesty is in Greenwich, having recently arrived from Scotland. At least that's what I read in the papers yesterday." Yesterday when she was in London, rifling through letters from her friend Effie, short for Euphemia.

What a difference a day made.

Tea, taken in a small shop a few blocks from the Pavilion, was excruciating. The sandwiches were stale and the conversation stilted. The four of them had apparently entered into an unspoken agreement to pretend it was perfectly normal that they'd met in Brighton, that the origin of Effie and Julianna's acquaintance was unremarkable.

They talked mostly about the Pavilion itself. Lord Marsden, she gathered, had a particular interest in architecture. Under other circumstances, Julianna's mind would be abuzz with ideas she might press him to write about, for he struck her as intelligent and thoughtful. "The Earl of Marsden on the Royal Pavilion." That would be the rare piece she and Mr. Glanvil would delight in equally. He might even allow her a colored plate.

The problem was that she couldn't sit and make idle conversation with Effie's friends while Effie himself sat silently on a chair to her left.

She had to amend an earlier thought. *Three* of them were endeavoring to pretend that everything was usual. Effie had not spoken a word in the hour-plus they had been together. He hadn't eaten anything, either. He had simply stared at Julianna over the rim of his cup as he drank methodically from it. She'd refilled it several times, and he hadn't even murmured a *thank-you*. Effie had sent her hundreds of poems over the years. To think of all those words flowing from this silent creature.

He was close enough to touch, yet he was also, somehow, farther away than he had ever been, even when he'd been writing her from Cornwall.

It was beginning to break her heart.

She should not have come.

To tea, to Brighton—any of it.

"It is stunning, truly," Lord Marsden said, summarizing his thoughts on the Pavilion. "However, though I am appreciative of His Majesty's support in several matters in Lords, I cannot help but feel a niggle of philosophical unease when I behold such a structure. What is it *for*?"

"It is a royal residence," Lord Harcourt said.

"Yes, I know. I meant the question in a more elemental sense. A *moral* sense. It's taken numerous years and an ungodly sum to build it. It's been expanded, and to hear it told, made over on the inside more than once to accommodate His Majesty's whim. The man already has any number of perfectly acceptable houses."

"One could argue, and many do, that the monarch's attention has raised Brighton's profile in the eyes of Englishmen and foreigners alike," Lord Harcourt said.

"Yes, yes, but . . ."

There was so much to unpack in every statement either of the gentlemen—the speaking gentlemen—made. *However, though I am appreciative of His Majesty's support in several matters in Lords . . .* This would seem to indicate that Lord Marsden was a Whig.

Normally, Julianna would be quite interested in this conversation, but she kept having to force herself to attend to it. Now the two earls were arguing good-naturedly about how many houses they each had and if criticizing the Pavilion was therefore hypocritical.

She sneaked a glance at Effie, and there he was, the same as ever, staring but silent. She wanted to rail at him. *Say something!* She understood that he could not treat her with the same familiarity that characterized their letters, but neither did he have to act as if she were a stranger—a stranger he didn't quite approve of, no less, judging by those assessing looks from behind the rim of his teacup.

The flash of ire that had her wanting to shout at him was suddenly quashed by the most ridiculous urge to cry. This wasn't the person she'd corresponded with all those years. The person who sent her poems, all of them good, even the ones she declined to publish. And what of his identity as Mrs. Landers? He gave such measured, encouraging advice, and he somehow managed to be amusing while doing so.

Where was *that* person?

Perhaps it had never been him. Perhaps, as she'd feared earlier, he was engaged in some kind of ruse.

The tears marshalling felt heavy, capable of displacing everything else—that ire from before. Her own sense of pride.

No. The last time Julianna cried was at her father's funeral. She'd awakened the next day, swollen and miserable, and decided that crying wasn't worth it. It achieved nothing. It hadn't made her feel better. It hadn't brought Father back. All it had done was make her look like a wet turnip. So she had turned herself into the kind of woman who never cried. And if Julianna were going to make an exception to the no-crying rule—which she absolutely was not—she *never* would have done it in front of them. Of *him*.

She merely had to get through tea. They'd drunk three pots and eaten all the mediocre sandwiches, so presumably it would be over soon.

Then she could go home. She *would* go home. Tomorrow.

She sat up straighter, and in so doing felt something inside her harden, as if her spine were being preserved in amber. Julianna wore invisible armor. She always had—an unmarried woman pursuing a career needed to protect herself from an unkind world.

Normally, she appreciated her armor. She needed it when she took meetings with Mr. Glanvil. When she was cast aside by her printer. When she listened in on Amy with her friends.

When she stopped working long enough to think about how alone she was in this world.

She had never—*never*—had to wear her armor when it came to Effie.

Again, the urge to cry rose. Again, she quashed it.

There was nothing for it but to don her placcate and her gauntlets and get on with it.

She physically turned away from Effie and ordered herself to attend the earls, who were still arguing about how many houses was too many.

Lord Harcourt surprised her by saying, apropos of nothing, "I have read and enjoyed your magazine, Miss Evans. You should be quite proud of yourself."

How . . . unexpected.

"I concur, though I admit I have only read Effie's poems," Lord Marsden said. "But anyone who prints his work is all right in my estimation."

Effie's friends had read his poems? Did that mean the verses *were* in fact his?

The gentlemen asked a few questions, and she found herself telling them about the magazine's history—her father's founding of it, the fact that she'd grown up underfoot, trained in all aspects of producing it. "The only thing I absolutely cannot do myself is draw or engrave."

"That plate in your September issue was really quite impressive," Lord Harcourt said. "It has inspired me to see about getting tickets to the play it depicted."

She resisted pointing out that for most of her readers, the plate would have to do.

"I am not much of a reader," he went on, "but I find myself turning the pages almost compulsively."

She smiled. "Thank you. I can think of no higher compliment."

"Truly. One reads a short story, and one thinks one will put the magazine down after that, but then on the next page one finds a compulsively readable column on how to dress pheasants. It's quite different from a newspaper."

"It is. In fact, I must take care not to report too directly on the news if I want to avoid the stamp tax." She paused, considering that she was in company with two members of the House of Lords. Ought she to press them for the tax's repeal? She decided against it. "To my mind, a magazine such as *Le Monde Joli* is the perfect form. I strive always to balance art and practicality, and I make no apologies for doing so. If a lady is fond of poems, she may read some of today's best in my pages. But if a lady wants to know what the latest fashions out of London or Paris are, she can learn that and skip the poetry. Or a gentleman, too, of course," she rushed to add. She was tickled that a man such as Lord Harcourt had read her magazine, but she told herself not to be. Why *shouldn't* he read it?

As much as the turn in the conversation had revived Julianna, she was aware that Effie had still not spoken. And that she was still wearing her armor.

Armor was so very uncomfortable.

"Perhaps we ought to be going," Lord Harcourt said after their conversation about the magazine dwindled.

"Yes!" Julianna cried, regretting the vehemence with which her agreement had been tinged. But she did so desperately want to leave. A day ago she would have said she had no fonder wish than meeting Effie in the flesh. That wish had become the imperative that had propelled her to Brighton. Now she wanted nothing more than to get away from him.

As they were beginning to stir themselves, Effie—Lord Featherfinch, or whoever he was—suddenly grabbed her hands again. Peeled the glove off the left.

She gasped. That made twice in one afternoon. Julianna did not like to think of herself as a gasper, but she prized logic, and what did two gasps in one day make one if not a gasper?

Effie twisted the ring she wore on her fourth finger.

"You are married."

"No!" she exclaimed, though again, she found herself regretting her pressed tone.

"No," she said anew, and with more control. She was startled,

possibly offended, that he could think she was married. Yet unaccountably glad that he had spoken. His voice had sounded . . .
well, she couldn't say it sounded usual because once again, she had
no history of hearing his voice. Yet somehow it sounded like . . .
Effie.

"You are not married," he said, and she wasn't sure if it was a
question or a statement. Regardless, he sounded uncertain.

Was it possible that his silence all this time had been masking
something else?

"You know that I will never marry. Besides, would I not have
told you if I was married?" she asked, though she did not take her
hand back. He kept twisting the ring, though the overwhelming
sensation was not the tin moving against her skin, but the touch
of his fingers. Gooseflesh rose all the way up her arm. She remembered that she prized logic and said, "If I were married, would I
not have signed my early letters, before we moved to addressing
each other by our Christian names, 'Mrs. Evans'?"

"Well, I did not tell you I was a man. I signed my letters with an
entirely different name."

"Point taken"—she smiled despite herself—"but I am unmarried, and I shall remain so. The ring is merely a decoy. A bit of
armor." Actual armor.

"How do you mean?" He was still holding the finger that wore
the ring, and he was looking at her with that same intensity she'd
observed in his countenance before, but now that he was speaking
along with looking, his regard felt . . . different. It reminded her
of the way his attention had felt via their letters. On paper, Effie
always wanted to know what she thought about everything. It felt
as if he were hanging on her replies, sometimes.

She considered his question. "Unmarried women on their own
are disallowed from so many experiences. They must have a father
or a brother, or at least a mother or a maid, if they want to do
anything."

Effie tilted his head. "Yes, why is that?"

"Everyone says it's so the innocent young lady isn't corrupted, but the degree of hysteria that accompanies the very idea of a woman alone in the world makes me wonder if perhaps it isn't the reverse that's true. Perhaps *they* are afraid of *us*. Perhaps it is we who have the power."

"Hmm." The head tilt deepened.

"Ahem."

Effie let go of her finger.

Oh, dear. That was the second time that Lord Harcourt had cleared his throat to draw their attention to how improper they were being. Not just with the hand holding—finger holding—but Julianna's speech just then. She'd meant it for Effie's ears only. Never in a million years would she have said such a thing in front of two peers she'd only just met.

All the lowering things were coming in twos today: gasping, having to be reminded that she had an audience, the feeling that she might cry.

At least she had Effie back.

What a ridiculous thing to think. She didn't "have him back." She'd never had him to begin with. He was a treasured correspondent, yes, but he didn't *belong* to her.

Julianna blinked as they stepped into the sunlit street. Tea had felt like an odd, not entirely pleasant interruption in the usual unfolding of time. Although nothing was usual about being here, she supposed.

What now?

"It was a pleasure to meet you, Miss Evans." Lord Harcourt sketched a bow.

Lord Marsden did likewise. "May we escort you to the Old Ship?"

She looked to Effie, who was back to being a silent, looming presence. She waited a beat. When he did not speak, she said, "Thank you, no. I can make my own way. I want to stop in a shop I passed this morning." That last bit was a lie. Julianna had neither the money nor the inclination for the shops, but she wanted to get away from the gentlemen as expeditiously as possible.

They said their goodbyes, and just like that, Julianna was walking—alone—back toward the hotel.

Until she wasn't.

"Wait!"

Her heart leapt as she turned to see Effie loping toward her.

He was back. The silent looming presence from the tea shop was gone and he was just . . . Effie. The relief was profound. But it was shortly followed by something else. Not anger, exactly, because as she'd just thought, Effie was Effie. She truly didn't give a fig that he was a man, an aristocrat. It was a kind of disappointment, a wariness conferred by the fact of his maleness, and his nobility, having been obscured.

He tripped over a cobblestone but righted himself, skidding to a stop in front of her. "Let's go sea-bathing!"

"I beg your pardon?"

"Sea-bathing! You have always wanted to try it, have you not?"

"I . . . have." Though she didn't remember telling Effie that. It must have been early in their correspondence. Before she'd read and reread every letter. Before she started keeping them in a box under her bed.

"Let us sea-bathe, then!"

She waited for more. A crackpot plan. Or at least a time and direction. He only kept looking at her, grinning.

"*Now?*"

He couldn't mean now, could he?

"Why not?"

She looked into his eyes, and they were alive. Dancing in blue and brown. Just the way she'd always thought Euphemia Turner's eyes would be.

She wasn't sure why she was surprised by his sea-bathing proposal. Effie was adventurous. Impulsive.

He started toward her as if he were going to take her arm but checked himself. Took a step back. She didn't like that. It felt like the wrong direction. "Aww, Jules, I'm sorry I was so odd back there. I'm just . . . overcome."

"By what?"

"What do you mean by what? By *you*, of course!"

Julianna was certain no one had ever been overcome by her before. She could feel her cheeks heating, though she wasn't sure if it was pleasure or mortification stoking the fire.

She stared at him, hands on her hips, and she gave over caring if to do so appeared odd, or improper. When he began to squirm, she asked, "Did you write all the poems you sent me?"

It was his turn to gasp. "Of course I did. How could you think otherwise?"

She merely had to raise her eyebrows for him to bow his head before her.

All right. She had established that most important thing between them had not been a lie. That was enough for now. "Sea-bathing, you say?"

She looked around for his friends. Reading her mind, he said, "They've gone back to the Pavilion. Simon didn't get enough of it, apparently."

She could feel herself smiling. The Effie she knew was adventurous and impulsive, and while a week ago she would have said that although she admired those qualities, she did not share them. But was that true? She was here, wasn't she, in Brighton? Perhaps Effie and his . . . Effieness was infectious.

Her smile deepened, as if mirroring some inner part of her, some primal core, that had already made her decision. "All right."

"Hooray!" He performed a little leap that was both ridiculous and endearing.

On the walk to the sea, Effie made up for his earlier silence. "Why are you here, Jules? Why didn't you tell me you were going to be here the same time I was? Though what if you had? Would I have responded by abandoning my plans?"

She waited for him to answer his own questions—that last one, anyway, but he did not. "I don't know why I'm here," she said, addressing his first. "And I didn't tell you because I didn't know I was coming until the morning I left—yesterday. It was a rather impulsive decision."

"That seems unlike you." He paused. The head tilt, which she was beginning to recognize as a signature mannerism of his—returned. "And yet in some ways, it is in character."

"I suddenly found myself with a dismayingly empty schedule." She told him about how printing problems had ensured she had nothing to do until next Thursday, and about the way she had found herself in an almost fugue state as she packed and bought her ticket for the coach. "I honestly don't know what came over me. I wasn't thinking at all!"

"Well, I'm glad you weren't!" He flattened her with that smile of his, and she was glad, too. Glad to be flattened.

At the beach, he said, "We shall have to part ways here. Ladies are on one side and gentlemen on the other."

Yes. She could see the nearby bathing machines marked with a sign that read "Ladies," and as she peered up the beach, she could see another cluster of machines in the distance.

"Can a person just walk up? Does one need to . . . make an appointment?" And what about attire?

"I have no idea," Effie said. "I've only ever swum by myself."

"Well," Julianna said, tilting her head to the sun and opening herself. Letting Effie's spirit of adventure fill her up. "Let us try."

"Excellent. Let us reconvene here in, say . . . I have no idea how long sea-bathing takes!"

"When you swim, how long does it take?"

"Oh, ages, but that's just me. Once I'm in the water, if it's calm enough, I can float on my back and gaze at the sky endlessly. But I suspect things are more circumscribed here."

Something about the image of Effie floating in the sea was . . . stirring. What would he wear—or not wear—while doing that?

"Let us meet there when we're done." He pointed to a nearby bench. "I will endeavor to make my immersion brief so as not to keep you waiting. You, though—you take your time. I will wait for you." He was staring at her again with that intense look. She didn't dislike it anymore. "Look at the sky while you're out there, Jules, and I shall, too."

The bathing machines dotting the beach looked like covered carriages that had been parked at the edge of the water. Inside, after changing into the bathing costume provided, Julianna discovered that was exactly what they were. She entered through one door from the beach and was towed out a way. Once situated, she emerged into the sea from the opposite door. Julianna laughed to think that she had been concerned she might not be "allowed" to sea-bathe on her own. In fact, the whole operation was designed for maximum privacy. The bathing machine itself shielded her from the beach and it from her. She could almost believe she was alone but for the dipper, a sturdy, red-faced woman who seemed profoundly uninterested in her charge. She didn't introduce herself, or even make a greeting. Julianna could have been anyone. She didn't need a mother, or a maid, or even her ring. It was refreshing.

Another thing the dipper didn't seem interested in was giving Julianna a chance to acclimate. She merely took Julianna's arm and marched her down the few steps to the seafloor. It was sandy beneath her toes—how wonderful. Julianna had never been barefoot in the outdoors before, not on grass or dirt, much less on the seafloor. She wiggled her toes and laughed as the sand oozed over them.

"Come on, then, ma'am," the dipper said brusquely, leading her farther out. Julianna wished her bathing costume wasn't so voluminous. It weighed her down as it got wet.

"Are you in search of a cure?" the dipper asked.

"I beg your pardon?"

"Sea water is the cure for so many things—the gout, all manner of glandular issues." She lowered her voice. "Some say it even helps the unfortunate lady who is unable to conceive."

"I am not in search of a cure," Julianna said. But . . . was that true? She could feel herself, lately, grasping toward something. Something more than control over her magazine. She sometimes felt as if something was missing from her life, but she couldn't articulate what it was.

She shook her head. She wasn't in search of a cure for anything that seawater could put to rights. "I am merely here for overall health and vigor."

"Well, shall we get on with it?"

"I thought we were?"

"Come out a way farther and lie back."

Julianna did as she was told. She closed her eyes as she allowed the dipper to lower her. The buoyancy conferred by the water was novel. Such a curious sensation. She wasn't exactly floating, as her attendant's arms stayed beneath her back, but she was nevertheless . . . light. She kept her eyes closed and concentrated on the way her body was moving. Gentle waves had her bobbing up and down. The effect was probably moderated by her minder, but it felt rather like being rocked.

A memory rose to the surface of her mind, suddenly, almost violently, like a whale clearing its blow hole. Her father, rocking her just like this. She'd been very young, and very sick. He had an issue of the magazine propped up on a stand, and he'd been reading it out loud. He had taught her that a final proofread was best done aloud. One could hear errors that one's eyes slid over when reading silently. She still employed that technique.

As she floated, Julianna thought about senses. About hearing birds one could not see. About how she had seen Effie speak without hearing him yet had known what he was saying.

How *he* had appeared to hear thoughts *she* had not spoken aloud.

Look at the sky while you're out there, Jules, and I shall, too.

She opened her eyes.

Chapter 5

Nightmare Scenario

Effie waited a long time for Julianna, but he didn't mind at all. In some ways, he had been waiting his entire life for Julianna, so what was a few more minutes?

The most surprising thing about all of this was that her hair smelled of roses. When he'd picked her up and twirled her around, there had been no mistaking the delicate floral scent. Effie hadn't expected that. If anything, he'd have thought her hair would smell of ink. But then, he hadn't expected *her*. Least of all here, in Brighton, but also in general. He had never expected to be confronted with Julianna in the flesh. He had never dared even to wish for such a thing. *You can't miss what you don't let yourself want.*

But then she was there. Julianna, whose hair smelled of roses and whose skin was pale like the linen paper she used for her letters.

Another unexpected detail: her laugh, as he'd twirled her. She had a high, girlish, lilting laugh that had been utterly shocking—a great deal more shocking than roses. The Julianna of his imaginings had a low, knowing laugh that was seldom heard because her standards for bemusement were uncommonly high.

She had smelled of roses and laughed easily and indeed had looked very little like his painted version of her, yet he had recognized her immediately. There wasn't a reason in the world he should have, but when his eyes saw a woman alone, gazing at the Pavilion, something inside him had been inspired to undertake further study. All the descriptive bits added up: the dark hair, the height, even the worn brown half boots—she'd written to him a few months ago about needing a new pair. The descriptive bits had been necessary to achieve a positive identification, but alone, insufficient. So he'd taken a step closer, and examined the nature of *her* examination. There was something about the quality of her attention as she gazed at the Pavilion with a mixture of wonderment and skepticism, something about *her*, something ineffable but simultaneously so very Julianna-esque, that had him calling out to her before he could think better of it.

And now he was here, on a bench waiting for her.

As before, he saw her before she saw him. She looked the same as she had when they parted ways, with her gray dress and her gray-ribboned bonnet. But beneath that bonnet, her hair must be wet, no? She must have coiled it or braided it and pinned it up while still damp. Julianna had always complained that she didn't like the way her hair curled when it was down. He could only imagine that tonight, with an assist from sea salt, and from having been pinned up wet, her curls would be extra chaotic. Wild.

He reached into his pocket to see if he had his fan with him. He often carried it in situations in which he wanted to make a fashion statement. It was a prop.

Now, though, he required it for function. He was very warm. He feared his face had turned as pink as the setting sun.

Once again, he wondered: *Is this desire?*

If so, desire was quite discomfiting.

She caught sight of him, and she smiled. Her smile was so at odds with her dreary attire that he almost laughed. Not at her, but at the contrast. And at the very idea that she had a secret smile. He wanted to flatter himself that the secret smile was reserved exclusively for him, but he could not reasonably do that. He would have to be satisfied that *this* smile, here and now, was for him.

He rose as she approached. "How did you find it?"

"I was transported."

He was so very, very glad. "Perhaps you can go in again. How long are you staying?" He should have asked that already. The answer to that question was everything.

"I'm not sure." She paused. "A few more days at least."

This was . . . all wrong. They sounded like they were making idle conversation at a party.

He'd gotten ahead of himself. Or fallen behind. Or something. He cleared his throat. "Did your fictional marital status hold up?"

"It did." She held up the finger with the dull ring. "I don't know that I needed it, though, or that the dipper who attended me even noticed. Nothing was said about it."

"What did you talk about?" He wasn't sure why he was asking, except that he wanted to be the one who'd been there, witnessing her first foray into the sea.

"Nothing beyond the necessary logistics. I should have preferred to be alone, though I appreciate that I don't know how to swim."

Before he could think better of it, he said, "I could teach you."

"You know how to swim? You must, as you previously referenced floating for long stretches of time."

"Yes, I adore swimming. I used to go quite a lot at my family's estate in Cornwall."

"Your family has an estate in Cornwall."

Something about her posture changed, stiffened ever so slightly.

He knew what was wrong. His immersion in the sea had allowed him to marshal his thoughts on the extraordinary events of the day. It had stung, when she'd suggested, earlier, that perhaps he hadn't been the true author of the poems he'd sent her. But he understood why her trust had faltered. "Julianna, I must apologize. Again. Properly." He hadn't been able to before, when they'd first encountered each other at the Pavilion, or later at tea, with the boys hovering like overzealous chaperones. And his attempt earlier, before they settled on sea-bathing, had been insufficient.

He leaned toward her, acting on an instinct to take her hand, but of course they couldn't do that here.

God damn all these bloody rules everywhere.

He took a fortifying breath. "I should never have deceived you."

"Indeed you should not have," she said tartly.

"I should like to say in my defense that I never lied to you about anything that was in my heart. About anything to do with sentiment, or poetry, or anything important."

"You don't think who you are is important?"

"Oh, Jules," he said, his heart nearly breaking. "You *know* who I am."

"Do I?"

"Yes!" he cried. But again, he could hardly fault her for doubting. "Let me explain." He told her the same thing he'd told the boys last night, about how thrilled he'd been when she accepted that first poem, and when she offered such excellent editorial suggestions. "I won't lie—anymore. Initially, I was miffed that you'd suggested changes. But I read your letter, and I knew you were right. I've gone on to trust your editorial judgment absolutely. There has been a time or two when I wondered if the printed poem ought to contain the names of two authors."

"Of course it shouldn't have. I was merely doing my job." She was trying and failing to suppress a smile. He thought she was flattered by his words, though he meant them not to flatter but to explain.

He went on to tell the rest: how the more poems she printed, the higher the stakes felt. How once their correspondence became personal, the stakes became *too* high for him to tell the truth.

"I was afraid of losing you," he finished solemnly. "I know lying is bad, but losing you would have been worse."

Did he imagine it, or did it appear for a moment that her eyes were welling with tears?

No, he had imagined it, for she smiled and turned her face toward the setting sun. The pinkness of the sky had deepened. It made her skin glow.

Her posture was less stiff than it had been before, and he felt it as a small victory.

"Did you look at the sky while you were sea-bathing?" he asked, though what he really meant was *Do you forgive me?*

"Yes," she said, still gazing at the sun, and he somehow knew she was answering both questions.

"Where the hell have you been?"

Effie felt dazed as he walked in late to dinner that night. His mind was at once slow and fast, racing back over every bit of his time with Julianna even as some part of him was still languorously floating under the blue Brighton sky.

"You made it back all right." That was from Archie, ever the worrier.

Effie answered the first question, which had been from the more direct Simon, as he seated himself. "I went sea-bathing." He turned to Archie. "I'm sorry I wasn't at our appointed meeting place."

"We waited an hour," Simon said, though the pique had gone out of his tone.

"I . . . didn't think." He had told Julianna he would wait for her on that bench, yet he hadn't spared a thought for his friends waiting for him. "It was ill-done of me."

"We were concerned about you." Archie served Effie some glazed beetroot and gestured to Simon to pass a platter of roast pork.

"No, we weren't," Simon said archly, though he did pass the plate. "You found Miss Evans, didn't you?"

"Tell me you did not go sea-bathing with Miss Evans!" Archie exclaimed.

"Where are the servants? Have you already had pudding?" There was a baked custard on the table, half demolished.

"We decided we rather liked the informal style of dining that circumstances forced us into last year—everything served at once, servants absent," Simon said.

Indeed, the remoteness of last year's holiday, and the lack of servants, meant the usual mode of dining in a series of removes had been abandoned. Effie murmured his approval through a mouthful of the custard. One of the other delights associated with this method was that one could eat the pudding first if one so desired.

"Tell me you did not go sea-bathing with Miss Evans," Archie said again, though this time he sounded less exercised and more resigned.

"I'm not sure why you're so scandalized," Effie said through a mouthful of pork. He hadn't realized how hungry he was.

"God's teeth, he *did* go sea-bathing with her." Archie turned to Simon, and they shared a look Effie could not parse.

"I didn't go *with* her. She went on the ladies' side and I went on the gentlemen's, and afterward we had a brief discussion about our respective experiences."

"Where?" Archie asked.

"What do you mean 'where'? Our experiences in the sea."

"No. Where did you have this discussion?"

"On a bench. Why are you so agitated?" Hold up. "Are you about to say because it wasn't proper?" Effie shot his friend a withering glance that froze him in the middle of lifting a glass of brandy to his lips.

Archie did not deny it.

"In fact," Effie said, purely to agitate the apparently easily scandalized Archie, "I invited her back to dine with us this evening, but she declined."

"Of course she did," Simon said. "Miss Evans seems a sensible sort."

Effie, confused and offended in equal measure, said, "It would have been much less scandalous than last year when Clementine and Olive joined our holiday—the whole holiday, not merely one meal."

"Yes," Simon said, "but last year we were in remote Cumbria and the house was staffed by an ancient woman and a girl who'd had a child out of wedlock."

Effie started to object, but Simon talked over him.

"I'm not saying it's right; I'm merely saying that circumstances this year are more delicate. You will recall that we were trying to cut a low profile—and that was *before* you took to sea-bathing with Miss Evans."

"What do I care if it gets out that I was seen associating with a common woman?" Effie said, offense winning out over confusion. "I can hardly fall further in my father's estimation."

"You don't care, but she might."

Ah. Indeed. Effie slumped against the back of his chair, ashamed that he hadn't thought about things from Julianna's perspective. It was akin to the letters. It had taken him far too long to understand that posting letters was, for many people, an unjustifiable expense.

Had he pressed her too hard, about the sea-bathing? He couldn't remember precisely what he'd said, only that he was so very intent that she agree. That . . . was not ideal.

"She wasn't wrong, before," Archie said, "when she was speculating about the restrictions faced by unmarried women."

"Wasn't that an *excellent* speech?" Effie's chest warmed thinking back on it. He was gratified that Julianna's wit was as pointed in person as it had always been in print. *Perhaps you ought to introduce yourself, too,* she'd said after he'd presented Archie and Simon to her. Oh, the delicious sharpness of the barb, the delight he took in being so lanced, even as he had been properly chagrined.

Realizing he was grinning like an idiot, he schooled his face. "I do take your point." He paused. "Perhaps that is why she declined my invitation." He resumed trying to see his recent interactions with Julianna from her perspective. "She insisted that she was only going to be in town a little longer, that she and I had met, which was her aim, and that I ought to spend the rest of my time with you lot." He curled his lip, and the boys laughed. "But was that an excuse? Was she worried that the servants would talk?"

Would they have?

Regardless . . . "How can I be here, and she be mere miles away? It isn't right. I know you think me ridiculous, and perhaps you're correct. But I love her."

"Did you tell her that?" Simon asked.

"Good heavens, no. I can't do that."

"Mm," Archie agreed.

"I'm sorry if we are acting like scandalized old biddies," Simon said seriously. "You know we only want you to be happy. We just . . . don't want you to ruin Miss Evans in the pursuit of said happiness. You have said how much you admire her work, and her desire to become a woman of independent means. I think you ought to take care not to jeopardize that."

Right. Simon was right.

"Still, you *should* see her again before she leaves," Archie said firmly. "We will think of something."

Effie told himself to be satisfied with that answer. He would have to be. It wasn't as if he could gallop off to the Old Ship under cover of night to demand an audience.

With a sigh, he served himself some creamed potatoes.

The rest of the evening was not unenjoyable. They ate, they retired to the drawing room they'd occupied last night, they drank and chatted. When Simon started making noises about retiring, Effie yawned and said, "I think I shall do the same."

"Pardon?" Archie asked. "Why?"

"Leander has been alone all day. And I am tired."

"Really?" That was from Simon, who looked as bewildered as Archie. "You are tired at"—he pulled out his timepiece—"half eleven?"

"Yes, really." Effie *was* tired, though he knew he would not sleep. Still, this day had worn out its welcome. He wanted to go to bed and stare at the ceiling and think about how to describe the way roses smelled. "Is that so unusual?"

"Yes," the boys said in unison.

He supposed that was fair. Generally, on these trips, he and Archie stayed up late. He gathered that Archie got up early and breakfasted with Simon. Goodness knew when Archie ever slept, but that was Archie. Who needed sleep when one had friends in want of company?

So, yes, it was unusual for Effie to be tired this early. Perhaps he should tell them. This was an Earls Trip, after all. The time of the year when secrets came out. And this year was apparently his turn.

"I am tired because I haven't been sleeping," he said carefully, trying to think how to broach a matter he didn't fully understand himself.

"What do you mean?" Archie asked. "You haven't been sleeping at all?"

"Not much. I sometimes attain a few hours toward dawn."

"You were always a night owl," Archie said.

"Indeed, but he also always lay abed until noon or later," Simon said. "Are you lying in as you usually do?"

"No. If I can manage a few hours of sleep, I consider myself lucky. But then I'm wide awake again. I've taken to stalking the city before the sun comes up, like some kind of madman."

"What do you think has changed to prompt these difficulties?" Archie asked.

"I am plagued by nightmares," Effie said. "I think some part of me resists sleep for that reason."

"You have often had stretches where you've battled nightmares, have you not?" Simon asked.

"Yes, but these are different."

"How so?"

"I have begun to . . . remember things." Was he really going to tell them about this?

"What things?"

Yes. Yes, he was. It was a holiday of confessions.

He took a breath to focus his thoughts. "I awaken from a nightmare and . . . Are you familiar with the sensation of trying to remember a dream even as its tendrils loosen their hold on you and begin to withdraw?"

The boys murmured their assent.

"This is the opposite of that. I wake up sweating, often shouting, and the dream is *right there*, a monkey on my chest."

"Ah. That is why you took down that painting that used to hang in your bedchamber," Simon said.

"Yes. I used to find comfort in that painting. It depicted the feeling of having a nightmare. The idea of a creature sitting on one's chest seemed a fitting metaphor, and one takes pleasure in fitting metaphors, doesn't one, even if they describe unpleasant experiences? But then this other type of nightmare started, and I no longer found the metaphor gratifying. Or that metaphorical, really. When I awaken from these episodes, I cannot breathe for a few moments."

"Are we talking about dreams or memories?" Archie asked. "You said just now that you have begun to remember things."

"That's the rub. I think the answer is both. In the dream, I find myself in a scene that later, once I awaken, I realize is a memory. I realize it *happened*."

Silence fell, and Effie knew they were struggling to understand. "You remember the two Christmases we all spent at school?" He thought back to those holidays with his friends, in an almost-empty school with a handful of other boys, a cook, and a supervising teacher, as some of the happiest times of his life.

"Your parents were traveling," Archie said.

"Only the first time. The second time, I wrote to them that I had taken ill so I could stay with you lot. I didn't want to go home."

"I don't blame you. Your parents are, not to put too fine a point on it, terrible."

"Yes, but I think they were perhaps more terrible than you knew." Effie paused. "Than I knew. My father, anyway."

The silence returned, and Effie was suffused with good feeling for his friends. They would wait as long as it took for him to speak.

"You both know that I am a perpetual disappointment to my father," he started, and the boys murmured their agreement—and their disapproval. "I used to try to please him."

"I do remember that month you voluntarily spent every evening summing vast columns of numbers."

"Indeed. And I used to follow him and Mr. Rodgers—Mr. Rodgers was the steward at Highworth before Mr. Nancarrow—around, trying to learn the art of estate management." He paused.

"While I can't say I ever relished the idea of inheriting—I was too interested in other pursuits for that—I was resigned to it. I suppose I still am, but there was a time during which I was keen on preparing for it."

He shook his head. He was getting off topic here. Why was this so hard to speak of? He hadn't even told Julianna, though she knew he had nightmares in a general sense.

"There were times, when I was very young, where I would say that Father expressed his disappointment in me with more than just words."

Archie, ever the protector, sat forward in his chair.

"I can give you examples. Once, when I was about seven, he locked me in my mother's wardrobe overnight."

"No!" Simon cried.

"Yes. They caught me trying on one of her hats."

"Oh, Effie," Archie said.

"And he killed my kitten once. I'd found a stray in the garden, a wee thing I nursed back to health. He'd been away, and when he came home and found me singing to it, he flew into a rage." He closed his eyes briefly, remembering. "It wasn't enough that he took her away, he had to march me to the sea and make me watch as he drowned her."

"Good God," Archie said, "that's—"

"He always hated my eyes." Effie hated to interrupt, but he wanted to get the rest of the story out now that he'd started. "Said they were the mark of the devil. He told me then that he ought to drown me, after the cat, to see if I'd float."

Simon blew out a breath. "I'm sorry I ever sought his support for—"

"And then . . ." He hated to keep interrupting his friends, but if he stopped talking, he would never have the nerve to finish. "There was a time a year or two later, between the first Christmas we all spent at school and the second, when he broke my arm."

"This was when you came back from term break with your arm in a sling."

"Yes. In that case, he found me playing naughts and crosses with the son of one of the tenants. We were using sticks to scratch the game into a patch of dirt. We were quite engaged in our pursuit and were bent with our heads together, and when I won in an upset, the boy threw an arm around me in congratulations." He paused. "I did not know my father was watching." Another pause. "I believe he thought I preferred the company of other gentlemen. Other boys. He sent the boy away and turned on me." He huffed a bitter laugh. "If only he knew how things have transpired."

"He would not approve of Miss Evans, either," Simon said gently.

"Indeed, he would not. But perhaps it would raise my estimation in his eyes all the same, for at least she is a member of the fairer sex. Not that I shall be breathing a word about her." No. He would not allow the poison that was his father to infect anything to do with Julianna.

"What about your mother?" Archie asked. "Where was she in all this?"

"She was there," Effie said. "Not at the naughts and crosses incident, but in general. She knew what was happening. When she was present, at the wardrobe incident, and when Father found me with the kitten, she would protest, but ultimately . . ." He shrugged. Ultimately, Mother would never defy Father. No one would. Not even Effie, could he have helped it. That was the problem, though: he couldn't. He defied simply by being.

"And you forgot about these episodes until recently?" Simon asked.

"Well, obviously I knew that I broke my arm, but I seem to have remembered it more as an accident. And as for the other incidents, yes, I'd plain forgotten them."

"And now they have returned as nightmares," Simon said. "How do you know they *are* memories and not mere nightmares? I am not doubting you, only seeking to understand."

Because he could smell the cedar of the wardrobe, feel the terror of being left alone. Because he could feel the particular mixture of indignation and shame—and searing pain—that resulted from the bone in his arm breaking. Now that these sense memories had been reawakened, they were with him all the time.

He didn't want to talk about that, though, at least not now, so he said, "I just do."

The boys nodded. They believed him. Of course they did.

"I have heard of this," Archie said. "Chiefly among soldiers returned from war. They somehow block out what has happened to them."

"You wrote a poem rather recently," Simon said, "that seemed to be about confinement. I'd thought it metaphorical, but perhaps it was literal."

"It was both," Effie said quietly. "I wrote that after the wardrobe episode . . . resurfaced."

"Do you think there are more episodes waiting to be unearthed?" Simon asked.

"I dread the thought."

"This is why you cannot sleep," Simon said. "You are avoiding additional unearthing."

Effie nodded.

"Do you remember last year, with the dressing gowns?" Archie asked, and they all laughed. Effie was glad for the levity. "You had yours made in pink, and we were surprised it wasn't black. You used to wear black all the time."

"I did. I felt black reflected my essential outlook on the world."

"But on our trip last year, you said something about being drawn to color. About being happier."

"Yes. I think that was the influence of Julianna. Miss Evans," he corrected, though he did not know why he was bothering with the boys.

"And that influence must have continued, because every time I see you these days, you are wearing a rather outrageous waistcoat."

"I suppose I contradict myself. I tell you on the one hand that these awful memories have come back, that they are keeping me from slumber. Yet on the other hand, it is true: I am happier than

I have ever been." He quirked a smile. "I know not what to say other than that I do indeed contradict myself." He grew serious. "In truth, I think it's *all* down to Julianna—the happiness and the memories. I think I started remembering because she began asking me about my childhood. She's the one who commissioned that poem 'A Summer's Day.' Do you remember that one?"

The boys, bless them, nodded.

"That was an interesting one," Simon said. "Given the title, one expected it to be a light bit of verse. And it was, to start, but then the mood took a turn."

Yes. "Do you remember the line 'broken bones, turned to stone'?"

"Oh, dear God," Archie said, "that was your arm!"

Effie shrugged. "It was and it wasn't. I think the memories, and the poems I've written about them, reinforce each other. One comes from the other and vice versa. When I try to think how to express something in verse, my mind . . . Oh, it is very hard to explain. It's as if my mind goes into a different place. As if a curtain is drawn back. Not always. Not often, actually. But the best poems come from when this curtain is drawn, allowing a glimpse into a different realm." He paused. "I am aware how ridiculous I sound."

"I don't think you sound ridiculous," Archie said.

"Nor do I," Simon said. "You know I haven't an artistic bone in my body, but I am not at all surprised that the process of creating poems is rather mystical."

"Sometimes, lately, it seems the curtain is drawn such that I can see into the past. No, I can . . . *feel* into the past."

"Is that a blessing or a curse?" Simon asked.

"I honestly don't know. On the one hand, I would rather not have these memories. It would be much more convenient if they'd stayed locked away. On the other hand, part of me dislikes the notion that my memory is hiding things from me. It's as if I don't know my own soul."

Effie felt better for having unburdened himself. He always did.

He wondered, for the second time in as many days, why he'd ever thought to keep secrets from the boys.

He was tired; he hadn't been lying about that. But when he got back to his room, he found himself possessed of a newfound energy. He let Leander out of his cage to stretch his wings and pulled out his stack of letters.

Dear Sartorially Sullied,

Stop giving your son castor oil. It's vile. As a happy consequence, you shan't have to do battle with castor oil stains ever again.

Sincerely,

Mrs. Landers

Much later that night, Effie was staring at the ceiling in his bedchamber, when his door creaked open. He could just make out the shape of Archie, who was carrying a candle, suspended in his doorway.

"What's wrong?" Effie whispered.

Archie slipped into the room. "Nothing. I awakened and thought to check on you." He set his taper on the nightstand. "Sleep eludes you, I gather?"

"Sleep eludes me," Effie confirmed. "What time is it?"

"Nearly four."

"I thought it must be. I usually try to avoid looking at my time-piece when I am battling my sleep demon, but—what are you doing?"

"Keeping you company."

Archie had pushed back the covers and was getting into bed with Effie.

"Keeping me company!" Effie, echoed, amazed.

"Well, trying to." Archie shoved Effie's shoulder. "Move over."

Oh, Archie. Was there a better man on this earth? Effie, a little overcome, moved over. If only one could bank kindness. Save it up when one encountered an excess of it, and pull it out later when it was in short supply. If that were possible, Effie would never run out.

"Speaking of preferring the company of gentlemen," Effie asked, "what will the servants think if they find us in bed together, or if they saw you sneaking in here?"

"Oh, who cares? Being an earl ought to be good for something. Besides, they are unlikely to find out. I told them you tend to lie abed in the mornings—that was before I knew that wasn't the case anymore."

"So we'll have a lie-in and, what? You'll climb out the window?"

"Do you know that I climbed in Clementine's window once last year, at Quintrell Castle?"

"You did?"

"Yes, and that was much higher off the ground, so your scenario does not daunt me."

"You always were rather a Corinthian."

Archie rolled his eyes and blew out his candle.

Effie turned onto his side, facing away from Archie. He thought he might be able to sleep now.

"You never fancied me, then?" Archie asked. "Or Simon?"

"Oh, for heaven's sake!" Effie turned back over, propped his head on his hand. It was too dark to make out Archie's expression.

"I merely wondered," Archie said mildly into the darkness. "If your tastes encompass men, and if you can only develop ardent feelings for those to whom you have an existing sentimental bond . . ."

Effie snorted. "Don't flatter yourself."

Archie chuckled. After a stretch of silence, he said, "I hope I have not offended. I am merely trying to understand."

That was Archie. Always trying to understand. To stretch the bounds of what he knew, and believed, in support of those he loved.

"I might have harbored a passing, *exceedingly* passing admiration for you that day you beat Nigel Nettlefell in that archery competition. You targeted him—no pun intended—because he'd been so beastly to me."

"I remember. He was beastly to everyone."

"But it dissipated," Effie rushed to add. "I promise you, it was gone the next day. You are my brother."

"Yes," Archie agreed mildly. "And you are mine."

Effie turned back over, and this time, he took the coverlet with him, yanking it from Archie's clutches. "Stop hogging the covers."

Effie did sleep in the next morning. When he awakened—to an empty bed—and checked his timepiece, it was just after ten. He felt more refreshed than he had in months.

He took the sheet off Leander's cage, opened the door, and offered his arm. Leander, like Sally, was quite happy to perch on Effie's hand, but unlike Sally, he wasn't affectionate. Whereas Sally used to nuzzle Effie's cheek and take apparent delight in playing games with him, Leander merely regarded him with his blank eyes.

"Is there anything in here?" Effie asked, rubbing Leander's head feathers. "I fear not."

"Go!" Leander chirped.

"Oh, so we've reverted to 'Go!' have we? All right, then."

It was just as well Leander had forgotten his recent foray into speaking in complete sentences; Effie didn't need the blasted bird announcing the contents of his heart like some kind of feathered newspaper boy. He arranged the sheets of linen Mrs. Mitchell had furnished and let Leander roam while he performed his morning ablutions.

Later, Effie found the boys lingering in the breakfast room, and as he helped himself to tea, he shot Archie a questioning look. *Had* he climbed out the window early this morning?

Archie merely winked.

"We were just about to walk to the village," Simon said. "Stretch our legs a bit. We thought we'd walk there, then visit the beach. We can discuss what to do about your Miss Evans."

She's not my *Miss Evans,* Effie wanted to say, but he also wanted what Simon said to be true, so he remained silent, and after he'd had eaten some kippers and toast, they set off.

The house they were borrowing was newish, its acreage carved out of farmland on the outskirts of the old village and situated on land that sloped down to the sea. It belonged to a friend of Simon's from Lords whose wife had taken a shine to the area. The family summered here but left the house empty most of the rest of the year.

"Have you been to the beach yet?" Effie asked. "Here by the house, I mean."

"We went after you stood us up yesterday," Simon said archly. "It's very quiet. Rather the opposite of the bustling seaside in Brighton. A shingle beach, with quite large stones. Mrs. Mitchell reports that the water is shallow."

The walk to the village was short, and as the September sun warmed Effie, that sense of lightness returned, of being able to relax in the steadfast company of his friends.

When he tripped over a loose cobblestone, he realized he had forgotten to put on his boots. He'd come down to breakfast in a pair of court shoes he'd packed and had unthinkingly left the house in them. He'd gone through a phase of wearing the flamboyant footwear last year, and this pair, which he'd had made based on a portrait of Charles II, was perhaps his pièce de résistance. He was mostly over the phase, but he did enjoy antagonizing the boys. And, really, these shoes, with their high red heels and riotous bows of silver lace and ribbon, were so much more pleasant to look at than plain leather boots.

"All right?" Archie said, reaching out a hand to steady Effie.

Simon, for his part, merely let his gaze fall to Effie's shoes and then lifted it to the sky as if applying for divine patience.

"What if I were to call at the Old Ship?" Effie said, returning to the topic of how he might see Julianna.

They discussed the possibility as they walked.

"What if she doesn't want to see me, though?" Effie asked. It was hard to imagine, given the tenor of their meeting yesterday, but she *had* decisively turned down his invitation to dinner.

"I feel certain she will want to see you," Simon said with a bit of a guffaw.

Effie wasn't sure what was so amusing. "How? How are you sure?"

"Because there she is."

Effie nearly tripped again.

"Good heavens, so she is," Archie said.

Sure enough, about thirty or so yards down Hove Street, dressed in a navy spencer and the same gray-beribboned bonnet as yesterday, was Julianna.

Effie was aware he should not be surprised by anything Julianna did. She was, after all, possessed of uncommon intelligence and wit. But to see her striding down the street here, where they'd purposefully hidden themselves from the bustle of Brighton, positively stopped him in his tracks.

She was wearing a dress of blue gray under the spencer—not the same purely gray dress as yesterday—and carrying an unadorned black reticule. She had a very . . . decided sort of walk, a long, strong gait, and she kept her gaze on her destination. Which, in this case, was apparently him. She looked like a governess intent on reaching a wayward charge.

"How wonderful!" he exclaimed.

"My lords," she said briskly, dipping into a curtsy as she came to a halt in front of them.

He wanted to tell her to stop that. She needn't curtsy. She *shouldn't* curtsy. Something about it felt terribly, terribly wrong. But before he could object, the boys were sweeping into bows, and what could he do but follow suit?

"Good morning, Miss Evans," Archie said solicitously. "How lovely to see you."

Instead of returning his greeting, Julianna said, "My lords, I have secured a tour of the Pavilion's interior. The public areas, anyway."

"You have!" Simon exclaimed. "How?"

"I merely called and introduced myself to the servant who answered the door as the editor of *Le Monde Joli*, a respected and respectable ladies' magazine, and explained that my readers, possessed of exquisite taste and being interested in decor and the latest fashion, would be delighted to read an account of the place. He invited me in and asked me to wait. Eventually, the butler appeared, and, after some conferencing with the housekeeper, it was decided that a tour could be offered tomorrow morning."

Effie beamed like a proud papa. She was so resourceful.

"How marvelous, Miss Evans," Simon said. "I would remark upon how lucky you are, but clearly it is enterprise and not luck at work here."

Exactly.

"Yes, and I thought you all might like to come. That's why I'm here, to invite you."

Simon came as close to having a fit of the vapors as Effie had ever seen—which was admittedly not very close, but still, his delighted gasp was so very un-Simon-like.

"Did you walk here?" Archie peered in the direction of Brighton.

"I did. It is not far."

"How were you planning to find us, had we not encountered each other here?" Simon asked.

"Lord Featherfinch told me you were staying at the home of one of your friends, Lord Marsden. I deduced that the friend in question must be Lord Haffert. You and he have voted the same on all matters I am aware of in Lords, and you are both engaged in trying to draft legislation related to prison reform for next year's session."

Simon's eyebrows flew skyward.

"And, knowing Lord Haffert has a house in Hove, a place I believe he became acquainted with thanks to his work in Parliament against smuggling, I thought when I got to the village, I would merely ask someone where it was." She shrugged as if this remarkable bit of sleuthing were an everyday occurrence. Perhaps, for her, it was. Perhaps that was why her magazine was so good.

"And you were merely going to knock at the door and ask for us?" Archie asked.

She looked between the three of them. "Should I not have? Would I have been unwelcome?"

Archie's hearty laugh peeled out across the sunlit day. "Not at all, Miss Evans. Not at all."

When she furrowed her brow in confusion—and hurt? Effie hoped not—Effie rushed to say, "He laughs because we have expended a great deal of effort in worrying about if I ought to call on you at the Old Ship. They were concerned my spending time with you would harm your reputation."

The furrow deepened. It was a decidedly perplexed furrow, though, not a hurt one.

"Or harm your livelihood," Archie suggested.

"I think," Julianna began slowly, "that you gentlemen are a trifle confused over what sort of person I am."

It was Effie's turn to be perplexed.

"I am not a refined lady whose reputation is a fragile glass bauble in need of protecting. That is your world, not mine."

Effie opened his mouth to say something, but, realizing he had no idea what that something might be, closed it.

"And, while I am hardly a newspaperwoman—though I was flattered that you thought to call me such yesterday, Lord Harcourt—I have in my time gone rather to extremes in pursuit of a story, so I hardly think being seen in the company of three gentlemen is a concern. In fact, isn't there safety in numbers? Isn't your hypothetical lady in need of reputational shielding in more danger from being discovered alone in close quarters with one gentleman than out of doors with three?"

Effie could not argue with that.

Neither, it seemed, could the others, for after a startled pause, they both smiled.

"Miss Evans," Archie said, "we were about to walk in the direction of home and visit the beach near the house. Would you care to join us? We can make our plans for the tour you've arranged."

She would, she said, and they set off. Effie's skin tingled from the pure pleasure of strolling with his three favorite people. Had he ever imagined a scene in which he would get to be with Simon and Archie *and* Julianna? He'd have sooner believed the sky really *had* turned chartreuse.

"You can't come as yourselves tomorrow," Julianna said after they'd walked a way. When she was met with blank stares, she added, "I thought you were trying to avoid detection while on holiday."

"We are," Archie said. "We are."

"While I do not fear any reputational harm from being in your company, neither do I want to call unnecessary attention to myself. If you attend as yourselves tomorrow, surely the news of your visit will get back to the king. The servants wouldn't fail to mention the three peers who came calling, asking for a tour, would they?"

"You are suggesting subterfuge," Simon said.

"I am."

"How exciting," Effie said, barely refraining from clapping.

"I am thinking that one of you is my assistant at the magazine," Julianna said. "One of you is an artist I have commissioned to take some sketches. The other is . . . Well, I haven't figured that out yet."

"A student of architecture," Effie said. "The person you have hired to write the story."

"Yes! Perfect!" She turned and beamed at him. Effie had thought yesterday that the rosy, slanted rays of the sunset had illuminated Julianna, but he could see now that hadn't been exactly correct. Julianna glowed from within. No amount of gray wool could contain that glow. It was stoked by the fires of her inner self. Her wit and ambition and goodness.

"Your student should be Simon," Effie said, beaming back at her, "for he can credibly opine about architecture."

"Yes," she said, turning to Simon. "I so enjoyed our discussion yesterday about architecture."

Julianna and Simon had had a discussion about architecture yesterday? Effie could recall no such discussion. But to be fair, he could recall little about their tea other than his singular focus on the idea that Julianna had been wearing a wedding ring. When he'd first degloved her, in the Pavilion garden, the shock of it had been visceral. As if that little bit of metal was a dagger and she'd shoved it straight into his heart. And then he'd spiraled: what right had he to feel betrayed over her being married when he had lied to her for years?

It was just that she'd spoken so forcefully against marriage, in her letters. The idea that she might have actually been married, even as she'd taken such a fierce stance against the institution, had made him feel rather ill.

The ring-dagger had then become a snake charmer, playing a tune that had him single-mindedly fixated—Effie was the snake in this unfortunate metaphor. He hadn't been able to focus on anything else. To hear anything else. So it was entirely probable that Julianna and his friends had had any number of conversations he had missed.

"You should be the artist," Archie said to Effie, "for you *are* an artist."

"No, I am the assistant," Effie said firmly. "I am Miss Evans's assistant." It felt like a true statement. He *did* aid her, did he not, by contributing to *Le Monde Joli*? "I know a fair bit about the magazine's production," he said, in case he needed support for his assertion.

"But that leaves me to be the artist," Archie said, "and I could not sketch to save my life."

"It matters not," Julianna said. "I have been told that I may not commission any plates of the interiors, only describe them in words. I shall tell them you are making rough sketches merely in order to aid the memory of my writer." She gestured to Simon, thereby anointing him the student of architecture.

"Well, then, it's settled," Effie said. "I am the assistant." What fun. What an adventure. Was it tomorrow yet?

They spent the next while skipping stones into the sea and making up names and histories for the characters they were to inhabit—histories almost certainly more elaborate than would be required. But the laughter flowed, and the stones skipped and they kept going.

"Perhaps I ought to write a poem about the Pavilion," Effie said, attempting to balance on a large stone. He had to admit that boring leather boots were more practical for beach frolicking than were court shoes.

"Or about three peers and a magazine editor who break into the palace in Brighton," Archie said.

"We're not breaking in," Julianna said. "We're gaining entry under false pretenses."

"Oh, I beg your pardon, that's quite different, then," Archie retorted.

He adored the way Julianna and the boys were getting on, teasing one another as if they were long-standing friends.

After an hour had passed, Julianna said she needed to be getting back. As yesterday, they offered to walk her; as yesterday, she declined. "You all have spent part of each of the last two days with me, and you're to join me tomorrow morning. I believe that's quite enough gate-crashing on my part. I will see you tomorrow at ten o'clock."

She started to turn away but swiveled her head back toward them. "Please endeavor to look less like the aristocrats you are." She frowned at Effie. "That goes doubly for you. For heaven's sake, find some reasonable footwear."

Chapter 6

Subterfuge

When Julianna arrived at the agreed-upon meeting space in the Pavilion gardens, the gentlemen were already there. Well, Lords Harcourt and Marsden were there, but they seemed to be accompanied by an older, white-haired gentleman wearing a bottle-green coat and looking as though he were visiting from the previous century. He was . . .

"Effie?" she exclaimed. And immediately corrected herself: "Lord Featherfinch!" It felt wrong to call him that, but what choice did she have? "What has happened?" She answered her own question: "You have cut your hair!"

"Yes, and powdered it." He kicked up a heel. "I thought it would complement the court shoes you told me not to wear."

"My . . . goodness." The long, shiny hair she gathered he was known for was simply gone.

"We tried to talk him out of it, Miss Evans," Lord Harcourt said. "The haircut and the entire . . . look."

"Well, I did," Lord Marsden said. "You didn't try very hard, Harcourt. He's wearing your coat."

"I have embraced the challenge of subterfuge," Effie, ignoring his friends, said.

"You certainly have." On the one hand, he looked nothing like himself. His dark hair had been cropped close to his head and, indeed, powdered quite thoroughly, making him look like an elderly Julius Caesar. He was wearing one of his famously outrageous waistcoats—this one was sunshine-yellow embroidered with red, which, she had to admit, matched the red heels on his shoes perfectly. With the addition of his borrowed green coat instead of the black he'd been wearing the two other times she'd seen him, he looked like a confection one might find in the court of Marie Antionette. Subtle it was not, but counterintuitively, it did work as a disguise.

"I have also decided that I'm your husband, not your assistant."

"I beg your pardon?"

"You are already wearing a ring."

"Yes, but . . ." But what? Why did it matter what roles they adopted for a brief tour that would be conducted by someone they would never see again? And more to the point, what was this feeling in her stomach? It was a slow sort of . . . churning. Yesterday there had been seagulls flapping through her head. Today it felt as if worms were coming to the surface of the soil after a rain, slow but insistent.

"I can be your husband *and* your assistant," Effie said. "Your husband who *is* your assistant."

"That would never happen," she said, choosing to focus on the minutia of the conversation at hand, rather than the upending of her insides. "More common in my industry is the husband is the proprietor of the magazine and the wife is the editor."

"No, no, I am not the proprietor."

"Well, you cannot be my husband who is my assistant. That would raise more suspicion than your"—she eyed him up and down—"personage."

"All right, all right. I shall merely be your assistant. I just thought if I was your husband, we might dine together after our tour. I know you said we're not meant to concern ourselves with your reputation, but I thought I could accompany you back to the hotel and . . ."

Julianna very much wanted to know how Effie had been planning to finish that sentence. But more than that, she wanted to dine with him after the tour. Her face was growing hot. She didn't care for that. She sniffed. "Very well, be my husband. Perhaps it shall be amusing to have one of those for a day. And we all know how accomplished you are at concealing your true identity." She did not wait for his agreement as his friends chortled at the barb, merely turned and said, "Come along, all of you."

They were met by a housekeeper, though Julianna imagined the role was more akin to that of a general, given the size of the house and the monarchical stature of its inhabitants.

The interior of the Pavilion—at least the handful of public rooms they were shown—was nothing short of astonishing. Never had Julianna seen, or thought to see, something so opulent, so extravagant.

They were led first to a grand, lushly carpeted gallery papered in a botanical pattern. Everywhere one looked, one saw bamboo tables and enormous vases. The elongated room was flanked on either end by grand staircases that were, they were informed, made of mahogany carved to look like bamboo.

"Can you tell us anything about the inspiration, or rationale, for the decor here?" Julianna asked the housekeeper. "It wasn't that long ago, I understand, that the palace was made over in the French style."

Julianna continued to question the housekeeper as Lord Harcourt "sketched" and Lord Marsden took furious notes, notes she suspected were real. Julianna's "husband" said nothing, merely followed a few steps behind her, though he offered his arm as they departed for the banqueting room.

The room's enormous table was geographically its center, but the eye was drawn everywhere else, seemingly all at once. Golden lampstands, pagodas, and all manner of luxury competed for one's attention. It would hardly matter what one ate in a room such as this, so absorbed would one's other senses be.

"The chandelier weighs one ton," the housekeeper informed them, causing Julianna to tilt her head back to take in a cut-glass chandelier hanging from a high, domed ceiling. It was held by a silver dragon.

She hardly knew what to say, where to look, so she kept looking at the dragon. In truth, she was feeling a little overwhelmed. She had been prepared for luxury but not to this degree. It was as if her mind couldn't make sense of such excess. She felt almost frozen.

"What a pity we can't include an illustration." Lord Harcourt sidled up to Julianna and showed her his sketchbook—but angled in such a way that she was the only one who could see his "drawing." The page was covered with scribbles, most of which were abstract, but she caught a glimpse in one corner of a clumsy drawing of a horse, and in another, a tree.

The absurdity of it tipped her out of her trance, and suddenly, it was all she could do not to dissolve into a fit of giggles. "How wonderful, Mr. Nasmith"—she managed to summon the agreed-upon alias for Lord Harcourt. "You have quite captured the essence of the space and your efforts will aid Mr. Hopkins"—"Mr. Hopkins," of course, being Lord Marsden's assumed name—"enormously in his essay."

The housekeeper asked if they wanted to see the kitchen. Julianna thought it odd she was offering, but she wasn't about to pass up the opportunity. It would certainly make for an interesting juxtaposition to all this luxury. Effie winked at Julianna as he once again offered a "husbandly" arm.

She was both right and wrong about the kitchen being less luxurious than that which had preceded it. On the one hand, it was clearly a functional space, lined with more copper pots and pans than Julianna could count. But it was also like no kitchen she had ever seen. "These are . . . trees?" Julianna asked, gesturing to one of several thin columns that reached all the way up to the high ceiling.

"Yes," came the reply. "Palm trees. Even the kitchen has not been overlooked in His Majesty's decor scheme."

The kitchen was clearly a point of pride, for they were treated to a lecture on its technological advancements, which included a steam-heated warming table and a range hood made of copper that was meant to draw cooking odors up and away.

Julianna was stuck on the trees, though. Imagine having four enormous decorative columns in one's *kitchen*. Imagine having a decor scheme for a room that was merely functional, a room that no one besides servants would ever see.

She stopped in her tracks, interrogating herself. Was she implying that servants deserved less beautiful surroundings than did His Majesty's guests dining on the other side of the door?

So lost in her thoughts was she that she had to hurry to catch the others, who were departing through a different door. Well, she had to hurry to catch Lords Harcourt and Marsden. "Mr. Evans"—because Julianna had already introduced herself when asking for a tour, they'd had to give Effie her surname—was hovering nearby, uxorious as ever.

"Shall we?" he asked gently, seeming to understand that the tour was unfolding at a more rapid pace than Julianna was capable of keeping up with.

Indeed, she had to force herself to pay attention to the saloon, and the music room, which were the penultimate and final stops on their tour. Red silk–paneled walls, an enormous sunflower carpet, pagodas, golden clocks, elaborate wallpaper, soaring ceilings.

Her mind was spinning.

When it became apparent that the tour was winding down, she searched her mind for any remaining questions and came up blank. There was too much detail to even know where to begin with questions of fact, and she could hardly ask whether the kitchen maids and footmen appreciated the palm trees in the kitchen.

After offering profuse thanks, and pledging to send a copy of the magazine, the foursome emerged blinking into the late morning—the interiors of the palace had been dim. As if by previous agreement, they strode across the gardens without speaking. It wasn't until they were out of view of the main entrance that they circled up.

The gentlemen regarded her keenly. They were, of course, looking to her for direction, for an opinion, for *something*. They were looking for her to speak, not be struck dumb by a royal palace.

"I knew, of course, that the decor was inspired by the East," she began slowly. "But to know is one thing, to see quite another."

Effie and Lord Marsden murmured their agreement, and Julianna, still blinking, said, "I'm afraid I wasn't able to take in enough detail to do the place justice."

She was genuinely dismayed by having fallen so short. How would she ever convey to her readers what she had seen?

Lord Harcourt cocked his head, regarding her with a concerned expression. "Perhaps I can help." He turned his sketchpad to face everyone, showing off his hash of a "drawing," which was both more elaborate and more absurd than the version he'd shown her inside.

Everyone burst into laughter.

There had been an odd sort of tension accompanying them on the tour, which Julianna hadn't realized until their laughter made it dissipate. She hadn't truly been afraid they'd be caught out, but one couldn't deny that they had gained entry under false pretenses.

"'Tis a good thing I'm only posing as an artist," Lord Harcourt said when they'd calmed themselves.

"I, by contrast, took genuine notes," Simon said, turning his journal toward them. It was indeed full of tiny, neat lines.

"You've done well, both of you," she said. "The housekeeper didn't suspect a thing about your true identities."

"What about me?" Effie struck a silly pose, kicking up one leg as if he were one of the flamingos she had featured last year in a travel memoir from Sardinia, a posture that made everyone laugh again.

"You, too, dearest. Good job."

Dearest? Oh no. How had that slipped out? No one seemed to think it odd, though. Perhaps they thought she was jestingly play-acting the role of the indulgent wife.

The more pressing question was why she'd thought of Effie that way. Not that she didn't think fondly on several people in her life. But she didn't call anyone *dearest.*

Well, she had once. She didn't anymore.

She didn't want to think about that, so she asked, "Lord Marsden, what did you think of the place?"

"I was transported by it." He huffed an impatient sigh. "Alas."

"Indeed," she agreed.

"Why alas?" Effie asked.

"Were you not listening the other day when we discussed the expense associated with its construction and reconstruction?" Lord Marsden said. "It's positively immoral. That one man, even a king, should require such a home—and it isn't even his primary home." Another sigh from Lord Marsden, this one more resigned than impatient.

"And yet . . . ," Julianna said.

"And yet," Lord Marsden agreed. "Additionally, I am well aware of the hypocrisy inherent in a peer making such a statement. It was simply so . . . beautiful."

Julianna said, "Da Vinci said, 'Beauty perishes in life but is immortal in art.'"

"What does that mean as applied to this case?" Lord Marsden asked. "That the beauty of the Pavilion transcends the circumstances surrounding its construction?"

"Perhaps. And—or—perhaps one can disapprove of the artist but appreciate the art?"

"Hmm." Lord Marsden nodded. "That is a fascinating notion. But who is the artist? The king? Or the architect Mr. Nash, perhaps along with his predecessors?"

"A good question." An idea dawned. "My lord, I wonder if I might prevail upon you to actually write this piece. I'd been planning to do it myself, but I fear my mind was moving too slowly to take in all the details of the place. Regardless, I think you would be better suited to the task."

"Oh, no, I couldn't. I have no experience with writing."

"You write bills," Lord Harcourt said. "Dismayingly long ones."

"I do not write them alone," Lord Marsden said, "and even I will admit that they are far from engaging reading."

"You would not have to write this alone," Julianna said. "I can help."

"She is an excellent editor," Effie said, and Julianna paused to smile at him. He was playing his role well. If only she could afford such a supportive assistant.

But no, she reminded herself, Effie was not playing the role of her assistant, but her husband, and she could *not* afford one of those. More to the point, she did not *want* one of those.

She turned back to Lord Marsden. "You can weave together a description of the interior, which is what most readers will be interested in, with a bit of analysis of the sort we were just undertaking."

"You want me to say that the Pavilion is immoral?" he asked incredulously.

"No, no, but perhaps you could speculate a bit on the use, and longevity, of art." She paused. "But by all means, if you want to say that the Pavilion is immoral, it will certainly sell a great deal of copies."

"Will Mr. Glanvil allow it?" Effie asked. He turned to the others. "Mr. Glanvil is the proprietor of Miss Evans's magazine."

Julianna adored the way he called it "Miss Evans's magazine" in the same breath that he explained that Mr. Glanvil owned it.

"Mr. Glanvil and I do not always see eye to eye on editorial matters," Julianna said, feeling that a mite more explanation was in order. "But I'm sure that if you sign your name to the piece, Lord Marsden, Mr. Glanvil will be happy to publish whatever you would like to say."

"But how can I sign my name if that visit was meant to be anonymous?"

"Ah. You are right, of course."

"I'm sure we can work something out," Lord Harcourt said. "Perhaps Marsden can write it, deliver it to Mr. Glanvil, and explain to him the need for anonymity. It wouldn't even be a lie. You wouldn't want to hamper your efforts in Parliament next year, would you?"

"No, indeed," Lord Marsden said.

"Perhaps," Effie suggested, "you could make it seem as if you are engaging him in a secret. Mr. Glanvil, from what I gather, likes to feel important. What could make him feel more important than a peer of the realm taking him into confidence?"

"I think something like that could work," Julianna said, smiling anew at Effie. He was so *good* at this. He knew the compromises required in the business of magazine-making. He knew Mr. Glanvil.

But, of course, that last bit wasn't strictly true. He'd never met the man. If Effie seemed to know Mr. Glanvil, it was because Effie knew *her*. Regardless, he was acting the true helpmeet, and it was immensely gratifying, though she had to tell herself not to grow accustomed to it.

"What do you say, Lord Marsden?" she asked, ordering herself to stop grinning at her counterfeit husband/assistant.

"I am flattered. If you will guide me, Miss Evans, I will give it a go."

After a bit more discussion, they made to part ways. The gentlemen, as she had discovered was their habit, offered to walk her back to her hotel. As was her habit, she declined. She truly believed she'd monopolized enough of their holiday.

"Ah, but your husband must walk you back," Effie said with a twinkle in his eye, "for isn't your husband going to the same destination? Aren't we to dine together?"

Oh. Her cheeks were heating. Was she . . . *blushing*?

No. It must be the uncharacteristically hot September sun. Julianna did not blush.

"Very well, then." She pressed her lips together. It wouldn't do to appear too enthused.

He offered his arm, as he had in the Pavilion. The difference was, they had no audience now for their pretense, so it was an unnecessary nicety.

Well, they did have an audience, in a sense. She wondered if the other gentlemen, given that they had previously been so concerned about propriety, would object, but they did not. In fact, they looked more like indulgent papas as they smiled at Effie and told him not to trip over his heels. Perhaps it had only been the *appearance* of propriety that concerned them earlier. Perhaps they truly cared about her reputation.

Why would they do that? She was a stranger to them. A common stranger.

She sneaked a glance at Effie, who somehow managed to look both handsome and ridiculous at the same time, with his powdery hair. She supposed the answer to her question was that the lords cared about her reputation because they cared about Effie, who in turn cared about her.

It was a heady feeling.

Which meant she needed to get a hold of herself. "Playacting at marriage," she said with a gaiety she hoped did not sound too forced. "As close as I shall ever come to the real thing."

She had playacted once before, if not at marriage, at love wrapped in an imagined domestic contentment. She had learned what a quick road to heartbreak such a masquerade was.

"So you have said on a number of occasions," Effie remarked. "You are awfully opposed to the institution."

"A woman my age may be a spinster, a wife, or a widow. I wouldn't mind being a widow, but not at the price of having been a wife first."

"Is that price so high, assuming you were to marry someone you loved? Someone who . . . lifted you up?"

Yes, the price was too high. What he was suggesting was an impossibility. It only led to being left behind. She didn't say that, though, turning instead to a more practical, though no less important argument against matrimony. "If I were married, all my property would become my husband's." She had told him this already.

"Your property is already your stepbrother's."

"But you know that is because the magazine was my mother's, and upon her marriage to Mr. Glanvil Sr., it became his."

"Yes, my point is merely that—"

"If I were married, I could not incur debt without my husband's consent."

"Do you generally go around incurring debt?"

"Quite a lot, actually. I don't pay my engravers until after they've done their work."

"I see. However, is it not—"

"I already have a man interfering in my business. I don't need another." She took a breath. She'd interrupted him twice. She was exercised over this topic, but there was no need to be rude. She was merely a bit frustrated because they had corresponded on the matter, back when she thought they were both women. Back when she thought he understood.

But he *did* understand, didn't he? Effie understood her perfectly well. He understood her in a way no one ever had.

She made to apologize for the interruptions, for her shortness of tone, but he did not appear bothered. "When you say you already have a man interfering in your business, you are speaking of Mr. Glanvil?"

"It's not that I don't understand the need to balance art and commerce. I understand it very well. I would go so far as to say that striving after that balance is one of my favorite things about my position. About ladies' magazines—mine in particular but also in general. But Mr. Glanvil is overly fixated on the commerce side of things. He fails to understand that an entire issue devoted to, for example, tips for keeping house would no longer be a magazine but rather a manual."

"You *were* speaking of Mr. Glanvil."

"Yes." She paused. Oh. Oh, dear. "Did you think I was talking about *you*?"

Effie shrugged. "Well, I *am* here forcing my way into your business by insisting on posing as that husband you don't want."

"No, no. You are biddable, and you always seem to know exactly what I want to do, to hear."

He winked. "I aim to please."

She wasn't expressing herself well. "You are . . . different from everyone else."

He mock-preened. "I should think so!"

He had been in jest, and he was in a lighthearted mood, so she didn't press the matter, but Effie *was* different from everyone else. Unlike so many men, Effie *listened*. More than that, he seemed anxious to hear what she had to say. Having met him in person, she could even say that he appeared at times to hang on her every word.

Perhaps that was how Effie had come to know her, in the way she'd just been thinking she so appreciated. It wasn't that complicated when one thought about it: if you listened to a person, carefully and for long enough, you grew to know them.

So why did it feel rather like magic?

She told herself to be careful. She had felt this way once before. She refused to get stars in her eyes over someone like Effie. She refused to get stars in her eyes over *anyone*.

They walked in silence for a while. It was such a lovely day. She'd enjoyed nothing less than a coup when it came to having talked her way into a tour of the Pavilion. And then in having convinced Lord Marsden to write about it. He would do an excellent job; she suspected the result would be one of the magazine's great stories for the ages.

Finally, and not least, she was walking arm in arm with the person she considered her closest friend. That was the important part, not magic or anything so melodramatic. Effie was her closest friend, and they had found each other.

It was a good day.

"Here we are," she said as they arrived at the Old Ship. "It's more elegant than any inn I've seen." Of course, she hadn't seen many.

"I find myself dismayed that it isn't shaped like a ship."

"How would a building be shaped like a ship?"

"How would an English palace be shaped like the Taj Mahal?"

"I take the point. I'd like to drop my notebook in my room before we dine."

Effie nodded his agreement, and she gestured for him to follow her, half waiting for someone to stop them, to stand in their path and proclaim their "marriage" a sham.

If they were on a ship, it was smooth sailing: they made their way to her room unmolested.

She spared a momentary thought, as she unlocked the door, for the disorderly state she'd left the place in. Julianna was not a natural housekeeper. She may even have left a shift hanging over the back of a chair. She tried to tell herself that surely Effie's regard was not contingent on her tidiness or lack thereof, but a competing thought got in the way. The notion of Effie seeing her shift was . . . doing something to her.

"Are you all right?" he asked as he followed her inside.

"Yes, why?"

"You were breathing rather rapidly there for a moment."

"No, I wasn't."

"All right."

His cheerful agreement was discomfiting. She was not accustomed to men agreeing with her, much less doing it with smiles on their faces.

She also wasn't accustomed to anyone watching her closely enough to notice changes in her breathing.

It had been a long time, anyway.

Effie began poking around the room, looking out the window, letting his finger glide over the handle of the ewer on the bureau, leaning over the bed to peek at a piece of paper—a theatrical review for December—she'd left there.

"Don't put your head on or near anything," she said, further discomfited by the way he was so openly and unabashedly curious about her surroundings. "I don't want powder on my things."

He looked up from the other side of the bed. "It's flour."

As if that were any better. "What did you do? Ask the cook for a sack of flour?"

He shrugged. "Sometimes needs must."

He looked so silly, so insouciant, so . . . Effie, that something swelled in her chest. It was warm, and buoyant, and she suddenly feared that it was going to lift her clear off her feet.

She didn't know what to do, so she picked up a pillow from her side of the bed and threw it at him.

She *threw a pillow* at him!

What had come over her?

He sputtered, but laughter moved in to replace shock. "I thought you didn't want my head to touch anything, and now I've contaminated your bedding." He retrieved the pillow from where it had fallen on the floor and slapped it, sending a fine mist of flour into the air.

"I don't—"

He threw the pillow back at her.

She emitted a sort of laugh-gasp hybrid. The nerve! Handily, there were two pillows on the bed. She threw the second back at him, making contact squarely with his head and sending another puff of flour into the air. She attempted to use a book from her night table as a shield, but he was too quick with his retaliation.

Soon they were engaged in an all-out pillow fight. She was gasping for air because she was laughing so hard, and Effie's low, rumbling chuckle was doing something, too, when it came to making her breathless.

"Ow, ow!" Eventually the laughing and the breathlessness made her stomach and chest start to hurt. "If I remove this pillowslip and wave it"—the pillowslip was white, and not just because of the flour—"will you consider it a proper surrender?"

"No, no." He dropped his pillow to the bed. "It is I who surrender."

Something about the way he said it, all low and knowing, intensified the pressure in Julianna's belly. *It is I who surrender.* It was, on the surface of things, a submissive thing to say. What was surrender but submission? But at the same time, there was an air of authority to the declaration, a decisiveness in the way he dropped both the pillow and the teasing all at once—they were like stones that had sunk in the sea.

She followed suit, with both pillow and book.

Which left them staring at each other, weaponless and shieldless. Nothing in between them. They were alone.

In some ways, they had always been alone together. In their letters, of course, but even here, in Brighton. That first moment they'd seen each other, that moment in which they'd communicated without sound and across distance. When he had taken off her gloves and examined her hands. There had been so many moments when the world around them had fallen away.

But it hadn't actually fallen, had it? It had merely felt that way. All those times, all those touches and glances, had unfolded in public.

But now.

For the first time since they'd met in person, they were alone together without an audience. The world actually *had* fallen away. Effie had made it so, with his ridiculous shoes and his ridiculous hair and his ridiculous scheming.

He was panting slightly, grinning as he stared at her with his kind eyes, blue and brown twinkling in equal measure, his dear face covered in flour. He was absurd. He was wonderful.

He was about to kiss her.

Or perhaps she was about to kiss him.

They were moving toward each other in nearly perfect unison, and hadn't it always been like that with them? Their letters. Their work as poet and editor. Their ability to communicate without words, even though their relationship had been built on words.

She told herself to be clear-eyed about what this was, and what it wasn't. To pin what was about to happen in time, in place. She was in Brighton on a beautiful summer day, and she and her best friend were about to kiss, and wasn't that an unlikely but lovely confluence of events?

And then Effie's lips were on hers. Or hers were on his. She would be lying if she hadn't, late at night under cover of darkness, imagined what it might be like to kiss Effie, but she had never imagined *this*. A strong mouth moving against hers—no, moving *with* hers. A deep, masculine groan when she pressed her tongue against the seam of his lips.

His hand came around to the nape of her neck, and she sighed. Desire pooled inside her, but, oddly, so did relief. She hadn't wasted her money coming to Brighton, or her time. She belonged here. For now at least, in this time and this place.

Belonging somewhere was a novel sensation.

What would happen, she wondered, if she tipped her body ever so slightly? If she . . . just made them fall. Would he come with her? Would they fall together?

He would, and they did, landing with a thud crossways on the bed.

"I am overcome," Effie said against her mouth.

Julianna was, too, but she didn't speak the words aloud.

"What are we—?"

"Shh." She did not want to talk about what was happening. Talking about it would mean talking about the future. Expectations. Declarations.

"But—"

She silenced him with another kiss.

He let loose another of those groans. It was so urgent, so at odds with his usual mild manner, his easy affability.

She let her mouth open slightly, to encourage him in. He came, and they kissed deeply and slowly. She never wanted it to stop.

It had to, of course, and it did, a minute or so later when, with another groan—a gratifyingly annoyed-sounding one—he pulled away.

He opened his mouth, but before he could speak, she said, quietly, "Leave it be. Can we leave it be?"

He nodded, though something passed over his face. She wasn't sure what, but it was dark. Uncharacteristically so.

He rolled onto his back and gazed up at the ceiling, allowing her to study him in profile. He had a Roman nose, and up this close, she could see the fine wrinkles in the corners of his eyes. The wrinkles were more prominent when he laughed, and Effie laughed a great deal.

But he also brooded.

So perhaps whatever dark thing she'd seen in his eyes a moment ago wasn't that uncharacteristic.

He turned his head, startling her. "Come swimming with me."

"I beg your pardon?"

"Swimming. I will teach you, like we said before."

"How?" she asked, though this was what she adored about Effie. He had a wild sense of adventure, an expansive view of what was possible. "Where? When?"

He quirked a smile. "How about we start with what is always the infinitely more interesting question, and that is 'Why?'"

"All right. Why?"

"Because the water cures you. Not in the way that the doctors yap on about. In a deeper way. You float on it—in it—and are reminded of how the world should be."

She wasn't precisely sure what he meant by that. She could ask him, and he would elaborate. He would very likely say something devastatingly true, and beautiful. But she, she who made her living commissioning words, surprised herself by not wanting any of them to answer her question. She wanted to know what the answer *felt* like. What did it feel like to float and know how the world should be? Would it be similar to the sensation she'd experienced two days ago, floating in the arms of her dipper? Probably that, and more, for it would be Effie's arms buoying her, rather than those of an unsmiling stranger.

Effie was staring at her with an intensity that made her eyebrows itch. She flashed him a smile and said, with a breeziness she did not feel, "How can a lady refuse such an offer?"

"She cannot. Therefore, I shall now answer your other questions. I know you care little for your reputation, but I think it better that we not be seen."

"I agree. Consenting to being seen with three lords on the street on a bright summer day is quite apart from being seen with one of them in the sea in a state of half undress."

He gave a curt nod, as if they were discussing a business matter. "I suggest our beach in Hove, where we ended our walk yesterday. In the very early hours, before the sun comes up."

"Very well. Tomorrow?"

"Yes. Tomorrow's Sunday, so everyone will be at church. Is six too early? The sun should just be coming up."

"Six is fine."

"Shall I collect you? I can take Lord Harcourt's carriage, or I could come on horseback. Do you ride?"

Did she ride? When would a woman like her have had occasion to learn to ride? Effie was such an endearing mixture of wise and obtuse. "I do not ride. I walk. I shall meet you there."

She could tell he wanted to object to the idea of her walking alone at such an hour. She held up her left hand and used her right to gesture at her ring. "I have my protective charm."

"Have you enchanted it?" he asked—seemingly seriously.

"Of course not. It was a figure of speech."

"I think you could, if you wanted to. I think you have so much more power than you know."

Why did that assertion make her throat tighten? She pretended to misunderstand. "I merely meant that being 'married' provides a certain degree of protection when I walk alone."

"I knew what you meant." Was it her imagination or did the smile he produced look a little sad? "Shall we dine before I depart?"

He rose from the bed. He must have begun perspiring at some point during their . . . exertions, for some of the flour that had migrated to his face had pilled, forming little dough balls.

She grinned, which caused him to grin. Any residue of wistfulness in the air was chased away.

She pointed at the mirror. "Fix your face before we go downstairs, husband."

Chapter 7

Nightswimming

Effie tried to sneak out of bed early the next morning, but Archie awakened.

"There's no need for *you* to use the window," Archie said drily, even as Effie perched on the sill, one leg already swung outside.

Drat.

In a repeat of the previous two nights, Archie had come to Effie's bedchamber and wordlessly gotten into bed with him, rolled over, and fallen asleep. Effie had, as on previous nights, been moved by the gesture.

Unlike previous nights, Archie's presence had not helped Effie sleep. But in this case, his inability to drift off was due to excitement, not melancholy. He hadn't wanted to oversleep his meeting with Jules, and he could hardly have asked a servant to wake him up. So he had remained wakeful, but contentedly so.

He summoned a carefree tone. "I am going for a walk." It was not, strictly speaking, untrue. He was going to walk to the beach.

And then he was going swimming with Julianna.

She would be wet.

Her clothing would probably adhere to her body.

If she wore any.

She *would* wear clothing, would she not? A shift or some such? He wasn't familiar, except theoretically, with what ladies wore beneath their gowns. Stockings. There would be stockings, he thought. Or perhaps—

"God's teeth, don't fall!" Archie called, and Effie saved himself from toppling off the sill. When he didn't say anything, Archie asked, "Do you want me to come with you?"

"No, no. You stay. I merely . . . need some air."

Also not a lie. Thinking of Julianna in various states of undress had made his head hot. He had a sudden memory of sitting by the fire in the kitchen after swimming at Highworth, angling his head close to the flames so his hair would dry. Father hadn't approved of swimming, so Effie would sneak down to the kitchen after an illicit outing, and Cook would set him by the fire and give him biscuits.

He hadn't thought about swimming at Highworth for years, not since he'd mentioned it to Julianna.

"Again," Archie said, "might I suggest the door, in your case?"

"Eh, I'm already here. You go back to sleep. And take the sheet off Leander's cage when you get up for the day, will you?"

He didn't wait for further interrogation, just hopped to the ground . . . whereupon he realized that although he'd gotten dressed, he had neglected to don any shoes.

Drat again.

"Archie?" he whispered, and when there was no answer, he dared to raise his voice a tad. "Archie?"

Nothing.

Archie always slept like the dead, dropping off the moment his head hit the pillow, almost as if he could will himself to slumber. As if to punctuate that thought, Archie let loose a single snore that Effie could hear all the way outside.

And then he heard another snore, one that sounded not altogether human. He smiled. If Leander had developed the ability to imitate snoring, perhaps there was hope for him after all.

Effie pondered his feet. Ah, well. Who needed shoes? He set off. He was unlikely to encounter anyone on the walk down to the water, and he certainly wouldn't wear shoes to swim.

What *would* he wear to swim, though? He'd been so consumed, moments ago, with imagining Julianna's bathing costume or lack thereof, that he hadn't spared a thought for his own attire. He was wearing a shirt over which he had thrown a waistcoat he hadn't yet buttoned. He wore no cravat and no stockings, the latter omission perhaps explaining why he had forgotten shoes.

Even though he was missing half of what passed for respectable attire, he could hardly go into the water wearing all this clothing, could he?

The sky was just beginning to lighten as he approached the shore.

She was already there. He'd thought to arrive first, and indeed, he was early, but she was earlier.

She hadn't seen him yet. She was standing with her back to him, staring out at the dark water. The way she was standing was familiar. He had the sudden realization that he'd seen her a day before they'd met at the Pavilion. A figure on the beach had drawn his attention that first afternoon. His initial fanciful notion that it might have been Julianna had been quashed by his—seemingly—better judgment. Unlike when they met at the Pavilion, her back had been turned, and she'd been quite far away. It made sense that he hadn't recognized her, but it *had* been her.

He huffed a quiet, delighted laugh. It couldn't have been her, he'd thought that day, extinguishing what he thought was a silly conceit with a silly answer, because the sky had been the wrong color. It had been a brilliant blue afternoon. And now it was morning, and the sky was pinky orange. Still the wrong color.

Yet there she was, once again silhouetted against the wrong color sky.

"Ha!" He'd been louder that time, and she turned. He regretted the outburst. He would have liked to study her undetected for a while.

He thought she would ask what he was laughing about, or greet him, but she merely let her gaze rake him and said, "I see you have left your ridiculous shoes at home."

He wanted to kiss her again—he had thought of little else during his self-inflicted bout of insomnia last night. Instead, he kicked one leg out in front of him, toes pointed, and examined his bare foot. "One doesn't need shoes for swimming."

"I am imagining you as a child, barefoot, happily running wild on your family's estate."

"That . . ." He lowered his leg. "Would be an incorrect image."

He walked so he was even with her. They stood side by side and stared out at the water, and a good minute passed before she said, "The barefoot part or the happy part?"

He waded into the shallows, so he didn't have to look at her as he answered. "Both."

She made a small noise that was part acknowledgment, part dismay. He did not turn, but after a beat she joined him. She held her skirts aloft, and she, too, was barefoot. She'd had on half boots before, and, he assumed, stockings. She hissed as she made contact with the cold water.

He regretted having missed her removing her stockings. There would have been garters involved, he imagined. She would have had to reach under her dress and unfasten them. He untucked his shirt and let it fall over his hardening prick. He had the notion he was meant to be embarrassed, but he wasn't. The arranging of the shirt was merely to spare *her* any embarrassment or discomfort.

He observed the physical phenomenon underway in his breeches with, on the one hand, a detached sort of curiosity. This had never happened spontaneously, out in the world.

On the other hand, he *wasn't* detached. He wasn't detached at all. He was inside the phenomenon. It was an urgent, not entirely pleasant feeling, a heaviness that, if he were to pay it too much mind, might make him mad with . . . something.

"I don't know you," she said suddenly, startling him.

"You *do*," he protested.

"You sound indignant."

"I *am* indignant. You know me."

"I don't. How can I know you if I was unaware that you had an unhappy childhood?"

"It was a long time ago. It is not relevant to who I am today."

"Hmm." It was a rather grumbly *hmm*.

"What do you want to know? I am an open book."

She was going to ask him why he'd been unhappy. He didn't want to discuss such matters, but for her, he would. He took another step seaward, the waves coming high enough to dampen the bottoms of his breaches.

She walked so she was even with him, damn her.

"Tell me about swimming when you were a child. Did you swim with your sister?"

"No. I swam alone."

"Who taught you?"

The question gave him pause. "I . . . don't know." Someone must have, though. "I can't remember."

"Hmm." This *hmm* was more contemplative than grumbly.

"It has recently come to my attention that I do not remember quite a lot of my childhood," he said.

"But you remember that you swam. You remember that you loved swimming. You told me that, earlier."

"Yes. I remember the *feeling* of swimming more than I remember the specific logistical circumstances surrounding it."

"What did swimming feel like?"

"This is what I mean when I say that you know me. I've given you the opportunity to ask me questions, and instead of asking about fact, you are asking about feeling. We are alike in this way. We have spoken intensely and frequently of *feeling*. That is what matters. Who taught me to swim, who my family are, where I grew up—all of that is unimportant."

"All right, then, but you still haven't answered my question, which was entirely about feeling and therefore ought to be something you are well prepared to address: What did swimming feel like?"

"Why don't you find out for yourself?"

She grinned, instantly lightening the mood. They hadn't been arguing, exactly, but they hadn't been entirely accordant, either. "What do I do? Do I go in in my dress?"

"That is a good question. I've never swum with a lady before."

"How do you know you've never swum with a lady, given your lapses of memory? Perhaps a lady taught you to swim."

He smiled. "Perhaps I was taught by a water nymph who enchanted me when we were done with our lesson, making me forget her."

She rolled her eyes in a fashion Effie dared to think was fond. "What do you wear when *you* swim?"

He raised his eyebrows. "Usually? Nothing."

It was shaping up to be a clear morning, but the look she shot him felt like a lightning strike. He rearranged his shirt and cleared his throat. "What did you wear sea-bathing the other day?"

"They had bathing costumes on hand. A sort of sturdier version of a shift." She paused. "I have to admit it was unpleasantly heavy once wet. I propose I remove my dress and wear my shift."

When she didn't say anything further, he said, "Are you asking me?"

"No, no."

"I *could* wear my dress," she went on, "but I only own two, and I shouldn't like one of them to get caught on a rock or . . . eaten by a fish. Do fish eat dresses? Probably not, but you take my point. I am keen to protect my dress."

Effie was taken aback by the idea of a lady owning only two dresses, but then he was ashamed that he was taken aback. He told himself to consider the situation at hand. The way Julianna was talking—rambling, really—with her head dipped almost gave the impression that she was shy.

How curious. He would never have thought to call Julianna shy. She seemed almost pinned in place, so he said, "I think when one is meeting in secret for a clandestine swim, one can wear whatever one wants."

She smiled and began hiking her dress up over her head.

He was fairly certain that he died for a moment. In any case, he blacked out for long enough that even though he'd only been standing there, he tripped over his own feet. He covered it by acting as if he'd been taking off his breaches, unbuttoning the fall, but then he remembered that he was wearing no smallclothes beneath them. He rarely did. He found them distractingly unpleasant. Something about the way they rubbed his skin.

He would leave his breeches on. He fixed them, removed his waistcoat, and began unbuttoning his shirt. By the time he was rid of it, Julianna had her dress fully off and was clutching it to her chest. Effie gathered his own extraneous garments to his chest in a similar fashion, turned back toward the beach, and hurled the bundle, smiling when it landed clear of the waves.

"I don't think I have the arm for that." Julianna walked back to the beach carrying her dress. He caught sight of her previously discarded stockings, for she set her dress beside them.

This should have been scandalous. She was wearing a shift, and he was wearing only breeches. When she returned to his side, he voiced the thought.

"This ought to be scandalous."

"Yet it isn't."

"It isn't, is it?"

It was a lot of things, including the single most erotic experience of his life, but it wasn't scandalous.

"It's because of the feelings," she said. "You said we have spoken frequently and intensely of feeling. That is why this doesn't feel scandalous."

"Because we already know each other so well, you mean."

"You were right about that, but you were also wrong."

He didn't know what she meant by that, but he'd had rather enough of this conversation—the metaphorical lightning strike from before had left the air charged, crackly—so he said, "Let's walk out a way, and I shall endeavor to instruct you."

They pushed out against the waves, Julianna inhaling sharply at various points. "It wasn't this cold two days ago."

"I think there must be something about the daytime, the sunshine, that changes the experience. Even if the water isn't actually any warmer during the day, the air is." Effie was a little ahead of her, and the water was up to his waist. "It's better to just get in all at once." He dived, letting the shock cool his head, and surfaced two dozen feet away. "But you oughtn't to try that," he called. "I'll come back and help you." He reversed course.

"You are a fine swimmer," she said when he surfaced by her side. "Perhaps no one taught you. Perhaps you are a changeling, a lost son of Poseidon who was born knowing how to swim."

Wouldn't that be lovely, to be someone else's son?

He stood, and while he hadn't been scandalized earlier, there was something about the way she was looking at his chest instead of his eyes as she spoke, that returned him to that heavy, vaguely unpleasant feeling. Or perhaps *unfulfilled* was the better word. It was a feeling that something was meant to happen, something that, frustratingly, *wasn't* happening. It was a sensation of being stuck.

"I think I may have been all talk," he said, just for something to say, and also because it was the truth. "I may be a capable swimmer, but I am realizing I don't know how to teach anyone else."

She told him about her experience with the dipper from the other day. "She held me as I floated, and while I appreciate that it wasn't swimming per se, it was glorious."

"That is where we shall start, then, with an assisted float."

Effie held out his arms and guided Julianna into them. "I'm going to walk out a way, beyond where the waves are cresting. It seems counterintuitive, but the waves will be gentler out there. I won't let you go."

"All right," she said, and he set off with Julianna, his Jules, in his arms. How extraordinary.

He found a good spot and held her lightly, letting her feel the rocking of the waves. "If you tip your head back, fill your lungs with air, and hold your breath, you may be able to float on your own."

"Let me try," she said. "But don't go anywhere."

"I shan't." If only he never had to. "You're doing it!"

She was floating perfectly, so cleverly and thoroughly had she taken his instructions.

A big wave hit, and she gasped. He could see her beginning to panic. He grabbed her, encouraging her to relax back into his arms. "You're all right."

They stayed like that for a while, Effie endeavoring to hold Jules tightly enough to buffer the worst of the waves but lightly enough that she might feel their motion. He wanted to ask her what she was thinking about, but he held his tongue.

"The dipper held me like this in Brighton," she said, startling him by answering the question he hadn't asked. "It reminded me then, as it does now, of a time when I was young, and ill, and my father rocked me."

"Is it a happy memory? I suppose not, if you were ill."

"I . . . don't know. I was so shocked by it—it came into my mind seemingly out of nowhere—that I didn't classify it." She had kept her eyes closed while she spoke, and the furrow in her brow deepened. "I miss him."

"Oh, Jules, he sounds wonderful." His heart clenched. "How lovely—and lucky—to have a memory of someone holding you up like that."

She opened her eyes and regarded him silently for a long while. "It is. It is also wonderful to have someone hold you up under a sunrise." She smiled. He wanted to flatter himself that she was smiling at him, but more likely it was merely the lightening sky that she found pleasing. It was streaked with pink and yellow, a formless watercolor.

"I have a painting of you at home," he said, though he had no idea why. "Or rather, I have a painting of the idea of you."

He expected a big reaction—an exclamation or an expression of disbelief—but she merely said, "What am I doing in it?"

"Nothing. You're standing against a sky the color of chartreuse, looking at me." He paused, wondering if he ought to explain what he meant by "looking at me," but decided she would understand. "I thought of it because now you are here, looking at me, and there is a pink and orange sky. I almost feel as if I have painted this scene into being, painted *you* into being."

"And yet, *I* am the one who came to Brighton looking for *you*."

"Perhaps we painted each other into being."

"I am not an artist."

"Perhaps we dreamt each other into being."

She smiled again. "Chartreuse like the liqueur? The sky may be many unusual colors"—she hitched a chin at the paintbox sunrise above them—"but I have never seen a green one."

"I don't know, except that it just came out that way."

"Mm."

"I blame you."

"Me!" she said with mock indignation.

"Yes, I think you made it happen somehow. You bewitched my paintbrush from afar."

"Drat. You've caught me."

She shivered. They should get out of the water.

"Swimming—or floating—feels like . . ." She trailed off, her forehead wrinkling while she searched for words. "It feels like freedom."

"Precisely," he said. "The weightlessness of one's body conferred by immersion seems to lead to an analogous mental state."

"Liberation," she said.

"Yes. If only the effect were more than temporary." He paused. "When you said, earlier, that I was right but also wrong, about us knowing each other—what did you mean?" He felt ready to know.

"You were right that we do know each other, intimately. But at the same time, we don't know each other *completely*. We cannot. What you said about your childhood having no bearing on who you are today—that isn't true, is it? It cannot be. For any of us."

"No," he said quietly, a sadness colder than the sea seeping into his bones, "It cannot be." Why else would all these nightmare memories be surfacing if childhood had no bearing on the present?

To his shock, she reached up and rested a palm on his cheek. "I am sorry."

"Whatever for?" He'd meant his tone to be light, but there was a catch in his throat.

"For whatever has hurt you." She paused. "Or whoever."

Tears sprang to the corners of his eyes. He supposed he ought to be grateful that they were disguised by the fact that his face was already wet.

"My father hurt me," he said carefully. "And my mother, too, but by inaction rather than by malice."

"Ah."

"I will tell you about it," he said, surprising himself by wanting to. "But I think we ought to get out of the water. It's becoming properly morning." The land that abutted the water was owned by Lord Haffert, and this section of beach had been deserted every time the boys had visited, but Effie and Jules, in their wet, half-dressed state, were pushing their luck post-dawn.

He carried her in a way, until he judged the water level would be below her waist, and set her on her feet.

She threw her arms around him. He'd have been less shocked if she'd planted a facer on him, though he wasn't sure why. They had *kissed* yesterday.

He returned her embrace, glad the cold water had led to some . . . shrinkage. Her body was long and lean, but her bosom was soft. She hugged him tighter, and he had to revise that thought. Her bosom was soft, but he could feel her nipples against his skin, through the wet muslin of her shift.

And *drat*, the shrinkage was . . . reversing.

She didn't seem to notice, just kept hanging on as she said, solemnly, "Thank you for teaching me to swim."

"I didn't teach you, in the end. I think proper swimming lessons are better conducted in more private waters, when one may immerse oneself for a long time, and under the high sun of the afternoon." If only he could invite her to stay at Highworth.

"Thank you for holding me up, then."

He took a step back, gently disentangling them. It was difficult. "Oh, you are most welcome for that, Jules. I would do that all day if I could."

"I should have brought some toweling," she said when they were back on the beach. She picked up her dress and shook it. " 'T'will be unpleasant to put a dry dress over a wet shift."

Effie had been trying not to look at the wet shift too closely. "Come back to the house." He spoke with his back turned, nominally because he was buttoning up his shirt. "You can dry off there."

She started to demur, but her speech was interrupted by an almost comically large yawn. She smiled when it concluded. "I can't imagine why I feel so exhausted."

"You walked here."

"It isn't a great distance, and I walk quite a lot, generally speaking. I suppose it's that I stayed up most of the night, not wanting to oversleep our meeting."

"I did the same." As if on cue, he yawned. "It seems your fatigue is infectious."

"Your friends"—another yawn—"won't mind if I pay a visit? Or the household staff?"

"They won't know," he said, though he had no idea how he was going to sneak her in.

The same way he had sneaked out, he decided. His bedchamber window was going to be harder to enter from the outside—jumping down had been one thing—but he could give Julianna a leg up. He'd helped his sister onto enough horses.

To his surprise, there was an actual mounting block sitting at the base of the window.

Oh, Archie.

They were able to scramble in, and there was no sign of Archie himself. Julianna had spent the short walk shivering, and he looked around for something with which to warm her. The bed was unmade, the servants no doubt believing he was still abed. He gathered up the counterpane and wrapped it around her shoulders, guiding her to sit on the edge of the bed. "Excuse me for a few moments."

He made his way into a small attached dressing room and quickly changed into fresh garments.

He had intended to make haste so he could get back to Julianna, but once he was changed, something kept him pinned in place, like a deer facing a hunter but unable to rouse itself to flee. Exhaustion, he supposed. But it wasn't just that. It was something else, too.

Wonder: Julianna was in the attached room, steps away. Julianna was *here*!

He wanted to kiss her again, if she wanted it, too.

He stepped back through to the room, buttoning his new, dry shirt.

She was asleep. Goodness, she slipped into slumber as easily as Archie.

A terrible fondness rose through him. She was slumped back against the headboard, and the counterpane had fallen off her shoulders. Gently, he attempted to rearrange her so she would be more comfortable, but she awakened.

"Mmph." She blinked, befuddled. He could see her preparing to rise.

"Shh," he soothed. "Stay. Rest a while. Get warm. You will not be discovered."

He thought she would object, but she only said, "I will rest if you will rest with me."

"Yes." He would do anything with her, anything she asked, and resting was easy.

She allowed him to fuss with the bedding, to tuck her in, then she shocked him utterly by holding up the covers, seeming to indicate that she wanted him to get in—that when she'd said "rest with me," she'd meant in the same bed.

When he didn't immediately move, she said, "Do I have to hit you with a pillow to get you to get in?"

He got in.

When he awoke who knew how much later—the sun was blazing through the crack in the curtain and his stomach was rumbling—Julianna was wide awake, lying on her side looking at him.

"I have awakened to find myself on Saturn," she said.

Effie had been writing to Julianna about Saturn's rings. He gathered the comment meant that as she'd come to consciousness and remembered where she was, she'd felt she may as well have been floating among those celestial wonders.

"You say the most marvelous things," Effie said.

"What do you mean?"

"You say things you mean metaphorically, but you say them with such lack of irony, such absolute unwavering steadfastness, that sometimes you give me pause, make me wonder momentarily if you aren't being literal. You say that you're on another planet. Or that your head burst into flame, or that your heart beat so fiercely it broke a rib. You describe the most extreme visceral experiences even as you maintain a facade of equanimity." He paused. "I am fairly certain you have never been to another planet. You have not experienced a broken rib, or the immolation of your head, have you?"

"I have not." The smile she'd been wearing faded. "Perhaps such similes are ill-done of me. I'm sure there are people who have experienced such grievous bodily wounds in a literal sense. Soldiers, for example."

"You are a kind of soldier."

She made a dismissive noise.

"You are always battling Mr. Glanvil for resources, and printers for time on their presses." He thought of Hamlet, tucked away in Archie's house. London felt so far away, in terms of both distance and experience.

"Come now, Effie, let us not get carried away. Such hyperbole is insulting to soldiers and to me. And to you. You're better than that."

Well, that stung. But that was why he adored Julianna, was it not? She never hesitated to voice her true feelings. Lots of people looked at Effie and saw the life of the party—the fashionable gentleman in the silly shoes always good for a witty remark. Effie had cultivated such interpretations. That was not what Julianna saw, though, or not all she saw. She held him to high standards, wanting him to live up to a potential she seemed to see more clearly than he did. This scrutiny of hers was both unsettling and thrilling.

"You know what I mean," he said. "You can't have imagined having to advocate so fiercely and continuously for the magazine your father started."

She nodded thoughtfully as she stared at the ceiling.

"Of course, you miss him as a person, too," Effie added, not wanting to reduce her relationship with her father to the magazine.

"You are correct on both counts," she said wistfully. "I do miss him, as I said. I miss him terribly, and sometimes it feels as though I miss him *more* as the years elapse rather than less. But the perpetual struggle over the magazine does throw into relief how different my life is compared to what I thought it would be. I think that—that gap—is the worst part."

"What do you mean?"

"Oh, I don't know. Father and I always planned for me to take over when he was gone. Neither of us foresaw Mother remarrying. I ought to be angry at her, I suppose, but I find I cannot be."

"You rarely speak of her in your letters." He knew about her sister, and her sister's family, and she often invoked her father.

"We aren't close. She is a woman who loves love, who hates to be alone. Glanvil Senior swept her off her feet." She shrugged. "To turn him down wouldn't have occurred to her. It would have been against her nature, and you can hardly fault someone for being who they are."

"So about this gap you referenced," he prodded. He was sucking up this information about her family like a thirsty robin in a birdbath, but what he really wanted to know about was this business of her life not turning out the way she'd imagined.

"Yes. I always saw myself running the magazine. I just didn't think it would be this hard. I didn't think I would be so . . ." She shook her head. "I don't know what I'm on about."

He didn't know precisely what she'd been going to say, but he had the distinct impression that the word she'd swallowed was one that would have broken his heart. *I didn't think I would be so unhappy*, say. *I didn't think I would be so lonely.*

Before he met her in person, he wouldn't have thought Jules was anything like that. She seemed so in control of all aspects of her life. How could such a person be unhappy, or lonely?

He knew she didn't want to talk about it. And perhaps he was incorrect. It was the height of self-regard, in a way, to presume to know how she felt, to speculate about which words she had inside her.

"Can we stay here forever?" he asked, both by way of distraction and because he would have loved for the answer to be *yes*. If only they could remain tucked into bed indefinitely. He could sneak out and procure food as required. Books. Whatever she wanted.

Her countenance turned wistful "I wish. I have wanted to meet you in person for ever so long, and how buoying it is to find, after a bit of initial confusion, that you're exactly as I imagined."

"Am I?"

"Well, apart from the minor detail that you are a gentleman, yes. Also, I hadn't expected you to smell like cloves."

Only Jules would consider the fact that he was a gentleman and not a lady a "minor detail." "What had you imagined I'd be like? What had you imagined I would smell like?" He smiled. "I hadn't expected you to smell like roses."

"So what you are saying is that neither of us smells right."

"I suppose I'm merely saying that the corporeal world has its advantages over the epistolary one, and *that* is not something I thought I'd ever say."

"We got most of it right," she said thoughtfully. "Or I did, anyway. I thought you would be intelligent."

Effie was certain no one had ever called him intelligent before.

"You would be thoughtful, and kind." She paused, considering him. She was so close, he could see that there were several different shades of green in her eyes, ranging from a deep forest to a bright moss. Next time he painted her against a chartreuse sky, he would be able to represent her eyes properly.

"You would have an eye for beauty, but also for pain," she went on. "That is what I thought you would be like, and it all came true. *You* came true."

Warmth flooded him as he considered her words. "My father would not agree with any of your assessment."

"Well, then, he does not know you."

"He does not care to know me."

"That is his loss."

It was time to tell her. "I cannot remember who taught me to swim, because I cannot remember a great many things from my childhood."

"How do you know you can't remember them if you can't remember them?"

Delighted, he huffed a laugh. She had such a keen mind.

"I *have* been remembering them lately, in bits and pieces. I've been having nightmares."

"So you have said."

"Yes, but I have led you to believe they are nightmares of the regular sort—phantasmagoric. Fanciful. Frightening but transitory. But they aren't. They're *true*. They *happened*."

"Your memories are coming to you as dreams."

"Yes." He went on to tell her what he'd told the boys, about the wardrobe and the broken arm and the drowned kitten. He told her *more* than he'd told the boys. There were so many examples. He hadn't thought it necessary to include them all the other night, in order to make his point, but something about Julianna's careful, unstinting attention made him want to tell her everything. To recite the whole brutal, mortifying list.

"That is why I never told you the whole truth about who I am," he explained when he'd finished his list of woes. "Because I don't want to be who I am."

Because of who I am, I can't have you.

He almost said that last bit aloud, but he reminded himself that it was only one reason among many he did not want to be the heir to the Earl of Stonely. And it was only one reason among many keeping him and Julianna apart. It was, given her fierce resistance to the very idea of marriage, a minor reason at that.

They lay side by side in silence for a long while until a scrabbling sound drew their attention. Julianna glanced in the direction of Leander's sheet-draped cage.

"Have you brought your *bird* on your holiday?"

"I have indeed. Leander is at a critical point in his education, and I didn't want him to backslide."

She chuckled. "Is he saying more words?"

"Alas, no. He has added 'Go' to the roster, but still no sentences, or even phrases."

That was a lie, and Effie had never lied to Julianna. But what choice did he have?

A terrible thought dawned: What if Leander said his one sentence in front of Julianna? *I am in love with a woman named Julianna Evans.*

He could only hope the creature would settle back down to sleep.

And/or that the sentence, which had never been heard since its singular utterance, had been an aberration.

"So he says, 'No,' 'Try,' and, now, 'Go,'" Julianna said, and Effie was tickled that she remembered from his correspondence such inconsequential details as Leander's previous syllables.

"That is correct."

"Why did you name him Leander? I never asked. Presumably he is named after the Greek hero? Leander who swims to his love Hero every night, guided by the light in her tower."

"I was inspired by the Keats poem that recounts Leander's drowning, but yes."

"Was she imprisoned in the tower? I can't remember."

"I don't know, but she must have been, else why would she let him drown trying to get to her?"

She slid off the bed. "May I meet your Leander?"

"Of course."

He led her to the other side of the room and slid the sheet off Leander's cage, praying the creature would stick to his single syllable du jour.

Julianna leaned over and out her face quite close to the bars. "He's lovely."

"Isn't he?" Effie cleared his throat. "Miss Evans, please meet Leander. Leander, this is Miss Evans."

"Hello, Leander," Julianna said warmly.

"Hello, Miss Evans!" Leander, that absolute bounder, said.

Chapter 8

More Subterfuge

"Good morning." Effie led Julianna into the breakfast room where his friends were seated at a round table and a maid was fussing with a chafing dish on a side table. "You gentlemen will remember my sister?"

The Earl of Marsden dropped his newspaper, and for a moment Julianna thought he might fall off his chair.

The Earl of Harcourt recovered more quickly as amusement replaced startlement on his face. "Yes, of course. *Lady Sarah*, how nice to see you." He shot a look at Lord Marsden that seemed to contain an instruction of some sort.

"We were so happy to hear you would be joining us," Lord Marsden said smoothly, apparently having received the silent directive.

"Father regrets that he could not stay," Effie said mildly, strolling over to help himself to some food, "but he asked me to convey his greetings to both of you." He glanced over his shoulder at Lord Marsden. "In truth, he is avoiding you, Marsden, because he doesn't want to talk to you about your gaols act anymore."

"Edward!" Julianna exclaimed, feigning disapproval.

"'Tis the truth, and we are among friends." Effie shot her a wink.

Julianna turned to the lords, continuing to play her part. "You will forgive my brother. Or perhaps it is my father who requires your absolution. One of the horses threw a shoe, which is why we arrived so late, and he was determined, despite the hour, to make the trip to Dover to catch his boat, which is set to depart this afternoon. Edward probably told you our father is sailing for the Continent to rejoin our mother in Italy." She lowered her voice. "He is mad for her, even after all these years, and will happily abandon his children in favor of his wife."

Effie snorted. They hadn't discussed that last little embellishment. Effie's playful demeanor had inspired Julianna to extemporize.

"I beg your pardon, Edward!" she said, affecting sisterly annoyance. "There is no call for such scorn. In truth, it is all rather romantic." She performed a mock swoon. "Except for the part where I've been dumped on you, brother mine."

The maid had gone and fetched the housekeeper, who'd heard the last bit of their exchange, and she began exclaiming over why no one had awakened her when Lady Sarah arrived. "I would have made up a room for you, my lady."

"Oh, it was very nearly dawn by the time I arrived. I couldn't possibly have slept. Edward walked me down to the sea, as my legs were in terrible need of stretching after the journey from Town."

"Well, I shall see to your accommodations immediately. How long will you be with us?"

Oh, dear. When Julianna awakened this morning in Effie's bed, she had been vulnerable—she had shed her armor with Effie as easily as she had shed her dress and stockings on the beach—so she had allowed his mischievousness, his spirit of adventure, to infect her. And she had so enjoyed spending time with his friends yesterday, so when he had beseeched her to spend the day with them, she had easily relented.

But she had been thinking only about today. About staying for breakfast, about spending a little more time with the gentlemen before she went back to her real life.

"Not long," she said, vaguely, because she had to say something.

"A night." She would invent an excuse to leave before night fell. Perhaps her "father" had missed his ship after all and would come back to collect her. Or perhaps she had an uncle and aunt who were to be fetching her to return to London. She would think of something. But not without consulting Effie. She had gone a little rogue just then, with her ode to their fictional parents' love, but it wasn't wise to be getting too off-script. Effie actually had a sister named Sarah. She had no idea what kind of aunts-and-uncles inventory he had.

"You're the one who made Father drive you here because you were bored in Town," Effie said tartly. "And now you're only staying one night?"

She shrugged with what she hoped was insouciance—Julianna had never been insouciant a day in her life. "'Tis a lady's prerogative to change her mind."

She breathed a sigh of relief when the housekeeper left, promising a room would be ready post haste.

Effie tiptoed to the door, shut it, and turned to the rest of them, grinning. Lord Harcourt made a show of applauding as if he were at the theatre, and Effie took an elaborate bow as if he were, too.

"Everyone did such a fine job," he said when he righted himself. "Even you, Simon. We ought to form a theatrical troupe."

Lord Marsden merely regarded Effie with his eyebrows raised.

"Oh, calm yourself," Effie said. "We went swimming very early this morning and entered the house through my bedchamber window. He turned and inclined his head in Lord Harcourt's direction. "Thanks for that, by the by."

Julianna had no idea what "that" was.

"We merely meant to dry off, but we fell asleep, and rather than having Miss Evans sneak back out the window—"

"Window sneaking being properly a one-way activity," Lord Marsden interrupted.

"Oh, *he* sneaked out this morning," Lord Harcourt said.

"How do you know that?" Lord Marsden asked.

"*Regardless*," Effie said, talking over them and turning to Julianna, "now that you are my sister, you may stay. The problem is we neglected to think through what 'staying' meant." He grinned. "I suppose you shall have to stay indefinitely. For the duration of your trip, I mean."

"No!" she protested.

"Miss Evans," Lord Harcourt said, "do not fret. We shan't keep you here against your will."

It wasn't that so much as she refused to be a permanent interloper, to intrude on the gentlemen's holiday beyond more than a short visit. "I have to be back in London by Wednesday at the latest." That was three days hence—three *nights* hence. She couldn't spend them all here.

Could she?

"You are welcome to stay as long as you please, but we can come up with a scheme to get you out of here whenever you like," Lord Harcourt said, and Lord Marsden murmured his agreement.

For his part, Effie made a vague noise of resigned acceptance. But, recovering quickly, he clapped his hands together. "What shall we do today?"

They spent the day gamboling. The cook packed them a picnic, and they rambled: through the village, along some roads that stretched out beside fields of barley and oats, and eventually back to the beach, where they set up their lunch.

"Oh, look, Effie, strawberries," Lord Marsden said. "Have you told Miss Evans your theory of strawberries and salt?"

Julianna was gratified that Effie's friends did indeed call him "Effie."

Effie shot Lord Marsden a quelling look.

"You haven't told her?" Lord Marsden, apparently immune to quelling looks, said. "Not even about the legs of lamb and pots of cream?"

"Oh, for heaven's sake," Effie said. "She isn't interested in that nonsense."

"Yes, she is," Julianna said.

When Effie didn't say anything, Lord Marsden turned to her and said, "We're all food. People are food."

"People are food?" she echoed, bewildered.

"*Simon*," Effie said, his tone laced with affront. "You're going to tell it all wrong."

Lord Marsden made a gesture to indicate he was yielding the floor to Effie, who heaved a put-upon sigh.

"It is a metaphor," he explained, "about how people sometimes find themselves born into the wrong families, and about how they might endeavor to find the people with whom they truly belong."

"Please do go on." She was terribly anxious to hear this theory. She hadn't known how to react to Effie's stories of his father's cruelties. Her instinct had been to provide a solution, a means of escape, though she understood and respected his assertion that he was trapped by the title he stood to inherit. But perhaps she needn't have fretted. Perhaps he had made his own way out of the mire with this theory of his—and these friends of his.

"Some people are strawberries, say," Effie said, "and some people are salt. If you're a strawberry born into a family of salt, you're out of luck. Or, I should say, you have your work cut out for you. For you must go out into the world and find people who are pots of cream."

Julianna was struck with the urge to laugh. She suppressed it. "I see."

"And what do the salt people do?" Lord Marsden prompted.

"They're off to find legs of lamb, which are improved by salting."

Julianna did laugh then. She hoped it hadn't come out as mocking. "How delightful and absurd."

"Absurd?" Effie echoed, and she was almost certain his affront was put on. "It is perfectly logical. Simon—Lord Marsden—calls it 'found family.'"

"Isn't that lovely?" she exclaimed, understating the matter entirely, for the phrase had lanced her chest.

"That's exactly what I said when he came up with it," Effie said.

If only it were so easy. If only one could "find" a family as easily as buying a newspaper. Julianna loved Amy and her nieces and nephew—she loved Mother, too, even if it was a more abstract sort of love—but she sometimes felt as if she didn't quite *belong* with them. She was lonely in a full house. And, of course, there was the hole in her life where Father had been.

But now was not the time for rumination, or grief. She turned to Lord Harcourt, who'd been watching the exchange with a kind of silent fondness. "What do you make of Lord Featherfinch's theory, my lord?"

"I think it brilliant, like he is."

What a fine answer. What good men. Though they needled one another, they also respected and esteemed one another.

After lunch, Lords Marsden and Harcourt proposed an outing to Brighton. "If I'm truly to be writing for your magazine, Miss Evans, I want to have another look at the Pavilion—the exterior, I mean," Lord Marsden said.

Effie begged off, so Julianna did, too, and soon she found herself alone with Effie at the sea. It was beginning to feel usual to find herself alone with Effie at the sea.

Until Effie took off his boots and proclaimed that he was going to wade in the water.

Julianna nearly swooned when she saw Effie's bare feet. She'd had the same reaction this morning on the beach, when he'd strolled up shoeless. She comforted herself, though, that this swoon was a trifle less . . . emphatic than the first had been.

Of course, all Julianna's swoons were interior. She was fairly confident that in general, she betrayed nothing of her true feelings. It was one of her particular talents.

There was something almost painfully intimate about seeing Effie's bare feet. On paper, it made no sense. She'd seen much more of him yesterday. He'd been bare-chested during their swim, and though she hadn't seen his manhood, she'd *felt* it when they embraced.

And she had been intimate with others. She had, to use a phrase she abhorred, given away her maidenhood—as if it were a flower that could be given only once before it wilted. She'd done it happily, knowing it was not a currency she needed, given that she had no plans to marry.

She was not a sheltered schoolgirl, was the point.

So what was it about a pair of feet—as nicely shaped as they were, they were just feet—that was making her wish she were the sort of woman who carried smelling salts?

She considered the concept of intimacy.

She had been intimate with others before, in the traditional carnal sense, but she had never, before Effie, been barefoot outside. She had never stepped into the sea, much less lain back in it and talked about liberation and the color of the sky.

And Effie was so attached to his fashionable footwear. For that reason, there was something about seeing him sans shoes that felt almost transgressive.

She smiled to herself, satisfied over having puzzled through the mystery of the bare feet. But then she sighed. Like a lovestruck young miss. How lowering. Effie was just so . . . everything. All the things she had said before: kind and intelligent and thoughtful. But also dashing and brave and capable of observing the world and reporting back on it in verse with a savage truthfulness that took her breath away.

They had embraced this morning, and kissed yesterday. They had slept in each other's arms. And not once had he dropped to one knee to exhort her to marry him. They'd merely kissed, or embraced, when they felt moved to, as if these things were part of life, part of their relationship, but not something to fixate on.

Effie was utterly unlike most men of her acquaintance.

Julianna had had two affairs in her life, the more recent one with Charles, one of the engravers she used with some regularity. Charles had, after their initial, spontaneous encounter, proposed.

"You don't want to marry me, and I don't want to marry you," she'd said—he had been a widower with no interest in a second wife.

When he'd apologized profusely and assured her that nothing untoward would ever happen between them again, she'd taken a leap and said, "I shan't be marrying, ever. But need it follow that I shall never know the joys of the marital bed?"

"I don't think they call it a *marital* bed for nothing," he'd replied, his quick wit reminding her why she liked him so much. She'd had to spend a great deal of time convincing him that she was in earnest. Once she succeeded, they'd gone on to enjoy themselves for a few months. Their affair had run its course, and Charles continued to provide excellent engravings for the magazine. She remained fond of him, and she suspected he felt the same about her.

And then there had been Edith. Her one true lady friend.

Her onetime love.

She had been a sister of one of Amy's friends, visiting for the summer. They'd talked endlessly about books, Edith eventually confessing to harboring secret aspirations of writing a novel. From there they'd progressed to reading aloud their favorite literary passages to each other. From there, they'd . . . progressed.

It had been wonderful, for a while, until the topic of marriage had come up.

"This doesn't count," Edith had said.

"What do you mean?" Julianna had braced herself, ready for the dagger.

She hadn't thought to put her armor on—she'd been young enough then that armor hadn't yet been her default wardrobe—so when Edith said, "This isn't the same as lying with a man; I can still say I'm coming to my future husband with my maidenhood intact," the dagger slid in, silent and lethal. Lady Macbeth herself could have been no more effective.

Julianna still had trouble understanding why she had been so hurt. It wasn't as if Edith could marry *her*. Still, some foolish inner part had wondered—hoped—that Edith's devotion to Julianna might have kept her from the marriage mart generally. Edith came from money; she didn't *need* to marry. Perhaps girlish Julianna had thought the two of them could be spinsters together.

She had been out of her mind.

After some time passed, Julianna's hurt had crystallized into something harder, darker. Anger, mostly, initially at Edith, but then at . . . everyone. Society. The rules they all labored under, which sometimes felt so arbitrary. So cruel.

Which she realized was absolutely ridiculous.

But she didn't regret any of it, not the anger, not the underlying hurt from which that anger had alchemized. For it had reminded her what was important—*the magazine above all.* The heartbreak wrought by Edith had made Julianna into the businesswoman she was. The woman who had been in earnest when she'd told Charles she didn't want to marry him.

So she was a wee bit worried about the way, when she was with Effie, she sometimes experienced that same out-of-her-mind sensation. Not that she was pining girlishly over him. It was a more literal sensation. Sometimes, Julianna's mind simply . . . emptied out when Effie was near. She was back to being that mindless starfish she'd been that morning she impulsively left Amy's house. With no thoughts left in the brainless void, all that was left was longing. Longing that felt disconcertingly familiar.

Effie loped back to the carpet she was sitting on and lay back, his hands clasped behind his head. "Do you think it a good thing or a bad thing that I'm suddenly remembering unpleasant childhood memories?"

Julianna had to take a moment to absorb the question, to wrench herself from memories of lovers past. "When did these memories start?"

"About a year ago."

"Was there any precipitating event?"

"Not that I can think of."

"Well, what was happening a year ago?"

"I suppose I was on an Earls Trip. We were in Cumbria. We

were joined—'tis a very long story—by Archie's now wife, Clementine, and her sister, Olive."

"Did you emerge from that trip with any revelations? Was anything different about your life after versus before?"

"Olive and I became bosom friends. Correspondents."

Julianna felt a twinge in her chest. Was she . . . jealous? No. Jealousy was for married couples, for people who had elected to tie themselves together permanently. As she had *just* been thinking, that wasn't what was happening here.

"Don't worry, Jules," Effie said. "It's not like you and me."

"I'm sure I don't know what you mean," she said, mortified she was so transparent to him.

"Olive and I are only friends."

"*We* are only friends."

He rolled onto his side, propped his head on one hand, and regarded her with an expression she could not parse. "Is that true?"

She didn't know how to answer. All her introspection just now hadn't really answered that question.

"Well," he said, after a few beats of silence, "if you and I are only friends, we are very different sorts of friends from Olive and I. You and I—" He sat up suddenly.

"What is it?"

"Olive and I became friends rather quickly. The setting made for an accelerated path to familiarity. I cannot say more without betraying a confidence. But I did tell her about many aspects of my life. I unburdened myself in a way I hadn't for some time." He glanced over his shoulder at her. "I told her about you."

"You needed to unburden yourself regarding me?" She wasn't sure if she should be miffed or flattered.

"'Unburden' is perhaps not the correct word. It is . . ." He shook his head. "I also told her about my father. That is the relevant point. She was the first person I told about how much of a disappointment I am to my father. Well, the boys always knew that Father and I didn't see eye to eye, but I'd never told anyone the extent of it. They thought I didn't mind being a disappointment."

"But you do mind," Julianna said, as gently as she could.

"I try not to mind," Effie said quietly.

I try not to mind. Oh, her heart ached for him.

"On that trip last year, I told Olive the true contents of my jumbled heart. And now that you mention a timeline, I think the nightmares—the nightmare memories—started after that. In retrospect, it was as if I'd opened a dam. Do you think that's possible?"

"I do indeed. I don't have anyone like that in my life, but I have often heard my sister say she feels better after having tea with a bosom friend who lives nearby."

"But I *don't* feel better. I can't sleep!"

"Is it possible you *will* feel better? Perhaps the dreams are coming now that the dam is open, but the water supply is limited? Perhaps it's spring and the water is high, but by summer the riverbed will be dry. Perhaps you merely need to survive the current flood." She shrugged. "I am no expert. As I said, I have never had a bosom friend like that."

Except you. She wanted to say it aloud but held back for reasons she couldn't articulate.

The thought wasn't quite correct, anyway. Effie was a bosom friend, but he *was* also something else, wasn't he, if she was being honest with herself? One didn't kiss one's bosom friends the way she and Effie had kissed.

One didn't turn into a mindless starfish around one's bosom friends.

Effie had been correct when he said that they were "different sorts of friends."

"I should like you to meet Olive," Effie said, drawing Julianna from her ruminations.

Julianna wanted to ask Effie about what was going to happen when they were back in London. She would meet Olive, and then what? They could hardly carry on the way they had been here, lazing about and bearing their souls, interspersed with the occasional kiss or ardent embrace.

Could they?

She and Charles had, for quite some time.

But no. Effie was the heir to an earl. One didn't carry on with the heir to an earl. The heir to an earl needed a *wife*.

And . . . there it was. Julianna couldn't get a breath in. The truth had pushed all the air out of her body. Earlier, she had observed that she couldn't understand why she had been so hurt by Edith, why her departure after that lovely summer had inflicted a wound that felt so much graver than garden-variety heartbreak. It had to do with marriage. Julianna had spent so much time thinking about marriage, even if only to resist it. She didn't want to marry. And even if she'd changed her mind on that front, she *couldn't* have married Edith.

So to have Edith flit off and marry her gentleman correspondent, to so easily assume the mantle of a conventional life, her "transgressions" with Julianna erased by her easy embrace of matrimony . . . well, yes, that explained a great deal to Julianna about her own mind. All that anger, at both Edith and at society.

And it explained what was going on here. Like Edith, Effie would eventually leave Julianna behind. Perhaps he wouldn't do it as blithely as Edith had, but he would have to.

Julianna blew out a breath, a bit overcome by having hit on a truth she hadn't realized was buried inside her.

But she could not betray this truth. None of this was Effie's fault, not even the fact that if they were to embark on a long-term liaison, he would one day leave her to marry another. He was as constrained by societal mores as she was. Perhaps more. At least she had her magazine.

The magazine above all. It had never felt truer, or more important.

"Olive would be exactly the sort of reader to appreciate your travel accounts," Effie said, apparently oblivious to Julianna's swirling thoughts. "She has a passion for traveling, a passion that has mostly gone unindulged. She did recently accompany her sister and Archie on their honeymoon to Italy, though."

Julianna told herself to set aside her revelation, at least for now. It wasn't going to do any good to dwell on it at the moment. Besides, her inner editor had perked up. "What part of Italy did Miss Morgan visit?"

"The north. Lombardi and Piedmont."

"Did she see the Shroud of Turin? If so, would she be willing to write an account of it?" Julianna had been thinking that one way to satisfy Mr. Glanvil's increasing interest in "moral" content—by which he meant biblical content—might be to disguise it as travel reporting.

"She did, and I believe she would be delighted to do so. However, I must warn you that she maintains some rather unconventional opinions as to the origins of the shroud. Some—not I, mind you—might even call them blasphemous opinions."

"All the better!" Julianna refrained from applauding but only just. "I shall write out a brief and have you pass it on to her, and if she is agreeable, she can send me her reflections directly. I will of course outline the terms. I don't pay first-time writers very much, but if she will accept . . ." Baroness Cartworth's report on the Lake District aside, Julianna was not accustomed to having members of the aristocracy write for her. "She probably doesn't mind how much I pay." Julianna could pay Miss Morgan half the magazine's monthly budget and it would be a crumb to her.

"Oh, no, I think she will mind exceedingly. She is . . . Well, it's not my place to say, but I don't think she would object to my telling you that she is saving up for something." He paused. "Not unlike you."

"You are referring to my fantasy of purchasing a press."

"I am indeed, but I wouldn't consider it a fantasy."

"It was always thus, but it became even more so when I took leave of my senses and came here."

"We need to move you out of the hotel!" Effie exclaimed. "How foolish of me not to think of it earlier. You can't be paying for it when you're staying with us."

"I can't stay with you!"

"Why not? You are my sister, and everything is very proper."

"I know, but—"

"I am happy to have you."

"But are the others? I gather that this trip has been a long-standing masculine tradition."

"If Clementine and Olive Morgan could gate-crash—that's your terminology, not mine—last year's Earls Trip, you may do the same this year." He smirked. "Perhaps next year will be Simon's turn." The smirk turned into a genuine guffaw.

"What is so amusing?"

"The idea of Simon doing anything so disrespectable." He shook his head. "No, next year's Earls Trip will be a return to form, just the three of us gents. I would bet my title on it."

Julianna refrained from pointing out that by his own admission, Effie didn't value his title very highly so perhaps he ought to find something else with which to wager in favor of saying, "What is disrespectable about my staying with you? You just got done explaining that I'm your 'sister' and that everything is in fact very proper."

"Everything is very proper as far as the household staff is concerned."

"But not as far as we're concerned?"

"Oh, pish, we don't care about propriety."

"We don't?"

"Are you not the one who made a speech on this very topic not two days ago?" He made a silly face as he raised his voice and mimicked her. "'I am not a refined lady whose reputation is a fragile glass bauble in need of protecting.'"

She rolled her eyes—fondly. She wished she had a pillow to throw at him.

He grew serious. "Of course you must not stay if you truly do not want to. And of course I care about propriety insofar as it is important to you." He paused before revisiting a previous question. "And we *are* friends. It's only that sometimes it feels as if you are a friend I can never be without. I am terribly afraid that when this trip is over, you will insist that we go back to the way we were before. That I'm to climb back into my cage and communicate with you only through letters."

She thought it was curious he'd used the image of climbing back into a cage. She herself had been thinking of them as birds in adjoining but separate cages. She had used the words *freedom* and *liberation* when they'd been swimming together. If she felt liberated when she was with Effie, did if follow that she was going to feel imprisoned when they parted ways? Which they were going to have to do, of course. Being left heartbroken was one thing. Being left heartbroken because your beloved had plans to marry someone else was quite another. Now that she understood that, she merely needed to integrate this truth into her conduct. Into her plans.

"Don't confirm my fear. Or deny it." His tone was growing increasingly urgent, and he took her hands in his. "Don't say anything. Just let me be with you, whether that's only for the rest of the afternoon, or until you have to go back to London.

"And if you are truly harboring fears that the others wouldn't welcome you, please set those aside. They themselves said only a few hours ago that they would be happy to have you, and they don't lie."

Julianna could feel herself softening. No, she was already soft. Effie made her soft and had been doing so for quite some time. What was happening now was a process by which she let him *see* that she was soft. Not knowing how to put any of this into words, she tried a small smile.

He heard what she wasn't saying and smiled back. "It's only three more nights, yes? You said you had to be back in London on Wednesday, in order to be at the printers for Thursday morning."

"Yes."

"So it's settled. Stay."

"All right."

How easy it had been to agree, to simply acquiesce. She ought to take that as a warning. She could stay for the rest of her holiday, but then she was going home—alone.

He rolled over onto his back and stared at the sky. "Now tell me about November. Or December."

He didn't have to ask her twice to get her to talk about the magazine, especially after her episode of inner turmoil and startling self-discovery. "I have the most wonderful fashion catalog planned for December. There is one dress in particular that is most extraordinary, or must be in person." Effie closed his eyes as if to better picture the dress she was about to describe. "The accompanying text explains that the overskirt is lemon yellow and the underskirt burnt orange. Can you imagine? The wearer would look like a sunrise."

"Like this morning's sky."

"Like this morning's sky," she echoed.

He grinned and opened his eyes. "I do so love your year-end fashion spreads."

"I do, too."

He rolled over, propped his head up on one hand, and regarded her with a quizzical expression.

"What is the matter?" she asked.

"Nothing at all! Just that even now, even after all our letters, after years of friendship, I occasionally encounter an aspect of you that remains mysterious. For example, I never thought you'd be the type to grow exercised over lemon-yellow silk. I'd have thought that was more my department."

"I wouldn't personally, but I *am* the type to grow exercised over the notion of pleasing my readers. And of selling magazines. But I do appreciate your point. You are noting the chasm between my apparent enthusiasm for fashion and the dull dresses I wear." At least she was wearing the blue-gray today rather than the merely gray.

"I wouldn't call them dull!" Effie protested.

"I would, and you should." Julianna didn't care for deluding herself. "I do like fashion, but I prefer to save my money for larger pursuits." Why was she so defensive? Effie knew about the printing press. And she wasn't ashamed of her paltry wardrobe. Her dresses were always clean and tidy, and she had a new one made every year or two, when one needed to be retired. But since she only had the two, she couldn't justify one of them being one of the outrageous confections she printed in her pages. Her wardrobe was another example of one of her adages in action: *You can't miss what you don't let yourself want.*

It occurred to her that she'd had the identical thought about sea-bathing. She hadn't let herself want to sea-bathe. Then she'd gone sea-bathing, and it had been a revelation.

She didn't quite know how she was going to go back to a life without it.

Back at the house, Julianna was shown to a graciously appointed bedchamber done in shades of cream and pink. It was rather like being inside a cross between a French pastry and a fluffy pillow, but she didn't hate it. French pastries were delicious, and fluffy pillows were cozy.

After Mrs. Mitchell left, Julianna lay back on the bed and considered her next move.

She thought about how relieved she'd been when Effie hadn't proposed after they kissed that first time, back at the Old Ship. How he hadn't seemed pressed to analyze their situation. He had said, *Just let me be with you, whether that's only for the rest of the afternoon, or until you have to go back to London.*

Until she had to go back to London. Yes. That was what she wanted.

She wanted him so very, very much. She *pined* for him, and she didn't think she'd ever pined for anyone or anything in her life. Except perhaps a printing press.

She just needed to keep whatever happened between them

contained. She needed Effie to be more Charles than Edith. Like Charles, except more time—and place—limited. They had three days left, after all, and she rather suspected the pining was mutual.

Could they do that? Could *she* do that?

Yes. She was no longer the naive girl she had been the summer of Edith.

Effie stuck his head in, almost as if she had summoned him. Perhaps she had. "Everything up to snuff?"

She sat up. It was now or never. "Yes, thank you. Everything is lovely."

"We dine at seven. Shall I ride to the Old Ship and collect your things? There doesn't seem any point in maintaining your room there."

"No. Well, yes, I would appreciate that. But would you come in first, please?"

He did as she asked, and when she added, "And shut the door behind you," his eyes twinkled mischievously.

She patted the bed next to her, and as he sat, he said, "Why do I get the feeling you are about to suggest a most amusing diversion?"

She smiled. "Because I am."

He performed the single clap she had come to understand was an expression of excitement.

She didn't see any reason to dissemble. "Would you come to me after dinner?"

"Of course. I— Oh." His eyes widened, "*Oh.*"

"If you like," she added, breaking with his gaze due to an unexpected surge of bashfulness. Followed by an expected surge of annoyance because Julianna did not do *bashful.*

By the time she got herself in order, Effie's eyes had gone from wide to knowing. Practically smouldering.

"Yes," he said. "I would like that very much."

Chapter 9

The Birds and the Bees

"I require your assistance," Effie said to the boys that night after dinner as they settled themselves in the drawing room with a bottle of port. They were alone. Julianna, pleading a headache he suspected was not real, had excused herself.

"I've already written to Stanhope as you asked," Simon said.

Effie had forgotten that he'd asked Simon to inquire about a hand press. That conversation, conducted before Julianna's arrival on the scene, seemed a lifetime ago. "Not that, though I do appreciate it. I require your assistance in . . . matters of a more delicate nature."

"All right."

Effie brushed an imaginary piece of lint off his sleeve. "I think Miss Evans and I will lie together this evening."

The boys whooped and made predictable, good-natured jeers. He had expected nothing less.

"Yes, yes. Now that you've got that out of the way, help me!"

Archie refilled their glasses. "What seems to be the problem?"

"I . . . don't know how to do it."

"What do you mean you don't know how to do it?" Simon asked.

"I never have," Effie said.

It took the boys a moment to absorb that fact. To their credit, neither laughed. Simon set down his newspaper, and Archie said, "I suppose that makes sense, given what you told us the other day about your history with love and desire."

"I am acquainted with the mechanics of the act," Effie said, "but I feel certain there is more to it than mechanics."

"*That* is certainly true," Simon said, and Effie was surprised. He would have expected such a declaration from Archie, who was utterly besotted with his wife.

"So? What do I do?"

"She may have some advice," Archie said.

"Really?" He had not considered that.

"Well, she is a decade older than you, is she not?" Archie asked.

"You think she. . . ?"

Archie shrugged. "If she has, you ought to take her advice over ours. She will know what would be most . . . expedient."

"Is expediency what I'm to aim for?"

"No!" Archie said rather vehemently.

"All right. Should I tell her I am a virgin?" Effie asked. "I get the impression it's something I'm meant to be ashamed of, but I don't understand why. We prize virginity in ladies; why not in gentlemen?"

Archie chuckled. "You and Clementine ought to talk."

"What do you mean?"

"She and I had many discussions over the concept of ruination when we were trying to shield her and Olive from that same fate last year. Why is it when a woman lies with a man to whom she is not married, she is ruined yet that same man is not?"

"An excellent question," Effie said, feeling a mite frustrated. Thinking about poetry was so much easier than trying to puzzle through these sorts of thorny societal questions.

"As an aside," Simon said, "perhaps our fixation on protecting the Morgan sisters from ruination last year explains why we were so invested in the idea of protecting Miss Evans's reputation this year." He smirked. "These trips do, of late, seem to be plagued with women on the verge of ruination."

"Don't they, though?" Archie said. He turned to Effie. "As to your dilemma, will you allow me to give you some advice?"

"Allow you? That is why I am here."

"I suggest you regard your primary role as bringing pleasure to Miss Evans."

"Yes, that *is* what I regard as my primary role. I just don't know how to do it." He refrained from rolling his eyes but only just. Here he'd thought Archie was so worldly, so wise. Effie had expected to be in receipt of actionable advice.

"The mechanical act, conducted in a merely cursory fashion, will very likely not achieve your aim," Archie said.

"All right," Effie said, no longer bothering to conceal his frustration. "What will, then?"

"A woman has a . . . bud."

"A woman has a bud?"

"Perhaps it's better thought of as a button."

"A button! As on a shirt?"

"No, not that kind of button."

"A larger button as on a boot?"

"No, no. Bud. Bud is better."

"Like a flower?"

"Not exactly."

Oh, for heaven's sake! "Will you speak plainly?" Effie turned and shot a quelling look at Simon, who was snickering.

"It is a nub of flesh," Archie finally said. "It is very sensitive." He explained how to find it, and Effie wondered if he ought to have brought a quill and paper, for it was sounding as if a map might be indicated. After a detour to warn against the dangers of getting a lady with child if one—or one's lady—had no desire to do so, Archie went on to explain how a man was meant to stimulate the nub in order to bring pleasure.

"This is the part where I suggest you speak to Miss Evans. Different ladies will have different preferences as to how much, and what kind, of pressure they prefer."

"And what about for how long?"

"How do you mean?"

"How long am I meant to . . . apply pressure."

"Oh, until the lady finds her release."

"What do you mean?"

"Effie, the night we arrived, you explained to us that you generally didn't feel desire."

"Oh, I do now, though." That was understating the matter entirely.

"Right. Well, had you, previously, ever . . ."

Effie knew what he meant. "Yes, of course. I'm not completely daft. I just never had the desire to do so in the company of another person before now."

"It is the same for ladies. Well, not precisely the same, but analogous." Archie went on to explain the mechanics of the female release.

Effie was dumbfounded. "Why did no one ever tell me about this?" He turned to Simon, who had been watching the exchange with poorly concealed amusement. "Did you know about this?"

"I did."

"Does *everyone* know about this?"

"I think not," Archie said. "Not all gentlemen, anyway. Or if they do, they don't care to concern themselves with it."

"Because of what you said," Effie said. "Because the female release is not necessary to the . . . proceedings."

"Correct. And perhaps also because the release in question can be elusive. One must apply oneself. Be prepared to settle in, perhaps for quite a while."

Effie could think of nothing more enjoyable than applying himself to Julianna for quite a while.

"I would suggest, though," Simon went on, "that the gentleman who *does* pay attention, who devotes himself to the cultivation of the female release, will be greatly appreciated by the female in question."

"I quite agree," Archie said.

"Good. Good." This was the kind of information Effie needed.

He still could not believe that he had attained eight-and-twenty years with no knowledge of this world of feminine mystery.

It occurred to Effie to wonder how Simon knew to make such a suggestion. Archie they had both seen making a fool of himself over Clementine last fall—and in the months sense. But what lady had been the recipient of all this knowledge of Simon's?

"How are you, Simon?" Effie asked.

"I beg your pardon?"

"How have you been? What is new in your life?"

"I am fine. Nothing is new."

"Are you sure?"

"What are you on about?"

"Nothing, nothing." Effie paused, ashamed that he had been so self-centered this trip. They'd talked and talked and talked about him and his woes, but he hadn't asked Simon a single question. He racked his brain. "The gaols act! That is new, isn't it?"

"You want to talk about the gaols act? Talking about parliamentary matters is against the rules of Earls Trip, is in not?"

"That never stopped you before."

"Effie, why don't you just go to Miss Evans?"

Effie looked at Archie, who nodded his agreement and said, "We will still be here in the morning for you to interrogate."

He didn't need to be told twice.

"Hello, my dearest," Effie said a few minutes later as he slipped into Julianna's room—but not before going into his own and turning the covers down and mussing the bedclothes so it would look as if he'd been there. If anyone came in later tonight, he hoped they would think he'd had a bout of sleeplessness and had gone for a walk. There was precedent for that. "How is your head?"

"My head is fine." She gestured him to the bed, as she'd done earlier, but this time she was wearing only her shift, the same one she'd worn to the beach.

"The headache was a ruse, wasn't it?" he asked, as he sat, his pulse kicking up.

"It was a ruse." She had been reading a sheaf of papers, and she set them on the night table.

"You were determined not to be seen as a gate-crasher."

"I was determined to have a nap!"

"And did you?"

"I did not. I meant to, but . . ."

"Yes?"

"I found myself too aflutter with anticipation."

That was flattering. And also the cause of a matching fluttering inside Effie. He decided to be direct. "I must tell you that I have never done this before. May I hope that you have so that at least one of us knows what she's doing?"

She lifted her head from where she had been blowing out a candle. There was a branch of them next to the bed, and she'd carefully blown out half of them, leaving the room cast in a warm glow. "You are remarkable."

"*You* are remarkable," he countered. He meant that in the most literal sense. He wanted to remark on everything about her, make a list, a catalog of her attributes. He could hang it on his wall at home, next to her portrait.

She smiled in a way he flattered himself was fond. "I have done this before, yes. There was a, ah, gentleman before you."

"Excellent."

"You are the only man on earth who would think so."

"What do you mean?"

"Most men would say I'm ruined. That I've given away my maidenhood. Their reactions would fall somewhere along a scale of stern disapproval to murderous outrage."

It was difficult to know how to respond to that. On the one hand, he wanted to honor her experience. On the other, he wanted to dismiss what she'd said as nonsense. He settled for the truth. "I approve of everything that brought you here to me, that brought us to this moment."

The next smile she graced him with was so unmistakably fond, so wide, it took his breath away for a moment.

When he recovered, he said, "Tell me what to do. *Show* me what to do."

The smile turned a little bit wicked. "Come over here."

He nearly tripped over himself to get to her. He'd been perched on the edge of the bed, but he scrambled across it so he was sitting cross-legged in front of her. She sat up, pushed back the covers and mimicked his position, and for a moment they merely stared at each other. Eventually, she reached forward and pulled his shirt out of his breeches—he had undressed to his shirtsleeves while with Simon and Archie—and up over his head. When she finished, she took up one end of the drawstring at the neckline of her shift and held it out. She wanted him to take it.

He pulled, slowly, the sound of string against string as the bow was untied, filling his head as completely as the waves on the shore had the other day.

When he had finished, she reached a hand inside her neckline and pushed the shift off one shoulder, then the other. He watched; his senses sharpened as if he were in danger. When the white linen fell to reveal small, pink-tipped breasts, he began to fear that perhaps he *was* in danger, though he could not quite articulate why.

He lifted the hem of his shirt, and before he could think what to do next, before his head was fully out from under the shirt, her hands were on him, stroking down his arms from shoulder to wrist, leaving a trail of gooseflesh.

"You may touch me, too," she whispered. So, after a beat, he lifted shaking hands to *her* shoulders, let them slide down to *her* wrists.

What followed was a slow, sensual game of sorts, whereby she touched him, and he, mirroring her, performed the same gesture. Her hands slid back up to his shoulders; his hands slid back up to her shoulders. Hers made their way then around nape of his neck; his did likewise with hers.

"I adored your long hair," she whispered as she slid her fingers up over the back of his head—he wanted to groan from the pure pleasure of her fingernails against his scalp—"but I think I like this better."

Wordlessly, he tangled his fingers in her hair. The flickering light of the candles glinted off it, making some strands look like shimmery onyx, others like warm mahogany.

With a sigh, she let her hands slide down the front of his face. It reminded him of the way he'd once seen a blind man greeting a brother after a long absence.

Her hands didn't linger, though; they continued their southward journey, down his neck, over his clavicle, and down the front of his chest.

Marveling that he had ever thought of desire as an abstract concept from which he was exempt—he was certain his prick had never been this hard—he replicated the path with his hands on her body. The textures of her were so exquisitely rendered: her collarbones, sharp as her wit; her breasts, soft as her heart. He was aware that she would not characterize her heart thusly, that her vision of herself did not include the word *soft*, but he saw a truth about her that others, including she herself, did not.

The knowledge that he possessed a singular view of her made him want to laugh and cry at the same time, made the pressure in his groin, and at the base of his spine, intensify.

He had been going to let his hands continue to fall, but she stopped him, putting her own over his so that they stayed in contact with her breasts. She hissed and let her head fall back. Experimentally, he kneaded the soft flesh, and she arched her back as if seeking more of his touch.

The hiss became a moan, and never had he heard anything so pleasing, so erotic, so *astonishing*. He was struck with the idea that he ought to replace one of his hands with his mouth. He could see himself from above, lips working over one of the pink nubs. They would make a gorgeous, obscene painting.

He made the image come to life, his own moan breaking free just before his mouth made contact. The nipple in his mouth was harder than the nipple in his hand. Experimentally, he flicked his tongue over it, and she took a rapid inhalation and held it. He did it again. Eventually, she exhaled—it was a ragged exhalation, almost akin to a sob.

He was growing more and more agitated. He saw another image in his mind, of her lying on her back, naked, his mouth on her neck. He began to make it so, gently encouraging her to lift her hips so he could remove the shift that had bunched around her waist.

He hadn't understood that making love was like painting, that when an image arose in his mind, he could make it concrete. They were a living canvas. Her pulse thudded under his lips, and when she sighed, he realized they hadn't kissed on the mouth yet. So he remedied that, changed the picture, lying atop her but keeping his full weight from her, kissing her deeply. She wrapped her legs around his waist, and he gasped in shock—she was painting, too—and gasped again when he realized the maneuver had put his manhood in contact with her soft center.

She began rocking her hips up and down, and he knew somehow that he was meant to rock with her. He had expected to have to have a conversation about making sure she did not fall pregnant as a result of their lying together, but it seemed they would not need to broach that particular topic, at least not yet, for this, this rocking as his prick nestled against her soft heat without entering it, was bringing him a degree of pleasure he had not thought to imagine. It was pressure and heat together, sensations that ought to have been unpleasant, but he wanted more of them; he wanted to rush toward them, profligate and blind.

Blind but not deaf, for he had never heard anything so maddeningly exquisite as the breathy moans Julianna was making. If only he could attend a symphony composed entirely of such moans.

"Keep going," she said, making him realize that although she was still rocking her hips, his had slowed, so focused had he been on the glorious symphony.

He rocked against her, and pure pleasure bloomed in his belly.

"Oh," she said, so low and quiet, she almost sounded like someone else. It was followed by another "Oh," the single syllable as different from the first incantation of such as it was possible to be. It was high and girlish and astonishing, and it made his eyes fly open.

Hers were closed, which afforded him the opportunity to watch in fascination as her face screwed up, almost as if she were in pain. Before he could fully register that expression, it was replaced by one of shock as her eyes and mouth alike opened. Her gaze latched on to his, and her body began to quake. It was glorious. *She* was glorious.

He was glorious, too. A great surge of pleasure moved through his body, and his hips bucked, losing their rhythm. If Effie had not known love, or desire, before, it was only because he was meant to know them here, now, inside this living painting. It was akin to what Simon had said about not wanting to catch a glimpse of the Pavilion before he was ready to contemplate its full glory. He shouted, and he felt the beauty all around them.

He could no longer hold himself up as he had been, keeping most of the weight of his upper body off Julianna, so he rolled to his side. He had spent partly on her stomach, partly on the bed and was now lying on the wet spot. He had never been happier.

She stayed where she was, and in fact took the space vacated by him to spread her limbs a bit, but she turned her head in his direction so they maintained eye contact. Neither spoke for a long while. They merely panted and smiled.

"What are you thinking about?" Effie finally said,

"Lately, I've been comparing myself to a starfish."

A great big laugh burst out of him. "That was the last thing I expected you to say."

"I keep finding myself sprawled out, having lost my wits. I was lounging exactly like this on my bed at home after you sent me *Archer's Lady's Book*, and before I knew it, I was on a Brighton-bound coach. Sprawling mindlessly with one's limbs akimbo brings to mind a starfish, though perhaps I defame starfish. For all I know they are quite intelligent."

"So you were thinking about the fact that you weren't thinking."

"I suppose I was. What were *you* thinking?"

"I was thinking that I was under the impression that I was meant to seek out a bud of flesh between your legs. Just now, I mean."

"You did."

"I did?" He held up a hand and considered it quizzically. Had he forgotten?

She laughed, rolled onto her side to face him, and took the hand in question. "You did it with your . . . member."

"I did?"

"Yes, when we were rocking back and forth, it provided just the right sort of continuous pressure."

"Well, that's all right, then." He paused. "It was just the right sort of continuous pressure for me, too." Another pause. "In case you couldn't tell." He grinned, knowing he was being ridiculous— she had on her stomach the very residue of his enjoyment. He took up his shirt, which was within arm's reach, and blotted.

When he returned his attention to her face, she looked . . . not sad exactly. Wistful.

"What is it?" he asked.

"Remember when you said just now that you approve of everything that brought me here?"

"Yes."

"If that is the case, I think I ought to confess something," she said, running her fingers up and down his chest in a way that was making him a little crazy. "Or, not that I *ought* to exactly, in the sense of feeling compelled, but I find myself *wanting* to."

"Please do." He was hungry for knowledge of her. He wanted more remarkable items for his list.

"You were my third, not my second."

Effie had meant what he said before. He was glad one of them had some experience. He didn't disapprove of her for having lain with others. He just . . . didn't want her to do it anymore. "Oh, so there were *two* lucky gentlemen before me. I wonder that one of them didn't come up to scratch."

"One tried. He was—is—one of my regular engravers. He proposed."

"And?"

"We have spoken of this several times. You know I am averse to the idea of marrying. The last thing I ever want is a man to propose to me. I declined."

"That was smart of you."

"You don't know anything about him!" After a brief silence, she laughed.

"What is so amusing?"

"I am laughing at myself. Here I am affronted on his behalf, even though I turned him down most fervently. But I suppose my point stands: you don't know anything about him, so you cannot say I was smart to rebuff him."

"I can, though!" She leveled a look at him. He winked and said, "If you had accepted, you wouldn't be here; therefore it was smart of you to decline."

Effie was careful to keep his tone light, teasing, but he meant every word. He meant every word most ardently.

She laughed again, which had been his aim, but he found himself desperate to know what she would say next. "I would have declined regardless, but he only asked because he was laboring under the weight of moral distress after our initial liaison. That is a terrible reason to propose marriage. We were not in love."

They were not in love. Was she implying that she would have accepted, had they been? No. She had *just* reminded him that her aversion to the idea of marriage itself had prompted her refusal.

He was safe.

No sooner he had that thought than it was replaced by another: Safe from what?

"And the other gentleman?" he asked, careful once again not to allow his tone to betray the urgency he felt. "What kind of numbskull was he to not want to propose to an incomparable such as yourself? I can't believe *two* gentlemen could make your intimate acquaintance and not fall in love with you."

"We were in love, in that case. At least, I thought we were. *I* was."

What Effie thought was *No.* What Effie said was "What was his . . . dilemma, then? Why didn't he come up to scratch?"

"He didn't come up to scratch because he was not a he. *Her* name was Edith." She studied his face. "Do you understand what I'm saying?"

Effie was set back on his heels, but when he stopped to think about it, he found he wasn't surprised. "I see."

"And?" Julianna prompted.

"And what?" *Am I supposed to say that I'm sorry you could not marry your love?*" He paused, trying to think what to say that was true but would not paint him in an unflatteringly possessive light. "I'm *not* sorry, because again, had you, you wouldn't be here."

"You're not scandalized."

"No." *That, at least was the truth.*

"Perhaps you . . . understand. Understand in a deeper way, I mean."

Oh. Yes. She had revealed something private, something she was afraid of being judged for. She was searching for understanding. And here he had been focused not on that aspect of her liaison, but the fact that she had fallen in love. That she had been in love with someone who wasn't him. That bit made him uncomfortable. Jealous. And being jealous made him feel . . . small.

"I do understand," he said, wanting to put her at ease, even if he was confused about his own feelings. "Theoretically. Until recently, Marsden and Harcourt apparently thought I favored gentlemen."

"And do you?"

"I think I favor . . . everyone. Theoretically. Is that possible?"

"I think so. I can't speak for society at large, but that is how I have always been."

"At the same time, though, historically I have favored no one. I find the expression of ardent urges impossible to imagine outside the context of a close friendship."

"Hmm."

"It is not the same for you?"

"I don't think so. While I certainly considered myself on friendly terms with both Charles and Edith, my desire for them felt . . . independent of that bond."

A terribly urgent question began coalescing in his mind. "Did you . . . remain friends with your past lovers?"

"With Charles, yes. We remain fond of each other, though the ardency has bled out of our connection."

"And Edith?"

She shrugged. "Summer ended, and she left. I had hoped she would write, but she didn't. I was terribly sad for a while."

Effie hated how jealous her words made him. He hated that he could intuit that "I was terribly sad" was Julianna understating the depth of her connection to Edith, and her dismay at its rending.

He forced himself to set his feelings aside and attend to hers. "One hears of gentlemen who are romantically inclined toward one another. They may live as friends. I suppose ladies might manage a way to do the same."

"Yes. I had . . . imagined a future in which that might have been the case." She pressed her lips together. "But when we parted ways, Edith was resigned to her fate, which at that point she believed was marriage. 'Resigned' is not even the correct word. I did not realize that she was corresponding that summer with a gentleman she had met briefly at a house party the previous Christmas. She was looking forward to meeting him again at the same party that year.

"She has three children now, I am told, and lives very happily in Somerset. I'm sure she never thinks about our 'transgressions'— that was her word for what had happened between us."

Effie had made an involuntary squeak, one he hoped conveyed his vicarious affront at the word Edith had chosen. Heartbreak was one thing; being left so blithely by someone who was planning to step immediately into another life was quite another.

"Yes," Julianna said sadly—his squeak must have done its job.

"I am sorry," he said quietly. It was only partially a lie. He was sorry she'd been hurt, but he wasn't sorry that her heartbreak had made her available: to write to him, to edit his words, to lie with him.

She smiled sadly. "Effie, you really are the most generous-spirited person."

"Come now." She would not say that if she knew about the discreditable, greedy things he was thinking.

"I never imagined telling anyone this. Not only that I have given myself to a man, but that I have given myself to a woman."

"And you have given yourself to me."

"And I have given myself to you."

"As I have given myself to you."

"Indeed."

He almost didn't want to ask, but he had to. The only way to discharge this knife-edge feeling of envy, was to speak openly. To ask the question he wanted answered rather than swallow it in fear. Still, in order to brace himself for what he was almost certain would be the answer, he phrased his question as an observation: "But you won't keep me."

She placed a palm on his cheek. "I am sorry, I won't. I can't."

It was not unexpected. He told himself he couldn't be hurt by having a future he had never counted on taken away from him.

He further told himself not to think of the future at all. Another of Julianna's maxims was relevant here, and he recited it back to her: "There is only now."

"Yes." Her smile struck Effie as a little wistful, though perhaps he was only seeing what he himself felt. She rolled away from him, and he wanted to tell her not to do that. He wanted to take her hand and place it back on his cheek.

She had lifted a candle, and she was gazing at the mantel across the room. "It is very likely past midnight, but it is too dark for me to make out the time on that clock. I am imagining you skulking out of here like a character in a Gothic novel. I think you shall be very well suited to such a task."

He suspected she was trying to lighten the mood.

It didn't work, but he pretended it did. He smiled and held out his arms and she set down her candle and rolled into them.

"It is a theatrical challenge I shall embrace, though 'tis a pity that if I am to be successful, it means I shan't have an audience." He spoke blithely and tried to make his heart light, too.

When she fell asleep, he knew he ought to go. And he would, just not yet. He slid off the bed and tiptoed to a small desk covered with papers. He smiled. She'd been here only a matter of hours, and already her editorial ephemera were everywhere.

He found paper and a quill and, arranging himself so he had a view of her, got to work answering a letter.

Dear Home for Christmas,

You must take your children and go. You are very lucky indeed to have a mother who loves you and whom you consider a friend. I hope you know how exceedingly rare that is.

Consider a scenario in which you do not go. Your mother dies alone, and you forfeit the chance to say goodbye. Perhaps your husband is satisfied, but once the disagreement is over, will he even notice, much less appreciate, that you have stayed to placate him?

Consider, too, the opposite scenario: You do go. You and your mother are both comforted by your presence at the end. Your husband is upset by your absence. Is his upset worth it? I must think so.

With my sincerest condolences,

Mrs. Landers

Effie reread his response several times, questioning himself. He was always telling these women to defy their husbands. Was it right of him to do that? He believed he was giving morally sound advice, but he was only thinking about the question immediately in front of him. He wasn't considering the repercussions that might follow when his correspondent took his advice.

He carried the letters back to bed, taking care not to awaken Julianna. His realization was not dissimilar to the one he'd had after that day on the beach with Julianna and the boys. Julianna had been bewildered by their concern for her reputation. *That is your world, not mine,* she'd said. He stared at the ceiling and pondered. Was he applying the wrong lens to the problems faced by his correspondent?

Effie and Julianna had initially found it endlessly amusing that "Mrs. Landers," the author of the magazine's "Advice for Married Ladies" column—an addition to the magazine that had been mandated by Mr. Glanvil—was not married. Julianna had seemed to relish deceiving Mr. Glanvil, though of course she, believing Effie to be a lady, hadn't known the true extent of the duplicity. They had both embarked on the enterprise as if it were a great big jest.

It had taken only one letter to sober Effie. It had been from a woman who was having trouble conceiving a child, and he would never forget the anguish woven through her words.

Other ladies' magazines of the day contained nominal advice columns, but they generally used a letter as a jumping-off point for a moral essay, and they almost never printed their readers' letters in their entirety.

Le Monde Joli took a different approach. Julianna printed several letters in each issue, and Effie was meant to give each reader genuine, and specific, advice. That first letter had been a lesson in the weight of that responsibility.

He had, from the start, tried to keep his not-lady-ness in mind, had endeavored to compensate for his sex. He was now realizing, however, that he had not spared much thought for the class he inhabited, or that of the women who wrote to him.

It had taken Julianna telling him she had only two dresses to jolt this awareness into him.

He remained ashamed of this oversight, but what could he do but try to be better going forward?

He considered "Home for Christmas." If his correspondent was a noblewoman wanting to visit her mother's deathbed, that was one thing. She could take her children with her and be assured of help both on the journey and at her destination. Her husband wouldn't suffer, not materially, by her absence. But if the woman was poor, that was quite a different scenario, was it not?

Luckily, he could ask his editor when she awakened. Which might be tomorrow.

Or—he turned to find her staring at him—it could be now.

His mouth formed itself into a smile without his conscious involvement. Her hair was mussed and her cheeks were pink, and who *wouldn't* smile at her? "How long have you been awake?"

"Long enough to observe that you look rather tortured."

"'Tortured' may be somewhat hyperbolic, but read this, will you? I could do with some advice."

She did, and he explained his dilemma, his recent realization.

"I see what you mean," she said. "I think, however, that your initial impulse was correct. She ought to go see her mother. Perhaps you needn't write such a lengthy answer. I adore the way you sometimes answer rather cheekily, often with a single sentence. You are familiar with the letters of which I speak?"

He explained his response to the "Sartorially Sullied" letter that was also meant for the December issue.

"Yes, precisely! While you can't answer 'Home for Christmas' with humor, suppose you take a similarly minimalist approach? Say something in the vein of, "Go home to your mother for Christmas. You will regret not doing it."

"But—"

"I know you are concerned about the larger circumstances, and that is to your credit. But we don't *know* the larger circumstances. If you will allow it, I will give you two pieces of advice."

"Please do."

"The letters we print have dual purposes."

Effie was so chuffed by that *we*, by the use of the plural pronoun, that he had to remind himself to attend to the rest of what she was saying.

"First, there's the immediate aim of the dispensation of advice. But the other purpose is to affect readers. To entertain them, or inspire empathy in them, to move them in some way. You are writing *to* your correspondent, but you are writing *for* all our readers."

"That . . ." Seemed eminently logical. Effie didn't know why he hadn't considered it from that perspective before.

"Take this current letter. Should you advise the correspondent to visit her mother, you are also telling everyone who reads it that this is the correct course of action. You will have done good in more settings than the life of the letter writer. Beyond that, even if the specifics of the scenario in question do not apply to the wider readership, the tone you take in a response may yet affect them."

Hmm. "This is the reason you appreciate amusing replies."

"Yes. They entertain our readers."

Our readers. There was another plural pronoun. He smiled. "Was there another piece of advice?"

"I see a thread weaving its way through your Mrs. Landers letters. A theme, if you will."

"You do? What is it?"

"You always take the part of the lady."

"I don't think I do that intentionally."

"I know you don't, which makes it all the more effective."

"It is possible—likely—that I am overcompensating for not *being* the lady I was meant to be when you gave me the job." He paused. "I am sorry. It is a consequence of my dishonesty."

She waved away the apology. "I do not believe you are overcompensating. That's not why you always take the part of the lady."

"Why do I do it, then?"

"Well, in some measure, I suppose because your charge is to help your correspondents. You are primed to be sympathetic to them. But also, in a larger sense, I believe it is because you are a good person."

"I am?"

She threw a pillow at him. "Yes, you fool."

He caught it. "Do say more."

He thought she would decline, tell him not to flatter himself overmuch, but she said, "You care about people. You put yourself in others' shoes, and you are willing to entertain the notion that your way of thinking may be incorrect. That's what you are doing here, is it not, asking whether your instinct is right in the case of this particular letter? Do you know how exceedingly rare such an attitude is, especially for a gentleman?"

Effie found himself choked up. Had anyone ever said such lovely things about him? To him? And she had said different but equally flattering things during their sunrise swim. Effie did not doubt that Archie and Simon respected him, and regarded him very highly. But much of that had to do with their shared history. And certainly his family had never said anything of the kind.

He thought of his peacock waistcoat. He felt like a peacock now, displaying his feathers, proud of himself.

He turned the paper over and tried another version of the letter while she watched, her head resting on his shoulder.

Dear Home for Christmas,

You must go. Your mother must not die alone.

With sympathy,

Mrs. Landers

"What do you think?"

"It's perfect."

She was perfect. *This* was perfect. Lying here with Julianna, working on the magazine in bed. *There is only now.* Perhaps her philosophy worked, after all.

The only thing that would make it more perfect would be to seal their editorial triumph with a kiss.

So he did.

Chapter 10

Unlatching

Julianna's past affairs had taken place in secret. Her liaisons had always been conducted in the dark—usually in the literal dark and always in the metaphorical dark. It was therefore utterly novel to be able to go downstairs to a sunlight-flooded breakfast room and have the other gentlemen know what was going on.

At least, she assumed they knew. Why else would Lord Harcourt have winked at Effie when she appeared? Why else would Lord Marsden, seated next to Effie, have looked even stiffer than usual, as if he were trying very hard to affect a pose of nonchalance?

They all stood and greeted her formally but warmly.

"Allow me to make you a plate," Effie said, encouraging her to sit.

"I have a newspaper if you would like to read it." Lord Marsden passed her this week's edition of the *Brighton & Hove Herald*. How lovely.

"What are your thoughts on kippers?" Effie called from the sideboard.

"I detest them," she called back, causing her tablemates to chuckle.

"Eggs?"

"Eggs would be lovely, thank you."

"Rashers?"

"Yes, thank you."

"Toast? With butter? Marmalade?"

Lords Harcourt and Marsden both appeared to be supressing laughter, and indeed Effie's methodical recitation of the contents of the breakfast spread was rather amusing. Julianna had the idea that normally, when one person made a plate for another, the first person knew what the second person liked. This was what she'd meant earlier, when she'd said that while in some ways, probably the ways that mattered the most, she and Effie knew each other, yet in other ways, they did not. She had not known about his father's cruelties. He had not known she didn't care for kippers. Not that she was equating kippers with cruelties. The point was, there were holes.

"Butter *and* marmalade?" Effie called when she neglected to respond.

"Use your judgment," Julianna said. "Regarding the toast, and the rest of it. Just no kippers, please. Or liver, should there happen to be any on offer."

"Clementine would find nothing to eat at this buffet," Effie remarked when he returned with Julianna's plate.

The men went on to explain that the countess did not eat meat.

"What about eggs?" Julianna asked.

"She eats them from our chickens at Mollybrook," Lord Harcourt said, "but eschews them when she is ignorant of their provenance."

"The hens at Mollybrook live in a veritable palace," Effie explained. "They are well fed and left to roam free. I would not be surprised to learn that the countess reads and sings to them, too." He smiled fondly. "We should all be so lucky."

"Does this have anything to do with that tract that was quite popular a few Seasons ago, *On the Moral Imperative of Not Eating Animals?* By a Theodore Bull?" Julianna remembered that pamphlet well. She'd seen hundreds of copies at her previous printer's establishment. In fact, the sudden vogue for Mr. Bull's ideas had delayed the production of the magazine more than once.

"What shall we do today?" Effie asked in an overloud voice that made Julianna wonder if she had said something wrong.

Lord Harcourt merely smiled and leaned closer to Julianna. "Yes, it does. My wife was at one time engaged to the author of that tract."

Julianna felt her eyes widen. She certainly hadn't expected *that*.

"While she is happily rid of the man, some of his . . . ideas endure."

Lord Marden said, "To be fair, and as Clementine pointed out, they aren't his original ideas. They have a much older intellectual ancestry."

"Yes," Effie agreed. "I seem to remember her saying something about the poet Shelley having written an essay on the topic before Mr. Bull came on the scene, so we ought to credit him rather than Mr. Bull. One likes to credit poets whenever one can; don't you agree?"

"Lord Harcourt," Julianna said, "do you think I might persuade your wife to write about her dietary philosophy for the magazine?" Julianna would have to invoke the nobility of its author to convince Mr. Glanvil to print it, but what a coup such a story would be. "I read Mr. Bull's pamphlet and found his tone unnecessarily strident. I would be quite happy to hear a similar argument made from a more even-handed perspective. And for the author to be a lady? All the better."

Lord Harcourt chuckled. "I shall ask her. I can almost guarantee that she will be thrilled by your commission, but of course I cannot agree to something on her behalf."

How remarkable. The way Lord Harcourt had phrased that, one would almost think he considered his wife an autonomous individual.

"What shall we do today?" Effie asked again as Julianna picked up her fork. "I admit I posed that question earlier partly to distract from the unpleasant topic of Mr. Shelley's intellectual descendant, whom I shan't be naming, but I really do want to know. It is a beautiful day."

194 / JENNY HOLIDAY

"What do you usually do on your holidays?" Julianna asked when no suggestion was forthcoming.

"The gentlemen looked at each other, seeming to consider the question. "Talk, I suppose," Lord Marsden said.

"Drink," Lord Harcourt said wryly.

"Archie usually sneaks away to hunt, and with any luck, he doesn't accidentally shoot anyone," Effie said, making a face at Archie.

Julianna gathered there was a story there. She was getting a sense, with these men, of a rich shared history. Of deep bonds stitched together with caring and humor alike.

"How about a ride?" Lord Harcourt asked. "The stables here are well provisioned."

"Haffert has encouraged me to make use of them," Lord Marsden said.

The gentlemen turned to Julianna.

"I've never been riding."

"Would you like to?" Lord Marsden asked.

"I could walk your horse," Effie said. "I wouldn't leave your side."

"I think I should find riding quite exciting," Julianna said.

Later, at the stable, Effie pulled the groom aside and said, sotto voce, "My sister has decided to attempt to overcome a long-standing fear of horses. Have you a gentle mare, perhaps, a creature who shall do right by her?"

Oh, dear. Julianna had not thought through the fact that Effie's sister, the daughter of an earl, ought to be an accomplished, or at least competent, horsewoman. But Effie, ever thoughtful, had come armed with a cover story.

"Oh, yes, my lord," the groom said. "I have just the horse."

Effie glanced over his shoulder and shot Julianna a secret wink. "I will gladly accept any expert advice you may have to soothe my sister's nerves."

The groom seemed thrilled with the prospect of making a con-

vert to the equine life, and he and Effie undertook an earnest discussion about saddles and terrain and the like.

The groom was beaming when he introduced them to a gentle
old girl called Poppy and explained to Julianna how she was meant
to mount. "You've got to explain it to me, too," Effie said. "I've
never paid any mind to side saddles."

Julianna managed to get herself situated and was only expe-
riencing a minor attack of nerves as Effie, on foot as promised,
took Poppy's lead. She could see why people enjoyed riding. The
prospect from up here was pleasing, as was the notion that she and
the horse were working together to achieve motion. Or, rather,
she could see how they *would* be, if only she could get a hang
of things. She kept forgetting the instruction to keep her right
shoulder back, and the cane the groom had handed her at the
last minute, telling Effie it would "stand in for the right leg when
cueing beyond a trot"—whatever that meant—was cumbersome.

Once they had cleared the property and turned onto a road
the groom had suggested, Effie stopped them. "Of course she's
expected to ride aside—I didn't think." He looked up at her. "I'm
afraid I'm not going to be much of a guide."

"Well, perhaps you can teach Miss Evans to fish, if not to ride,"
Lord Marsden said. He and Lord Harcourt had brought fishing
rods and had quizzed the groom about a pond a mile or so hence.

Which was how Julianna found herself on a grassy bank next to
a murky pond digging for worms.

"I must say, Miss Evans, you are an awfully good sport," Lord
Marsden said when she held up a big fat one. "You're not squea-
mish at all."

She shrugged and allowed him to model how to twist the worm
onto her hook—Lord Harcourt had lent her his rod. In fact, he'd
been quite insistent that she take it. Effie had told her the man had
all but given up hunting, despite the fact that he used to be mad
for it, in deference to his wife's animal-loving ways. Perhaps he'd
given up fishing, too.

Lord Marsden demonstrated how to cast the line and reel it in.

"What an ingenious little contraption this is," she said, referring to the geared mechanism by which one reeled in the line.

"Invented by the Americans just recently."

Goodness, these Americans with their innovative reels and their flashy magazines.

Lord Marsden, having insisted Lord Harcourt take his rod while he was helping Julianna, refused its return and said he would go sit by Effie for a bit.

His departure left Julianna and Lord Harcourt standing side by side in companionable silence, occasionally reeling their lines in and recasting. Julianna noticed that Lord Harcourt was casting without having baited his hook. At one point, he noticed her noticing, and, with a twinkle in his eye, made a shushing gesture with his finger against his lips. She smiled and nodded, miming buttoning her lips.

When she reeled in her line and found the hook empty, she baited it with a new worm.

"I suppose I ought to actually bait mine if I mean to keep standing here going through the motions," Lord Harcourt said.

"You needn't on my account," Julianna said, but he was already done by the time she finished her sentence.

She glanced over her shoulder to check on the others, who were several yards away lounging on a patch of grass. Lord Marsden was talking earnestly about something, but the wind was such that she couldn't hear what. Effie was twirling a long reed or cattail of some sort—beyond the flower-arranging advice the magazine occasionally ran, Julianna did not know plants—and nodding as Lord Marsden spoke. He must have felt her regard, for he turned his head and shot her a wink.

She smiled and returned her attention to the pond, to the meditative act of casting and reeling. As she repeated the motion over and over again something inside her . . . came unraveled. Not in the distressing way the phrase generally implied, as in the destruction of a garment one had spent a great deal of time knitting and/

or was relying on for warmth. No, this was an unraveling of something that had become so tangled as to form a solid mass.

Perhaps the better word was *unlatching*. An unlatching of a gate she normally kept closed, a gate she normally *had* to keep closed.

The sun was warm on her face—the benevolent fairies were doing their agreeable prickling—and she was struck with the urge to remove her bonnet. She suspected no one here would mind if she did.

"Lord Harcourt," she said, "would you think it terribly shocking if I took off my bonnet, and if not, will you hold my rod as I do so?"

"No, and yes," he said mildly.

"I suppose I've done things far more shocking in your brief acquaintance with me," she remarked as she de-hatted herself.

"No and yes," he said again, drawing her attention.

She had been jesting. She was aware that spending the night in the gentlemen's borrowed house ought to, by polite standards, be considered shocking. Scandalous. As should impersonating Effie's sister. Swimming with Effie.

Lying with Effie.

Lord Harcourt's tone just now had been temperate, but had there been a rebuke in his response?

"It would take a great deal more than a glimpse of your hair to shock me," Lord Harcourt said as he accepted her rod.

She waited for more, for an explanation of the "yes" part of "no and yes," but he said nothing further, so she loosened the ribbons of her bonnet and pushed it back off her head.

It wasn't until a few minutes later, when she had her rod back and was entering again into that state of calm contentment conferred by fishing, that state of *un*, that Lord Harcourt said, "What I find shocking, Miss Evans, is how well you seem to know our Effie. How you . . . appreciate him."

"Yes, well, there is much to appreciate about . . . Lord Featherfinch."

How she hated calling him that. Lord Harcourt had called him "our Effie" just now, but Julianna did not know if she was included in that "our." It felt safer to err on the side of formality.

"There is, isn't there?" Lord Harcourt said, again with the appearance of mildness. Yet Julianna felt certain there was an observation underlying the seemingly inconsequential question, perhaps even a warning.

"Effie gives his trust, and affection, so easily," Lord Harcourt elaborated. "And following on that, his loyalty."

"I am not sure I agree with that." It probably wasn't her place to say so, but the objection wouldn't stay in.

There, *that* had shocked him—his eyebrows had flown up. "What do you mean?"

"You may think he gives those things easily, but that may be because you have always had them."

"Effie is quite close to my wife's sister, Miss Olive Morgan. They became fast friends from almost the moment they met."

"I do not think giving one's affections rapidly is the same as giving them indiscriminately. I believe Lord Featherfinch is in fact quite picky about on whom he confers his regard. His circle seems small, for a peer."

"Hmm. I suppose my point is that regardless of the circumstances of the bequeathment of Effie's affections, once bestowed, the recipient has power to injure him greatly."

"There I concur. Lord Featherfinch is very sensitive. That is what makes him such a good writer. He opens himself to the world, to experience, in a way and to a degree that is really rather remarkable."

"Yes. Perhaps that was what I was trying to say."

Julianna waited for more, but nothing was forthcoming. She didn't need words, though, to understand that there *was* a warning of sorts being issued. Lord Harcourt didn't want to see Effie hurt.

She would never hurt Effie.

Would she?

"Oh!" A sharp tug on the line startled her out of her thoughts.

Lord Harcourt got a bite, too, and he showed her how to reel the line in slowly, a little at a time.

Effie and Lord Marsden joined them, speaking words of encouragement. Soon, Julianna had a surprisingly large fish dangling from the end of the line. She kept her attention on it as it flopped and fought, its gray-gold scales glinting in the sun.

Effie, who'd come to stand nearby, applauded. "I say, Jules, splendid job!"

He shouldn't be calling her "Jules." "Julianna" was one thing, but "Jules," in front of his friends? Perhaps Lord Harcourt had been correct. Perhaps she had more power here than she'd realized.

Lord Marsden removed her fish from its hook. Lord Harcourt did the same with his, and he threw it back into the pond with a plop that created a big enough splash to dampen the hem of her dress.

"A fine carp, Miss Evans," Lord Marsden said. "Shall we keep it?"

It had never occurred to her that they wouldn't. Wasn't the whole point of catching fish to *catch* them?

Perhaps this was another quirk of the aristocracy. They wore impractical shoes, and they caught fish only to throw them back. But then she thought of Lord Harcourt's hook, which had remained unbaited for so long.

"I think," she said, "that I ought to follow Lord Harcourt's example and let the creature return to its watery home."

"Have you had enough fishing, Miss Evans?" Effie asked earnestly. She was back to being "Miss Evans." That "Jules" of earlier must have been a slip of the tongue. She missed being "Jules," though she knew formality was for the best.

"I think so, yes," she replied. The meditative contentment of before seemed far away.

"Then I've a proposition. Marsden and I have cooked up a scheme whereby we swap your horse for his. He and Harcourt will take your horse back to the house, and you and I can go for a proper ride. I hadn't thought through that of course you were going to be mounted aside. I think you would find great enjoy-ment in riding the proper way. There's nothing like a good gallop. We can ride together, on the same horse," he added, anticipating her objection, which was that although she had been keen to try riding in a circumscribed way, she felt quite unqualified for a solo "good gallop."

She glanced at the other gentlemen. Lord Harcourt's counte-nance was friendly and open as he proclaimed his approval of the plan. Perhaps the cautionary issuance she'd perceived earlier had only been her imagination.

"All right, then," she said. "A good gallop. Though I admit to some trepidation about the 'gallop' part."

"A good trot, then," Effie said with a smile as wide as the sky was blue.

Riding, it turned out, was like fishing: rhythmic—almost lulling—and capable of putting one into a deeply contemplative state. It was not dissimilar to what sometimes occurred when Juli-anna attempted her flame-visualization exercise.

"All right?" Effie said, speaking into her ear. He was mounted behind her. After saying goodbye to his friends, Effie had seated Julianna in the saddle of a pretty white horse called Genevieve and himself behind her. He'd taken the reins, which had the effect of closing her in his embrace as they set out at a sedate pace.

"Yes," she said. "More than all right."

"Would you like to try a trot?"

"Would Genevieve like to try a trot?"

He laughed, but she had been in earnest. "Genevieve would like to do what we would like to do."

"Isn't it painful, or at least awkward, for her to bear two riders?"

"I wouldn't recommend we embark on a cross-country journey two astride, or charge into battle, but for this short time, and given that our combined weight is not terribly high, she will be fine."

"All right, then. Let us trot."

Trotting was less contemplative than walking, and more jostling. "I am not sure I care for this. I feel as if my insides are slosh-ing around in a way that is less than pleasing."

"The next gait is a canter, and although it is faster than a trot, it is smoother. Shall we try?"

She was feeling adventurous. "Yes, but hold on to me."

"Always, Jules, always."

The fervency with which that declaration had come out brought to mind her discussion with Lord Harcourt.

Was she . . . doing wrong by Effie?

"Ahh!" She could think no further on the matter for suddenly, they were *flying*. The wind was whistling in her ears, Genevieve was snorting and breathing, and Effie was, as instructed, holding her tight.

Julianna's senses filled with cloves and liberation.

She laughed. She wasn't sure why, exactly. Out of joy, yes, but it was a visceral sort of joy. She felt it in her chest, where her heart thumped at twice the usual pace, as if it were manned by a drum-mer anxious to get to the end of a song. She felt it in her arms and legs, too, in her fingers and toes—all her extremities vibrated like emphatically rung bells. There was an entire percussion section inside her. ·

Cantering was *not* like fishing. Gone was the orderly beat of fo-cused attention, it having given way to a linear, insistent trajectory. It did have in common with fishing that same sense of unraveling, unlatching.

Brighton was making her shed her armor, or Effie was. Or per-haps it was some alchemical result of being with Effie in Brighton.

Riding was ultimately more akin to sea-bathing, she decided. She could go anywhere. Ride away. Float away.

Escape was an illusion, though. Soon, far too soon, Effie did something with his legs and with the reins that prompted Gen-evieve to ratchet down through the dreaded trot and into a walk.

"We are nearly back at the house. I suppose we ought to get off and walk, in order to keep up the ruse."

"Thank you," she said, retying her bonnet as they set out on foot. "That was very exciting. I can't think when my heart has raced so."

Effie grabbed her hand and kept it, swinging their arms back and forth as they walked. "Challenge accepted."

"I beg your pardon?"

Instead of answering, he shot her a wicked look.

"Oh." She grinned.

"Indeed. I shall endeavor to apply myself this evening to the task of making your heart race."

She thought again of Lord Harcourt, and her sense that there had been a warning implicit in their discussion about Effie. "Why did Lord Harcourt throw his fish back in the pond?"

"Why did you?"

"Because he did!"

Effie laughed. "Not out of some high-minded sense of morality?"

"No! I was looking forward to eating my fish. I've never caught my own dinner."

"I believe he is persuaded by his wife's arguments regarding the eating of animals."

"He must be." Julianna found this kind of devotion extraordinary.

It must have been the man's devotion to Effie that had prompted him to issue that coded warning.

"I did not want to distress Lord Harcourt," she said, "so I followed his example."

"I don't think he would have been distressed. He watches Simon and I eat animal flesh at dinner and remains unaffected."

"What if he *were* affected? Would you stop?"

"Of course."

Once again: evidence of extraordinary devotion.

She shook her head, wanting to exit this conversation, though she was the one who'd instigated it. "Well, perhaps I shall have another chance to catch my own dinner."

She would not, though. It had been a daft thing to say. She was leaving the day after tomorrow. She would never fish again. Or ride again. Or sea-bathe again.

Or lounge in bed with Effie talking about editorial strategy.

This was why it was better not to know what one was missing.

You can't miss what you don't let yourself want.

Her old adage wasn't rolling off the tongue like it used to.

Effie did apply himself to making Julianna's heart beat fast that evening. Once again, she left the gentlemen to their port after dinner and retired to her bedchamber. Once again, he came to her after midnight, tapping on her door lightly before letting himself in.

Were two nights enough to constitute a pattern? If so, this was quite an enjoyable one. She very much looked forward to another night with Effie, exploring each other's bodies and talking about the magazine. And if she followed her own directive to remain in the now, she would be able to abandon herself equally to both endeavors.

Effie broke the pattern, though. Instead of being his usual charming, talkative self, he began shedding his clothing the moment the door closed behind him. There was no "Hello, my dearest," no earnest confessions, just the *swish* of silk against linen as he shed his waistcoat, a relatively staid—for him—yellow silk embroidered with tiny white daisies. Then the *thud* of boots hitting the carpet.

This was . . . unsettling. She eyed him, not sure what to make of this silent, determined version of Effie. Soon, he had disrobed entirely, and as he stood in front of her—she was in bed, reclined against her headboard wearing only her shift—she could not read his expression.

She sat up straight, a little alarmed. Not knowing what Effie was thinking, feeling—she didn't like it. Inscrutability didn't suit him, at least when it came to her.

But then he smiled.

Those perfectly mismatched eyes lit up, almost, it seemed, in spite of himself.

He still did not speak, but that was all right. The smile, the light in his eyes, reassured her. As she had done last night, she extinguished half the candles on her night table. She had the vague notion that many ladies preferred carnal activities to occur in the dark, but not Julianna. She wanted to *see*.

She began working her shift off, struggling with the fabric as it tangled with her arms over her head. She thought he would assist, but he did not.

When she freed herself, he was still standing at the edge of the bed staring at her, seemingly unaware of his own state of arousal, or at least unaffected by such. She might have thought him simple if she didn't already know him to be the wittiest of men.

The loveliest, too. He was tall and lean, his skin uniformly pale. The flickering of the candles cast his features, which appeared somehow sharper with his short hair, in a warm glow.

A wicked idea took root. He had surprised her by being so silent. Perhaps she could surprise him, too. She eyed his prick. Charles had always enjoyed this.

Before she could think too much on the matter, she shimmied to the far side of the bed and took him in her mouth.

"Dear God!" he shouted, and she smiled around his length. Finally, she had gotten him to speak.

"Julianna!" he exclaimed, and she smiled again at the scandalized tone. Just for a moment, though, before applying herself to the task at hand—the task at mouth.

She wrapped her hands around him, kneading his arse as she worked him over. She wasn't taking him particularly deep—she and Charles had only done this a few times, and she wasn't sure how . . . rigorous she was meant to be.

Her inexperience didn't seem to matter, judging by the noises Effie was making—he sounded dismayed, but she knew better because she knew *him*. Charles hadn't made those sorts of noises. He hadn't made *any* noises. There was something about this sort of response, so honest and insistent, that made her own desire spiral up and up. She almost thought she might find her release without Effie touching her. Without touching herself.

"Oh, God!" Effie cried, and he took a deep breath in and held it. Pushed her gently off him and spent.

She smiled as his release coated her neck—even as he began apologizing.

"Hush." She took her turn to gently push him away—he was hovering and making to wipe her neck clean, and she needed a moment to collect herself. "Lie down. Catch your breath." She had a handkerchief on her night table, and she used it to clean herself.

When she turned back to him, he was sprawled in a way that called to mind her starfish pose. He looked very satisfied, like a cat who'd had his fill of cream. He was a starfish-cat.

"I didn't know about that," he said as she lay next to him, propping her head on her hand.

"Did you enjoy it?"

"No," he said promptly. "Not at all."

She swatted his chest—or she meant to, but before she could retract her hand he captured it, pressing it against his chest with his own. He was back to being silent, but it wasn't the stern, impenetrable silence of before. It was harmonious, fond.

She let the quiet unfold for a few minutes as his breathing returned to normal. Eventually, he heaved himself up and shimmied down the bed, stopping when he was lying on his stomach, his head level with her hips.

He pushed her legs open and let his fingers lazily stroke her folds, watching her closely. When he found what he was looking for, she gasped. It was a genuine gasp, but it also seemed to work to signal him that he had arrived at his destination. It made sense. He had spoken yesterday about wanting to find this spot on her body.

And then he shocked her by lowering his mouth to it.

Pleasure—still laced with shock—sliced through her, making her back arch off the bed.

He followed her pelvis with his head, using his hands on her hips to guide them back down to the bed. Reapplying himself, he began kissing her, gently at first and then more insistently.

"How did you know to do this?" she heard herself saying. She wanted to kick herself. Why was she asking this question *now*?

He lifted his head. "Should I not be? Is this wrong?"

"Not at all." Nothing had ever felt more right, in fact, but she couldn't quite make herself be that effusive. "Please continue."

"I simply thought that if your mouth on the source of my pleasure was so shattering, perhaps my mouth on the source of yours would be, too. Are you certain I am not incorrect?"

"I am certain!"

"In truth, I have been finding being with you not unlike the act of painting. An image arrives in my mind. In this case, it is an image of you prostrate, me with my head between your legs. The image . . . begins to overtake me. And then I make it manifest."

"You, my friend, are the most remarkable man I have ever met."

"If that is true, I worry for the state of men."

He was back to his usual charming, self-deprecating self. That was a relief.

Wasn't it?

She put on her best seductive smile. "Perhaps we can debate the state of men later, if you don't mind."

She thought he would launch a witty rejoinder, or perhaps flash her one of his signature Effie smiles and return to his task, but he did neither. He cocked his head and stared at her for a long moment before saying, "Will you take your hair down?"

Her hair was still up—somewhat—in the chignon she'd worn to dinner. She worked the pins out and combed through the tangles with her fingers. It was likely to be a curly, wild mess. "All right?"

He nodded, but he sat up and guided her back to the pillow, where he spent a moment arranging her hair against it. She understood now. He was making his painting. Making *their* painting.

When he was satisfied with his handiwork, he nodded and slid back down between her legs.

"You'll tell me if I'm doing anything you don't like, won't you, Jules?"

She murmured her agreement, and that was the last word she spoke for a very long time.

Julianna awakened sometime later and reflected upon the fact that she had never fallen asleep as readily as in recent days. There was something about the utter satiation she felt after an encounter with Effie that tipped her right into a deep, dreamless sleep. She let herself return to wakefulness slowly—she was on holiday, after all—luxuriating in relaxation and contentment.

She reached for Effie, but the bed was empty. Cold. She threw on her wrap. Julianna had been given fine accommodations. Her bedchamber was effectively two rooms, a sleeping area connected by a short, boxy corridor of sorts to another space she had used as a sitting room. Though she supposed it was properly meant to be a dressing room—in addition to a settee and a pair of wing chairs, it contained a collection of mirrors in the corner that would allow a lady to examine her reflection from all angles as well as a dressing table where a lady more refined than she would perform her toilette.

Effie, wearing only his breeches, was perched on the latter piece of furniture and staring into the mirror. He didn't notice her. He appeared melancholy.

She shifted in place a bit and, when that did not get his attention, said, quietly, "Have you had a nightmare?" If so, she felt badly—she had been sleeping too soundly to notice.

He transferred his gaze to hers, via the mirror. It took him a long time—too long—to answer her question. "No nightmares." His face didn't change. It scarcely even moved as he spoke. "I haven't had any since I've been here."

"Well, that is good."

208 / JENNY HOLIDAY

They continued to stare at each other. For the second time this evening, Julianna couldn't read Effie's expression. Before, his signature good nature had eventually reasserted itself. Perhaps she could encourage that to happen again. She held out her hand. "Come back to bed?"

"I can't," he said somberly. She hadn't noticed that the rest of his clothes were on top of the dressing table. He slipped his shirt on. When he was done, he met her gaze in the mirror again. She wanted to tell him to turn around, to look at *her*, not her reflection, but once again, something stopped her. What was it? This was *Effie*. Her dearest friend, and for one more day, her lover. Why was she holding back?

She didn't know her own mind, and she didn't like it.

Perhaps the problem was that she couldn't know her own mind without knowing his. Perhaps they had grown that interdependent. It was an alarming thought.

"I can't stay," he said again.

She was disappointed, but it was likely almost morning. She must have slept longer than she'd realized. "All right. I shall see you soon, then."

"Yes," he said, but there was a sadness in his tone. In his eyes, too. "I shall see you soon."

Chapter 11

Mythology

"Does anyone remember the myth of Leander and Hero?" Effie asked after dinner the next night—the last night. Well, not the last night of Earls Trip, but the last night with Julianna in attendance.

Once again, Julianna had retired after dinner, leaving Effie to pass some time with the boys. She no longer pled a headache. They all seemed to have accepted a certain rhythm to their days—and nights. Today, as yesterday, they had all ventured out together, spending most of their time on the beach, and had taken their evening meal together.

After spending some time with the boys and a glass of port, Effie was meant to go to Julianna. For the last time.

"You're the poet among us," Archie said.

"And the one who owns a bird named Leander," Simon said.

"I've got the basics of it from the Keats poem," Effie said. "Or the ending, anyway. He drowns trying to get to his love, Hero. But I can't remember what led to that."

"You can't imagine *I* know," Archie said. It was true; Archie had never been a scholar.

"You're in luck, because I do," Simon said, and when both Effie and Simon looked at him in surprise, he held up his hands and added, "I've been expanding my reading of late and have recently dipped into Greek mythology."

Was it Effie's imagination, or was Simon being somewhat defensive? Greek mythology certainly was out of character for him. Effie had only ever seen Simon read newspapers. Though come to think of it, he *had* been reading *Sense and Sensibility* in the coach. Effie made a mental note to think more on this exceptional turn later, but for now said, "Do go on."

"Leander and Hero fall in love, despite the fact that she is a priestess of Aphrodite and has taken a vow of chastity," Simon said.

"Why would a priestess of Aphrodite take a vow of chastity?" Archie asked.

"Why did the Greeks do anything?"

"I take the point."

"Regardless, she is forbidden to marry. And she and Leander live on opposite sides of the Hellespont, she in a very high tower overlooking the sea."

"I would expect no less for a priestess of Aphrodite," Archie said wryly.

Simon shot Archie a quelling look. "Leander convinces Hero that he should swim across the channel every night to pay her a visit. She agrees, though she is fearful."

"Of Aphrodite's wrath?" Effie asked.

"I suppose so. Or perhaps she is concerned about the treacherous swim. There are various versions of the story. I'm sure we all read Ovid at school."

Effie had only a vague memory of that, and the characters of the various myths blurred in his mind. Someone was always drowning or burning or being pecked to death by birds.

"Hero is meant to hang a light in her window every night to guide Leander on his swim," Simon continued. "Which she does, and he makes his nightly crossing, though there is a detour in Marlowe's accounting where he gets mistaken for someone else by Neptune—this is the Roman version—and if I recall correctly, there's a magical bracelet involved."

"Isn't there always?" Archie said.

"Will you hold your tongue?" Simon said. Archie smirked as Simon continued. "Marlowe ends his poem there. He died before he finished it, apparently."

"You've been reading poetry?" Effie asked.

"I wouldn't say I've 'been reading' poetry. I read *a* poem."

"But why?" Not that a person needed a reason to read poetry, but it was out of character for Simon.

Simon ignored the question. "In other versions of the myth, the lovers agree to part ways at the end of summer. The waters will be too treacherous to swim come wintertime."

The lovers agree to part ways at the end of summer.

"How? How did they agree to part ways? Did they simply say, 'Well, that was diverting. Have a lovely summer,' and go on their merry ways?"

Simon and Archie were both looking at Effie strangely. Effie gestured for Simon to continue.

"But then one winter night, Leander sees the light in Hero's tower and takes it as a summons."

"That seems rather a leap," Archie said. "Perhaps Hero is engrossed in a novel she can't put down. Perhaps she has forgotten all about Leander and taken another lover. Perhaps she merely fell asleep with the light burning."

Simon turned to Effie. "You're the one who asked for this tale. Can you make him stop?"

Archie held up his hands and made a show of closing his mouth.

With a short sigh, Simon resumed his tale. "Leander starts across the strait, but it's a terribly stormy night and the light is extinguished. He loses his way and is drowned. Hero, seeing that, drowns herself too."

"If she could see him drowning, could she not see that her light had gone out?" Archie, apparently unable to help himself, said.

"I repeat: Who knows why the Greeks did anything?"

"And then," Effie said, "Keats says of Leander's death, 'Nigh swooning he doth purse his weary lips for Hero's cheek and smiles against her smile.'"

Smiles against her smile.

How lovely. How devastating.

"What is the point, do you think?" Effie asked, after taking a moment to collect himself. "Love across a chasm such as the Hellespont is doomed?"

As doomed as between the heir to an earl and the editor of a magazine? As doomed as between the heir to an earl who can't marry the editor of a magazine and the editor of a magazine who won't marry anyone?

"Don't take vows of chastity you don't intend to keep," Archie offered.

"I should think it's more 'Do not anger the gods,'" Simon said.

Perhaps it wasn't that high-minded. Perhaps it was simply, *Only fools willingly swim to their deaths.*

Effie dallied in going to Julianna that night. The past two nights, he had appeared in her bedchamber sans coat—the first night sans waistcoat, too. He had merely gone to her in whatever he had been—or hadn't been—wearing by the end of his evening session with the boys.

Tonight for some reason he found himself fussing over his cravat. Which was ridiculous. It was going to come right back off. It was only that he wanted their last night together to be memorable. He wanted to present himself in the best possible light.

Or perhaps, he thought, as he took a third go at the perfect waterfall knot, it was more that he needed some armor.

He had come to understand that the more time he spent with Julianna, the deeper he fell in love with her. And the deeper he fell in love with her, the worse the pain was going to be when she was gone.

He already felt it, this pain. It had been creeping up on him all day. Since last night, really. After she'd fallen asleep yesternight, he'd been seized with a terrible melancholy. He'd stared at his reflection in the mirror and hadn't recognized himself. He'd told himself that it was the short hair, but it wasn't. Something inside him had awakened, some tender, vulnerable core he hadn't realized ran as deep as it did had been exposed to the light, and it *hurt.*

There is only now.

Effie could not slice life up into such clean segments, as if he were surgically removing a wedge of cake from the whole, making a clean cut with no icing smeared on the knife. For him, there was overlap: love and pain coexisting. Tomorrow, when she left, the pain would increase in magnitude, and the next day, the first day without her, it would grow even more. Would a day arrive when pain was all there was? When it displaced everything that had previously stood in its path: love, yes, but also friendship, imagination, and beauty? In other words, all the things he held dear?

No, no. He was being hyperbolic. She was going home, tomorrow, yes, and he would miss her. But he'd be back in London shortly. Of course, he wouldn't see her every day when they were back in Town. Perhaps he ought to ask how long her liaisons with Edith and Charles had lasted. Then he would have something against which to benchmark his expectations.

No. He needed to stop thinking about such details. Effie had clearly failed to properly embrace Julianna's philosophy of living solely in the present, but he did have only one night left with her here, on holiday, and he would be a fool to waste it brooding.

He blew out his candles, hurried to the door, and yanked it open—and found Julianna on the other side of it, her knuckles raised to knock. She froze. He froze. The clock struck two.

"Effie?" she whispered, looking strange, almost otherworldly, as the flame of her single taper threw shadows across what had been familiar features.

Oh, his heart. He loved her so.

"Come in," he whispered, and after what looked like a moment of uncertainty, she did.

She came to stand by the bed. "Did you fall asleep?" she asked, smoothing her hand over the tidy counterpane. The bed was in pristine condition, so she knew the answer to her question.

He knew that her question had been a proxy for another, unarticulated one: *Why didn't you come to me?*

"No," he said gently. "I wasn't asleep."

He saw the hurt in her eyes, even in the dim light, or perhaps he only sensed it. They had been so concordant since they had met here in Brighton, reading each other's moods without the need for speech or worldly senses. Perhaps that was what was so painful, being that attuned to one another. Having almost all of her, but at the same time, not having her at all.

Perhaps this madness would recede when she was no longer physically present in his life every day. Perhaps that was one consolation to be taken in the days and weeks to come.

"Come," he said, opening his arms.

Another moment of uncertainty: she hadn't set down the candle, and she wasn't meeting his eyes.

He held his breath.

Slowly, so slowly, she set her candle on the night table next to the branch he'd just extinguished. She paused there, and just when he thought he would have to say something—though he had no idea what that something should be, and not knowing what to say to *Julianna* was a very unsettling feeling—she turned and threw herself at him. As his arms tightened around her, he thought for a moment he heard a hitch in her breath, but when, after a few moments, he broke the embrace to hold her at arm's length, nothing about her expression or the way she carried herself seemed out of sorts. He must have imagined that hitch.

Still, everything felt very serious. The air was charged with a kind of solemnity.

That wasn't going to work—he would never survive the night that way. He rallied. It was a great effort, but he let his gaze roam her body, looked down at his own, and when he once again returned his attention to her, he winked and said, "Each of us is wearing entirely too much clothing."

The flippant remark cracked the ice of the pond they were

stuck under—it wasn't time for drowning yet. There was still a light in the tower.

They began fumbling off their clothing. Effie, shucking coat and waistcoat, cursed himself for having dressed so thoroughly earlier. The dratted cravat seemed determined to make him spend as much time removing it as he had tying it, so he switched to tugging off his boots, and when he returned to shirt and cravat, Julianna was naked.

He paused, a mixture of frustration and lust swirling inside him as he gazed on her. He would not see her like this for some time. And when they did manage a liaison, it would have to be in secret. Where? The magazine's office? He could sneak her into his house, he supposed. Certain gentlemen probably did that sort of thing all the time. But the prospect seemed so . . . tawdry.

He also worried about what she would think of his house. It was rather grand, and for the first time, its casual opulence embarrassed him. He had told her the truth about his family, his title, but that didn't mean he wanted to highlight the strait between them.

Stolen time, hidden spaces: this was what was ahead for them.

Well, he would simply have to embrace the necessary sacrifice. The subterfuge. Hadn't he, mere days ago, been encouraging everyone in exactly that? If he could cut off his hair to sneak into the Royal Pavilion, he could do a great deal more in order to see Julianna.

More to the point: he was brooding again. He would have plenty of time to brood later. For now he needed to—"Oof."

Julianna must have grown impatient during his reverie, for suddenly she was pressing on his chest, walking him back toward the bed. When they arrived, she pushed him unceremoniously onto his back and climbed on top of him. She worked his shirt loose from his breeches, but she, too, was defeated by his cravat.

"I was attempting a waterfall knot," he said, "and now it's tightened beyond removing. I fear I shall have to cut—"

She stopped his mouth with a kiss, laying herself over him.

All right, then; that worked, too.

They kissed for ages. Effie told himself to savor it. For although subterfuge was fine if needs must, it was less than ideal. A comfortable, warmly lit bedchamber in a house full of people who understood: this was their last taste of that life.

She pulled away before he was ready. He wanted to kiss her forever. He didn't want to spend; he didn't want her to find her release. That would mean the night was over.

His prick had other ideas as she straddled his thighs and stroked it. "Uhn," he groaned.

When she did that, he became temporarily paralyzed. He became the mindless starfish.

He had been rendered slow-witted enough that he didn't catch on to what she was doing next until it was almost too late. "Wait!" he cried, finding his voice just as she was about to sink down onto him.

She stopped, and he felt a fool.

He hadn't thought they were doing that, was the thing. He had taken to heart Archie's advice about the dangers of an unintended pregnancy, and there had been no discussion of their coming together in this way, nor any sense that it was even on offer.

He had thought she would be more comfortable with mouths and fingers and such.

Hell, *he* might be more comfortable with mouths and fingers and such.

"What is it?" she asked as she sat back onto the tops of his thighs.

"It is too dangerous. You cannot have a child. *I* cannot have a child."

"Why can *you* not have a child?" she asked, a question he thought was rather beside the point at the moment.

He answered anyway. "Because if I had a child, presumably I would love it. And if I loved a child, how could I put him in line for the earldom?"

"You do realize it's rather unusual to hear a person such as yourself declaim that he does not want to inherit land, power, and riches. That he does not want to consign a child to such."

"I suppose I am an original," Effie teased, fluttering his eyelashes for comic effect.

"You do not really have a choice, though, do you? I appreciate the many ways in which you are unconventional. You *are* an original. But you shall have to produce an heir, shan't you?"

"I suppose so." Honestly, he preferred not to think about it, and so far that strategy had proven sufficient. Someday, his parents would probably begin haranguing him over the succession, but that day had not yet arrived. "But I would like to think you of all people would understand why the prospect feels rather like a yoke to me. A cage."

"I do, but I feel I ought to point out that you can be whatever sort of earl you like. You can be a poetry-writing, court-pump–wearing earl. Regardless, there is very little risk of getting me with child."

His first impulse was to ask how she knew that, but he swallowed the question. He had to assume she did—it was her body, her future, on the line here. He settled for saying, "Very little risk is not no risk."

"Can you pull out? When you're close, I mean?"

Yes. He hadn't realized that was an option, but of course it was. And now that it was, he wanted it. He yearned for it with every word of every poem he'd ever written.

"But of course if you don't want to, we won't," she said, leveling him with a look so tender it brought tears to his eyes. She started to pull away.

He clamped a palm down on her forearm. "I can do that."

The smile she graced him with was equal parts wicked and guileless, which should have been impossible, but many things about Julianna, about Julianna and him together, should have been impossible.

"We should switch places," she said, glancing down at his hand keeping her anchored to him.

"I beg your pardon?" He didn't understand, but he removed his hand all the same. It wasn't polite to hold a lady against her will.

Once freed, she flopped onto her back.

"You are starfishing," he said fondly.

"I appear to be starfishing, but I am in my right mind. Starfishing requires the temporary departure of one's senses. To reduce the risk of this encounter resulting in a child neither of us wants, you must pull out before you spend. That is more likely to be successful if you are on top. You shall be able to move away from me unimpeded."

You shall be able to move away from me unimpeded.

Effie didn't care for that sentence.

He shook his head. He was overthinking this. He wasn't writing a poem here.

He was making a painting.

He closed his eyes and pictured it. Him moving over Julianna, her eyes closed in ecstasy. He could angle himself the way he had the first night, when she said the pressure was just right. Except this time, he would be inside her.

He opened his eyes. He might not survive the encounter, but he was ready.

He kissed her again. And again and again, pausing only long enough to inform her, "We are going to kiss for ages." She smiled, and he smiled against her smile—like Leander from the Keats poem? No, of course not. No one was drowning here.

And so they kissed for ages. It would be the last time they had ages to spare.

She kept attempting to move things along, but Effie was coming to understand the pleasure to be had in delayed gratification. It was difficult, but the best things often were. Eventually, he moved down her body, kissing her neck, stroking her breasts, flicking her nipples the way he'd learned she liked. He allowed her to stroke his body all over, too, but when her hands found his prick, he swatted them away.

"I said 'ages,'" he teased.

"It's *been* ages." She tried to pout, but she was laughing, and then he was laughing.

"Edward," she said after their laughter died, and his formal Christian name on her lips shocked him to his core. *"Please."*

A bolt of lust shot down his spine, and suddenly he *didn't* have ages.

There is only now.

"You will have to guide me," he said. He had meant it in a general sense, but she grabbed his prick, lined herself up with it, wrapped her legs around his waist, and, using his body for leverage, thrust upward.

And there they were. Together. Ages would not be long enough.

"You might like to move," she whispered, and he realized he had been frozen.

Part of him wanted to stay frozen. Stay like this forever, closer to Julianna than he had ever been or would ever be to anyone else. But once she planted the seed of the idea, this notion of moving inside her, his body began undulating. He remembered the rocking she had enjoyed before, and he tried to replicate that, but some relentless need inside him was overriding his conscious will and he could not help but begin thrusting.

She didn't seem to mind. She hung on to him with both arms and both legs and met his every thrust.

"Effie," she said, and if he didn't know better, he'd have thought she was distressed.

"Jules," he answered.

They stared at each other. One of her hands had slid around to the front of her body and was rubbing the magical nub of flesh. He moved his own hand to join hers, adding his first two fingers next to the two she was using.

She moaned again, and for a moment, her eyes slipped closed. But they opened just as quickly, opened wide, as if in disbelief, and she went perfectly still.

Nothing had ever flattered him more, or made him feel more powerful. He could have a thousand poems published, or he could have this, and he would choose this every time.

He pressed down a little harder with his fingers and, knowing he was close to his own precipice, gave a great thrust. The quaking began. It started with her. He felt her shivering where their bodies touched, and soon her shivering became his became theirs.

There was only now, and there was only them.

Julianna fell asleep, as she had been doing during their nights together.

In their correspondence, she had always sympathized with Effie about his insomnia, telling him that she had so often lain abed and resisted sleeping for thinking about the magazine that she feared she had trained herself *not* to sleep, even when she wanted to.

But she certainly fell asleep readily here. Tonight, they hadn't been lying panting for five minutes before he realized that she wasn't panting so much anymore as she was lightly snoring.

Effie would have enjoyed flattering himself that it was his presence, but it was more likely the generalized effect of a holiday. Distance—both physical and sentimental—from one's cares, even if one did not perceive one's cares as burdens, as was certainly the case with Jules and her magazine, had a restorative effect.

But . . . *Was* she distant from her cares here? He certainly was not. He had been, moments ago, but *There is only now* had become *What happens next?*

He had been distant from his cares when their holiday began, the relief of confiding in his friends and the giddiness of his early encounters with Jules conspiring to create a profound contentment deep inside him. That state hadn't lasted, though. Cares, they had a way of seeping in.

Regardless, he was glad Julianna was sleeping well. Perhaps she could bank some of it for when she had to go back and do battle with Mr. Glanvil and the other men of her world, the ones who didn't respect her talents or consider her feelings.

He levered himself off the bed gingerly, so as not to wake her. Pulling on a dressing gown, he peered into Leander's cage, willing the bird, who was awake, to remain silent.

"Do you want to come out?" he whispered, opening the door and presenting his wrist.

Leander stepped out with a burble that was not loud enough to wake Julianna, and Effie took him to a bureau in the corner on which sat a wash basin and ewer. Leander liked to perch on the edge of the basin and drink the water—that it was from the same source and therefore identical to the water furnished him in his cage was a fact to which Leander was indifferent.

Effie lit a candle and studied his reflection. For some unfathomable reason, he expected he would look different than he had an hour ago, when he'd been tying his cravat.

He was unchanged. He had even grown accustomed to the short hair.

What had he expected?

Frankly, as illogical as it was, he had expected the upheaval he'd experienced these past few days to be visible somehow. He had expected to look like a man whose heart was at once soaring and half broken, like a man who had everything and was about to return to a life wherein he had to settle for a sliver of everything. For shadows.

He didn't know how long he stood there, staring at his reflection while Leander preened, only that he was startled when Julianna's reflection joined his.

She was fully dressed and holding her own candle. She was ready to go back to her room, and in the morning, she would leave. They had cooked up a fiction by which they would hand off "Sarah" in Brighton to a fictional aunt and uncle who would then escort her back to London.

This was the second time Effie and Julianna had met like this, in the mirror. Perhaps he ought to take it as a sign. Perhaps their relationship worked better when it was mediated by something like a mirror. Letters. Perhaps they needed a degree of remove.

For the first time, Effie wondered if this had all been a mistake. Previously, he would have said no, even considering the pain that was coming—the pain that was already here. Meeting Julianna was the single most exciting thing that had ever happened to him. That first day, when they embraced in front of the Pavilion, he would have said meeting her had been worth any price, any pain. But that was back when he felt pain with his heart. His soul.

Julianna had introduced him to his body. Not his body alone but his body as conjoined to his heart and soul. She had made him one, made him whole. He was subject now to an entirely new sort of pain.

This pain was everywhere, and was suddenly more than he thought he could bear.

"What will happen now?" he asked Julianna's reflection carefully. He had been following her directive, as well as he could, to live in the present, but it was time to discuss the terms of their ongoing relationship.

"I expect I ought to go back to my room," she said glibly. "I believe I heard the clock chime four."

"That's not what I mean."

She cocked a head. "What do you mean, then?"

"You know," he said, not bothering to tamp down the pique in his tone. He was hurt that she would pretend to misunderstand his question, and he didn't care if she knew it. "And please do me the respect of refraining from saying, 'There is only now.'"

Her countenance shifted. "What *can* happen? We can hardly carry on as we have here. Your absence from my bedchamber earlier meant you knew that, did it not? That is why you were dallying, not because of that cravat." She nodded at the silk he was still wearing around his neck. It was starting to feel like a noose.

"We cannot carry on as we have here, seeing each other intensely and frequently, all right," Effie said, "but that doesn't mean we shan't be able to see each other at all."

When she didn't answer, he began to panic. He tried not to show it, but Leander must have been able to sense it, for he hopped around the edge of the basin until he was facing Effie, and squawked.

The bird seemed to spur Julianna to speech, though she didn't spare Leander a glance. "When would that happen? Under what circumstances?"

Under less-than-ideal circumstances, he wanted to say. *In shadows. In haste.*

It was better than nothing.

Wasn't it?

"It's not as if we run in the same circles," she said, when he didn't answer. There was enough light in the room to see something in her eyes dim.

No. We do not run in the same circles. How can we? There is a strait between us.

He needed to start speaking out loud. Apparently they could no longer read each other's thoughts.

He hated to push her, but what choice did he have? "What if I were to bring my next poem, or my next column, to your office? Hand you my pages rather than mail them to you."

"But you write those pseudonymously."

Was she worried someone would see him at her office and identify him as the author of "Advice for Married Ladies" and/or the odd poem?

"What if I were to require help with a poem? We could have an 'editorial meeting.'" He hoped she caught his meaning. She looked . . . not vexed, but discomfited. She was tapping the fingers of one hand mindlessly against the fingers of another.

"What is wrong?"

Did she not *want* to see him?

"What are you thinking?" he pressed.

"What happens after the editorial meeting?" she asked.

"I'm not sure I follow."

She stopped fidgeting and looked right at him in the mirror. "I haven't time for an affair."

He had to reach out for the edge of the bureau to steady him-

self. That she could turn away from all that had transpired between them because she was *busy* had him reeling. The statement
lanced him, another instance of the power she had to hurt him, to
hurt every part of him, body, soul, and heart together.

He wanted to ask how she had found time for the other two affairs she'd had, but the question would be laced with affront, even
malice, and to meet hurt with hurt was beneath him.

He took a step back from the bureau. He did not turn to face
her but kept his gaze on hers in the mirror. He was stepping back
because he wanted to get farther from the light. He didn't want
her to see the wild thudding of his pulse, which had been easily
visible in his neck. For the first time, he regretted having shorn his
hair. His long hair would have been a curtain right now, one he
could hide behind.

There was a stab in his stomach, a rush of sourness. The idea of
hiding from Julianna—hiding his true feelings, hiding *himself*—
was anathema.

"I am sorry," she said, breaking the connection between their
gazes and looking at the floor.

What was she saying? He could not lose her entirely. "Let us
resume our correspondence," he said carefully. "We shall see how
things feel."

Julianna wouldn't have him, not even in the shadows, apparently, but would she have his letters? She had to. He could not give
up their correspondence.

"So we write to each other as we did before."

"No. We shall write to each other with no pretense between us.
You know who I am now, who I really am. And . . ." An idea was
forming. "Will you allow me to furnish you with funds to pay for
your letters to me?"

"Why would I do that?"

"Because it would make me happy." Or at least it would make
him less bereft than if he neither saw nor had word from her ever
again.

"I ought to say no."

"You ought to say yes."

"Why?"

"So you may write me every day. If you want to." He started again. "So you may write me as often as you would like. So I may have the pleasure of reading as many letters as you would like to send me." He paused, wondering if he should say the rest. Well, hell, why not? He was on the verge of losing her entirely. "And because my father has been very cruel to me and though it is petty of me, I take pleasure in the idea of using his money for such."

She met his gaze again, and her eyes were a little lighter. "Then I say yes."

All right. There was something. A lifeline. He took a shaky inhalation. He still did not want her to see the true nature of his distress, though he still hated this impulse—this need—to hide anything from her.

He smiled sadly, feeling as if he were being shut back inside a cage. No, he was voluntarily retreating to it, which was something he was willing to do because he was—

"I am in love with a woman named Julianna Evans!"

Leander. Speaking a full sentence. His only sentence. *The* only sentence.

Effie and Julianna were still looking at each other in the mirror. Initially, he thought her eyes lightened even more. He almost fancied he saw a spark there. But no. Whatever he'd thought he'd seen was gone, replaced by an expression he could not read, and an unreadable expression on Julianna's face was worse, to his mind, than one of sadness, or anger.

He had no earthly idea what to say. Should he deflect? Pretend innocence? *The silly bird, how he lies!*

He had the terrible feeling that Leander's outburst had sealed his fate: He would not see her again, and she would not write to him, either.

"I see," she said, before he could think how to try to salvage the situation. "I shall go, then. I never wanted to hurt you."

But she had.

Did intention matter? If someone didn't want to hurt you but they did anyway, did that make the hurt somehow less?

If you got into a cage willingly, did that make your incarceration any less painful?

A terrible sadness had come over him. He was a hollow man. Everything light and joyous and careful had been scooped out of him, leaving him a shell.

"I had hoped to go sea-bathing again," she said quietly. She took a step back, toward the door, but she kept her gaze on his.

It took him a moment to adjust to the mundane statement. "Yes, we'd planned to, hadn't we?"

"I got . . . caught up in our nights together indoors."

He supposed he could suggest that they go now. He could give her one more swim at dawn before she left him.

He thought of Leander—the mythical hero, not the bird—drowning, and he said nothing.

Unlike Leander, Effie had some sense of self-preservation. It was somewhat shocking to realize it, but it was true.

He could not swim across the stormy strait if Julianna wouldn't hang a light for him. He could not make such a journey when he knew the outcome would be a watery death. Even for her, he could not do it. His hollow body was riddled with holes, with injuries he'd accumulated over a lifetime and in recent days. If he attempted such a swim, he would sink to the seafloor like a stone.

"I am in love with a woman named Julianna Evans!" Leander said.

"Yes," Effie said to the bird. "We heard you the first time."

After holding his gaze in the mirror for another long moment, Julianna left.

Chapter 12

Advice for the Heartsick

Effie stayed up, keeping a vigil of sorts in the dark. At various points, he told himself to stand down. The problem was, he didn't know *how* to. How could he possibly sleep in this last stretch of hours before she left? How could he do anything with her under the same roof, here but as good as gone? He was in limbo, in a terrible purgatory of his own making.

An idea took root. He pulled out the last letter he had yet to answer for December.

Dear Miss Heartsick,

I probably ought not to answer your letter, not because you are unmarried and appealing to the author of a column entitled "Advice for Married Ladies," but because I am unqualified to do so. I do not know if it is possible to die of a broken heart. Plays, and poetry, tell us it is possible. Why, I wonder, did Shakespeare write tragic lovers whose fates ended in death and comedic lovers who were united in marriage by play's end but nothing in between? Where is the story of the brokenhearted fool who picked himself up and kept going? The spurned lover who did *not* drown?

Perhaps you can write such a story for yourself. I hope so.

Yours,

Edward Astley

228 / JENNY HOLIDAY

He knew he could not sign the letter with any version of his real identity for publication, but for now, it felt good to affix his name to the sentiment.

Having been somewhat calmed by the act of writing a letter, Effie thought of his dear friend Olive Morgan, to whom he had *not* written as he'd intended. He had been too caught up in the events of the past week. Olive, no stranger to heartbreak, once told him that when she was in despair, she forced herself to act like a happy person. *I put on a bonnet—the more outrageous the better—and take myself to the park and smile at people who smile at me. I'm not really smiling, mind you; I'm merely molding my lips into the shape of a smile, but no one knows the difference. Eventually, and for increasingly long stretches of time, I myself forget the artifice.*

Comporting himself as a happy person was not within Effie's reach. He wasn't that good an actor. But he could act like a person who cared about himself. He thought about what Olive would do in this situation, or Archie and Simon. What Archie had done by sneaking into Effie's room at night and sleeping next to him to ward off nightmares. He was lucky enough to have people in his life who cared about him. He needed to act that way toward himself.

That person, he decided, would change into a freshly laundered nightshirt. That person, understanding that sleep was restorative, that it, as Shakespeare said, "knits up the raveled sleave of care," would fluff up his pillows and pull the covers up over his body.

That person would then lean over and blow out the candle on his night table and try to rest, even if dawn was just around the corner.

When the vigil was over and light began to slice in through a gap left in the curtains he hadn't properly closed, Effie got up. Put one foot in front of the other and took himself to the breakfast room. He was the first one there, which was novel. He wondered if the boys or Julianna would turn up first. He wondered which option he preferred.

Everyone appeared at the same time, and there was a flurry of morning greetings in which he did not participate.

Neither did he make a plate for Julianna, as had become his habit. It wasn't that he wanted to be hurtful, just that *he* was so hurt, so set back on his heels, he couldn't bring himself to consider what she would like, to deliver her a plate of the choicest morsels, as if this were a morning like any other.

The conversation was somewhat stilted. Archie carried the brunt of it, asking Julianna technical questions about the printing and distribution of the magazine. Julianna kept looking at Effie as if she were waiting for him to chime in, and indeed, on other occasions, he would have been very happy to participate in a conversation about such matters—he had learned a great deal being in her orbit all these years—but this morning, he felt as if he were separated from the conversation by a pane of glass. A wavy pane that, in addition to muting sound, warped sight. He was outside looking in.

He checked his timepiece. "I suppose we ought to go if we're to"—he glanced around, noting that there was a maid in the room clearing the remains of their breakfast—"meet Uncle and Aunt at the appointed time." In truth, Julianna was planning to take the eleven o'clock Brighton-to-London coach, and he didn't want her to miss it.

Well, he *did* want her to miss it. But he didn't. He wanted her to want to miss it.

He was as befuddled as he'd been on the journey here.

The boys stood when Julianna did. Effie got to his feet as well. There was a brief moment of discomfiture while they all stood staring at each other around the table.

Archie broke the silence by turning to Effie and asking, "Shall we accompany you and Lady Sarah to meet your aunt and uncle?"

"Yes, thank you." He could tell Julianna was surprised, but he wasn't going to turn down the company of his friends on this painful errand.

"All right?" Archie whispered, after Julianna had gone to fetch

230 / JENNY HOLIDAY

her reticule. Archie, who was always insisting he wasn't smart, had an uncommonly high degree of acumen when it came to sentiment and relationships.

"Not really," Effie said. He would tell them the rest later. Or perhaps he wouldn't. He still had that feeling of being isolated behind a pane of glass. He'd have thought that feeling would be limited to Julianna, but he felt it as regarding the boys, too.

They took Archie's coach, and the silence that settled as they rumbled out of Hove was dismayingly awkward—or it would have been had Effie not still been tucked away behind his glass. The protective pane ratcheted the discomfort level down to mild.

"Miss Evans," Simon said, "I've been thinking about my piece on the Pavilion, and I wonder if I might ask you a few questions, just to focus my mind before I begin it in earnest."

"Of course."

They talked, and while Simon was, ostensibly, speaking to Julianna, he kept eyeing Effie. Occasionally, he made brief eye contact with Archie.

When they alit, Julianna thanked them for allowing her to impose upon their holiday.

"I assure you, it was no imposition," Simon said. "I ought to be thanking you for that tour you contrived."

"Well," she said, hitching her reticule into the crook of her elbow, "I've had the most wonderful time." She was speaking to all of them but looking at Effie.

The boys echoed her sentiments and started to fall back. Simon succeeded, but Effie managed to grab Archie's arm to keep him by his side. He probably looked like a right fool, but he didn't care. He needed reinforcements.

"I have finished my Mrs. Landers letters for December." He held them out, but Julianna merely looked at them as if he were holding a strange object she didn't recognize. "You may as well take them now."

"Thank you," she said after shaking her head as if to rouse herself from a daydream. "I am sure I will return to the office to find a stack of new entreaties. I will send you the lot of them so you may begin thinking about January." She paused. "A new year."

"Yes," he said, and he didn't know which statement he was agreeing with—that he could start the January letters, or that January would be the start of a new year. He decided on the latter. "A new year."

A new year in which everything would be the same as ever. He would still be behind his glass. In his cage.

Oh, such maudlin comparisons. He would have laughed at himself were he not so deep inside his own overwrought metaphors. At least he wouldn't be meeting his watery end in a painful drowning.

"Goodbye, Miss Evans," Effie said, suddenly needing this leave-taking to be over. Addressing her so formally hurt him, but sometimes a smaller hurt had to be tolerated in order to protect against a greater wound.

Well, he'd already sustained the greater wound. Perhaps the smaller hurt was a way of dressing the existing laceration, staunching the bleeding.

What he hadn't banked on was that it would hurt her, too. Her eyes filmed with tears. She pulled herself together quickly, though: she straightened her spine, adjusted her posture, and said, "Goodbye, Lord Featherfinch."

Yes. It *was* painful, wasn't it? Julianna had referred to him as "Lord Featherfinch" a few times, but it had always been in company, when it would have been improper for her to have used anything but his title. In those instances, she'd been talking about him, to the boys. *Lord Featherfinch told me you were staying at the home of one of your friends.*

What do you make of Lord Featherfinch's theory, my lord?

She had never addressed him directly by his title.

He couldn't truly be upset, though, could he? He had started it.

After a long moment of silence, Archie stepped forward and helped Julianna into the coach—she was the last passenger to board, and everyone was waiting on her.

The coach rolled away, and that, apparently, was that.

"Do you want to talk about it?" Archie asked gently, as their own conveyance rumbled off.

"Do I want to talk about what?" Effie said—disingenuously, he knew.

Archie raised his eyebrows.

Effie sighed. "I'm not sure what there is to talk about. Everything has unfolded as expected."

"What does that mean?"

"Julianna and I cannot be together, for all the reasons I enumerated when we first spoke on the matter."

"And nothing about the past week changed any of those reasons?"

"She certainly seemed not to mind that you were a man," Simon said with a smirk, "and if I recall correctly, you identified *that* as an 'unscalable obstacle.'"

Effie moved his mouth into the shape of a smile, because that was what one did when one's friend said something amusing—he was attempting to follow Olive's advice about acting. "Indeed, but I am still me, and she is still her, and that is that."

Effie had the novel experience of wishing the holiday would end. Usually, he dreaded returning home. Usually, being with Simon and Archie, wherever they were, felt more like home than Number Twenty Berkeley Square.

Now, though, with several days of holiday yet before him, he longed for the silent, sterile halls of the London house. For the sanctuary of his bedchamber within it. Would he take down the chartreuse-sky painting? He would have to. It would hurt too much to look at it.

Would he return to having the nightmares? They had been absent here, but was that because someone, be it Julianna or Archie, had always been sharing his bed? Or did he dare to hope they were permanently gone?

So many questions.

He pasted on another of Olive's non-smiles. "Mrs. Mitchell tells me there is a Druidic stone of some note nearby. Shall we go see it?"

The boys both eyed him skeptically. They hadn't excepted him to suggest a benign outing.

But what would a happy person do on holiday? A happy person would go see a stone in a field. What else? A happy person would catch up on his correspondence—his real correspondence, not his pseudonymous, advice-dispensing correspondence.

By which he meant he would write to Olive.

He probably ought to write to Julianna, too. He had said he would. He'd urged her to resume their correspondence, even offering to pay for it. He had, at the time, thought of writing to her as a lifeline. She didn't want him as a lover anymore, but, he'd reasoned, they could still be friends. Correspondents.

He was no longer sure if that was true.

Still, he wasn't the kind of person who made promises he didn't keep. So he would write to her. Once, at least. It would probably take up a great deal of time. Striking the right tone would prove challenging.

And then perhaps he would take the boys sea-bathing.

Sea-bathing, letters, a great big stone: it was good to have a plan.

On their way to view the stone, Archie said, "You have been holding out on us."

"I have not been," Effie protested. Lord, he didn't want to talk about this anymore. "We can't marry. Well, I can; she *won't*. She also doesn't want to continue our liaison in any form whatsoever, so I'm not sure what more there is to say."

"Not that, *Mrs. Landers*," Archie said. He turned to Simon. "It seems, that in addition to writing poetry for Miss Evans's magazine, he's also dispensing advice for married women under yet another pseudonym."

Archie and Simon laughed heartily, and Effie said, "Yes, yes," as he waved away their good-natured jeers.

It was good to know, though, that he still had his friends, that he still had their good-natured jeers.

They alit a while later in a farm field and contemplated a rather unimpressive rock.

"It's a lump of sandstone," Simon said.

"It's no Stonehenge," Archie agreed.

"The story," Effie said, "has something to do with the devil being angered by everyone converting to Christianity in . . . the past at some point." He hadn't been listening that closely to Mrs. Mitchell, though normally this would have been exactly the kind of attraction he would have found fascinating. "He was digging a dike to drown all the ancient villages around here, and he stubbed his toe on this stone and abandoned his heinous plot."

"All it took for the devil to give up his scheme was a stubbed toe?" Archie asked.

"This is the same devil who rained curses on Job?" Simon asked.

"And beheaded the faithful and what have you?" Archie said.

"Oh, and wasn't there a terrible dragon with seven heads sweeping the stars from the sky?" Simon asked.

"Perhaps, and what about plunging people into a river of fire and boiling blood?"

"I believe that's Dante, not the Bible."

"Oh, my mistake."

"Regardless, the point stands," Simon said, turning to Effie. "A stubbed toe would not deter Lucifer."

It was possible Effie's smile at that point was a tiny bit genuine.

"Do you think I ought to let Leander go free?" Effie asked three nights later, when they were settled in with their post-dinner drinks. It was something he'd been thinking about the past few days.

"We are speaking of Leander the bird, not Leander the doomed mythological hero?" Archie asked.

"Yes."

"Can a tropical bird such as Leander survive in England?"

"I don't know."

"I can't think that he would live a long life in our climate."

"Even so, perhaps he would rather be free." Effie was in his cage, in his glass-encased prison, but did Leander need to be?

"I fear Leander may be too stupid to survive in the wild," Simon said with a smirk.

"That may be true," Effie said. "But even if the weather and/or his own dullness of mind means it would only be a brief taste of liberation, perhaps he would still rather be free. Perhaps Sally would rather have been free."

"What has brought on these thoughts?" Simon asked.

"Oh, I don't know," Effie said. "I am being maudlin, I suppose. I was lying awake last night contemplating going home and thinking about the fact that I am alone. And then I thought, *Well, at least I have Leander.* But *then* I thought, *Am I using him as a sort of psychic crutch? Is it fair to keep him inside all the time and locked up nearly all the time?*"

"You are not alone," Archie said. "You have us."

"Yes." Effie bowed his head. He did have the boys, and he hadn't meant to minimize that. In fact, they'd been managing, these past few days, to cheer him somewhat, to start chiseling away at the glass separating them. "I am alone in my family, I meant."

"As am I," Simon said.

"Indeed," Effie agreed. Simon's elder twin brothers passed unexpectedly years ago, and his mother had yet to get over it, and by extension, her disappointment that Simon had inherited the title. As for Archie, his father passed years ago, and his mother descended further each day into the fancies of her own mind. It was daft to proclaim that he, Effie, was alone in his family when all his immediate relations were alive, whereas the boys had lost parents and siblings.

"I rather think my situation is different, though," Simon said. "I am alone because my family is indifferent to me. You are alone because your family is cruel to you."

"Only Father, to be fair."

Simon shrugged as if he disagreed but wasn't going to press the matter. Simon wasn't entirely wrong. Effie had thought, these recent months, about how his mother had been conveniently absent during the worst of his father's rages.

"Well," Archie said, "to answer your original question, Leander seems perfectly content to me."

Yes, Leander *seemed* perfectly content. Effie's mouth was still in the shape of a smile. It was possible to *seem* perfectly content but not *be* content.

Chapter 13

Editorial Interdependence

You can't miss what you don't let yourself want.

Julianna should have heeded her own advice.

If she'd never gone to Brighton, never seen the Pavilion and its wonders, never floated in a blue sea under a blue sky, she wouldn't have known what she was missing.

If she'd never met Effie, she wouldn't have known what she was missing.

She ordered herself to stop ruminating. What was done was done. She *had* seen the Pavilion and she *had* swum and she *had* met Effie.

And she had been changed by it all.

But some things didn't change. She tried another precept, one that had held up better to the storms inside her: *The magazine above all.*

That was still true. It was still a bulwark.

October was done. Mr. Cabot had had a copy ready for her inspection when she arrived, as agreed. She'd made a few corrections, and now it was a week later and she was in the office with her newest creation in hand.

Traditionally, this was the part where she paged through and marveled that everything had come together so well. The chaos— usually but not always of the organized variety—that characterized the production process had been tamed and yielded this: a magazine. The perfect way to pass an evening.

Usually, she felt a pleasant brand of proud exhaustion at this stage.

Now, though? She felt exhaustion, yes. But there was nothing pleasant about it. She merely felt . . . blank. Empty. She wasn't even particularly proud of October, though she recognized objectively that it was a fine issue. It contained many wonderful stories, and she had even "forgotten" to implement a correction Mr. Glanvil had wanted to make to the moral essay, and though she would pay for it later, she should be feeling that small triumph right now.

She felt nothing.

She tried again, paging through from back to front. "Advice for Married Ladies" ran on the last page, and Effie's letters, were, as per usual, exquisite. Witty and compassionate and heartfelt.

She thought back to the letter he'd been working on their second-to-last night together. It seemed a lifetime ago. That letter, about whether the writer should spend Christmas at home with her mother, would run in December, along with the castor oil letter, and two or three others. They had gotten to the point where Julianna forwarded Effie a stack of letters and he chose which to respond to, sending them back along with his replies. She printed all that she had room for, and while in the beginning he'd overshot, answering too many letters, over time he had honed his ability to know how many letters to address, and how long to make his collective replies. To wit, October's four letters fit perfectly onto the column's page.

It was a bit startling to realize that she had begun willingly handing over even a small part of the magazine to someone else. Not that she didn't always do that, in a sense. Other people wrote the content of the magazine. But when had she decided she trusted Effie not only to write Mrs. Landers's responses but to choose the letters to which he would respond? When, in other words, had she handed off editorial authority? The only other person who had that was Mr. Glanvil, and she had not parted with it willingly in his case.

She shook her head. It mattered not. She performed her usual tasks with the few dozen copies she'd had delivered to the office. She kept some for the archives, and she prepared a few copies to mail to distant correspondents. She wrote Mr. Glanvil a note—designed to manage his expectations—to attach to his copy. She set aside a copy for Amy and a copy for herself to take home.

Then she moved on to a review of November. Most of the stories were done, and the rest were in hand. She made a few notes—ideas for layouts, preliminary thoughts about which stories to feature on the cover, that sort of thing.

So . . . November was as done as it could be at this point. She knew what came next. She was tempted to go home and start worrying about December tomorrow, but the Christmas issue was always a great deal of work.

Just because you *wanted* to avoid something didn't mean you could.

She took a fortifying sip of tea that had long since gone cold and began by going over what she already had on hand.

She had her latest installment of the serialized novel she had commissioned—the whole "novel" was done, so she merely needed to decide where to cut off December's installment. She used the word *novel* loosely because the tale of the runaway heiress turned lady adventurer captured by benevolent pirates was not entirely coherent. Readers didn't seem to mind though, or perhaps the serialized nature of the story made it easier to overlook inconsistencies, for the story was quite popular.

She had a piece on innovations in table ornamentation with a particular eye toward Christmas entertaining.

She had a recounting of a tea tasting, in which two ladies described and vociferously debated the merits of Darjeeling versus Earl Grey. She'd been planning to hold that one for January, but a story she was waiting on from America for December—an account of alligators in the Mississippi—was looking as though it might not arrive in time. If that was the case, she would run the Great Tea Debate in December. She did realize that tea was tremendously less exciting than alligators, but one did what one needed to do.

There was her quarterly column by "The Actress," which was meant to be a glamorous and slightly scandalous account of a life treading the boards. Julianna had fought Mr. Glanvil to keep the column, and in fact its retention had been assured by agreeing to the addition of the monthly moral essay. She was thinking of sacking "The Actress," though. While the lady was indeed an actress, she had never accepted a carte blanche and tended to write more about the text of the plays she was in than the social scene surrounding their performance. And she always turned her columns in early, which struck Julianna as beside the point if she was meant to be reporting on the latest on-dits. Perhaps it was time to switch authorship to "The Opera Dancer." She made a note to ask around to see if she could find someone suitable.

Finally, she had Mrs. Landers's letters.

She pulled them out of the desk. When Effie had handed them to her unexpectedly as she was leaving Brighton, she'd shoved them into her reticule—and, later, into her desk—without reading a word. She had told herself that October and November required her attention more urgently.

That had been an excuse. It would have taken her mere minutes to skim the letters.

In truth, she was afraid of them.

She missed him. She missed him so very much. There was a great big chasm in her chest, and it had grown wider every day she was away from him.

And now that the mad dash to get October out the door was done, now that she was in a state of equilibrium with November, there was nothing with which to fill that chasm. But what could she do about it? She would have to trust that time would mend things. It was time to read the Mrs. Landers letters for December. *The magazine above all.*

She was afraid, though, that reading Effie's letters would widen the chasm inside her even more, indeed, that it might tear her apart entirely. And if there was no Julianna left, there would be no magazine to prize above all, would there?

With shaking hands, she smoothed the pages written in the familiar loopy hand that was so dear to her.

She had seen "Home for Christmas" and "Sartorially Sullied." Both letters had received concise rejoinders.

Then there were two letters she had not seen, one from a woman who was at her wit's end with child-rearing. Effie's response was typically kind, thoughtful, and practical. It made Julianna's throat tighten.

And then. Oh, and then. A missive from a lady who had been left at the altar. Effie's response was *not* typical here. It provided no solace, no actionable advice.

It did commiserate, if not explicitly.

And he had signed it "Edward Astley." His real name. Not his title. Not the nickname she and his friends knew him by.

Julianna never cried.

And yet, Julianna cried.

The next day, a letter arrived for Julianna at home, posted from Brighton.

She would have wagered the balance of her printing press fund that she wouldn't hear from Effie, despite their agreement to resume their correspondence. She had clearly broken his heart, and what person in possession of a broken heart voluntarily wrote to its breaker?

She went to open the seal, but it gave her some trouble. It was larger and thicker than usual. After successfully prising it open, she discovered a shilling beneath it.

Dear Julianna,

She paused. What had happened to "My dearest Jules?"

She supposed you did not say "My dearest Jules" to the person who had broken your heart.

I write to you on the final evening of Earls Trip 1822. We have been having a fine time since you left.

Effie had been having a "fine" time?

Why did that sting? Did she want him to be having a poor time?

Perhaps she had been mistaken about how deeply she had wounded him. Perhaps it had only been a glancing blow and he had already shaken it off. It was hard to imagine, given how painful their parting had been. Both of their partings: the nighttime one, in which Leander had blurted what Effie, thankfully, had not, and the daytime one, in which Effie had done everything he could to avoid talking to her, or even looking at her.

We learned about the existence of a Druidic stone called the Goldstone and went to see it. It was indeed gold, if you looked closely enough at it. Well, it was sandstone, I think, shot through with flecks of gold. But it wasn't very large, and it wasn't shaped or honed in any particular way. It was just a big lump of rock. Still, one tries to see Druidic stones when one is in the vicinity of them.

I did manage to get the boys to come sea-bathing with me. It was very refreshing.

I trust you have taken delivery of October and that all is well.

Sincerely,

Edward.

Edward. She supposed if she was *Julianna*, instead of *Jules*, he was *Edward*, instead of *Effie*—at least he had not addressed her as *Miss Evans*—but she didn't care for it one bit.

She also didn't care for his report. He had seen an underwhelming rock. The Effie she knew would have made up a fanciful story about the rock's origins, or invested it with imaginary powers.

And sea-bathing had been "refreshing"? That was the best her favorite poet could do?

Sea-bathing was not refreshing! It was life-changing. Profound. She still remembered what he'd said when he'd been trying to convince her to go the first time. *Water cures you. Not in the way the doctors yap on about. In a deeper way. You float on it—in it— and are reminded of how the world should be.*

Where was *that* Effie?

The answer to that question sat like the Goldstone in her gut. That Effie was gone because she had banished him. Now she had Edward, who called her Julianna and reported on superficialities.

And not a word about the shilling, which she assumed was meant to cover the cost of her next letter to him. She could send several for that sum.

She wanted to rail at the unfairness of it all. That he was being like this, so formal and distant, was maddening. But she couldn't by rights be angry with him. It wasn't his fault he'd . . . fallen in love.

She assumed. Effie had never spoken any words of love; his bird had.

Effie's *actions* had spoken of love, though. His tenderness and the obvious delight he had taken in her company. The way he'd cut his magnificent hair as if it were nothing, simply because it bought them some time alone.

She understood why he was holding himself back in this letter, why his words felt so superficial.

She had told him she was too busy for an affair. She *was* very busy. But all the same, that had been a lie. She hadn't seen a way to explain her reticence to him. She had only just discovered for herself the source of her unease.

No, the source of her *fear*. Here, alone, she should call it what it was. If she took up with Effie, he would eventually leave her. He would have to. On the evening of their final coming together, she had remarked outright that he would need an heir. He hadn't contradicted her, had replied with an "*I suppose*" that had been almost Edith-esque in its offhandedness.

An earl in need of an heir didn't marry a woman like Julianna. Even if he did, if he *could*, she wouldn't want that. All the practical reasons she had recited to him regarding her opposition to marriage—her inability to take on debt in her own name, for example—remained true.

But what was also true, and what explained why she couldn't entertain even a time-limited dalliance with him as she had with Charles, was that she was afraid of the pain that would necessarily accompany the end of such a dalliance. As with Edith, Effie would leave her to marry someone else. It was one thing to have one's heart broken, but to watch the breaker hie off and get married to someone else was not something Julianna could do a second time.

Bloody marriage. It ruined everything.

It was better that they go back to being friends. Effie was her dearest friend in all the world, and the intensity of their bond had confused her such that things had spilled over. It was time to tidy up that spill. She needed her friend back.

She set the shilling on its edge and spun it. How could she make that happen?

Dear Effie,

She refused to call him Edward.

If you should care to write a poem about your underwhelming Druidic stone, consider it commissioned. You may think I am in jest, but December is looking a little slim. I am not sure the American alligators we spoke about will make it in time.

Your shilling was a surprise. While I did agree that you might use your father's money to fund our correspondence, you have overestimated my epistolary endurance. It would take me days to write a letter long enough to cost that much! But I thank you for your generosity. It is very like you.

Do you know that the first night I was back at home, as I lay in my familiar bed and closed my eyes, I could have sworn I was still rocking in the waves? In some ways, I am right back at it with the magazine, but in other ways, it has been wrenching to be here, rather than in Brighton. Rather than in the sea.

She almost added "Rather than with you," but she stopped herself. Her aim was to get their friendship back on solid footing, not to lead him on. Not to lead *herself* on—not to want what she couldn't have.

I was so pleased to receive your letter. I hope you will write me again and tell me about any other mediocre rocks you might have encountered in my absence.

Yours,

JE

P.S. What about a geology column? Is that a good idea, or would engravings of rocks be orders of magnitude more disappointing than the real thing?

Chapter 14

Dream On

After Effie returned from his holiday, two curious things happened.

First, he and Julianna began writing to each other.

Well, it wasn't so much that they *began,* he supposed, for they'd been corresponding for years. But they . . . began anew. A few days after he arrived home, he received a slightly more formal than usual but perfectly warm letter from Jules. She'd done a better job than he in striking the right tone. She'd started out with some small talk about the magazine, but by the end she was confessing to being discombobulated by her re-entry into society. He felt the same.

And then there had been:

Yours,
JE

As with the first time she had signed off with her initials, a shiver ran through him. The sight of those two letters implied a familiarity he would never cease to find thrilling.

He got out his supplies and sat down to write her back.

He did consider that perhaps he should not be so easily won over. That last night in Brighton, he had all but begged, even in the face of her rejection, that they should remain friends, and resume their correspondence. He had said he would write to her, and so he had. But a bit of time and distance had him questioning whether he could in fact be her letter-writing friend. Whether it was wise to remain entangled with her in any form. He had his pride to consider. And his poor heart.

But here was her letter. She was so intelligent, so charming, so *herself.* Case in point: a geology column. What an absurd, wonderful idea. If anyone could make rocks interesting, it would be Julianna.

And so it began again, back and forth, and rather furiously, too, letters being exchanged almost every day. She often wrote him two pages, which she had never done before. He sent her another shilling. She protested that she hadn't spent through the first yet, but he wanted her to have the means to write him a novel if she so chose.

One day, about a fortnight after he'd returned to Town, a letter arrived in which she asked about his nightmares. Had they come back?

They had.

Not as intensely as before. He had not unearthed any new memories, though—no more nightmares-that-actually-happened. He was redreaming some of the old ones, the wardrobe imprisonment in particular. Curiously, the more he had the dream, the less distressed he felt upon awakening. It was almost as if the dream were working its way out of his system, as if, as Julianna had suggested might happen, the riverbed was running dry.

Since her query about the nightmares had seemed genuinely meant, he told her a little bit about the new-old nightmare. She queried some more. He told some more. She wrote some more.

What if you could change the dream?

He put the letter down. She had taken leave of her senses. He shook his head and returned to it.

I know you are going to think I've taken leave of my senses.

He laughed. They were attuned as ever.

But consider what I am about to say as a thought experiment. You say the wardrobe nightmare is back, but that it is less intense than before.

Years ago, my father ran a series of essays on the ancient Greeks. I can't say they were overwhelmingly popular, and he only ran three installments in a planned six-part series. I had a niggling sense that there was something in one of them about dreaming. I went into the archives and sure enough, there was this quote from Aristotle:

"Often when one is asleep, there is something in consciousness which declares that what then presents itself is but a dream."

And that book I told you about, the one from which I learned my flame-visualizing exercise, makes mention of the ancient practice of Yoga nidra, which, as far as I understand it—which admittedly isn't very far—is the cultivation of a state of consciousness between waking and sleeping.

Here we have two suggestions, from disparate places and cultures, that it might be possible for a dreamer to be aware that he is dreaming.

I wonder, could control follow awareness?

In other words, is there a way for you to realize that you're dreaming while you're dreaming, and if so, can you then change the outcome of said dream? Could you, say, open the wardrobe from the inside and simply walk out? Remove yourself to somewhere calming. Perhaps go for a swim (for this incident took place at your family's country estate, yes?).

Again, I realize I probably sound daft. But one of the lovely things about you is that I can say anything to you.

He set the letter down again, astounded by its contents.

Could he do as she suggested?

Well, he could certainly try. How, though? He returned to reading.

The question is, how would one attempt to enter into a dream with awareness that one was dreaming?

Another laugh, at how alike they remained in their thinking.

I haven't the faintest idea. I tried for myself, thinking that perhaps if I made an attempt, I might be better positioned to advise you. I have been dreaming of my father since Brighton. I haven't told you this, and I'm not sure why, apart from the fact that I am inexplicably sheepish about it. Then in turn annoyed, for what, I ask myself, is there to be sheepish about? It would seem a perfectly ordinary thing for a person to dream of one's beloved departed father.

I have been having the same dream almost nightly, and it manages to be both extraordinary and mundane at the same time. In it, I arrive at the office in the morning to find my father there, just as he used to be, although in those days we would have traveled together from our shared home. We used to have desks pushed up against each other so that when we sat in them, we faced each other. I still have those two desks, but after Father passed, I moved his to a corner of the room. It hurt too much to have it in my direct line of vision, to have to perpetually be reminded of his absence.

In the dream, he is at his desk in the old spot carrying out routine tasks related to the magazine. In one dream, he will be marking up a story. In another, he is bent over the accounts. So in that sense, the dream differs night to night.

What does not differ is that I am overwhelmed with sentiment to see him. I call his name. He looks up, and I realize he is the same age as when he died a decade ago. I have aged, but he has not. We are still father and daughter, but not in the same way as before. I have gained on him, which is a rather uncanny sensation.

He smiles at me. We are happy to see each other. I go to

him, exclaiming, but I can't quite reach his side. Something invisible stops me. He seems to know what it is and opens his mouth, presumably to explain, but no sound comes out. He seems surprised by his muteness and tries again, to the same (lack of) effect.

The dream takes a sinister turn then as he keeps attempting and failing to speak. I, however, can speak, and I begin to question him. How are you here? What are you trying to say? I bombard him, even though I know my queries, and his inability to answer, are distressing him.

Last night, after I blew out my candle, I closed my eyes and tried to see an awake version of the dream. I pretended I was mounting a stage play and Dream Julianna was an actress I could direct. In my dream play, Dream Julianna sat down across from her father and greeted him calmly. Then he told Dream Julianna whatever it was he'd been trying to say.

I fell asleep, and I had the dream again, but it didn't follow the script I'd "written" while awake. Perhaps you shall have better luck than I.

Effie put down the letter, overcome—by the recounted dream, by the fact that she had shared it so readily, by her attempt to influence it so she could help him with *his* dreams.

He would try her method, he decided.

The second curious thing that happened was that Effie went to a ball.

It was an annual late-October soiree of some renown held by the Duchess of Edenshire. Sarah had written him from Italy—an unusual occurrence, as the siblings didn't generally correspond—and begged him to attend. She had planned to go herself, but Mother and Father had decided they were staying on in Italy for at least an extra fortnight. Since Sarah could not go, she entreated Effie, would he please do so and report back? Would he pay particular attention to the following gentlemen? What did they wear, with whom did they dance, that sort of thing.

Effie had no desire to attend the ball, but how could he say no? Sarah, quite a bit younger than he, was heading into her second Season, and he could appreciate that she was, to use her words, "stuck in Italy with our parents, and one can eat only so many olives and see so many ruins before one goes slightly mad."

"This is only the second ball I've attended in months," Effie remarked when they were en route in Archie's coach. Clementine, having learned Effie was bound for the same ball she, Archie, and Olive were attending, insisted he ride with them. He resolved not to repeat the mistakes he had made last time. No dancing with any lady more than once. No playing cards with Mr. Lansing. In fact, he would avoid the game rooms altogether.

"I know, and I am told that's very out of character for you," Clementine said. "By all accounts, you used to be a lover of parties and spectacles and what have you."

It was true. Effie used to like nothing more than a party, a ball, a musicale. Somewhere to see and be seen. Flowers, music, wine. He used to consider it all food for the senses.

"And he used to be off to Vauxhall at least weekly," Archie said.

"What happened?" Clementine asked.

What happened was that he started staying home to write letters. Or reread letters. Or wait for letters to arrive. His focus had shifted from outward to inward. He had substituted ink for champagne.

"Nothing happened," Effie said blithely, "except that I suppose my tastes have changed."

"Well, you are going to be the star of this ball," Clementine said.

"Am I? Why?"

"I think what my sister is trying to say," Olive said, "is that you're an unmarried heir to an earl."

"And a handsome one at that," Clementine said.

"I wouldn't have said 'handsome,'" Olive said with a wink. "Especially with that ghastly haircut."

Olive was teasing, but she was right, about his popularity at least—Effie had no opinion on his own beauty or lack thereof—for he was mobbed from the moment he stepped in. Meddling mamas, mostly, and before he knew it, his name had been scrawled on more dance cards than he could count. He was struggling to put eyes on the gentlemen Sarah wanted him to observe.

"I think I have made a strategic error," he said to Archie a few hours in, when he had a blessed break in his dancing duties and stood by a punch bowl panting. "Perhaps more than one."

"Have you?" Archie said. Olive merely smirked.

"Yes, the first was in coming at all. The second was in not working in to conversation the lie that I won't be home the rest of the week. I fear I may be as mobbed by callers as I have been by the mothers of prospective dance partners." At least the Lansing siblings had not been in attendance.

In some ways, though, he was glad he'd come and had a miserable time. It had taken this ball to show him, once and for all, that he wasn't the man he used to be. Brighton had changed him.

"I say," Archie said, "have you decided what you want to do with the broken printing press that is still in my library?"

"Oh, dear." Effie had forgotten about poor Hamlet. "You may dispose of it."

"Are you certain?" Archie searched Effie's eyes in a way Effie struggled not to find annoying.

"I am certain. I have no further use for it."

Brighton had changed him, but it hadn't changed Julianna.

Mrs. Moyer knocked on Effie's bedchamber door a week later.

"I told you, I am not at home to callers," he called through the closed door. "I am not at home to callers unless it's Miss Olive Morgan," he clarified when Mrs. Moyer popped her head in. He had been trying—unfruitfully—Julianna's method of stage-directing his dreams, and he wanted to see what Olive made of it all, so he had invited her to call.

"It is Mr. Nancarrow, my lord," Mrs. Moyer said.

Effie's skin tightened. "Is my father with him?"

"He is not."

Hmm. Effie couldn't begin to think what Mr. Nancarrow wanted with him.

"Mr. Nancarrow," Effie said, joining him in the drawing room he'd been stashed in. "I am surprised to see you in Town when my parents aren't." He paused. "They are not, are they?"

"Your parents are still in Campagna."

Effie relaxed somewhat.

"My lord, you will forgive my abrupt appearance, but I must speak with you on a matter of some urgency."

"All right." Effie sat, feeling a twinge of nerves.

"I haven't known how—or whether—to broach this subject, but I think it is something you ought to know. It's a delicate matter. But you know you can trust me, because . . ."

"Because you made a printing press vanish at my behest."

"Yes." Mr. Nancarrow smiled, and there was something strangely reassuring about that smile, the way one corner turned up a little farther than the other.

"Your father is ill," Mr. Nancarrow said.

Oh. That wasn't what Effie had expected. "Has anyone called a doctor?"

"That is why he returned early from Italy after having made that initial trip. He had an episode of some sort there and came back here to consult with his doctors."

"He ought not to be traveling, then. He ought to choose Highworth or here and stay put so he can recover."

"He . . . is not going to recover. Which is why he went back to join your mother and sister."

"I beg your pardon?" Effie couldn't have heard that correctly. The Earl of Stonely was just fifty-three.

254 / JENNY HOLIDAY

"He is dying, my lord," Mr. Nancarrow said gently. "That is why they haven't come back. He is too ill to travel now."

Effie got to his feet, propelled upward by a silent tug as if he were a bird being carried on an air current. He grasped the back of the settee, momentarily concerned that he might actually take flight.

"I can see you're upset," Mr. Nancarrow said.

The truth was, Effie wasn't upset that his father was dying. Which was probably ill-done of him. The boy in the wardrobe would have been upset, but Effie was not. He was no longer that boy, he supposed. Which was itself a kind of triumph.

But if he was no longer that boy, and he was no longer the kind of man who enjoyed being the center of attention at balls, who was he?

"There's something else," Mr. Nancarrow said, his voice sounding uncharacteristically ragged.

"All right." Effie sat again, noticing that Mr. Nancarrow's hands, which were folded in his lap, were gripping each other so tightly his knuckles had gone white.

"I was born in Calecastle," Mr. Nancarrow said, naming the village closest to Highworth. Mr. Nancarrow jutted his chin out slightly. "My mother has no husband."

Had that chin jut been defensive? Did he think Effie was judging him? "Well, your mother's marital status is hardly your fault." Effie had to admit that his views on the matter had been shaped by his conversations with Julianna, and by his work as Mrs. Landers, and he was glad they had been.

"Some would say it matters not whose fault it is, that I bear the consequences of my mother's sin: I was born on the wrong side of the blanket, and that's all there is to it."

"Well, you've managed to make something of yourself. You went to university, did you not?"

"I did."

"What did you study?"

"Botany."

"See? Very impressive. I'm not sure how you managed that; it's really rather remarkable."

"I managed it because your father paid for it."

"He did?" Effie was, frankly, shocked. He had heard his father make unkind remarks about natural-born children before, and about the women who gave birth to them.

"He did. He always made sure I—and my mother—had what we needed."

"Well, that's rather surprising. I can't think why he would do that."

Mr. Nancarrow smiled, a little sadly, Effie thought. "Can't you?"

"I can think why anyone else would do it. Charity. Fellow-feeling." The possession of a functioning heart in one's chest. "But my father? No." There was no reason Effie could conjure to explain why his father would take such an interest in a by-blow, to the extent that he would send him to univ—

Oh, dear God. He looked closely at Mr. Nancarrow, and with a gasp, he understood. The lopsided smile that had soothed him: It was as if he were looking at a close relation of Sarah's. No. It wasn't *as if* he were looking at a close relation of Sarah's, he *was* looking at a close relation of Sarah's. Father had that sort of smile, too, where one side curled up farther than the other, though Father rarely smiled.

Effie, by contrast, took after his mother, had her dark hair and aquiline nose. Sarah—and Mr. Nancarrow—had ashy-blond hair. As had Father before his had gone white.

Effie examined his heart. His first response to this astonishing news was happiness. Mr. Nancarrow was a fine fellow. What would it be like to have a brother? A true brother?

Though of course he would not be a true brother in the legal sense of the word, but Effie didn't give a fig about that.

"I am sorry," Mr. Nancarrow said solemnly. He must have realized that Effie had got his meaning.

"Why are you sorry? None of it's your fault."

"I want to assure you that I have no designs on anything that isn't my right."

That was curiously phrased. Did Mr. Nancarrow have designs on something he believed *was* his right?

The idea pierced Effie like a bullet. If he'd been a bird borne up by a current before, now he'd been shot out of the sky by a hunter with deadly mark.

"Mr. Nancarrow," he said, speaking slowly despite the fact that his mind was reeling, "might I ask how old you are?"

"I am eight-and-twenty, my lord." He paused. "Like you."

"When were you born?"

"The eighth of January."

Mr. Nancarrow was six months older than Effie.

"Was my father married to your mother?"

If Mr. Nancarrow was legitimate, he was the next earl. Hope flared in Effie's chest, though he quickly extinguished it.

"They never married." He paused. "As far as I know."

Effie didn't know whether to be disappointed or relieved.

"Your father came round rather a lot when I was a child," Mr. Nancarrow continued, "and it wasn't to see me, if you get my meaning."

"I do indeed."

"I am sorry."

"I do wish you would stop apologizing!"

"I am sor—" Mr. Nancarrow clamped his mouth shut.

"My good man, were you about to apologize for apologizing?"

Mr. Nancarrow's sheepish smile became genuine, and they shared a chuckle, which went a significant way toward breaking the tension.

"I was happy when your father asked me to become steward of Highworth," Mr. Nancarrow, now clearly more at ease, said. "The work suits me, it pays well, and it confers a respectability that should allow me to marry someday, to have children, to . . . have a normal life."

To have a normal life. How lovely that sounded.

"He told me you were disinterested and disinclined to take the reins," Mr. Nancarrow said.

"He probably told you a great deal more than that," Effie said tersely.

"He did, and having had several occasions now to make your acquaintance, I question whether any of it was true."

Tears pricked the corners of Effie's eyes. Knowing that Mr. Nancarrow had taken the measure of him thusly was surprisingly moving.

Knowing that Mr. Nancarrow was his *brother* was surprisingly moving.

He cleared his throat. "I am disinterested, but that was not always the case."

"Ah," Mr. Nancarrow said, infusing an inordinate amount of understanding into that single syllable. If only Leander's single syllables were so empathic.

Effie wasn't sure why, but he opened his mouth and told Mr. Nancarrow everything. He recounted his childhood interest in learning about the estate and explained how his father always rebuffed his ideas. Rebuffed *him*. He shared a few examples of the childhood cruelties.

Through it all, Mr. Nancarrow listened. He listened deeply, studying Effie's face as if he were a fascinating painting, and when Effie was done, he said, "Thank you for telling me all this, my lord."

"You ought to drop the 'my lord.' We are brothers, are we not?"

We are brothers. How extraordinary.

"My friends call me Effie," he went on. "But if you don't care for that, you could call me Edward."

Mr. Nancarrow smiled. He really did have the nicest smile. On the surface of things, it was the same as Father's, but it managed to confer the opposite effect on its audience.

"And you should call me Kenver." The smile disappeared. "At least in private."

Oh. Yes. Effie supposed this was the part of the proceedings where the simple, profound joy of having discovered a brother would slowly be poisoned by the fact that they were sons of their specific father. "He is not prepared to acknowledge you, of course."

"I . . . don't know," Kenver said, though Effie hadn't meant his statement to be taken as a question. He'd have thought there was no way Father would acknowledge a by-blow, but he also wouldn't have expected Father to put a by-blow through university and retain him as his steward.

"I found a document that I am . . . concerned about." Kenver was speaking uncharacteristically haltingly. "That is why I'm here today. I want to show it to you."

The paper Kenver handed Effie was a lance through his chest. Dear God. "I thought you said my father—our father—and your mother were never married!"

"I did say that."

"But these are marriage lines!" A copy of the lines that would have been entered into the parish register book. The parish was the one encompassing Highworth, and the date before Effie's own parents' marriage.

Effie's mind reeled and his heart beat wildly. He closed his eyes and tried to see Julianna's flame. It worked, at least enough for his thoughts to un-jumble themselves and for his heart to slow. He opened his eyes. "If you made a claim with this at the Committee for Privileges, you'd be named heir."

"Possibly."

Effie eyed Mr. Nancarrow—he supposed he ought to revert to calling him Mr. Nancarrow now that it seemed he was being threatened. Blackmailed, perhaps.

The very idea made him want to weep. It was positively gutting to have had what felt like a breakthrough of fellow-feeling only to have it snatched away.

Well, the joke was on Mr. Nancarrow. Effie dropped the document on the table between them. "Well, have at it."

"I beg your pardon?"

"I don't want it. I don't want any of it—the title, the estate."

"If this plan of your father's were to succeed," Mr. Nancarrow said, "it would make him a bigamist in the eyes of society—and the law. It would mean you and your sister would be deemed il-legitimate. God knows what it would mean for your mother."

Effie hadn't thought of that, so carried away had he been by the momentary hope that he had stumbled on a way to escape his fate—and by the whiplash of having found a brother only to lose him—but of course Mr. Nancarrow was correct. Mother would have been quickening with Effie when Mr. Nancarrow was born. Effie wasn't close to his mother, but he did feel a pang of sympathy for her. He thought of Sarah, and her hope for the future, the list of gentlemen she'd prevailed upon him to spy on.

Effie was surprised by the extremes Father was apparently pre-pared to go to, though upon further reflection, he wasn't sure why. Was this any worse than locking a child in a wardrobe overnight?

"Why would he do this?" Kenver asked, his tone uncharacter-istically strident.

"Because he hates me. Were you not listening to the stories I told you earlier?"

Kenver's brow knit in confusion. "He hates you enough to ruin the rest of his family?"

"Yes. If it comes down to the family versus the title, the title wins every time."

"Even if it means having a bastard earl?"

"Better a bastard than me. But you *wouldn't* be a bastard; you would be the long-lost heir. Handsome and rich and eligible. And what does Father care about the rest of us if he's about to die?"

Effie tried to think, to encourage reason to rise above sentiment. He was as cornered as he'd ever been. He should not have told Mr. Nancarrow to have at it. He could not allow Father to ruin Sarah and Mother. So he would have to pay off Mr. Nancarrow. He'd have to allow himself to be blackmailed *and* he'd have to be earl.

And he would have to find a new steward, one as good as Mr. Nancarrow.

Effie straightened his spine and lifted his chin. "What do you want? Name your price."

"My lord, those are *forged* marriage lines!" Mr. Nancarrow cried, suddenly aghast. He gentled his tone. "I am almost certain of it. My apologies; I thought that part was clear. I should have led with that."

Effie took a breath, struggling to adjust to this new piece of information. "How can you tell? The parish is correct. The date is logical."

"Well, for one, I spoke to my mother about it."

Effie couldn't help but smile. "I suppose the good lady would remember a wedding."

"And the marriage lines are always given to the woman, are they not?" Mr. Nancarrow said.

"I . . . don't know."

"They are, proof of a married state being much more important to a woman than to a man."

"I see." Effie thought of Julianna, and her particular reasons for wanting to remain unmarried. He was beginning to understand how thoroughly women had to rely on their relationship, or lack thereof, to a husband to get what they wanted. "So you have come to me to tell me you do not want the riches that have effectively landed in your lap? Do you not want *anything*?" People were not this naturally good, were they?

"Well, perhaps . . ."

Aha. People were *not* this naturally good. "I will pay whatever you ask, give you whatever you like." Still, he appreciated that Kenver had come to him.

"What I would like is . . . to have a brother."

Effie shook his head, scarcely able to believe his ears. "You had an earldom in your grasp, man!"

"I don't want an earldom. I just want to be happy."

Astonishing. "You don't think an earldom would make you so?" He could sympathize.

"I think what makes men happy is honest work. Family and friends. I have the former. I could use more of the latter."

Effie hardly knew what to say.

"My lord—"

"Effie," Effie corrected. "Or Edward."

Kenver dipped his head. "Effie. My intent in coming here was to assure you I plan to destroy this document."

"But is that document all there is?"

"I have searched high and low at Highworth and found nothing else that might be associated with this plot. But looking back at the year or so, I am reinterpreting a number of conversations I've had with your father—"

"Our father," Effie corrected. "I am sorry to keep interrupting you, but when we are alone, I should like us to call things what they are."

Effie was graced with another lopsided smile. "Our father. He has said a few things I now see as evidence that he was planning something like this. But I believe he thought he had more time."

"Yes, let's talk about that." Effie had momentarily lost sight of the fact that this conversation had begun with news of his father's imminent death. "You will forgive me my lack of sentiment, but what is the matter with him, and do you know how much time he has?"

"He has a disease of the liver. Apparently his condition worsened when he was abroad initially. When he came back here, he said it was because he wanted to consult his London doctors. But he appeared at Highworth for a night. I now wonder if it was to place that"—he nodded at the document that still rested between them—"among his papers. I am quite familiar with the contents of his office, and I can confidently say it was not there before. He then announced his intention to return to Italy for the rest of the planned holiday. Your mother has since written me that he has worsened yet again and they are unable to travel and so have extended their stay. She did not outright say it, but the implication was that when she and your sister return, it shall be without your father. Our father. She told me he wished me to look in a certain drawer in his desk and that he trusted I would do the right thing with what I found there."

"So you were meant to find the false document and use it to seize the title." Effie paused. "Did my father know you at all?"

Kenver shrugged.

"Clearly not," Effie said, "though in an ironic twist, if there *were* a way for you to seize the title without ruining my mother and sister, I would be quite happy for you to do so."

"Would you truly? It is difficult to fathom."

"I would." Effie, reasoning that he had already told Kenver almost everything, decided to finish the job. "I am in love with a woman named Julianna Evans." He smiled, thinking of Leander's recitations of the same. "She is completely unsuitable on a number of fronts. She is also completely wonderful on a number of fronts."

He went on to tell Kenver the rest. Well, he omitted the details of their intimate encounters, but he told him about the letters, about having met for the first time in person in Brighton, about the age and class gaps, and about Julianna's adamant opposition to the institution of marriage.

"Because of that last point," he finished, "it matters not at all, but if I were a normal sort of man, not an earl, I wonder if I could convince her to . . . be with me in some fashion."

"But you're not a normal sort of man. You are a man in a cage, as surely as your macaw is in one."

"Yes." Kenver understood. "Which is why if you wanted to present your claim to the earldom and it was only I who would bear the consequences, I would be quite happy for you to do so."

"I cannot lie to a committee of Parliament," Kenver said. "I have taken genuine pleasure and pride in overseeing Highworth, but I don't want any of it under false pretenses."

Effie sighed. "I know you don't." He had been thinking earlier, how quickly Kenver had taken the measure of him. It seemed the reverse was true, too. They knew each other, somehow. Perhaps it was because they were brothers. He kept returning to that single astonishing fact.

"There is more," Kenver said.

"Oh, splendid."

Kenver smiled sadly and said, "Your observation about the parish and dates being plausible is correct. During our father's sudden return to England a month ago, he also had me arrange a meeting with the vicar."

Ah. "I grasp what you are implying." The vicar at Highworth was new, a young man who had only recently been awarded the living—the living provided by Father. "The marriage lines would have been entered into the parish registry book."

"And if they were not at the time of the marriage, which they almost certainly were not, I imagine they are now."

"As if by magic," Effie said wryly.

"Or by money," Mr. Nancarrow said, matching Effie's tone.

Effie couldn't help but chuckle. He liked Mr. Nancarrow's forthrightness. "Can you check the book?"

"I have been trying to figure a way to do so. I think I shall be able to manage something. In the meantime, I wanted you to know what was afoot, for I have no idea what more your father—our father—is planning. Will he indeed die in Italy? Will he somehow rally enough to come home and wreak havoc here? How much does your mother know?"

"To your last question, I expect she knows nothing. Historically, my mother has acquiesced to our father in all matters, but I can hardly see her aiding in the destruction of her own life and that of her unmarried daughter, so I suspect he has not made her privy to his plot. To your other questions, I know not. I suppose all we can do is wait and see."

"Should I destroy this?"

"I think you should hold on to it. If he does come home, perhaps you can assure him that you have understood his intent."

"I was thinking that would be the best course of action. Let him think his plot will be successful. Then when he is . . . gone, we will destroy this document."

"Mm."

"In the meantime, I had thought to give you this." He handed over a leather pouch.

"What is it?"

"All the money I have in the world. Well, all that I have save what I need for the next month. I've been saving diligently. I have been wanting to buy my mother a little cottage, one that's not . . ."

"Paid for by our father," Effie supplied. He understood. "Why would you give me this?"

"So you know you can trust me."

Effie did trust Kenver, but he appreciated that Kenver's honor demanded he accept—temporarily—the promissory gesture. "All right. I shall keep this safe for you."

Kenver nodded. "And I shall keep the forged document safe for you."

"For the record, I should like to say that when Father is gone, I . . ." Effie trailed off, unsure if it was safe to speak around Kenver the way he spoke around Archie and Simon, expressing sentiment that for some inexplicable reason was regarded by society as unmanly. Well, why not? If they were to be in each other's lives in any meaningful way, which Effie very much hoped they were, Kenver would eventually catch on to what sort of person Effie was. He cleared his throat and spoke confidently, if a bit defensively. "I should very much like to have a brother generally, and to have you for a brother especially. I shall be proud to call you mine."

There went the lopsided smile again, though it was quite a bit bigger than before. "I should like that, too, more than you know. I have never had any family, apart from my mother, who—" It was Kenver's turn to clear his throat, and Effie realized with a start that this conversation was making Kenver feel as sentimental as it was Effie. "I was going to say that I should very much like you to meet my mother, though I know that is impossible."

"Impossible? It would seem the opposite. She is in Calecastle, is she not? While we should perhaps wait until our father has passed, once that has occurred, it would seem the easiest thing in the world for me to meet her next time I am at Highworth. In fact, I should like to make a trip for the express purpose of meeting her as soon as it is convenient for you both."

"You would?"

Effie smiled. It seemed he had managed to astonish the unflappable Kenver Nancarrow. "I would. I believe I am familiar with this sentiment of wanting one person you care about to meet another person you care about. In my case, I have never been close to my family of origin, though Sarah and I are, I think, fond of each other in a distant, vaguely exasperated sort of way. I consider my real family to be my close friends, the Earls of Marsden and Harcourt. I should be honored to introduce you to them. Properly, I mean, not just standing in the foyer while we plot to hide a printing press."

Kenver lowered his head on an exhalation. Effie supposed no one had ever been honored to introduce Kenver to anyone, given the circumstances of his birth. When he raised it again, he said, "I can think of nothing I'd like more than to meet your friends properly."

Chapter 15

True Colors

Julianna's life had returned to its previous rhythms on both its major fronts: the magazine and Effie.

The November issue had come and gone and she'd been quite satisfied with it. December was in hand. The American alligators had not come in early enough, alas, but she had resigned herself to swapping in the Great Tea Debate. Julianna and Mr. Glanvil were arguing about color plates. In other words, magazine life continued apace.

On the other side of things: Julianna and Effie had resumed their correspondence.

It was curious, though, that she thought of her life as having two major fronts. For so long there had been only one: *the magazine above all*. But, she reminded herself, friendship was important. After that initial dose of formality bordering on frostiness in Effie's first—first new—letter, she and Effie had regained their previous degree of intimacy. Everything was well. Except . . .

Everything was also very unsettled.

Which was curious, because she never used to feel that way. Her work fulfilled and stimulated her. She loved her sister and her sister's family, even if living with them was sometimes awkward. She had been happy with and proud of the life she had made for herself and had felt settled. Rooted.

She no longer felt that way. In fact, she felt the opposite: restless. Easily distracted. The world seemed drabber than it used to, as if it were a plate in need of the color that Mr. Glanvil would not allow.

She suspected she knew what was wrong: it was the dream. The one in which Father visited the office and seemed to want to tell her something but found himself unable to speak. She had it nearly every night now. Her advice to Effie regarding controlling one's dreams had been featherbrained. It didn't work at all.

"Hello? Jules?"

But perhaps Effie had managed to get it to work? To invade *her* dreams? For she must be dreaming now. There was no way Effie was here, in her office, at two o'clock on a dreary Thursday in early November.

"Miss Evans, I have come to seek your counsel regarding my treatise on the Pavilion."

Hmm. Unless Effie had managed to bring a friend with him on his nocturnal wanderings, Julianna was not, in fact, dreaming, for that last sentence had come from Lord Marsden.

She rose unsteadily from her desk. "Goodness. Effie. Lord Marsden." She was flustered. Julianna had never been flustered in her life.

Effie looked . . . different. Still himself—he was wearing a scarlet waistcoat embroidered with black thread—but he was blurry.

"I say, Jules, what a smashing eyepiece. You look like a scientist, or a deep-sea explorer."

Oh, yes. Effie was blurry because she was wearing a magnifying glass fashioned in the style of a monocle over one eye—she used it to proofread stories because she had discovered she found errors more reliably when she examined the text up close.

She fumbled it off, and the gentlemen came into focus.

"I know you're up to your eyeballs in December, perhaps literally." Effie quirked a smile. "But Simon was agonizing over his assignment—something to do with parapets, I think?—and, knowing I would be no help, I suggested we call on you."

She wasn't sure what to say. On the one hand, she was so unaccountably happy to see him. It was all she could do to refrain from throwing her arms around him. On the other hand, she had asked that they not see each other in person anymore, and here he was, on the flimsiest of excuses. On the third hand—and she was well aware that she did not have three hands—the Pavilion story was going to be a centerpiece of a future issue, and she welcomed the opportunity to shape it.

"Mind you," Effie continued when she did not speak, "initially I'd thought he said *parakeets*, and I was well-prepared to opine on that topic, but no, it turns out a parapet does not fly through the air and chirp, so I lost interest."

Effie was speaking blithely but eyeing her closely. He opened his mouth again, as if to keep rambling—he was talking because he knew she was discomfited and was buying her time.

She gathered herself and said to Lord Marsden, "We also have to decide what to do about your byline, my lord."

"Speaking of December, is this it?" Effie walked over to a large table covered with papers, each marked with a number, in a spread-out mock-up of the issue.

"Yes."

He walked around, eyeing the pages. "Where is the famous sunrise dress? As I've said, I do adore your year-end fashion spread."

"So do my readers. The Christmas issue always sells well, and while Mr. Glanvil thinks it is because of our Lord and Savior, I think it's because of the dresses."

Lord Marsden snickered. Julianna went to stand next to Effie and pointed at the dress he was asking about. "See this ruffle? It is meant to be a kind of transitional color between the orange and yellow I told you about. A sort of apricot shade, if you will."

Effie cooed appreciatively. "So you will have that plate colored, I suppose."

"I thought to. Mr. Glanvil won't allow it, though, as he favors coloring an illustration that will accompany a piece on Christmas tabletop ornamentation."

"A pity."

"Yes, but it is an improvement on his initial plan, which was to reserve color for the nativity scene. I made quite the impassioned speech to try to save the sunrise dress. *The nativity scene, which we have all seen a hundred versions of in a hundred different places, including last year in this very magazine, is to be in color, but the triumph of the Season in Paris, which was a fleeting moment, is relegated to black and white?* I asked. He responded by offering the compromise of using color for the tabletop piece. I thought it a modest triumph. The holly-bedecked branch of candles will make for a striking illustration. I console myself that the sunrise dress has enough embellishments that it will render well enough in black and white. At least I am not wasting color yet again on the Holy Family and assorted barn animals."

Lord Marsden chuckled, startling Julianna. She had forgotten that she and Effie were not alone. She turned to Lord Marsden. "My lord, may I have a look at what you've brought me?"

The two of them sat together, and as Julianna skimmed the draft, she was vaguely aware of Effie poking around the office.

After she and Lord Marsden were done discussing his piece, Effie asked, "Who are your neighbors? A dressmaker downstairs, I saw. And it seems you have a solicitor across the hall. But what about above?"

"Flats."

"Who lives there?"

"Professionals, mostly. The solicitor you mentioned. The dressmaker from downstairs along with her husband, who owns the building."

He performed one of his single Effie claps. "Well, Simon, if Jules has got you all straightened out, we ought to be going."

That was it? He had arrived in her office like a cyclone, and now that she'd sorted Lord Marsden, he was leaving?

Although perhaps he hadn't come in like a cyclone. Perhaps she'd only felt him as such. He had been calm and perfectly measured in his demeanor. Friendly. Because they were friends.

You can't miss what you don't let yourself want.

Her old adage surfaced in her mind, but it had long ago ceased to be true.

What Julianna wanted, she decided over the next week—what she wanted and could actually have—was company.

"I miss Father," she said to Amy one afternoon when she'd knocked off early and sought out Amy only to find her in the garden dyeing a dress from last Season. A yellow muslin was becoming navy—refashioning garments was one of Amy's particular talents.

"I miss Mother," Amy said, surprising Julianna.

"Why don't you go see her?"

"Why doesn't she come see us?" Amy countered.

"I . . . don't know." It was odd, now that she thought about it, how rarely Mother visited.

"It is much easier for her to travel here than for me to pack the children up and go to her." Amy stirred the dark water in the washbasin rather more aggressively than seemed called for. "It's one thing for you to go on your own, but it's harder for me."

Julianna felt guilty for having lied to her sister, but not guilty enough to confess. "It is indeed easy for Mother to come here, yet she never does," she observed. "She didn't even come for Christmas last year. Why do you think that is?"

"The truth? I don't think she likes the children."

Julianna started to protest, but Amy cut her off.

"Mind you, I believe she loves them, but I don't think she enjoys spending time with them, and Oliver is rather a handful. I don't think she's constitutionally suited to babies. I hold out hope that as they get older, she might take more of an interest in them, as she seemed to do with us."

Julianna never would have come to this conclusion on her own, but now that Amy had pointed out this tendency of Mother's, it could not be denied. Mother had been somewhat distant when

Julianna was young, but Julianna had put that down to having had more in common with Father.

"I am sorry," Julianna said, and she meant it. "It must be terrible to be missing a beloved parent who is nearby yet . . . absents herself." She tripped over her own words.

"I miss Father, too, of course, but in a different, less immediate way. It was Mother I spent all my time with. It was always Mother and me, and Father and you. I'm sorry you still miss him so terribly."

"It isn't that I still miss him, although I do, it's more that he's been . . . on my mind lately."

"How so?"

Julianna told Amy about the dream, though to do so did not come naturally. "And that's how it always ends," she finished, "with him trying and failing to speak."

"You are probably trying to say something to yourself."

"I beg your pardon?"

"Well, it isn't as if you believe Father is actually trying to speak to you." She set down her paddle. "Do you?"

"No."

"Say that as if you mean it." Amy laughed, but not unkindly.

Julianna smiled. "Of course I don't think he's trying to tell me something in a literal way. He isn't sitting on a cloud looking down at us. I just . . . never considered your interpretation. But now that I have, I believe you are correct."

"So the question is, what are you trying to tell yourself?"

"I don't know."

"Sister, may I ask why you are here today?"

"I live here."

"Yes, but why are you here in the middle of the day on a Thursday? It's unlike you."

Julianna's chest had felt heavy all day. "I think I am lonely." Either that or she had come down with consumption.

"Oh, Julie." Amy laid a hand on Julianna's arm. "You've chosen a lonely life."

Was Amy referring to Julianna's refusal to marry, or the fact that her chosen vocation required such an investment of time? It hardly mattered, for the point stood. Julianna suppressed her habitual reaction, which was to bristle, to be defensive, and considered that not only did Amy mean well, she had spoken the truth.

"Yes, I suppose I have. The rub is that it's never felt lonely before." Julianna used to spend hours alone in the office not even noticing the passage of time.

"What's different now?"

Everything.

"Nothing."

"Well, I am delighted to see you with the sun shining down on your lovely face. I am so fatigued come evening. It's rare that we get to spend time together without Arthur or the children, and I should like to do more of it."

"Truly?" Julianna was touched.

"Yes. Perhaps that is what you are trying to tell yourself in the guise of Father. *Spend more time with your sister.*" She had lowered her voice as if imitating Father on that last bit, and they both laughed.

A fanciful idea landed, made a little dent in the rock in Julianna's chest. "Do you think I could dye the ribbon on my bonnet navy? I could run and get it now."

Amy agreed, and a few minutes later she plopped said ribbon into her cauldron. "I'm not sure going from gray to navy is going to make much of a difference, if a change is what you're after."

"I just thought it would be a little less drab. And I have that navy spencer."

"Oh, yes, it will look smart with the spencer."

"But I think I would like a change. Perhaps it is time to have a new dress made."

"Oh, yes! And may I suggest a departure from your usual palette?"

"By which you mean 'not gray.'"

"By which I mean 'not gray,' Amy confirmed. "Green would be just the thing. It would go so well with your eyes."

Julianna was wearing her new moss-green dress three weeks later when Effie came back. Once again, he was not alone. He was accompanied by Lords Marsden and Harcourt and two ladies.

"Hullo, Miss Evans."

She managed to be less flustered by his appearance this time.

"We are here to paint page four," he said blithely.

Julianna shot to her feet from where she had been sitting at her desk—so much for less flustered. "Pardon?"

"The more I thought about it, the more I couldn't abide the sunrise dress being rendered in black and white. Won't Mr. Glanvil be surprised that there are two color pages in this issue?" He tilted his head as Julianna gaped at him. "Though perhaps it might be better to give him a copy without the dress colored."

Julianna remained unable to find words, but it didn't seem to matter, for Effie kept speaking. "I've brought some friends. 'Many hands make light work'—isn't that something people say? I know the magazines are coming off the press today. What would normally happen after that? Do they somehow get posted from the printing house? They mustn't, though, because they have to be colored. I admit I don't know what the normal process is, but I am keen to learn."

Effie proceeded to introduce her to the Countess of Harcourt, and her sister, Miss Olive Morgan.

Julianna was stunned. So much so that she forgot to curtsy. Or to blink. She still could not speak.

"In summation," Effie said, "I propose we get as many copies of December here as we can, and get to work."

"We brought fortifications," Miss Morgan said, setting a picnic basket on Julianna's desk and pulling from it a bottle of wine.

"Perhaps that is better saved for when we are done," Lady Harcourt said. "I have never undertaken this kind of work, but

I imagine a steady hand is needed—perhaps wine and watercolor don't mix."

Miss Morgan responded to her sister's supposition by producing a glass. "Oh, pish."

Everyone looked at Julianna then, all of them all at once, as if they were a flock of birds flying as one and she their leader.

Overwhelmed by . . . everything, Julianna ordered herself to find her voice. She elected to answer Effie's question of fact. "I have a few dozen copies of December here, and the rest are at the printer, but I could have them delivered here."

"Splendid." Effie performed his signature single clap. "And I for one would adore a nip of wine." He came close to Julianna and whispered, "I've brought my January Mrs. Landers letters, too, though I don't know why I'm whispering. Everyone here with the possible exception of the countess knows I am she."

Much to-ing and fro-ing followed. The gentlemen moved stacks of magazines into piles on the desks and table. The countess distributed paintbrushes and watercolor sets. Miss Morgan poured wine.

Once they were situated, each person furnished with a beverage and a paintbrush, there was another lull in activity and conversation, and Julianna realized everyone was looking to her to say something.

All she could think of to say was "You lovely, lovely people."

And, belatedly, once she had a paintbrush in hand, "I have no idea how to do this."

"I thought you'd say that," Effie said, "but how hard can it be? Didn't you once tell me that your previous printer had his children doing color work?"

"You are the painter among us," Julianna said. "I propose you make an initial attempt, and if successful, the rest of us shall mimic you."

"Olive ought to do it. She has quite the eye. You should see some of her embroidery."

And so they began, Julianna huddling with Miss Morgan and reading aloud a description of the dress. Together they consulted on color gradients, and in short order Julianna was contemplating a beautiful version of the sunrise dress.

"I can see why it's called the sunrise dress," the countess said as they all began attempting to reproduce Miss Morgan's efforts.

"I don't think it is called that in any official capacity," Julianna said. "It's just a moniker that came to mind when I read the textual description of the dress."

"'Tis Miss Evans's innovation," Effie said, and everyone agreed that it was the perfect name for the dress.

Soon, each person was bent over a stack of magazines. The countess and the gentlemen were seated at the large worktable and Miss Morgan and Julianna side by side at Julianna's desk, which afforded them a little privacy. How novel to meet Miss Morgan, about whom Julianna had heard so much—both in Brighton and via Effie's letters.

"I am so glad to finally meet you, Miss Evans," Miss Morgan said. "For I have heard so much about you."

Julianna laughed. "I was just thinking the same thing."

"I am mad for your magazine, you know."

"Oh! Are you?"

"Yes, even before Lord Featherfinch relayed your inquiry about whether I would write an article about Turin—and I will, happily; nothing has ever flattered me more than being asked—I was a regular reader." She leaned in and whispered, "I was a regular reader even before I understood I ought to be paying special attention to the *poetry* you print." She hitched her head toward her sister, and mouthed, "She doesn't know."

"Really?" Julianna whispered, "I'd have thought since Lord Featherfinch has told his friends about his poetical bent, and one of those friends is her husband, that the lady would know."

"No." Miss Morgan performed another gestural nod, this one aimed at the gentlemen. "Those three would sooner die than betray each other's confidences. They're very loyal that way."

They were, weren't they? How lovely. How lucky.

"Miss Evans, would you care to come to tea sometime?"

"Yes, I would like that very much."

She really would. She hoped it was not one of those "invitations" that was merely a vague suggestion of a future event unaccompanied by any specifics suggesting that the event would actually occur.

"Would Saturday at four o'clock suit? Please tell me if that isn't ideal. Lord Featherfinch tells me you work long hours. I, by contrast, am a lazy lie-about, so if you counter-propose a time that better meets with your approval, I am certain I can accommodate."

Julianna felt herself flush with pleasure as she said, "Saturday at four suits just fine, thank you."

Julianna could scarcely believe she had two earls, a viscount, a countess, and a sister to a countess coloring her magazine. And a tea date Saturday with the latter.

"I say, this is rather nice," Lord Harcourt said. "Calming. Pleasantly repetitive. It focuses the mind."

"Like your beads," Effie said.

"Perhaps better than my beads." Lord Harcourt explained to Julianna, "I have a string of beads I use to help settle my mind. It is superficially akin to the rosaries of the Catholics, though it does not hold any religious significance. I find the repetitive nature of moving the beads calming."

"Well, my lord, you are welcome anytime, and I shall give you repetitive calming tasks."

They worked late into the evening, and as the piles of magazines shrank, so too did the heaviness in Julianna's chest.

Chapter 16

Daydream Believer

"I have met your Miss Evans for tea," Olive said on Sunday, sweeping into the drawing room Effie was sitting in pretending to read.

"She's not *my* Miss Evans, and why did you not invite me?" Effie put down his prop book and smiled. He hadn't been able to read because he couldn't stop thinking about Julianna. He wanted to see her again, but if he couldn't do that—he had yet to come up with another excuse to visit her office—a secondhand account of time spent with her would be a compensatory way to pass an afternoon.

"I wanted to get the measure of her," Olive said.

"I've already told you the measure of her." But he would gladly tell her again.

"I know, but you'll forgive me for saying I wasn't certain I could trust you to be objective."

"How do you mean?"

"I say this with great affection, my dear friend, but you have been known to attach yourself to notions that are more fanciful than practical." As he began to object, she glanced pointedly down at his shoes—he was wearing the red heels.

Effie could not help but smile. "And? Did you find Miss Evans up to snuff?"

Olive's eyes danced. "I did indeed."

He would have been relieved except he knew there could have been no other outcome. "Perhaps I am overly vulnerable to fanciful ideas, or fashions"—he kicked up one of the red heels—"but my taste in people is beyond reproach. Shall I call for tea?"

"Yes, please."

Olive poured the tea when it came, and Effie sipped happily, once again relishing the prospect of talking about Julianna. He had spent ages *not* talking about her, *years*, and from this vantage point, he couldn't think why. "Isn't Miss Evans so intelligent?"

"She is, very."

"What did you talk about?"

"Oh, all kinds of things. I couldn't even begin to recount them. I think we have, in a short time, become genuine friends. Though I admit to being a trifle intimidated; she really is so very knowledgeable about so many things."

"Yet her erudite nature coexists so delightfully, so apparently congruously, with a flash of a whimsical disposition."

"I wonder if her whimsical disposition is reserved for you, for I did not witness it."

"Oh, do you think so?"

Olive set down her teacup. "Effie, have you told Miss Evans that you're in love with her?"

Effie set down his. "I have."

Or at least his macaw had.

The message had been delivered, was the point.

Olive clearly had not expected that answer, for she opened and closed her mouth a few times without any words coming out. Her interlude of muteness was followed by a great peal of laughter.

Effie laughed. Her mirth was contagious, even if he had yet to discover the source of it.

"I thought I was coming here to read you a stern lecture on the topic," she said when she'd recovered.

"Did you? Well, let's have it. I wouldn't want a stern lecture to go to waste."

"Oh, I can't deliver such a lecture now. We shall have to move on to plotting."

"Plotting?"

"Yes, for your happiness and that of your future bride."

"Clearly you and Miss Evans are not the bosom friends you believe yourselves to be if you haven't been enlightened as to why that is an impossibility."

"Your father can't be made to come around?"

"No, but it's got nothing to do with that." He went on to explain that despite the ways in which Julianna and he were entirely unsuitable as a match—despite the strait between them—the fact remained that she wouldn't have him. "She won't marry me," he finished. "She is vehemently, one might even say violently, opposed to the institution of marriage."

"Hmm." Olive twisted the string of her reticule as she stared into space. She did this sometimes, disappeared for a moment as she retreated into her scheming. "She won't *marry* you."

"Yes. That's what I just said."

You said it differently. "You said, 'She won't marry me,'" with each word given equal emphasis. I said, 'She won't *marry* you.'" She winked. "Do you catch my meaning?"

"I do catch your meaning, and I tried that already!"

"How so?"

"I proposed we continue to see each other. She has—" He'd been going to say 'She has done it before,' and though he was certain Olive would not be overly scandalized by that tidbit, it really wasn't his tid to bit. "She was not open to the suggestion." That still stung, that she had carried on with her prior lovers, for a time at least, but wouldn't do the same with him. "I assure you, I would have taken whatever was on offer. I still would."

Olive set down her cup, leaned forward across the table, and laid her arm on his sleeve. "Oh, Effie, I'm so very sorry."

He shrugged. "At least we have regained our previous friendship." They had, yes? "She was as warm as ever when we went to her to help with the coloring, was she not?" He suddenly required reassurance.

"She was very warm. I can't speak to 'as ever,' as that was the first time I'd seen you interact, but I got the sense of the two of you as long-standing . . . friends."

"And we are writing to each other more than ever. I daresay we are writing to each other *furiously*." It was enough. It would have to be.

She came around and sat next to him on the settee and laid her head on his shoulder. He slung an arm around her.

"You know what I appreciate about you, Olive?"

"I assume there are so many answers to that question that we'd be here all day if you were to recite them all."

"You understand heartbreak. You're a schemer, and a bit of a romantic, I daresay, beneath your blithe exterior, but you know when to fold. You know when a cause is hopeless."

She began to speak, but he cut her off. "It's not all doom and gloom, for although I have indeed lost the love of my life, it turns out I have gained a brother."

"I beg your pardon? Are you and the earls opening your brotherhood to another? That's rather hard to fathom."

"No. A long-lost brother." He hadn't been planning to tell anyone about Kenver yet, but he found himself moved to confide in Olive. "A literal one."

"What?" she shrieked.

"Indeed. He's been right under my nose for a while now, and it turns out he is rather wonderful."

He told her everything, and his bearing grew lighter as he did so. He was walking around with a broken heart, but the key bit was that he was walking around. He had the boys—and a new brother. He had Olive. He had a sister he probably ought to pay more attention to, and he resolved to do so when she came home. He had already written to her with his report of the ball.

He had Julianna, too, didn't he? His friend, Julianna. It would be enough. If he just kept walking around, perhaps his heart would mend, bit by bit.

"I feel that you are at a crossroads," Olive said.

"What do you mean?"

"Something is about to change. Perhaps you aren't going to get exactly what you want, but I have the oddest feeling that you are going to be all right. Better than all right."

It started the same way it always did, with disbelief. Incredulity. Surely, they hadn't locked him in the wardrobe and left? After an initial interlude of shouting and pounding on the inside of the door, Effie ceased his efforts. Father was trying to make a point. It would probably go better for him if he sat quietly for a while, ceased his struggling. Acted like a wayward boy who had learned his lesson.

It was a game. Effie was very good at games. He had in fact recently won a spillikins tournament at school, his patience and steady hand beating everyone, even that miserable toad Nigel Nettlefell. Even the graceful and dextrous Archie.

So he closed his eyes and counted as high as he could. He was somewhere in the hundred thousands when he opened them.

It was dark.

It had been dark before, of course, but it was *dark* now. The slice of light that had been visible around the edges of the door was no more, and he couldn't see his hand in front of his face.

It was cold, too. Usually his mother's room was toasty in the winter, its large fireplace kept perpetually stoked. Clearly, they'd let it go out.

Panic started to rise in his chest. It was the middle of the night. Where was Mother?

He still had the hat, though it had been destroyed in the tussle. He clutched its remains to his chest, trying to find the grosgrain ribbons he knew to be violet. He didn't need light to see them, and he thought stroking them might be calming. He closed his eyes and tried to make his mind fill in the images that should accompany what his fingers were feeling.

It worked for a while. Until it didn't, and the panic started creeping back.

He began knocking again on the inside of the door. Surely enough time had passed that someone would let him out.

Knocking became pounding, shouting became screaming, crying became hyperventilating.

He had to use the necessary. He was so hungry, so frightened, so cold.

Panic became terror as he began flailing about.

Flailing will not help.

He stopped moving. Looked around futilely. Where had that voice come from?

Get up.

He considered this voice. It was insistent but not unkind. He had never heard it before, yet it was familiar somehow.

Get up.

He got up.

Open the door.

He started to talk back. *I can't.*

He had already tried every possible means of escape. He had rattled, pushed, pounded. He had attempted to break down the door with his shoulder but had managed only to injure himself.

Open the door.

He stood, the wardrobe being just tall enough for him to do so. He reached his hand toward the door, and suddenly, oddly, there was a bit of light. It should have been impossible. The door was still closed. It was surely the dead of night.

But somehow, some way, there was just enough light for him to see that there was a hook and eye lock on the inside of the wardrobe. That had *not* been there before.

Open the door.

The hook slid easily and silently from the eye, as if the mechanism had been freshly oiled.

He opened the door and surveyed the room. Mother's room, but she wasn't present, as he had surmised from the cold. She must be sleeping elsewhere.

He stepped down, and he was free.

It should have been impossible.

What now?

He could go back to his own room, he supposed, and slip under his covers. Ask for flannel-covered bricks to be sent up. Or he could go to the kitchen, for he hadn't eaten since breakfast.

He wasn't tired, though, and he wasn't hungry, though he had been both mere moments ago.

What did he want to do?

The answer rose in him as if it had always been there, just below the surface. It felt logical, even though it was December.

He walked: out of Mother's room, down the big mahogany stairwell, out the front door.

People saw him. Servants, initially, then Mother and Father and Sarah. No one stopped him, though. No one even questioned him.

Outside, he wasn't cold, though he wore no coat and no shoes.

The walk to the sea from the house generally took thirty minutes, yet he found himself approaching the water in thirty seconds. The moon lit his way, though earlier he'd had the sense of it being a moonless night.

There was something about the lack of shoes, here on the beach, that was familiar.

He stood, staring out at the dark water, at the pinned-up stars above it.

What do I do now? he asked the night.

The answer came not from the night but from inside him. *You can do whatever you want.*

He went for a swim. The water was warm.

After that extraordinary dream, Effie wrote to Kenver and asked him to pay a visit.

I have recently had occasion to reevaluate a few things about my life, and I should appreciate your counsel. Might I prevail upon you to come as soon as it is convenient?

A few days later, he was receiving the man.

"I'd like to speak some more about the succession," Effie began.

Kenver made a shushing noise. "May we go somewhere more private?"

"More private than this?" They were alone in a drawing room. Effie glanced at the door through which Mrs. Moyer had retreated. It had been left slightly ajar, but he could close it.

"Yes," Kenver said, still whispering but emphatic.

"My goodness," Effie said, gesturing for Kenver to follow him, "one would almost think intrigue was afoot."

"One can never be too careful."

"Is everything all right, my lord?"

It was Mrs. Moyer, appearing out of nowhere as the gentlemen mounted the stairs, which Effie supposed was a case in point.

"Yes, indeed. I'm merely taking Mr. Nancarrow upstairs to . . . show him a painting."

"There is actually a painting in here," Kenver said, crossing Effie's bedchamber to the picture of Julianna—placeholder Julianna, impressionistic Julianna—against the chartreuse sky. Effie had not been able to bring himself to take it down. Kenver spent a long moment examining it. "This is extraordinary."

"Thank you."

Kenver turned, inquisitive. "You painted it?"

"You needn't act so surprised."

"I'm not. Well . . . I am. But it's because I am only just getting to know you. I didn't realize you had artistic talent."

"You should read my poetry."

"May I?"

Effie was not accustomed to conversing with people who were so earnest.

He regrouped. There would be time for poetry later—he hoped. For now, he wanted to make his proposal. "Here's the thing, Kenver. I don't want to be the earl."

"Well, you hardly have a choice in the matter, my lord."

"Will you *stop* with the my-lording!"

"Well, you hardly have a choice in the matter, *Effie*," Kenver said, rolling his eyes ever so slightly in a way Effie found brotherly and therefore thrilling.

When Effie didn't say anything, Kenver held up his hands. "What are you implying? I don't want to be the earl, either."

Effie threw up his own hands. Who was this purehearted? "Truly? You truly do not? Why not?"

"Why don't *you*? Once our father is gone, I mean."

Effie had asked himself that question. Father would be gone soon, apparently. Effie couldn't marry Julianna, apparently. So what was stopping him from being the poetry-writing, court-pump–wearing earl that Julianna had teased him about?

He even had a brother-steward who would help him, of that he had no doubt.

"Because I have other interests." Of course, his chief interest was Julianna herself. Since that was not an interest that could go anywhere, he was determined to develop some others. Beyond writing poetry that he sent to Miss Julianna Evans for her consideration.

Perhaps he should not have been so hasty in instructing Archie to dispose of Hamlet. He had already prevailed upon Simon to write again to the Earl of Stanhope.

"I have other interests, too," Kenver said.

"What are they?"

Kenver looked stricken and did not speak.

"See? You don't have other interests; you're just inordinately attached to some antiquated notion of propriety."

"If I am inordinately attached to anything, it is the idea of not committing a criminal and moral offense."

Effie smirked. Apparently some people *were* just that pure-hearted. "Well, my plan doesn't require the commission of any offense, criminal, moral, or otherwise. It merely requires a bit of creativity. I propose we enact a ridiculous plan by which we . . . enact Father's ridiculous plan."

"Have you been listening to anything I've said?"

"We enact it in our own, perfectly legal way," Effie amended. "I'll be the earl in name; you'll be the earl in practice. You agree to keep my sister and mother in the style to which they are accustomed, and you can do what you like with the rest of it. Well, you've got to look after the tenants, and the servants too, of course."

Kenver blinked a few times. "What about you?"

"I am planning for a new sort of life."

"Whatever can you mean?"

"I will tell you, I promise, but not quite yet."

"Whatever kind of life you want, you can have it. We can all live more than comfortably from the estate's income. You won't have to wait much longer, and then you can do whatever you want."

You can do whatever you want.

Effie smiled. The refrain was everywhere lately. As if it had been there all along, just below the surface.

What he wanted was to be his own man.

"I'm making it sound more dramatic than it is. I'll come round and visit. Well, I'll come round and visit you. I'm not sure Mother and Sarah will want any part of me."

"What about Lords? You'll have to vote."

"Right." Effie hadn't thought about that. "Well, that's fine. I can do that." He would only ever have voted how Simon told him to anyway.

"And what happens when you die?" Kenver asked. "You will forgive my bluntness."

"Cousin Herbert becomes the next earl. Or his son does, should I outlive Herbert."

"What if you have a child?"

"Why would I do that?"

"Last time we met, you spent a considerable amount of time singing the praises of a certain lady."

"Oh, yes, but she won't have me."

"You sound strangely cheery about that fact."

"I'm not. I am in fact heartbroken about it, but one must move forward, mustn't one?"

"All right. What if you have a child some other way? With some other woman."

"I shan't."

"One cannot always plan these things."

"Kenver." Effie laid his hand on Kenver's sleeve. "It isn't going to happen."

"So, you're the earl in name; I'm the earl in work."

"It sounds like a perfectly awful arrangement for you, but yes."

"You forget that my other option is a scrabbling life of disrespectability."

"Yes, I do, don't I?"

Kenver rolled his eyes in a way Effie dared think was affectionate. "If you are determined . . ."

"I am determined. Do we have a deal?"

"I still don't understand why you must make such a decisive break from the title, but trusting that you will enlighten me in time, yes, we have a deal."

Effie went to Julianna's office the next morning without an excuse. He didn't have Simon and his parapets in tow. He had no army of colorers.

He just wanted to see her, to tell her about the dream.

And, he reasoned, he didn't need an excuse. She was his friend. People called upon their friends all the time. He was building a new life, and he wanted her friendship to be part of it.

Or at least that's what he told himself as he climbed the stairs to the magazine's office. They hadn't talked about their relationship since she'd told him, in Brighton, that she didn't want it to continue in person. So perhaps he *wouldn't* be welcome without an excuse. Perhaps she would see the truth: he was attempting to worm his way back into her life.

"Effie!" She pushed back from where she'd been sitting at her desk. "What are you doing here?"

She was wearing the same green dress as last time he'd seen her, when they'd colored the December issue. It matched her eyes, and it was stunning.

"I thought to pay a visit to a friend," he said, choosing his words carefully.

"Come in." She smiled and beckoned him from where he was hovering in the doorway.

He breathed a sigh of relief as she gestured for him to follow her to the big worktable. "I'm finishing up January."

"Are your alligators in?" he asked as he took the seat she offered him. "And were my letters fine?"

"Your letters were fine—they were exquisite as always. And my alligators remain at large!" She walked around the table and pointed to a blank page on which she'd written "Alligators." "I am afraid I may have to wait for February for the alligators. I am already pushing it with the printing deadline for January."

"I shall write the February Mrs. Landers letters over Christmas." He had yet to finish—he had yet to start—his letters for February. He had been too busy overhauling his life. "I don't get the impression that my parents are coming home for the holidays, so it shall be a quiet Christmas at home. Plenty of time for letter writing." Plenty of time to draw up investment proposals, too, to enact new schemes.

"Oh, yes." She waved a hand dismissively. "I have no concerns over your February letters."

The conversation came to a halt there. Normally, he would have had no trouble coming up with something to say, but there was something about the way she was staring at him that had him at a loss for words. She pulled out a chair opposite him at the worktable and sat, regarding him the whole time. He began to wonder if he'd said something wrong. Done something wrong. When he could stand her scrutiny no longer, he said, "What?"

"Can we go to the sea?"

"I beg your pardon?"

"Southend-on-Sea. I have been looking into it. There aren't frequent coaches as there are to Brighton, but it's so close."

What in heaven's name was she on about?

He shelved that question in favor of a more mundane one, though he wasn't sure why: "How would we get there?"

She sent him an appealing look.

"We would take one of my family's conveyances," he said, putting words to that look.

"Since your parents are away . . ."

"I could drive, I suppose." That way they would only have to take the landau. They would not need servants to accompany them.

What was happening here? Transportation options were beside the point. He was still struggling to absorb the notion that she apparently wanted to go away with him, and to parse his own reaction to her proposal. A month ago, a week ago, that reaction would have been elation. Now it was . . . not elation.

It was the dream. The dream had impelled him to change everything.

"Do you drive?" she inquired.

"I can." He preferred not to, historically. He was more comfortable as a passenger. As a passenger, one could daydream and such.

But suddenly the image of himself as a passenger, in, say, his father's coach, seemed more akin to the image of a bird in its cage. He sat forward in his chair. "Do you remember Sally?"

Her brow knit. Fair: he had confused her with the abrupt change of subject. "Your parrot?"

"Yes, dear departed Sally."

"I do. I never had the pleasure of meeting her as I did Leander, but you used to write about her rather a lot."

"Do you think she was happy?"

"I don't know anything about parrots, so I couldn't possibly say."

"I loved her. I believed that she was made happy by my loving her. I no longer know if that was true. Or if it *was* true, if it was enough."

Her brow knit even more. He shook his head. He was getting off track, and he was confusing her. "Where would we lodge on his holiday you are proposing?"

She offered a tentative smile. "There is a pub right on the sea called the Castle where we might find a bed. And I understand that as of a few years ago, there are steamboat rides. Can you *imagine*? I would adore an account for the magazine."

Effie was stuck on a phrase she'd tossed off earlier. *Where we might find a bed.*

"How many beds might we find at the Castle?" he asked carefully.

His question was entirely in earnest, but she must have thought he was being flirtatious, for her smile contained a hint of wickedness as she said, "One, of course."

Part of him wanted to agree. *When may we leave and how long may we stay?*

But then he thought of the fragile peace between them. The hard-won peace within his own heart. The peace that had inspired him to come here in friendship, to tell her about the changes he was planning to make in his own life. He had no doubt that if they went to Southend on Sea, that peace would be upended. They would have a wonderful time. She could wear her decoy wedding ring, and they could pretend to be husband and wife. He would, for a time, be allowed to love her.

But then what?

They would come back, and he would have to start anew the process of mending his broken heart. Archie and Simon told him that bones that have been broken knit back together stronger, but that must only be true the first time. It defied logic to think a person could keep breaking in the same place, in the same way, and not eventually stay permanently broken.

"And then perhaps in the summer, when the July and August issues are combined," she went on, "we could make another trip. Somewhere further afield. Lyme Regis, perhaps."

A trip where he would break again, and have to knit himself back together upon his return.

How curious it was to be offered exactly what one thought one wanted and to find it not enough.

He spoke carefully: "I thought you said you hadn't time for an affair."

Her lips quirked upward. "I find myself inspired to make time."

Right.

"And honestly . . ." Her tone had dropped, grown more serious. "I missed you. I began to question why I had been so adamant, in Brighton, that there could be nothing further between us. Wasn't being away from London—from life—so lovely? What if we could do that once or twice a year?"

Effie was suddenly so tired. So sad. Not sad in the way he had been in recent weeks, not gutted and desperate. More that he was resigned to being at the beginning of a long journey, a reinvention. He had thought he could share that journey with Julianna to some degree. As friends.

Her proposal had forced him to peer even deeper into his weather-beaten heart and to face the fact that she had been right, that last night in Brighton: this thing with them, whatever it was, had to end. It had to end entirely.

He thought about letting her down gently, about saying something vague. He didn't have time to make a trip to the sea. He had to spend Christmas with family.

A lie would have been so easy.

"I won't go to Southend-on-Sea with you," he said, because some part of him knew that the truth, no matter how much it hurts, sets you free.

Chapter 17

Manic Pixie Dream Earl

Julianna had not expected Effie to decline her proposal. She was set back on her heels. Perhaps she had misunderstood him. Had he said "I *can't* go" or "I *won't* go"? There were nuances there that led to disparate interpretations.

"I exist for more than your gratification," Effie said quietly.

Her mind began to spin. He had said *won't*.

How? Why? What had changed? Could he lose his regard for her so quickly?

She took a breath. "I beg your pardon? Where is this coming from?"

He rested his elbows on the table and steepled his fingers. "I am not a character you invented."

"Of course you aren't. If I was any good at inventing characters, I'd be a novelist, not an editor."

"You are being glib, and I'm trying to say something important. Something that's important to me, in any case."

He might as well have thrown cold water on her, so shocked was she. She, seated across from him, physically recoiled, leaning back in her chair as far as was possible. Once there, the cold turned hot as shame flooded in.

"By all means, speak."

"Ofttimes, it feels as if I am but a character for you to take out and play with when the urge strikes. Or perhaps the better metaphor is a doll. I am pretty and amusing and good for a laugh—until you tire of me. Then you may put me back on the shelf until next time."

She tried to object, but he spoke over her, which was unheard of from the usually solicitous Effie.

"I have twisted myself trying to be that doll. Trying to be what I thought you would like. Initially, it was my pleasure to do it. It would have remained so had I felt we were building something. An alliance, a partnership. I would never have forced you into marriage, but *something*. It wouldn't have *been* twisting, in that case. It would have been something more like . . . bending.

"You once remarked on how biddable I was, how I always seemed to know exactly what you wanted to do, or to hear. I should have listened better when you said that. I thought I was being gentlemanly. I thought making you happy would make me happy—and it did.

"But that only works if you want me as much as I wanted you."

Wanted. Past tense. Julianna blinked rapidly so that she would not cry. She had cried enough tears in recent weeks that she could no longer credibly claim she was not a crier, but she still found herself resisting.

"You have this idea about who I am," Effie said. "An aristocrat."

"You *are* an aristocrat," she could not resist pointing out.

"Yes, and I used to wish I could change that." He smiled. "Ironically, perhaps I can, in a way."

She had no idea what that meant, but she didn't have an opening to ask, because he kept going, the pace of his speech picking up.

"I understand I can't make you want me—truly want me, for something enduring, for something more than once or twice a year—and so I've got to stop trying. It's a small revelation, in the scheme of things, but it's a rather large one for me personally."

"Effie," Julianna said, unable to disguise the anguish in her voice. "I am so very sorry. I never meant to make you feel unappreciated. I never wanted you to twist yourself to please me. And I *never* thought of you as a doll."

"I know," he said quietly, sadly. "But does it matter what you meant, what you thought? Or does it matter what you *did*?"

Oh, dear heavens. Julianna had never experienced such misery, not even the day Father died. Her body felt heavy with it.

She wanted to ask why this was all coming out now. Why hadn't he told her any of this before, back when she could have modified her behavior?

"I had the dream again," he said, "and this time it worked differently."

"You were able to control it?" she asked, struggling to adjust to the change in topic but understanding, somehow, that he was answering her unarticulated question about what had prompted him to make that devastating speech.

"In a manner of speaking. It wasn't as you said—as Aristotle says. I had no awareness that I was dreaming while I was dreaming. But there was a voice in the dream. A voice that had never been there before. It guided me up and out of the wardrobe."

"That's wonderful," she said, and meant it. "Whose voice was it, do you think?"

"I did consider that perhaps it was yours, because after I got out of the wardrobe, I went for a swim, and you were the one who suggested that."

Something inside Julianna lurched toward him. She wanted the voice to have been hers. She wanted to be the one helping Effie in his time of need, the one who appeared in his dreams.

"But as I was floating in the waves—which was curious because it was December in the dream, yet the water was warm—I realized the voice was *mine*.

"You think I'm a specific kind of man. The kind who will try to control you, or your magazine, which I sometimes think you care about more than yourself.

"I can't make you see that I'm different." He unsteepled his fingers and sat back again. "Or perhaps I'm not different; perhaps to think so is only self-flattery. It matters not. The point is, I cannot go to the seaside with you and give you everything and then come back and withdraw everything because you only want me in certain circumstances."

He stood. She, having been struck dumb—again—by his speech, stood, too. It was all she could think to do.

"I will write the February Mrs. Landers letters, but after that you should find someone else to do it."

The sob was beating at the door of her chest. She swallowed it. "Will you still send me poems for consideration?" She couldn't bear it if Effie stopped sending her poems.

He smiled—a little sadly, she thought. "No. I will send myself poems."

She didn't know what that meant, but she was too desperate to query him further, for she understood that he was saying goodbye—he was carrying himself toward the door. "You can't even be my friend. My correspondent?" She heard the desperation in her tone but could not do anything about it.

He must have heard it too, for he turned with his hand on the door, his expression exquisitely gentle. How the tables had turned. "No. I am sorry. I know I contradict myself. I know I was the one who suggested we keep up our correspondence even as we set aside our affair. I came here today in that spirit, to pay a friendly visit. But I didn't understand."

"You didn't understand what?"

"I didn't understand that for me, being your friend is nearly as painful as being physically intimate with you but not being able to truly belong to you."

Julianna inhaled sharply. He might as well have slapped her. Never in a hundred lifetimes would she have imagined Effie forsaking her. But what could she do? She couldn't make him stay. If she had indeed been bending him to her will as he'd suggested, she could no longer allow herself to do so. "So this is goodbye."

"This is goodbye." He nodded as if punctuating what he'd just said. He stared at her for a long time.

"I am sorry," she said. "I truly am."

"I know you are. Goodbye, Jules."

It was early, and dark. Julianna didn't expect anyone to be in the office this early on a Sunday.

He looked up from where he'd been bent over his desk—his desk that was in the center of the room, flush with hers, the way it used to be.

"Father!" she cried. What was he doing here? *How* was he here?

His fond smile pierced her chest. Oh, how she missed him. Oh, how she missed the magazine they used to make together, without the meddling of any Glanvils.

She was hit with a wave of exhaustion so fierce, her limbs grew weak. She had been working so hard. Sometimes, producing the magazine in the Glanvil era made her feel as if she were pushing a boulder up a hill—alone. Father having returned threw into sharp relief how terribly lonely she was.

But she didn't have to be anymore. He was here. She didn't understand *how*, but he was. She made to go to him, but something stopped her. There was a barrier between them, nothing she could see or feel, but it was there all the same. She tried again, approaching from the other side of his desk. She could not get close to him.

He was trying to speak. He seemed to know what this invisible barrier was. She stopped trying to surmount the barrier so she could listen. So he could explain.

"Would you repeat that, Father?"

His lips were moving, but no sound was coming out. Julianna began to grow agitated.

"I can't hear you! Speak up!"

Father kept "talking," but no sound came out. The longer it went on, the more her distress intensified.

Tears gathered. Julianna tried so hard not to cry. She wasn't certain where this extreme aversion to crying had come from, except that she feared that once she started crying, she would never stop.

Usually, she had some amount of control. When Mr. Glanvil's actions threatened to summon tears, she thought of the larger picture. *The magazine above all.*

Here, now, though, she feared she could not hold back the tears. As with the time she had read the letter from Effie that closed with his formal name, they were too strong, too powerful. She was at the bottom of a massive waterfall with an insufficient parasol.

She brushed them away angrily. She was angry with herself, for crying. She was angry with Father, for not being able to make himself heard. She was angry with Effie, for . . . for what? Why was she angry with Effie, who had given her everything she could ever want? A brilliant trove of Mrs. Landers letters each month. The sea.

His heart.

As she was swiping tears off her cheeks, her fingers grazed against something unfamiliar near her ear.

What was that?

She checked the other ear. It was there, too, something soft but foreign.

She pulled.

She had scraps of muslin balled up inside her ears! No, not scraps, a long, thin piece in each ear. She kept pulling and pulling. As she neared the end of each length, she began hearing her father.

"You don't have to be alone," he said.

Except, it wasn't his voice coming out of his mouth; it was her own.

"I beg your pardon?" she said, shaking her head and giving one last rub to each now-empty ear.

"You don't have to be alone."

Again, it was Julianna's voice coming out of Father's lips.

Extraordinary.

She awakened with a start.

Frantically, she checked her ears. They were empty.

After fumbling to light a candle, she got out of bed and hurried from her windowless room. She went outside and stood in front of her sister's house and looked up at the starless city sky.

Amy had been right. It hadn't been a message from Father she'd been struggling to hear; it had been a message from herself. From herself, to herself.

And it hadn't been that Father had been unable to speak; it had been that she had been unable to hear.

She had heard now. The question was, what was she going to do about it?

No, the question was: Was she too late?

Chapter 18

A Dollar and a Dream

"Thank you all for coming," Effie said as he stood by the fireplace in a drawing room in the London house and contemplated his closest friends—Archie and Simon, of course, but he had also invited Olive. "I have some news I wanted to share with you in person."

"Does this news involve a certain Miss Evans?" Olive asked with a twinkle in her eye. The others snickered like school boys.

"It does not," Effie said solemnly, and they fell silent.

He had made the right decision, he assured himself, in rebuffing Julianna's invitation to go to the sea. It hadn't merely been an invitation to go on holiday. It had been the introduction of a pattern. A template for what being together would be like, if one could even call it "being together."

The rest, he wasn't so sure about. Was he really just never going to see her again? Never write to her? It had felt like the right thing at the time. But could he live without her?

He had avoided thinking about it by putting his plan into action, because whatever else happened, he had set his mind on this. The living part.

"We are soon to be joined by Kenver Nancarrow," he said by way of introduction, and also by way of distraction—he didn't want to talk to them about Julianna. Not yet. The wound was too fresh.

"The Highworth steward?" Archie asked.

"Mm," Effie murmured, for that was a correct if incomplete characterization of Kenver. "He wrote that he would be arriving tonight with some news, and I asked him to come at eight o'clock."

"That is still an hour off," Archie said.

"Yes. The news I have to tell you concerns him, so I wanted to speak to you before he arrives."

"Well, let's have it, then," Simon said.

Effie took a sip of his wine to fortify himself, for he felt as if he'd sprinkled gunpowder around the room and was about to drop a lit match.

"Olive already knows this, but Kenver Nancarrow is my brother."

The room went dead silent until, after a long beat, Simon said, "I beg your pardon?"

"Well, I suppose he is my half brother, if you want to get technical, which I do not. It seems my father dallied with his mother for quite a few years. He is six months older than I. Father put him through university and hired him as steward, and he has of late uncovered evidence that Father has arranged his affairs to make it look as if he had married Kenver's mother before I was born—with the expectation that Kenver would then claim the title after Father passes."

He paused for a breath—that had been an overly long sentence. Julianna would have told him to break it up.

"Oh, and I forgot to tell you that Father will pass soon. He is by all accounts on his deathbed in Italy, too unwell to return home."

He went on to explain the details of the plot Kenver had uncovered—the marriage lines, the probable bribe of the rector—and when he was done, he was met with another silence. It was shorter this time. After a heartbeat, the room erupted in exclamations.

"I am astounded that your father would do this," Simon said when the cacophony died down.

"Are you, though?" Olive asked. "Are you really?"

Simon made a conciliatory gesture, and everyone turned their attention back to Effie.

"Better to have an illegitimate earl than a soft one," Effie said. The truth didn't hurt anymore. Not since the dream. "Kenver and I are aligned in our thoughts on the matter. He will not make a claim on the title. We have allowed Father to think he will, but he won't."

"How do you know you can trust him?" Simon asked.

Effie didn't bother explaining about the surety Kenver had offered in the form of that pouch of coins, because that pouch of coins was immaterial. "I just am. You will be, too, when you meet him."

"What says your mother of all this?" Archie asked. "Sarah?"

"I do not know. Mother writes to Mr. Nancarrow from Italy, but her letters are limited to the facts of the matter. 'Father is declining rapidly. The weather is lovely. At least his final days shall be filled with the beautiful golden light of Campagna. Et cetera.' I do not know if she knows about his plan, or if she knows the truth about Kenver. I doubt it, on both counts. I shall have to speak with her when she returns.

"None of this is the point, though. The point is that I have a brother. Huzzah!"

Everyone lifted their glasses and congratulated him and said how much they were looking forward to meeting Kenver.

"Well, that I have a brother is the precursor to the point. The true point is that having discovered a brother who is adept at estate management has worked rather in my favor."

"I should think so," Archie said. "But I should also think if he is as decent a man as you suggest, he will be willing to teach you." He paused. "In perhaps a way your father was not."

"I'm sure he would, but I have decided that the life of a peer isn't what I want. It never was. I'd reconciled myself to it and therefore sought to learn about it, but now I am presented with someone who truly enjoys doing it. Kenver and I have therefore decided that he will carry out all the duties associated with the title."

"That is not unheard of," Archie said. "It is not unlike the arrangement I have with Mr. Hughes," he said, naming his own steward. "We meet once a week when I am at Mollybrook, and I do my best to contribute, but I would be lost without him."

"That is . . . not precisely what I am imagining." Here was the point, the point Effie kept dancing around. He cleared his throat. "I am looking to make a rather large change."

They were all regarding him with open, inquisitive expressions. Oh, how he loved them. He was blessed when it came to friends. Over-blessed.

"I am going to move out."

"Of this house?" Archie asked. "Are you going back to Highworth?"

"No," Olive said, eyeing him closely. She was getting it, even if she didn't yet know precisely what "it" was.

"I have found rooms to let. On Grub Street. One for me to live in, one from which I shall operate my business."

He had stunned them. Well, he had stunned the boys, whose mouths had dropped open in tandem. Olive merely regarded him with raised eyebrows.

"I plan to be a poet."

"You are already a poet," Simon said, "and is poetry a 'business'? And what about Lords? Mr. Nancarrow cannot vote for you."

"I want to publish my poems myself. In a chapbook, as you yourself have often suggested. A book with my name on it. My true name." He took out his fan. "The idea is nearly enough to make a person swoon."

"That's wonderful," Archie said, beaming like a proud papa.

"And I want to print them myself," Effie added. Now they were finally at the crux of the matter. "I want to be in charge of every aspect of their creation and production."

"I think I begin to understand," Simon said. "You're going to buy a press, aren't you? This is why you've been pestering me about Stanhope. Here I'd thought you wanted the press for Miss Evans."

"I did. But I've rethought matters. If I own a press, I can print whatever I like. My own poems, but also other people's words. Other people's paying words. To do that, I need money."

"You have money," Archie said.

"Not really. It isn't mine. Not properly."

"I begin to understand," Simon said.

"I want to do this on my own," Effie said. "I do have some money that's mine. I never cashed any of the bank drafts Miss Evans has sent me over the years for my work for the magazine. I mean to do so now. That will get me started. But I need *more* money. I need *investments.*"

"Are not our gains as ill-gotten as yours, if we are to follow your logic?" Simon asked.

That gave Effie pause. "I . . . suppose they are."

"You men and your logic," Olive said dismissively. "I shall invest. I haven't much, but I have been bleeding Father of pin money rather ruthlessly for years."

"But you are saving that for—" Effie cut himself off. That was another bit of knowledge that wasn't his to share.

"I am saving it for a lucrative investment opportunity," Olive said firmly, "and I know one when I see it."

"Of course we shall give you whatever you want," Archie said. "I shall have to speak with Clementine, but I know she won't object."

"You can count on me, too," Simon said, "though I notice you didn't answer my question about Lords."

"I don't want you to *give* me money. I want you to *invest*. I used that word for a reason. I want you to be part owners, at least initially." He turned to Olive. "And you, too, if you like." Returning his attention to Simon, he said, "Yes, of course I'll vote for your act. I'll vote however you tell me to."

"Oh, what a delicious scandal it shall be," Olive said. "The poet-earl emerging from his Grub Street hovel to carry out his Parliamentary duty."

"It's not going to be a *hovel*, thank you very much." Effie sniffed but shot Olive a wink.

They were off, then, discussing his plans. Everyone had an opinion, it seemed, which Effie supposed was what you got when you had investors. At least they were better than Mr. Glanvil.

"Are you sure this isn't about Miss Evans?" Olive said when the conversation died down.

"Only in the sense that she inspired it. She inspired me as a poet. She introduced me to the technical side of magazine production, and printing. And more to the point, she opened my eyes to the dignity and satisfaction to be had in making one's own way in the world, even in the face of obstacles."

"So it has everything to do with Miss Evans," Olive said wryly.

"I suppose you are right. But I'm not doing it *for* her, if that's what you mean." He paused. Perhaps he did need to tell them about his recent break with Julianna, in broad strokes, anyway. "She and I have parted ways."

It took a moment for the room to absorb that bit of news. He had expected them to object, to launch an interrogation, but they merely stared, agog.

"Must you, though?" Olive finally said. "I can appreciate that you're not doing it for her, but rather for yourself, but must that mean she has no involvement at all?"

Everyone was waiting in silence for Effie to answer Olive's question. Drat. He was going to have to tell them more. "Miss Evans and I have differing opinions on what the nature of our relationship ought to be going forward." He tried to think how to explain it in a way that wouldn't require him to turn himself inside out, that wouldn't land him back behind a pane of glass.

"There is a strait between us, you see, and it turns out not to be traversable. And so I have determined that it's best to . . . stop staring at the water." He almost laughed. What a heavy-handed metaphor. Would the boys recognize in it the tragic story of Leander and Hero?

Apparently not, for after another discomfiting silence, Simon said, "This plan of yours is truly extraordinary. You realize it is going to mean an abrupt lifestyle change?"

Effie was grateful to Simon for changing the subject. "I do." He winked. "You lot shall have to subsidize me on future Earls Trips. That's as far as I'm willing to take your money not in the form of an investment."

"You aren't going to be able to live in the style to which you have become accustomed," Archie said. "What about your love of beautiful clothing?"

"You know what else is beautiful?"

Archie raised his eyebrows, and everyone regarded Effie inquisitively.

"Freedom."

"This is Kenver Nancarrow, my brother," Effie said a while later, positively bursting with joy at the coming together of his historically favorite people with his new favorite person.

Kenver tried to issue the "half brother" correction, but Effie protested loudly against the qualification. Olive herded Kenver to a chair and handed him a glass of wine while telling him to brace himself for the "delightful disarray" of keeping company with Effie. Archie began peppering Kenver with questions about his plans for the holidays.

It took Simon to cut through the chaos. "Effie," he said loudly, "You'd better tell Mr. Nancarrow your theory of salt and strawberries."

"Yes!" He ought to have done that ages ago. He turned to his brother—he turned to his brother!—and said, "Harcourt, Marsden, and I have a theory of family. It goes like this: Some people are salt, and some people are strawberries. Which you are is random, left to Lady Fate. So you might end up a cellar of salt in a family of strawberries, or a leg of lamb baked into a cake."

"A leg of lamb baked into a cake!" Olive exclaimed while Archie made a retching noise. "That is a new one."

Kenver looked confused, which was fair. "So what you're meant to do," Effie explained, "is find your people. If you're a strawberry, you need to find a cake. If you're salt, you need to find a leg of lamb, or something else that needs salting."

Kenver did not appear enlightened. His brow furrowed. "And what am I?"

"I don't know, but you're something that goes with whatever I am."

Kenver's brow smoothed, and he looked bashful as he said, "All right, then. I've never cared for lamb, so I suppose that makes me cake."

"Then I'm a strawberry," Effie said triumphantly.

"You're ridiculous, you know," Simon said, though there was affection in his tone.

"That's why we love him," Olive said indulgently.

It was Effie's turn to feel bashful. This was what he meant when he said he was over-blessed when it came to friends. If only his broken heart would mend. He had to trust that time and distance would continue to do their good work—he already felt more clear-headed than he had just after Brighton. Regardless, this conversation was becoming a little too sentimental, even for him. He turned to Kenver.

"You said you had an important matter to discuss? Shall we withdraw? If it matters, I've told my friends everything regarding my father's illness, and his plot."

"No need to withdraw. I've merely come to tell you I've had a letter from your mother. She reports that your father is bedridden and awake only a few hours a day. During these hours he apparently asks for you, and requests that you journey to his bedside."

That was an unexpected development. "Ought I to go, do you think?"

No one spoke initially. After a few beats of silence, Kenver said, "That is a complicated question."

"And here I thought it required only a yes or a no."

Kenver narrowed his eyes at Effie. Effie adored that Kenver knew him so well that Kenver knew he was being glib when glibness was not called for.

Effie had indeed been glib, but only to distract from the swirling mass of sentiment that the summons from Father had stirred up. "You are right. It is a complicated question—which is why I asked it, I suppose. One hears tales of the dying repenting their sins, of estrangement giving way to acceptance and mutual forgiveness and understanding."

"One does hear that," Kenver said noncommittally.

"What do you all think?" Effie said, turning to the others.

"Is there anything *he* needs to forgive *you* for?" Simon asked.

"What do you mean?"

"You said *mutual* forgiveness."

"Well, I certainly haven't been the son he wanted."

"So you need forgiveness for being who you are," Simon said. On the surface of things, his tone was mild, but Effie, having known him since they were boys, could hear the affront in it.

"I think," Kenver said quietly, "you ought to put aside questions of atonement and try to imagine how seeing your father might feel. Would it provide any sort of comfort to *you*? A valuable sense of closing the door on a chapter of your life?"

Effie gave it some thought. It was hard to imagine being comforted by proximity to Father regardless of the circumstances, and what was he doing now, with the plan to change his life but providing his own sort of closing of the door on a chapter? "I don't think so. But perhaps I ought to say goodbye nonetheless."

"If you want to, by all means," Archie said. "But I should like to remind you that your father never saw any need to say goodbye to you when he left you at school over the holidays. He never felt the need to say goodbye before leaving you locked in a wardrobe overnight."

There was affront in Archie's tone, too, and it was overt.

"But I am a better person than he." Effie didn't want to be boastful, so he added, "The bar, of course, being quite low."

He'd been attempting a jest—more glibness—but no one laughed.

Olive said, "I hear you saying that a deathbed visit would not provide *you* any comfort, or sense of reconciliation. Which means you would be attending the death in order to bring *your father* comfort, or the sense of a satisfactory ending, or at least to offer him the opportunity for such."

"It is also possible," Kenver said, "that the summons isn't about any of this. He could merely want you out of England to smooth the way for what he assumes will be my claim at the Committee for Privilege. In that sense, I agree with Miss Morgan: You ought to go only if so doing will serve *you* in some way."

"I think," Effie said slowly, "that I shan't go." He blew out a breath, feeling shaky but exhilarated.

"Well, then, that's that," Archie said. "Shall we have another round of drinks?"

Once glasses were refilled, Olive said, "Have you told your brother about your plan to move to Grub Street and start a printing company?"

Kenver chuckled. "I have yet to be enlightened as to details, but I suspected something akin to that was afoot. I've told him his own income can finance such an endeavor."

"And *I've* told *him*," Effie said, "and the lot of you, that I want to make it on my own."

"It's both astonishing and maddening, isn't it, Mr. Nancarrow?" Archie asked.

"I'm not sure I agree that it's maddening, my lord," Kenver said. "Astonishing, yes. Perhaps also admirable."

Everyone murmured their agreement.

"May I offer a suggestion?" Kenver said.

"Of course," Effie said.

"If you are going to completely upend everything, if you are going to effectively leave your life behind to become a poet and printer, why not also leave your life behind to marry your entirely unsuitable lady?"

The room erupted in good-natured jeering followed by a cascade of agreement.

"I've told you all this a thousand times. Because she won't have me."

"Are you sure about that?" Kenver asked.

"Of course I'm sure."

"Have you told her about your new business venture?" Archie asked.

"Have you told her about your new rooms in Grub Street?" Simon asked.

"Have you told her you love her?" Olive asked.

Effie's mind reeled as they pelted him with questions. All he could do was offer an answer to that last one.

"My macaw has told her I love her."

Chapter 19

Free as a Bird

Julianna unlocked the door to the office. It was early, so it was dark. It was cold, too, it being January first. A new year.

She was alone this time, as she'd known she would be.

She hadn't had the dream again.

She didn't need to locate her father's desk in the space to know whether she was awake or asleep.

It should go back in the center of the room, though. She went to it and began attempting to drag it from where it had rested against the wall since Father's death. If she was successful in her planned speech to Effie, he might want to sit there, from time to time. *She* wanted him to sit there.

She grunted as she put all her weight into attempting to pull the desk away from the wall. She wanted to have every detail attended to before she made her move. She wanted everything to be perfect.

That was what she told herself, anyway.

It was possible she was procrastinating.

She stopped pulling.

She was scared. Terrified, really. That was why a fortnight had elapsed since the dream—the version in which she finally heard "father."

What if she was too late? What if he didn't want her anymore, under any circumstances?

She struck a match, intending to light a candle, to catch her breath and fortify herself for the task ahead, but she stopped and stared at the flame. The adages she lived by marched through her mind. She had spent so long hewing to them, organizing her life around them, for fear that if she didn't, she might . . . unravel.

But she'd unraveled anyway, had she not?

There is only now.

There was only now, until there wasn't. Until "now" wasn't enough. Until you met a person who wanted your future, who made the pleasure of his ongoing company contingent upon being part of that future.

You can't miss what you don't let yourself want.

That one only worked when the power of your will was stronger than the power of your desire. That had always been the case for Julianna. Until, again, it wasn't. And once you flipped, once the wanting became all-consuming, so too did the missing.

The magazine above all.

She had been ruminating on Effie's comment, the day they parted, that he sometimes thought Julianna cared more about the magazine than she did herself. Did *the magazine above all* make sense when she, her very being, was included in that *all*?

What was she *doing*? Why was she *waiting*? Because of fear, yes, but she was no longer accepting that as an excuse. Time was passing. Opportunity was diminishing. Effie was not Edith. Perhaps that should be a new adage.

A wave of impatience crested inside her, coming out her mouth and snuffing the flame just before the match burned all the way down. It was time to go to him. It was time to ask him the question that frightened her more than anything ever had before.

"What if you could change the dream?"

Or, it was time to turn toward him, for he was here.

Hadn't it always been like that with them? That day, at the Pavilion, she had turned, and there he'd been. That last night together, she'd lifted her hand to knock on his door, and he had opened it before her knuckles made contact.

"What if I could change the dream?" she echoed, struggling to shift her attention from the astonishing yet not at all surprising fact that he was here—*he was here!*—to the content of what he'd said.

"That's what you asked me, in a letter, when you introduced the idea of trying to control my nightmares, change the outcome of them."

"I remember, but I'm not sure I follow what you mean saying that now, in this context." She stepped back and gestured him into the dim office.

"I changed the dream."

"Yes, you told me."

"I'm still changing it—the awake one."

"I don't understand."

"You have been speaking about marriage as if it is something that happens to you." He perched on a table. He looked like he belonged here.

No, he didn't "look like" he belonged here. He *did* belong here.

Julianna had so often felt, in recent days, a lack of belonging, as if she didn't fit in anywhere. She hadn't seen a way to ameliorate that. *You've chosen a lonely life*, Amy said. Julianna had chosen the magazine above all else, and she had—she'd thought—accepted the lonely consequences of that decision. She hadn't, historically, even regarded those consequences as lonely.

Until him.

Once again, her mind was undergoing such a rapid reckoning that she had to force herself to consider his words. *You have been speaking about marriage as if it is something that happens to you.*

"For women," she said, "it usually is."

"I am aware, but you are not an average woman. I have never met someone, woman or man, so utterly in control of her destiny."

"You are wrong. If I were in control of my destiny, I would not have to fight my mother's late husband's son for control of my magazine." That might be beside the point here, beside the reckoning, but she could not resist pointing it out. "I would not have needed to control the person who is dearest to me in all the world as if he were a doll." The shame was still fresh.

"It is true that you and Mr. Glanvil are frequently at odds, but I do not take that to mean you are not in control of your destiny. I suppose I am speaking more of your temperament, your mental posture. You make things happen. For example, that Pavilion tour. You don't hesitate to tell people when they're being daft. For example, the boys and I and our over-worry about propriety in Brighton."

He paused. Smiled. "And as for the rest, you have an idea of what marriage would mean for you, but I think you're discounting the *you* part of the scenario. That's what I'm saying about you being in control of your destiny. It's as true in matters of sentiment as it is in matters of business. You have impeccable judgment. I'm not saying there is no risk of heartbreak when one considers matrimony, but I'm also not asking you to marry me."

The anti-proposal: it stung. The fact that she was disappointed was telling, wasn't it?

"I have come to tell you that I've made some changes in my life, largely inspired by you," Effie said. "I've left home. Not that it was ever home, not really. I've left my father's house."

He proceeded to spin the most amazing tale. He'd found a brother, and she was so happy for him on that account. He had rented rooms. He was, effectively if not legally, leaving his title behind. It was all very astonishing. It was all very brave. But Effie was very brave, wasn't he?

"I'm not asking you to marry me," Effie repeated. Also repeated: the pang of disappointment in her chest. "But I do have two questions. First, will you go into business with me?"

"I beg your pardon?" What could he mean?

"I was meant to appear here with an item that would make my case better than I shall be able to, but that plan proved impractical. It turns out when you're changing your dream in the corporeal world, large objects can't float up several flights of stairs as easily as the ghosts that haunt them."

"What are you speaking of?" Why was this all so befuddling? "You were meant to appear here with 'an item'?"

"Yes. I bought a hand press."

"You bought a hand press?" Julianna was aware that she was doing nothing more than parroting what Effie was saying. At least she was better spoken than Leander.

"I confess I did not grasp that although Stanhope's version is smaller than Gutenberg's, it still isn't something one can transport in one's pocket. It's currently in Simon's orangery, but we can arrange to have it moved here." He paused. "Or to my rooms in Grub Street. Depending on what you decide."

"You . . . bought me a hand press?"

"No. I bought myself a hand press. Well, that's not strictly true. I finally cashed all the bank drafts I've earned from you over the years, but as you well know, that wasn't nearly enough. Simon and Archie and Olive bought me a hand press." He quirked his head, and her heart twinged at the familiar mannerism. "That's not exactly right, either. Simon and Archie and Olive invested in the endeavor I am launching. I'm going to print things. Books—my own, to start. But also, perhaps, magazines?"

"No!" She was beginning to understand.

"Well, not if you don't want to."

"You can't just . . . print my magazine!" After all she had done to him.

"I'm sure I don't know why not. But that is not what I'm proposing. I suggest we operate the press together. We print your magazine and my books and whatever else. The "whatever else" is key to the profitability of the enterprise." He winked. "I am told that 'profitability' is what a man of business ought to aim for."

"But why would you offer *me* this press when *you* have funded it? Or, I suppose I should say, you and your investors."

"Yes. They're investors, and I might opt to keep them as such. *We* might opt to keep them as such, should you care to join me. Or, we might elect to pay them back according to the terms outlined in a dismayingly dull document I signed last week."

"You aren't answering my question. What would *I* bring to this proposed partnership?"

"I have a press, but I don't know how to use it."

"I . . . well, I suppose I know. In theory."

"And more to the point, you know people who know. You also know people who might bring their business to us. The way I see it, I supply the infrastructure, and you drum up the business. And the labor, should we require any. See? I don't even know about that. Do we need pullers? Or can we do it ourselves?"

The notion of physically operating a press with Effie was . . . Well, it was nearly enough to make Julianna swoon, especially when she thought of her own magazine coming off it.

"You're saying we could print *Le Monde Joli* on your press."

"On *our* press, yes."

She had to close her eyes for a moment to forestall the swoon. She needed to not get ahead of herself. She needed to know everything. And *say* everything. Because he needed to know everything, too. "You said there were two questions."

"Right. Well, the second isn't really a question. I merely want you to know that I love you." He smiled, and the sight was so incredibly dear to her. "I am almost certain you already know, but I wanted you to hear it from me and not Leander."

Julianna gasped. And then began to cry. Two things Julianna allegedly never did.

At least she managed to stave off the swoon.

"I always said I would never marry," she said through her tears.

"Which is why I'm not asking you to. So don't cry, Jules, at least not on my account. My question isn't contingent on my declaration. I still want to be business partners, if you do. It's just that I can't . . . go to the sea with you. You understand? I could live in a room in Grub Street with you, or in a"—he glanced around— "cold, dark office with you, but I can't have you and then not have you. I won't be used and discarded." He shook his head, and his countenance softened. "So we shall be friends. And business partners, I hope."

Oh, Effie. He *was* proposing, in a way. He was proposing something short of marriage, something he thought she might find acceptable, and what lengths he had gone to in order to be in a position to do so.

"You gave up everything for me," she said incredulously.

"I didn't. I didn't know what you were going to say. I still don't. I gave up everything for *me*. And I'm not sure I would describe it thusly. I gave up some things, yes, but I did that so I could get another thing."

"And what is that thing?"

"Freedom."

Yes. When you unraveled yourself, or unlatched yourself, you were free. To start over.

An idea was forming, an idea that was at once radical and completely obvious. "What if I . . . started a new magazine? What if *we* started a new magazine?" That was what she should have said. That was what she meant.

"I think that's a fine idea." His eyes twinkled. "*Evans's Lady's Book*, perhaps?"

She dried her eyes. "Only self-regarding braggarts have their names in the titles of their magazines."

"I take the point. Well, your name will be on the inside, as editor and proprietor."

"And your name?"

"Perhaps I shall be your assistant?" He paused. "When I have time. I shall be awfully busy writing and publishing my poetry." He winked. "Now who's the self-regarding braggart?"

"So you shall be my assistant but not my husband."

"You were right before, in Brighton, when we were discussing our roles in that whole breaking-and-entering scheme."

"It wasn't breaking and entering."

He waved a dismissive hand. "You wanted me to be your assistant, but I insisted on being your husband. You were right. In fact, I think you may have had a prophetic vision."

Here it was: her opening. Her heart thumped—with fear or love, she wasn't sure. Perhaps both. "Perhaps *you* were right when we went breaking and entering in Brighton. Perhaps you ought to be my assistant *and* my husband."

A slow smiled blossomed on his orchid lips. "Julianna Evans, are you proposing to me?"

This was it. As usual, Effie had smoothed the way for her. All she had to do was say . . . "Yes."

That wasn't right, though. Well, it was right. It was her answer, the true answer, but it wasn't enough. She owed him more than that. He'd started to speak but she held up a hand. "I would like to say something to you, if you will allow it."

"Of course. Your speech is not for me to allow or disallow."

"I want to say that I love you, too."

He dipped his head, looking adorably flustered.

"I didn't tell you before because I don't think I realized it myself. Or I didn't let myself name it. And that was because I was afraid. The bit where it came off as though I was toying with you—the doll business—" He started to object but she shushed him. "You were right about that. It was because I wanted you, but I was afraid. All the reasons I always gave for wanting to avoid marriage were true, but they weren't . . . comprehensive. There was another one, a big one, one that had nothing to do with laws, or money, or the magazine. I was afraid that if I loved you, when you left to marry someone else—"

"Like Edith did," Effie said quietly. "I understand."

"But I have come to realize that you are not Edith. One of the great gifts you have always given me is your careful attention. You have always listened to me. I ought to have done the same for you, really listened to what you said. *Believed* you when you said you weren't fussed about the earldom, or the lineage."

She took a breath. That hadn't been nearly as difficult as she'd imagined. She felt lighter already, even without knowing how things were going to turn out. "I'm sorry I didn't listen. I'm sorry

I appeared fickle. I *wasn't* fickle, in my heart. I just wasn't allowing myself to know my own heart. I hope it's not too late. I had intended, today, to come to you and suggest that we begin an affair. A long-term, poorly hidden affair on terms we find mutually agreeable."

She took another fortifying breath. "But in light of your changed affairs, and of your fine speech just now, I believe that, yes, I am proposing to you." She paused. "Proposing *marriage*, if that wasn't clear."

He didn't speak for a long time. Fear began to assert itself, and Julianna made a gesture of impatience.

Effie smiled. "I am merely having trouble adjusting to such a declaration. You once said the 'last thing you wanted' was a man to propose to you."

"If it helps, I said I didn't want a man to propose to me." She grinned. "I never said I didn't want to propose to a man."

"I ought to call that quibbling," he said fondly.

"I was in jest, but I find that perhaps direction makes the difference. Of course, *you* make the difference. That whole business about you being you, wonderful you. But also, direction seems to matter. How interesting."

"Direction?"

"I am the proposer here. The question is flowing from me to you. I am doing the asking."

"And I am doing the answering."

"Yes. And soon, please? I am not sure I ever appreciated how difficult it is to make a suit of marriage."

"Are you afraid I'll say no?"

"Of course I am!"

"Oh, goodness, I was just teasing."

"Does that mean. . . ?"

"You do understand that regardless of who is doing the asking, if we were to marry, you would be marrying into a title. You would be a countess."

"In name only, though, yes? Just as you plan to be an earl in name only?"

"You could be whatever kind of countess you like. But in the eyes of the law, you would still be one."

"I would like to be the kind of countess who lives in a room in Grub Street and publishes a magazine with her husband who is also her assistant."

He grinned. "I would like that, too. I would like that very much."

Julianna tried to return his smile, but something still nagged at her.

"What are you brooding about?" he asked. "Oughtn't this to be the part where the happy couple embrace and what have you?"

He was teasing, but the thing, the nagging thing, was coming into focus. They had discussed this briefly, in Brighton, in the context of needing to prevent conception, but this context—the context of marriage—was quite apart from that. "Some people . . ." She paused, gathering her thoughts. "Some people, myself perhaps among them, would say that I am too old for you."

"Too old! What does that mean? Is anyone too old for anything? If an old man desires to dance a quadrille, he need only find a willing partner."

"And how does an old man at a ball find a willing partner?"

"He asks ladies until one deigns to dance with him."

"No. He has money."

"I beg your pardon?"

"Young ladies deign to dance with old men because they have money."

Effie burst out laughing, and oh, how she had missed that sound. "I suppose that is true."

"And some people *are* too old for some things." She paused. She had hinted at this that night in Brighton, but she hadn't outright said it. "Some women are too old to bear children."

"Why would I want a child?"

"Why wouldn't you?"

"We discussed this. Because a son of mine would have to be Earl of Stonely someday."

"I take your point, but aside from that, you would make a perfectly wonderful father."

"Do you think so?"

"I know so."

"Be that as it may—and believe me, I am mightily flattered—the first thing a father ought to do for his children is protect them." He was speaking fervently, and she knew what he was thinking about. "And the only way to protect my children from their fate is not to have them to begin with."

"I suppose my point is more that most people would not allow such high moral standards to prevent them from doing something else they wanted to do, especially when that something else is to have children."

"Julianna, I am unsure how we have ventured so far down this conversational path. I never imagined myself having children, because I never imagined myself falling in love. I felt no regret over that fact. But here I am now, in love. With you, in case you missed that. Perhaps I should have brought Leander along so he could shout it in your face again. So if you're trying to tell me that you can't have children, please believe me that I am taking that news in stride. It's not that I don't care. If you care, I care. But I care because you care. I don't inherently care."

"I wonder," she said laughingly, feeling the weight of the moment start to lessen, "if you could conceive of a sentence that uses the word 'care' more times than your previous?"

"I think I attained the upper limit of the number of 'cares' that may be in a single sentence. In fact, I think you should give me a prize."

She kissed him.

But only for a moment.

He squeaked his displeasure when she pulled away. "I am eight-

and-thirty. My menses are irregular." She narrowed her eyes at him. "Do you know what menses are?"

He rolled his eyes. "Yes, I know what menses are."

"Well, you do rather tend to live in your daydreams, and you were a virgin when I met you."

"I will have you know I was a virgin due to inclination, not lack of opportunity. In fact, the very day I left for Earls Trip, I fended off not one, but two suitors." He was laughing as he spoke, and she smiled along with him.

"My point is, I want to make it utterly clear that I believe it is too late for me to have children."

"*My* point is, *as I told you*, I have no desire to consign a child of mine to become the earl of Stonely. None."

"What if you had a daughter?"

"He threw up his hands. If you don't want to be with me, Julianna, just say it."

"I can't say it." She wasn't doing a very good job proposing, was she? She regrouped. "I have made a hash of this. I should like to say it's because you're the writer and I'm the editor. But that is merely an excuse. I do not have your way with words, but it shouldn't take that many to say what is in my heart. Even your dim-witted bird can do it." She took a breath. "I love you, Euphemia-Edward-Effie. More than I've ever loved anyone. I want to marry you, most desperately, and I find that fact terrifying."

His countenance went utterly soft. "I know you do, dearest."

"I am going to need a new adage, aren't I?"

"Indeed you are," Effie said with a wink. "Once you are a married woman you can hardly go around proclaiming 'the magazine above all else.'"

He was teasing, but the thought was still so . . . upending. "Why is it so easy for you to love?"

He grew serious once he realized that she hadn't joined him in his jesting. "I don't know. I suppose because of my friends. Who will be your friends, too, if you will allow it."

"I have been so afraid to lose the magazine. But I think that was a proxy for my real fear, which was to lose . . . myself. I realize that makes very little sense."

"No, it makes perfect sense. But if we are to follow the metaphor . . ." He turned up his palms. "If you will allow me?"

"Of course. Metaphors are your department."

"Your magazine has been chipped away at over the years by the Glanvils. You have been trying to protect it, but it has put you in a terrible position of constantly being on the defensive."

Yes, that felt right. And it was so exhausting to be constantly on the defensive.

"And perhaps," she said, speaking slowly, for she was articulating new thoughts as they formed, "in being so focused on the minutia of defending it, I have lost sight of the larger mission."

"Yes." He beamed like a proud tutor. "And what is the larger mission?"

"The larger mission is love. Belonging. Trusting that the people I love—the person I love—won't leave."

"Oh! Now we are off the magazine metaphor and on to sentiment!"

"Well, let's say the larger mission is love *and* a new, better magazine.

"Love and *Evans's Lady's Book.*"

"We are *not* calling it that."

"Perhaps we ought to speak to our investors about titles. Perhaps we ought to speak to them tonight, over dinner. That might help with the 'belonging' bit of the equation."

"Perhaps we ought to," she agreed. "To return to what I was saying, though—to close it off, I hope—I just want to make sure you know what you're . . . getting with me."

"I know what I'm getting with you."

"You're getting a woman who cannot give you a child." She wasn't sure why she was belaboring this point, except that it seemed impossible that she was on the verge of having everything she'd ever wanted. Everything she'd never allowed herself to want.

"I am getting a woman who can give me everything. I am getting a woman who changed the color of the sky," Effie said. "I am getting a woman on a beach under a chartreuse sky."

And *she* was getting everything she'd never let herself want. How extraordinary. "Oh. All right, then."

"However," Effie said with a twinkle in his eye, "I don't believe I've actually heard you articulate the question."

"The question?"

"The question in question."

"I thought you were a poet."

"Apparently not when a lady is making a suit of marriage. Apparently then I take leave of my literary senses. But I am not wrong. You have said you are proposing—more than once. But I never actually heard a question, did I?" His strange-beautiful eyes danced.

"Effie," she said, her heart close to bursting. "Will you do me the honor of marrying me?"

"Yes," he said, and Julianna was free.

Epilogue

One month later

The voices pierced through Simon's peace.

"There you are!" Archie, making quite the racket with the heavy oaken door from the vestry, exclaimed.

"Goodness!" Effie, sounding affronted in the way only Effie could, followed Archie up the aisle toward Simon. "What on earth are you doing in *here*?"

"Here" was church. The chapel at Galecroft, in particular. Simon had always liked it. Set apart from the main house and situated in a copse of silver birches, it had been a refuge for him as a boy. When he'd had to spend summers at Galecroft he'd tended to pass his days here, cool stone walls and a canopy of trees providing a double layer of shelter. Here, he could imagine a world in which the good and the right prevailed.

He didn't know why the boys were so surprised to find him in the chapel. People—even Archie and Effie—tended to forget that he had been bound for the Church before his elder twin brothers died and he inherited.

He closed the book he had been reading.

"It is cold, but it's a beautiful sunny day," Archie said, sliding into the pew beside Simon.

"The ladies want to row across the lake, where I am sure it will be colder than it is on land, but the novelty of being on the water should distract us from the chill," Effie said, sitting in the row ahead and twisting to face them. "They want you to accompany us." He grinned. "And by 'they,' I mean Clementine, Olive, and *my wife.*"

"Far be it from me to disappoint *your wife.*" Simon smiled, for Effie's excitement was infectious.

Effie and Julianna had wasted no time having the banns of marriage called once they'd gotten over themselves and accepted what the rest of the world could see plain as day—they were meant for each other. The banns had taken three weeks, of course, so they were still very newly wed. Hence all the *my wife*-ing. Simon had offered them the use of Galecroft for a post-wedding trip, it being close to London and therefore ideal for a quick escape between the wedding and the upcoming opening of Parliament, but somehow that had evolved into everyone coming along. "Earls-Plus-Girls Trip," Olive Morgan had dubbed it. "Consider it an intermezzo," she'd said. "An off-season compliment to your autumnal 'sacred masculine tradition.'"

Simon wished he *could* disappoint the ladies. As much as he liked them, he had come to the chapel to brood. He was quite worked up about the upcoming session of Parliament.

"I am for London tomorrow," he said, sliding his book under a Bible resting on the pew next to him.

"So soon?" Archie asked.

"Yes," Simon said emphatically, though he'd only that moment decided to decamp. "I have some books in the London house I need to consult."

"Ah," Effie said.

He knew they thought him overserious. Simon believed that if a man was fortunate—or unfortunate—enough to be born into wealth and privilege, he ought to approach his duty with an earnestness of purpose. He ought to work to make sure that the good and the right prevailed, not just sit in a church wishing for it. He would make no apologies for taking his responsibilities seriously.

He didn't have to make any apologies, though, not to these two. They might think him overserious, but they would never judge him for it. They understood him. Their friendship had always been, and remained, a balm.

"You two stay as long as you like, though," he said.

"We will indeed, thank you," Effie said. "And pray tell, what is that book you're attempting to hide under that Bible?"

"I am hiding nothing," said Simon, who had been doing exactly that.

"Let's have it, then." Archie reached over Simon and extracted the tome. "*Persuasion*! You have become quite the devotee of Miss Austen of late."

"Yes, well, she writes very astutely about social mores."

"Did Miss Brown give you that one, too?" Archie asked. "She and Clementine are positively mad for Miss Austen's novels."

"I can't remember where I got this," Simon lied. "As I said, please stay on after my departure, but you'll both be back in Town by the fourth, yes?" February 4 was when Parliament opened. He was asking partly to distract the boys from the topic of where he'd gotten his book, but also to impress upon them the importance of returning to Town in time.

"Yes," Effie said with affectionate exasperation. "We will be back, and we will do exactly what you tell us to do as it relates to voting and such. But you know I plan to be absent as much as I can this session. I'm quite busy!"

Effie *was* busy, and Simon was happy for him. His father had died in Italy, and his mother and sister had returned only last week, whereupon Effie dropped the bomb on them regarding his plans to marry Julianna, move to rooms in Grub Street, and become a printer and poet. The family had been thrust into chaos. Well, Effie's mother had been thrust into chaos. His sister, Sarah, after recovering from her initial shock, was reportedly, "Coming around. Possibly. As long as my 'antics' do not hamper her own matrimonial prospects. And as long as the eye-wateringly large sum Kenver proposed to allow her every month remains eye-wateringly large."

The events of the past month really had been something to witness. Olive Morgan reported that news of the scandal was beginning to make its way through society, and Simon himself had fielded several questions disguised as "concern," at a party he'd attended last week. Effie seemed not to mind whatsoever, and Simon and Archie were following his lead.

The newlyweds were in fact living in two rooms on Grub Street—"one for us and one for the press." Amusingly, Effie had dubbed the new contraption Cordelia. "I took your point, Simon, that naming a press after a man haunted by the ghost of his dead father and driven to his death by said haunting might have been, in retrospect, a poor idea. Cordelia, by contrast, opposed her father even when everyone was against her so doing, even when it had terrible consequences. She held her head high. Of course, she died tragically in the end, too, that being one of the aforementioned terrible consequences, so perhaps I should have gone with the jolly Falstaff. Though he dies, too, doesn't he?"

Kenver was trying to persuade Effie to allow the purchase of nicer accommodations, but Effie was so far resisting, adhering to his vow to make it on his own. "I am not, however," he had proclaimed to Archie and Simon, "at all above accepting accommodations and comfort from you lot." Hence the jaunt to Galecroft. Hence Effie's gleeful anticipation of this autumn's Earls Trip. "It's going to be ever so much more luxurious," he'd said, "now that I'm coming from lowered circumstances." He had paused. "Lowered materially. Raised in every other sense."

"I think Clementine and Olive and I will join you in departing tomorrow," Archie said. "Or perhaps the ladies can travel to Town with you? I need to get out to the hunting box before I have to be back for Lords."

"The hunting box?" Effie queried. "I'd've thought if you were going anywhere, it would be to Highworth to see your mother. I know it is increasingly difficult for you to be away from her."

"Normally, I would, but I'm building a plunge pool at the hunting box, and I am apparently needed by the foreman to rule on a few matters before the excavation can begin."

"You are building a what pool?" Effie asked.

"A plunge pool. You're familiar with Royal Tunbridge Wells?"

"Yes. I took the waters there once. It was quite diverting."

"It's the same water, under my property," Archie said. "Same benefits but without the crowds. I thought it might help Mother. It was Clementine's idea, actually, and Miss Brown's. They were talking recently about how bathing seems to calm Mother, and Clementine mused about the possibility of taking her to Royal Tunbridge Wells. Miss Brown thought the crowds would produce agitation sufficient to override any benefit the waters might have. I started thinking about how I'd heard the Duke of Greenworth had dug his own pool on his estate in Glastonbury—I gather there are spring waters thereabouts, too. And *then* I started thinking about how close the hunting box is to Royal Tunbridge Wells and dispatched Mr. Hughes to travel there and oversee the digging of a test hole. Water was struck, and low, now I'm digging a pool."

"How extraordinary," Effie marveled.

"Let's go there," Simon said, an idea overtaking him with some urgency.

"*You're* the one so intent on making it back to Town," Effie said.

"Not now," Simon said. "In autumn. Earls Trip 1823. Will your pool be done by then, Archie?"

"I should think so. It's literally just a hole in the ground."

"Well, then it's settled," Simon said. "We'll all go. You and your wives, and your mother, too, Archie." And Miss Brown. She would be needed by Archie's mother.

"What about the sacred masculine tradition?" Archie asked. "The ladies are always mocking it, but 'tis a real thing! It's called Earls Trip for a reason. And it's not really a trip, is it, if we merely spend it at one of our houses?"

"Things change," Simon said. "You two are married. Your mother is ailing, Archie. Earls Trip in the form we know it is a relic of our younger years, when we were bachelors, when we bore fewer responsibilities. Times change, and we must evolve along with them, mustn't we?"

"I for one," Effie said, "find the prospect of lounging about in a pool without having to engage with society at large immensely appealing."

"Perhaps," Archie said, "we can work out a compromise whereby we spend a week ourselves, and then the ladies join us. Or perhaps, given that I've laborers there already, I could have a simple outbuilding built, where we could stay apart from the main lodgings."

"Of course," Effie said with a smirk, "the aforementioned lounging about shall have to remain a distinctly masculine pursuit. We lot seem to have shocking low standards of decorum in recent years, but we can hardly take the waters with the ladies."

Simon picked up his copy of *Persuasion* and fanned himself.

"All right." Archie stood. "Let us consider the destination settled and we shall discuss details of when—and who—later."

Effie stood, too. "Off we go to take the water—in a different way—with the ladies. It's been ages since I've been in a boat."

They filed to the back of the chapel. There was a stained glass window along the back of the structure, and through it Simon could see the ladies approaching.

He decided to beg off. He didn't begrudge them an afternoon of gaiety on the lake, but he wasn't keen to share it. "At the risk of disappointing the ladies"—he turned to Effie with a smile— "*your wife* among them, I shan't join you. I'll see you later, when we dine."

"Are you sure?" Archie asked.

"Yes. I've some preparations to do for next week."

The boys rolled their eyes affectionately as they exited. Simon watched them meet up with the ladies. Archie offered one arm to his wife and the other to his sister-in-law, and they set out across the lawn between the chapel and the house.

Effie and Julianna followed. They appeared to be discussing

something with great fervor. Each was gesturing animatedly until Effie threw up his hands and stopped. He drew Julianna to him, and she came laughingly. They kissed.

It was only then that Simon realized with a start that he was looking at them through a green pane in the stained glass. Effie and Julianna were kissing under a chartreuse sky, and if that wasn't an example of the good and the right prevailing, he didn't know what was.

Author's Note

There was no such magazine as *Archer's Lady's Book*. I originally intended for Julianna to be interested in seeing a copy of the then-new *Saturday Evening Post*. The *Post* began publishing in 1821, and I was delighted by how perfectly this lined up with my timeline. Alas, it turns out it didn't become the iconic, illustrated-cover publication we think of it as until sometime later. (And of course it didn't start up with the Norman Rockwell covers until much later.) And there don't appear to be any women's magazines in the New World at the time. So I made one up.

It is perhaps odd that I have gone to such pains (I am not, generally speaking, a fan of the author's note as a concept) to confess to you a minor manipulation of fact when the entirety of this book takes a great deal of liberty with the idea of an authentic tale from Regency/Georgian days. It is of course true that friendship groups comprised of young, handsome, emotionally intelligent and mutually supportive aristocrats with good teeth and high standards of personal hygiene . . . probably did not exist. I suppose I see a difference between emotional truths, which I consider more malleable, and literal truths to do with time and space and the nature of reality. In today's precarious world where opinion is so often elevated to the status of fact, I feel compelled to confess my literal and literary lies.

So anyway, I made up the magazine.

Acknowledgments

I relied on a number of books on Brighton, printing technology, and women's magazines in the writing of this book, particularly *Life in Brighton* by Clifford Musgrave, *Women in Print: Writing Women and Women's Magazines from the Restoration to Queen Victoria* by Alison Adburgham, and *A Magazine of Her Own? Domesticity and Desire in the Woman's Magazine 1800–1914* by Margaret Beetham.

I am indebted to the various libraries and universities that have made accessible the contents of some of the women's magazines of the era (which would have been Julianna's competitors). Particularly useful (and a delight to browse) was an extensive index of *Lady's Magazine; or Entertaining Companion for the Fair Sex* by Professor Jennie Batchelor, Dr. Koenraad Claes, and Dr. Jenny DiPlacidi out of the University of Kent.

The watercolors in *Views of the Royal Pavilion* by John Nash were immensely helpful, but no more so than an actual tour of the Pavilion and its gardens, which I highly recommend and which can be undertaken via the Brighton & Hove Museums. A walking tour from Real Brighton Tours helped with the history of the surrounding city.

The brilliant Rose Lerner did some research for me to establish that the king was not in fact, going to be in Brighton when my gentlemen were. But more than help with fact, she educated me and helped me think through some larger issues. Several conventions of historical romance would have been *so* much more convenient for my story (if only Effie could renounce his title! If only "not taking up one's seat in Parliament" were actually a thing!), but even in Ted Lasso–inspired historical romance, reality matters (see my author's note for my thoughts on types of truths!). Of course, any errors in the book are mine.

Everyone at Kensington has been so lovely. Elizabeth May and Sarah Selim really got Effie and Jules, and they helped me get a much better handle on Julianna in particular. Their enthusiasm for this book meant so much. Jane Nutter, Lauren Jernigan, and Alex Nicolajsen have done such great work promoting this series.

Dawn Cooper, under the direction of the art folks at Kensington, made another fantastically delightful cover.

Sandra Owens read an early draft and provided her usual steadfast, humor-inflected support. I am not sure what I would do without my daily dose of her friendship.

As always, none of this would have been possible without Courtney Miller-Callihan, who brought to the table her signature mix of cheerleading and editorial acumen. Cheyenne Faircloth also provided editorial feedback and social media support that was much appreciated.

Finally, my sister, Erin. There is something about this series that's all tied up with my sister! In this case, she, then a resident of the UK, took me to Brighton. We had gluten-free afternoon tea, walked on the beach, and only had to move rooms once so I wouldn't expire of heat exhaustion. It was a much-needed break during an inordinately stressful time, a stressful time that she and I uniquely understood, and as with Effie and his earl friends, isn't it such a balm to be with people you don't have to explain anything to?

Go back to where it all began, in Archie and Clementine's love story:

EARLS TRIP
by Jenny Holiday

The first in a sparkling Regency-era series with a delightfully modern feel, set against the irresistible backdrop of an annual trip taken by three handsome earls . . .

Even an earl needs his ride-or-dies, and Archibald Fielding-Burton, the Earl of Harcourt, counts himself lucky to have two. Archie (the jock), Simon (the nerd), and Effie (the goth) have been BFFs since their school days, and their annual trip holds a sacred spot in their calendars. This year, Archie is especially eager to get away—until an urgent letter arrives from an old family friend, begging him to help prevent a ruinous scandal. Archie's childhood pal Olive Morgan must be rescued from an ill-fated elopement—and her sister, Clementine, must be rescued from rescuing Olive. Suddenly the trip has become earls-plus-girls.

This . . . complicates matters. The fully grown Clementine, while as frank and refreshing as Archie remembers, is also different to the wild, windswept girl he knew. This Clem is complex and surprising—and adamantly opposed to marriage. Which, for reasons Archie dare not examine too closely, he finds increasingly vexing.

Then Clem makes him an indecent and quite delightful proposal, asking him to show her the pleasures of the marriage bed before she settles into spinsterhood. And what kind of gentleman would he be to refuse a lady?

Read on for a preview of the very first chapter . . .

Chapter 1

The Boys Are Back in Town

What happens on Earls Trip, stays on Earls Trip.

Usually.

In 1821, on the eighth annual Earls Trip, things took a bit of a turn.

When Archibald Fielding-Burton, the Earl of Harcourt, arrived at Number Seven Park Lane to collect his friend, Simon Courteney, the Earl of Marsden, Marsden was waiting in front of his town house.

"Hullo," Archie said, hopping out of the coach. "Ready?"

"He's been ready since seven this morning," said Mr. Janes, Simon's valet, who was stationed at attention behind his master.

"Of course he has." Archie shot an affectionate look at Simon, then a placating one at the long-suffering Janes. "Has he also been standing here since seven this morning?" Archie took the valet's sniff as affirmation. "Poor Janes. Marsden, you ought to wait inside like a properly bred person."

"Well, remember," Simon said mildly, "I'm *barely* a properly bred person."

Archie chuckled as small muscles in Janes's jaw visibly tightened.

"Mr. Janes, what will you do with yourself for a fortnight without your wayward earl and his wretched wardrobe to wrangle?"

"I look fine," Simon said, and a muscle in Janes's jaw twitched.

Strictly speaking, it was true. There was nothing wrong with Simon's current ensemble or any other in his wardrobe. It was more that he tended toward the bland in all matters material, be they sartorial, culinary, or bodily. He always had. Today he was wearing a pair of buff breeches and a brown coat cut in a style that had been the height of fashion five Seasons ago when he'd ascended the earldom, and his hair . . . Well, his hair was best not discussed. Archie himself was no dandy, but he tried to keep up appearances.

As Janes supervised the loading of a small trunk into the coach, Archie picked up a valise resting on the bottom step of Simon's house—and nearly tore his arm off. "Oof. What's in here? Bricks?"

"Books." Simon climbed into the coach.

"Ah, yes." Archie was flooded with affection for his friend.

Simon was so very much himself. He used to try to smuggle books out of the Winchester College library on term breaks. He was still doing it, apparently. "Where's Effie?" Simon asked when Archie joined him inside.

"I'd've thought you'd have collected him first, as his house is between mine and yours. Now you'll have to backtrack."

Simon disliked inefficiency, but perhaps not as much as he appreciated a logical argument, so Archie made one: "Yes, but unlike you, he won't be ready. He may not even remember that we're to make the trip at all. Either way, he almost certainly won't have done his packing. I'd rather go out of my way and have some company for the extraction process, since it's likely to be laborious."

"A fair point." Simon heaved an enormous sigh and slumped back against the squabs.

Archie examined his friend, cataloging the darker-than-usual circles under his eyes and the paler-than-usual cast of his skin.

"All right, then?"

"Yes, yes, but I am sorely in need of respite. I've been run off my feet of late. I've been—" He cut himself off. "It is of no mind."

Archie smiled. He understood perfectly what Simon meant, because he understood Simon perfectly. The uneasy earl tended to reside in the caverns of his mind and had to be wrenched out of them periodically by his friends, which was a process he both abhorred and relished. It was as if something inside him knew he needed the respite he'd referenced, but something *else* inside him resisted. He was a man at war with himself. He always had been, and it had only gotten worse since he'd unexpectedly inherited the earldom.

Janes popped his head into the coach and closed his fingers around a stack of newspapers resting on Simon's lap. "Shall I take these, my lord?"

Simon's hands flew to the opposite edge of the papers, and a polite tug-of-war ensued.

"It's no use, Mr. Janes," Archie said. "He shall have to be weaned slowly from them, like a man from the poppy."

"Thank you, Janes. That will, uh, be all," Simon said in the voice he used when he was trying to project authority in the domestic sphere, over the staff who would always think of him as the painfully shy, seldom-seen third son of their late lord. Archie had told Simon a hundred times to use his Parliament voice at home, but somehow Simon didn't, or couldn't, and he ended up sounding like a boy playing at manhood.

Janes shot a dismayed look at Archie.

"Worry not, Mr. Janes. I shall keep his lordship in line at the posting inns, and once in Cumbria, we shall be completely alone." Archie couldn't wait. Town made him jumpy and irritable. His lungs were crying out for fresh air, his trigger finger was itching for a good hunt, and, not to put too fine a point on it, his soul was in need of a prolonged dose of exposure to his best mates.

Speaking of. One down; time to collect Effie. He rapped on the ceiling, and the coach rumbled off.

"Shall we wager on how long it will take to wrest Effie from his papers?" Archie asked a while later, as they turned onto Berkeley Square. "Or his paints. Or merely the dark depths of his imaginings?" He chuckled. "Surely there will be some manner of wresting required, is my point, and shall we lay a wager on it?"

"I'd have to be bound for Bedlam to take that wager." Simon bent his head to join Archie in peering out the window at Number Twenty. "God's teeth! Who's died?"

"I don't know!" Archie exclaimed, alarmed. The steps of the town house were strewn with straw and the door bedecked with the black ribbons of mourning.

"You don't think . . . ?" Simon's voice reflected the horror that had taken root in Archie's gut.

"*No*," Archie said, though he was all too aware that wishing something weren't true had no bearing on whether it actually was. "We'd have heard if the earl died," Archie said to himself as much as to Simon. Effie would have come to them straight away.

It occurred to Archie, though, that someday, the old earl was going to die, and his son, Edward Astley, Viscount Featherfinch, would inherit the earldom. It also occurred to Archie that no one, least of all Effie himself, was prepared for that day. As they approached the door, Archie, trying to regain some equilibrium, said, "I wager it takes us seventy minutes to extract him."

"Considering that he planned this year's trip," Simon said, "I'm going to give him the benefit of the doubt and say three-quarters of an hour."

"We shall see. Loser sits backward on the journey."

"If there's even going to be a journey," Simon said as the straw crunched beneath their feet. "*Someone* has clearly died, and we can't go without Effie."

"Indeed." Well, they could. But they wouldn't. "Then we're here to pay our respects, I suppose. Still, I maintain he would have told us if something terribly dire had happened." Although Effie did tend to live in his head. Not in the same manner Simon did. Simon lived inside his Parliamentary arguments; Effie lived inside his daydreams. Whereas Simon could usually be counted on to remember to do things like eat and bathe—he saw them as necessary annoyances—often Effie could not.

Archie's knock was answered by a footman he did not recognize. The man was not wearing a mourning armband and greeted them as if nothing were amiss.

"We're here for Featherfinch," Simon said.

"I'm afraid the viscount is not at home to visitors at the moment."

"He's at home to us." Archie started for the stairs. "He's expecting us." Or, rather, he *should* be.

"I *beg* your pardon!" the footman called after them.

The housekeeper appeared, no doubt drawn by the commotion. Archie paused in his ascent. "Ah. Mrs. Moyer. We're here to collect Featherfinch for our trip."

"Your trip?" she echoed blankly before recovering herself and curtsying to them. "My lords." That caused the footman to stand straighter.

"Our trip to Cumbria?" Archie tried, though he knew full well what had happened here. Effie hadn't told any of the household staff, never mind any of his family, about his travel plans.

Mrs. Moyer wrinkled her brow and said, predictably, "I'm afraid I don't know anything about such a trip, my lord."

"The trip we take every year the second fortnight in September?" Honestly. Was Effie's dreaminess like the plague, capable of infecting the rest of the household?

At least Archie was going to win the wager.

"Mrs. Moyer, a good morning to you." Simon, able to sense Archie's rising frustration, spoke soothingly to the housekeeper. "May I ask who has passed?"

Mrs. Moyer tilted her head to one side, as if she were searching for words but coming up short. "Perhaps you ought to ask Lord Featherfinch about that."

"Are the earl and countess well?" Simon pressed.

"Oh yes, quite. They're at Highworth," she said, naming the family's Cornish estate.

"Let's go." Archie mounted the stairs and made for Effie's room, trusting Simon would follow and reflecting on what a poor job the staff was doing keeping people from Effie if they had, in fact, been instructed that he was not at home to visitors.

"Featherfinch!" Simon called as Archie knocked.

Archie, not waiting for a response, pushed open the door. "Unless someone very important has died, you had better be at the ready, or I shall—"

Edward Astley, Viscount Featherfinch and heir to the Earl of Stonely, was not at the ready.

He was also not dressed.

Visit our website at
KensingtonBooks.com
to sign up for our newsletters, read
more from your favorite authors, see
books by series, view reading group
guides, and more!

BOOK CLUB
BETWEEN THE CHAPTERS

Become a Part of Our
Between the Chapters Book Club
Community and Join the Conversation

Betweenthechapters.net